The tunnel seemed endless, yet the end was upon him almost before he realized it, and he lunged up another ladder. The shaft was sealed, but he was already probing at it, spotting the catch, heaving it up with a mighty shoulder. He burst into the night air . . . and his senses were suddenly afire with more power sources. More combat armor! Coming from behind in the prodigious leaps of jump gear and waiting in the woods ahead, as well!

He tried to unlimber his own energy gun, but a torrent of energy crashed over him, and he cried out as every implant in his body screamed in protest. He writhed, fighting it, clinging to the torment of awareness.

It was a capture field—not a killing blast of energy, but something infinitely worse. A police device that locked his synthetic muscles with brutal power.

He toppled forward under the impetus of his last charge, crashing to the ground half-in and half-out of the tunnel. He fought the encroaching darkness, smashing at it with all the fury of his enraged will, but it swept over him.

The last thing he saw was a tornado of light as the trees exploded with energy fire. He carried the vision down into the dark with him, dimly aware of its importance.

And then, as his senses faded at last, he realized: It wasn't directed at him—it was raking the ground behind him and cutting down the mutineers who had pursued him. . . .

MUTINEERS' MOON

DAVID WEBER

MUTINEERS' MOON

This is a work of fiction. All the characters and events portrayed in this book are fictional, and any resemblance to real people or incidents is purely coincidental.

A Baen Books Original

Baen Publishing Enterprises
P.O. Box 1403
Riverdale, NY 10471

ISBN: 0-671-72085-6

Cover art by Paul Alexander

First printing, October 1991
Fourth printing, November 1999

Distributed by Simon & Schuster
1230 Avenue of the Americas
New York, NY 10020

Library of Congress Catalog Number: 96-11391

Printed in the United States of America

Book One

Chapter One

The huge command deck was as calm, as peacefully dim, as ever, silent but for the small background sounds of environmental recordings. The bulkheads were invisible beyond the projection of star-specked space and the blue-white shape of a life-bearing world. It was exactly as it ought to be, exactly as it always had been—tranquil, well-ordered, as divorced from chaos as any setting could possibly be.

But Captain Druaga's face was grim as he stood beside his command chair and data flowed through his neural feeds. He felt the whickering lightning of energy weapons like heated irons, Engineering no longer responded—not surprisingly—and he'd lost both Bio-Control One and Three. The hangar decks belonged to no one; he'd sealed them against the mutineers, but Anu's butchers had blocked the transit shafts with grab fields covered by heavy weapons. He still held Fire Control and most of the external systems, but Communications had been the mutineers' primary target. The first explosion had taken it out, and even an *Utu*-class ship mounted only a single hypercom. He could neither move the ship nor report what had happened, and his loyalists were losing.

Druaga deliberately relaxed his jaw before his teeth could grind together. In the seven thousand years since the Fourth Imperium crawled back into space from the last surviving world of the Third, there had never been a mutiny aboard a capital ship of Battle Fleet. At best, he would go down in history as the captain whose crew had turned against him and been savagely suppressed. At worst, he would not go down in history at all.

The status report ended, and he sighed and shook himself.

The mutineers were hugely outnumbered, but they had the priceless advantage of surprise, and Anu had planned with care. Druaga snorted; no doubt the Academy teachers would have been proud of his tactics. But at least—and thank the Maker for it!—he was only the chief engineer, not a bridge officer. There were command codes of which he had no knowledge.

"Dahak," Druaga said.

"Yes, Captain?" The calm, mellow voice came from everywhere and nowhere, filling the command deck.

"How long before the mutineers reach Command One?"

"Three standard hours, Captain, plus or minus fifteen percent."

"They can't be stopped?"

"Negative, Captain. They control all approaches to Command One and they are pushing back loyal personnel at almost all points of contact."

Of course they were, Druaga thought bitterly. They had combat armor and heavy weapons; the vast majority of his loyalists did not.

He looked around the deserted command deck once more. Gunnery was unmanned, and Plotting, Engineering, Battle Comp, Astrogation. . . . When the alarms went, only he had managed to reach his post before the mutineers cut power to the transit shafts. Just him. And to get here he'd had to kill two subverted members of his own staff when they pounced on him like assassins.

"All right, Dahak," he told the all-surrounding voice grimly, "if all we still hold is Bio Two and the weapon systems, we'll use them. Cut Bio One and Three out of the circuit."

"Executed," the voice said instantly. "But it will take the mutineers no more than an hour to put them back on line under manual."

"Granted. But it's long enough. Go to Condition Red Two, Internal."

There was a momentary pause, and Druaga suppressed a bitter smile.

"You have no suit, Captain," the voice said unemotionally. "If you set Condition Red Two, you will die."

"I know." Druaga wished he was as calm as he sounded, but he knew *Dahak's* bio read-outs gave him the lie. Yet it was the only chance he—or, rather, the Imperium—had.

"You will give a ten-minute warning count," he continued, sitting down in his command chair. "That should give everyone time to reach a lifeboat. Once everyone's evacuated, our external weapons will become effective. You will carry out immediate decon, but you will allow only loyal personnel to re-enter until you receive orders to the contrary from . . . your new captain. Any mutinous personnel who approach within five thousand kilometers before loyal officers have reasserted control will be destroyed in space."

"Understood." Druaga could have sworn the voice spoke more softly. "Comp Cent core programs require authentication of this order, however."

"Alpha-Eight-Sigma-Niner-Niner-Seven-Delta-Four-Alpha," he said flatly.

"Authentication code acknowledged and accepted," the voice responded. "Please specify time for implementation."

"Immediately," Druaga said, and wondered if he spoke so quickly to avoid losing his nerve.

"Acknowledged. Do you wish to listen to the ten-count, Captain?"

"No, Dahak," Druaga said very softly.

"Understood," the voice replied, and Druaga closed his eyes.

It was a draconian solution . . . if it could be called a "solution" at all. Red Two, Internal, was the next-to-final defense against hostile incursion. It opened every ventilation trunk—something which could be done only on the express, authenticated order of the ship's commander—to flood the entire volume of the stupendous starship with chemical and radioactive agents. By its very nature, Red Two exempted *no* compartment . . . including this one. The ship would become uninhabitable, a literal death trap, and only the central computer, which *he* controlled, could decontaminate.

The system had never been intended for this contingency, but it would work. Mutineers and loyalists alike would be forced to flee, and no lifeboat ever built could stand up to *Dahak*'s weaponry. Of course, Druaga wouldn't be alive to see the end, but at least his command would be held for the Imperium.

And if Red Two failed, there was always Red One.

"Dahak," he said suddenly, never opening his eyes.

"Yes, Captain?"

"Category One order," Druaga said formally.

"Recording," the voice said.

"I, Senior Fleet Captain Druaga, commanding officer Imperial Fleet Vessel *Dahak,* Hull Number One-Seven-Two-Two-Nine-One," Druaga said even more formally, "having determined to my satisfaction that a Class One Threat to the Imperium exists aboard my vessel, do now issue, pursuant to Fleet Regulation Seven-One, Section One-Nine-Three, Subsection Seven-One, a Category One order to *Dahak* Computer Central. Authentication code Alpha-Eight-Delta-Sigma-Niner-Niner-Seven-Delta-Four-Omega."

"Authentication code acknowledged and accepted," the voice said coolly. "Standing by to accept Category One orders. Please specify."

"Primary mission of this unit now becomes suppression of mutinous personnel in accordance with instructions already issued," Druaga said crisply. "If previously specified measures fail to restore control to loyal personnel, said mutinous elements will be destroyed by any practicable means, including, if necessary, the setting of Condition Red One, Internal, and total destruction of this vessel. These orders carry Priority Alpha."

"Acknowledged," the voice said, and Druaga let his head rest upon the cushioned back of his chair. It was done. Even if Anu somehow managed to reach Command One, he could not abort the order *Dahak* had just acknowledged.

The captain relaxed. At least, he thought, it should be fairly painless.

". . . ine minutes and counting," the computer voice said, and Fleet Captain (E) Anu, Chief Engineer of the ship-of-the-line *Dahak* cursed. Damn Druaga! He hadn't expected the captain to reach his bridge alive, much less counted on *this*. Druaga had always seemed such an unimaginative, rote-bound, dutiful automaton.

"What shall we do, Anu?"

Commander Inanna's eyes were anxious through her armor's visor, and he did not blame her.

"Fall back to Bay Ninety-One," he grated furiously.

"But that's—"

"I know. I know! We'll just have to use them ourselves. Now get our people moving, Commander!"

"Yes, sir," Commander Inanna said, and Anu threw himself into the central transit shaft. The shaft walls screamed past him, though he felt no subjective sense of motion, and his lips drew back in an ugly snarl. His first attempt had failed, but he had a trick or two of his own. Tricks even Druaga didn't know about, Breaker take him!

Copper minnows exploded away from *Dahak*. Lifeboats crowded with loyal crew members fanned out over the glaciated surface of the alien planet, seeking refuge, and scattered among them were other, larger shapes. Still only motes compared to the ship itself, their masses were measured in thousands upon thousands of tons, and they plummeted together, outspeeding the smaller lifeboats.

Anu had no intention of remaining in space where Druaga—assuming he was still alive—might recognize that he and his followers had not abandoned ship in lifeboats and use *Dahak*'s weapons to pick off his sublight parasites as easily as a child swatting flies.

The engineer sat in the command chair of the parasite *Osir*, watching the gargantuan bulk of the camouflaged mother ship dwindle with distance, and his smile was ugly. He needed that ship to claim his destiny, but he could still have it. Once the programs he'd buried in the engineering computers did their job, every power room aboard *Dahak* would be so much rubble. Emergency power would keep Comp Cent going for a time, but when it faded, Comp Cent would die.

And with its death, *Dahak*'s hulk would be his.

"Entering atmosphere, sir," Commander Inanna said from the first officer's couch.

Chapter Two

"Papa-Mike Control, this is Papa-Mike One-X-Ray, do you copy?"

Lieutenant Commander Colin MacIntyre's radar pinged softly as the Copernicus mass driver hurled another few tons of lunar rock towards the catcher ships of the Eden Three habitat, and he watched its out-going trace on the scope as he waited, reveling in the joy of solo flight, for secondary mission control at Tereshkova to respond.

"One-X-Ray, Papa-Mike Control," a deep voice acknowledged. "Proceed."

"Papa-Mike Control, One-X-Ray orbital insertion burn complete. It looks good from here. Over."

"One-X-Ray, that's affirmative. Do you want a couple of orbits to settle in before initiating?"

"Negative, Control. The whole idea's to do this on my own, right?"

"Affirmative, One-X-Ray."

"Let's do it, then. I show a green board, Pasha—do you confirm?"

"That's an affirmative, One-X-Ray. And we also show

you approaching our transmission horizon, Colin. Communications loss in twenty seconds. You are cleared to initiate the exercise."

"Papa-Mike Control, One-X-Ray copies. See you guys in a little while."

"Roger, One-X-Ray. Your turn to buy, anyway."

"Like hell it is," MacIntyre laughed, but whatever Papa-Mike Control might have replied was cut off as One-X-Ray swept beyond the lunar horizon and lost signal.

MacIntyre ran down his final check list with extra care. It had been surprisingly hard for the test mission's planners to pick an orbit that would keep him clear of Nearside's traffic *and* cover a totally unexplored portion of the moon's surface. But Farside was populated only by a handful of observatories and deep-system radio arrays, and the routing required to find virgin territory combined with the close orbit the survey instruments needed would put him out of touch with the rest of the human race for the next little bit, which was a novel experience even for an astronaut these days.

He finished his list and activated his instruments, then sat back and hummed, drumming on the arms of his acceleration couch to keep time, as his on-board computers flickered through the mission programs. It was always possible to hit a glitch, but there was little he could do about it if it happened. He was a pilot, thoroughly familiar with the electronic gizzards of his one-man Beagle Three survey vehicle, but he had only the vaguest idea about how this particular instrument package functioned.

The rate of technical progress in the seventy years since Armstrong was enough to leave any non-specialist hopelessly behind outside his own field, and the Geo Sciences team back at Shepherd Center had wandered down some peculiar paths to produce their current generation of esoteric peekers and pryers. "Gravitonic resonance" was a marvelous term ... and MacIntyre often wished he knew exactly what it meant. But not enough to spend another six or eight years tacking on extra degrees, so he contented himself with understanding what the "planetary proctoscope" (as some anonymous wag had christened it) did rather than how it did it.

Maneuvering thrusters nudged his Beagle into precisely the proper attitude, and MacIntyre bent a sapient gaze upon the read-outs. Those, at least, he understood. Which was just as well, since he was slated as primary survey pilot for the Prometheus Mission, and—

His humming paused suddenly, dying in mid-note, and his eyebrows crooked. Now that was odd. A malfunction?

He punched keys, and his crooked eyebrows became a frown. According to the diagnostics, everything was functioning perfectly, but whatever else the moon might be, it wasn't *hollow*.

He tugged on his prominent nose, watching the preposterous data appear on the displays. The printer beside him hummed, producing a hard-copy graphic representation of the raw numbers, and he tugged harder. According to his demented instruments, someone must have been a busy little beaver down there. It looked for all the world as if a vast labyrinth of tunnels, passages, and God knew what had been carved out under eighty kilometers of solid lunar rock!

He allowed himself a muttered imprecation. Less than a year from mission date, and one of their primary survey systems—and a NASA design, at that!—had decided to go gaga. But the thing had worked perfectly in atmospheric tests over Nevada and Siberia, so what the hell had happened now?

He was still tugging on his nose when the proximity alarm jerked him up in his couch. Damnation! He was all alone back here, so what the *hell* was that?

"That" was a blip less than a hundred kilometers astern and closing fast. How had something that big gotten this close before his radar caught it? According to his instruments, it was at least the size of one of the old Saturn V boosters!

His jaw dropped as the bogie made a crisp, clean, instantaneous ninety-degree turn. Apparently the laws of motion had been repealed on behalf of whatever it was! But whatever *else* it was doing, it was also maneuvering to match his orbit. Even as he watched, the stranger was slowing to pace him.

Colin MacIntyre's level-headedness was one reason he'd been selected for the first joint US-Soviet interstellar flight crew, but the hair on the back of his neck stood on end as his craft suddenly shuddered. It was as if something had touched the Beagle's hull—something massive enough to shake a hundred-ton, atmosphere-capable, variable-geometry spacecraft.

That shook him out of his momentary state of shock. Whatever this was, no one had told him to expect it, and that meant it belonged to neither NASA nor the Russians. His hands flew over his maneuvering console, waking flaring thrusters, and the Beagle quivered. She quivered, but she didn't budge, and cold sweat beaded MacIntyre's face as she continued serenely along her orbital path, attitude unchanged. That couldn't possibly be happening—but, then, *none* of this could be happening, could it?

He chopped that thought off and punched more keys. One thing he had was plenty of maneuvering mass—Beagles were designed for lengthy deployments, and he'd tanked from the Russkies' Gagarin Platform before departure on his trans-lunar flight plan—and the ship shuddered wildly as her main engines came alive.

The full-power burn should have slammed him back in his couch and sent the survey ship hurtling forward, but the thundering engines had no more effect than his maneuvering thrusters, and he sagged in his seat. Then his jaw clenched as the Beagle finally started to move—not away from the stranger, but towards it! Whatever that thing on his radar was, it was no figment of his imagination.

His mind raced. The only possible explanation was that the blip had stuck him with some sort of . . . of *tractor beam,* and that represented more than any mere quantum leap in applied physics, which meant the blip did not come from any Terran technology. He did not indulge himself with any more dirty words like "impossible" or "incredible," for it was all too evident that it *was* possible. By some unimaginable quirk of fate, Somebody Else had come calling just as Mankind was about to reach out to the stars.

But whoever They were, he couldn't believe they'd just happened to turn up while he was Farside with blacked-out communications. They'd been waiting for him, or someone like him, so they must have been observing .Earth for quite some time. But if they had, they'd had time to make their presence known—and to monitor Terrestrial communication systems. Presumably, then, they knew how to contact him but had chosen not to do so, and that suggested a lot of things, none particularly pleasant. The salient point, however, was that they obviously intended to collect him, Beagle and all, for purposes of their own, and Colin MacIntyre did not intend to be collected if he could help it.

The exhaustive Prometheus Mission briefings on first contact flowed through his mind, complete with all the injunctions to refrain from hostile acts, but it was one thing to consider yourself expendable in pursuit of communication with aliens you might have gone calling on. It was quite another when they dropped in on you and started hauling you in like a fish!

His face hardened, and he flipped up the plastic shield over the fire control panel. There'd been wrung hands at the notion of arming a "peaceful" interstellar probe, but the military, which provided so many of the pilots, had enjoyed the final word, and MacIntyre breathed a silent breath of thanks that this was a full-dress training mission as weapon systems came alive. He fed targeting data from his radar and reached for the firing keys, then paused. They hadn't tried talking to him, but neither had he tried talking to them.

"Unknown spacecraft, this is NASA Papa-Mike One-X-Ray," he said crisply into his radio. "Release my ship and stand off."

There was no answer, and he glowered at the blip.

"Release my ship or I will fire on you!"

Still no reply, and his lips thinned. All right. If the miserable buggers didn't even want to talk . . .

Three small, powerful missiles blasted away from the Beagle. They weren't nukes, but each carried a three-hundred-kilo warhead, and they had a perfect targeting setup. He tracked them all the way in on radar.

And absolutely nothing happened.

Commander MacIntyre sagged in his couch. Those missiles hadn't been spoofed by ECM or exploded short of the target. They'd just ... vanished, and the implications were disturbing. *Most* disturbing.

He cut his engines. There was no point wasting propellant, and he and his captors would be clearing Heinlein's transmission horizon shortly anyway.

He tried to remember if any of the other Beagles were up. Judging by his own total lack of success, they would be none too effective against Whoever-They-Were, but nothing else in this vicinity was armed at all. He rather thought Vlad Chernikov was at Tereshkova, but the flight schedules for the Prometheus crews had grown so hectic of late it was hard to keep track.

His Beagle continued to move towards the intruder, and now he was turning slowly nose-on to it. He leaned back as nonchalantly as possible, watching through his canopy. He ought to see them just about ... now.

Yes, there they were. And mighty disappointing they were, too. He didn't really know what he'd expected, but that flattened, featureless, round-tipped, double-ended cylinder certainly wasn't it. They were barely a kilometer clear, now, but aside from the fact that the thing was obviously artificial, it seemed disappointingly undramatic. There was no sign of engines, hatches, ports, communication arrays ... nothing at all but smooth, mirror-bright metal. Or, at least, he assumed it was metal.

He checked his chronometer. Communications should come back in any second now, and his lips stretched in a humorless smile at how Heinlein Base was going to react when the pair of them came over the radar horizon. It ought to be—

They stopped. Just like that, with no apparent sense of deceleration, no reaction exhaust from the cylinder, no ... *anything.*

He gaped at the intruder in disbelief. Or, no, not disbelief, exactly. More like a *desire* to disbelieve. Especially when he realized they were motionless relative to the lunar surface, neither climbing away nor tumbling closer. The fact that the intruder could do that was somehow more terrifying than anything else that had happened— a terror made only worse by the total, prosaic familiarity of his own cockpit—and he clutched the arms of his couch, fighting an irrational conviction that he *had* to be falling.

But then they were moving again, zipping back the way they'd come at a velocity that beggared the imagination, all with absolutely no sense of acceleration. His attitude relative to the cylinder altered once more; it was behind him now, its rounded tip barely a hundred meters clear of his own engines, and he watched the lunar surface blur below him.

His Beagle and its captor swooped lower, arrowing straight for a minor crater, and his toes curled inside his flight boots while his hands tried to rip the arms off his couch. The things he'd already seen that cylinder do told his intellect they were not about to crash, but instinct was something else again. He fought his panic stubbornly, refusing to yield to it, yet his gasp of relief was explosive when the floor of the crater suddenly zipped open.

The cylinder slowed to a few hundred kilometers per hour, and MacIntyre felt the comfort of catatonia beckoning to him, but something made him fight it as obstinately as he had fought his panic. Whatever had him wasn't going to find him curled up and drooling when they finally stopped, by God!

A mighty tunnel enveloped them, a good two hundred meters across and lit by brilliant strip lights. Stone walls glittered with an odd sheen, as if the rock had been fused glass-slick, but that didn't last long. They slid through a multi-ply hatch big enough for a pair of carriers, and the tunnel walls were suddenly metallic. A bronze-like metal, gleaming in the light, stretching so far ahead of him even its mighty bore dwindled to a gleaming dot with distance.

Their speed dropped still further, and more hatches
slid past. *Dozens* of hatches, most as large as the one
that had admitted them to this impossible metal gullet.
His mind reeled at the structure's sheer size, but he
retained enough mental balance to apologize silently to
the proctoscope's designers.

One huge hatch flicked open with the suddenness of
a striking snake. Whoever was directing their flight
curved away from the tunnel, slipping neatly through the
open hatch, and his Beagle settled without a jar to a floor
of the same bronze-like alloy.

They were in a dimly-lit metal cavern at least a kilometer across, its floor dotted with neatly parked duplicates
of the cylinder that had captured him. He gawked
through the canopy, wishing a Beagle's equipment list
ran to sidearms. After his missiles' failure he supposed
there was no reason to expect a handgun to work, either,
but it would have been comforting to be able to try.

He licked his lips. If nothing else, the titanic size of
this structure ruled out the possibility that the intruders
had only recently discovered the solar system, but how
had they managed to build it without anyone noticing?

And then, at last, his radio hummed to life.

"Good afternoon, Commander MacIntyre," a deep,
mellow voice said politely. "I regret the rather unortho-
dox nature of your arrival here, but I had no choice. Nor,
I am afraid, do you."

"W-who are you?" MacIntyre demanded a bit hoarsely,
then paused and cleared his throat. "What do you want
with me?" he asked more levelly.

"I fear that answering those questions will be a bit
complicated," the voice said imperturbably, "but you may
call me Dahak, Commander."

Chapter Three

MacIntyre drew a deep breath. At least the whatever-they-weres were finally talking to him. And in English, too. Which inspired a small, welcome spurt of righteous indignation.

"Your apologies might carry a little more weight if you'd bothered to communicate with me *before* you kidnaped me," he said coldly.

"I realize that," his captor replied, "but it was impossible."

"Oh? You seem to have overcome your problems rather nicely since." MacIntyre was comforted to find he could still achieve a nasty tone.

"Your communication devices are rather primitive, Commander." The words were almost apologetic. "My tender was not equipped to interface with them."

"*You're* doing quite well. Why didn't *you* talk to me?"

"It was not possible. The tender's stealth systems enclosed both you and itself in a field impervious to radio transmissions. It was possible for me to communicate with the tender using my own communication systems, but there was no on-board capability to relay my words

17

to you. Once more, I apologize for any inconvenience you may have suffered."

MacIntyre bit off a giggle at how calmly this Dahak person produced a neat, thousand percent understatement like "inconvenience," and the incipient hysteria of his own sound helped sober him. He ran shaky fingers through his sandy-brown hair, feeling as if he had taken a punch or two too many.

"All right ... Dahak. You've got me—what do you intend to do with me?"

"I would be most grateful if you would leave your vessel and come to the command deck, Commander."

"Just like that?"

"I beg your pardon?"

"You expect me to step out of my ship and surrender just like that?"

"Excuse me. It has been some time since I have communicated with a human, so perhaps I have been clumsy. You are not a prisoner, Commander. Or perhaps you are. I should like to treat you as an honored guest, but honesty compels me to admit that I cannot allow you to leave. However, I assure you upon the honor of the Fleet that no harm will come to you."

Insane as it all sounded, MacIntyre felt a disturbing tendency to believe it. This Dahak could have lied and promised release as the aliens' ambassador to humanity, but he hadn't. The finality of that "cannot allow you to leave" was more than a bit chilling, but its very openness was a sort of guarantor of honesty, wasn't it? Or did he simply *want* it to be? But even if Dahak was a congenital liar, he had few options.

His consumables could be stretched to about three weeks, so he could cower in his Beagle that long, assuming Dahak was prepared to let him. But what then? Escape was obviously impossible, so his only real choice was how soon he came out, not whether or not he did so.

Besides, he felt a stubborn disinclination to show how frightened he was.

"All right," he said finally. "I'll come."

"Thank you, Commander. You will find the environment congenial, though you may, of course, suit up if you prefer."

"*Thank* you." MacIntyre's sarcasm was automatic, but, again, it was only a matter of time before he had to rely on whatever atmosphere the voice chose to provide, and he sighed. "Then I suppose I'm ready."

"Very well. A vehicle is now approaching your vessel. It should be visible to your left."

MacIntyre craned his neck and caught a glimpse of movement as a double-ended bullet-shape about the size of a compact car slid rapidly closer, gliding a foot or so above the floor. It came to a halt under the leading edge of his port wing, exactly opposite his forward hatch, and a door slid open. Light spilled from the opening, bright and welcoming in the dim metal cavern.

"I see it," he said, pleased to note that his voice sounded almost normal again.

"Excellent. If you would be so kind as to board it, then?"

"I'm on my way," he said, and released his harness.

He stood, and discovered yet another strangeness. MacIntyre had put in enough time on Luna, particularly in the three years he'd spent training for the Prometheus Mission, to grow accustomed to its reduced gravity—which was why he almost fell flat on his face when he rose.

His eyes widened. He couldn't be certain, but his weight felt about right for a standard gee, which meant these bozos could generate gravity to order!

Well, why not? The one thing that was crystal clear was that these . . . call them people . . . were far, far ahead of his own twenty-first-century technology, right?

His muscles tightened despite Dahak's reassurances as he opened the hatch, but the air that swirled about him had no immediately lethal effect. In fact, it smelled far better than the inside of the Beagle. It was crisp and a bit chill, its freshness carrying just a kiss of a spicy evergreen-like scent, and some of his tension eased as he inhaled deeply. It was harder to feel terrified of aliens who breathed something like this—always assuming they hadn't manufactured it purely for his own consumption, of course.

It was four-and-a-half meters to the floor, and he found himself wishing his hosts had left gravity well enough alone as he swung down the emergency hand-holds and approached the patiently waiting vehicle with caution.

It seemed innocuous enough. There were two comfortable looking chairs proportioned for something the same size and shape as a human, but no visible control panel. The most interesting thing, though, was that the upper half of the vehicle's hull was transparent—from the inside. From the outside, it looked exactly the same as the bronze-colored floor under his feet.

He shrugged and climbed aboard, noticing that the silently suspended vehicle didn't even quiver under his weight. He chose the right-hand seat, then made himself sit motionless as the padded surface *squirmed* under him. A moment later, it had reconfigured itself exactly to the contours of his body and the hatch licked shut.

"Are you ready, Commander?" His host's voice came from no apparent source, and MacIntyre nodded.

"Let 'er rip," he said, and the vehicle began to move.

At least there was a sense of movement this time. He sank firmly back into the seat under at least two gees' acceleration. No wonder the thing was bullet-shaped! The little vehicle rocketed across the cavern, straight at a featureless metal wall, and he flinched involuntarily. But a hatch popped open an instant before they hit, and they darted straight into another brightly-lit bore, this one no wider than two or three of the vehicles in which he rode.

He considered speaking further to Dahak, but the only real purpose would be to bolster his own nerve and "prove" his equanimity, and he was damned if he'd chatter to hide the heebie-jeebies. So he sat silently, watching the walls flash by, and tried to estimate their velocity.

It was impossible. The walls weren't featureless, but speed reduced them to a blur that was long before the acceleration eased into the familiar sensation of free-fall, and MacIntyre felt a sense of wonder pressing the last panic from his soul. This base dwarfed the vastest human installation he'd ever seen—how in God's name had a bunch of aliens managed an engineering project of such magnitude without anyone even noticing?

There was a fresh spurt of acceleration and a sideways surge of inertia as the vehicle swept through a curved junction and darted into yet another tunnel. It seemed to stretch forever, like the one that had engulfed his Beagle, and his vehicle scooted down its very center. He kept waiting to arrive, but it was a very, very long time before their headlong pace began to slow.

His first warning was the movement of the vehicle's interior. The entire cockpit swiveled smoothly, until he was facing back the way he'd come, and then the drag of deceleration hit him. It went on and on, and the blurred walls beyond the transparent canopy slowed. He could make out details once more, including the maws of other tunnels, and then they slowed virtually to a walk. They swerved gently down one of those intersecting tunnels, little wider than the vehicle itself, then slid alongside a side opening and stopped. The hatch flicked soundlessly open.

"If you will debark, Commander?" the mellow voice invited, and MacIntyre shrugged and stepped down onto what looked for all the world like shag carpeting. The vehicle closed its hatch behind him and slid silently backwards, vanishing the way it had come.

"Follow the guide, please, Commander."

He looked about blankly for a moment, then saw a flashing light globe hanging in mid-air. It bobbed twice, as if to attract his attention, then headed down a side corridor at a comfortable pace.

A ten-minute walk took him past numerous closed doors, each labeled in a strangely attractive, utterly meaningless flowing script, and air as fresh and cool as the docking cavern's blew into his face. There were tiny sounds in the background, so soft and unintrusive it took him several minutes to notice them, and they were not

the mechanical ones he might have expected. Instead, he
heard small, soft stirrings, like wind in leaves or the distant calls of birds, forming a soothing backdrop that
helped one forget the artificiality of the environment.

But then the corridor ended abruptly at a hatch of that
same bronze-colored alloy. It was bank-vault huge, and
it bore the first ornamentation he'd seen. A stupendous,
three-headed beast writhed across it, with arched wings
poised to launch it into flight. Its trio of upthrust heads
faced in different directions, as if to watch all approaches
at once, and cat-like forefeet were raised before it, claws
half-extended as if to simultaneously proffer and protect
the spired-glory starburst floating just above them.

MacIntyre recognized it instantly, though the enormous bas-relief dragon was neither Eastern nor Western
in interpretation, and he paused to rub his chin, wondering what a creature of Earthly mythology was doing in
an extra-terrestrial base hidden on Earth's moon. But
that question was a strangely distant thing, surpassed by
a greater wonder that was almost awe as the huge, stunningly life-like eyes seemed to measure him with a calm,
dispassionate majesty that might yet become terrible
wrath if he transgressed.

He never knew precisely how long he stood staring at
the dragon and stared at by it, but in the end, his light-
globe guide gave a rather impatient twitch and drifted
closer to the hatch. MacIntyre shook himself and followed with a wry half-smile, and the bronze portal slid
open as he approached. It was at least fifteen centimeters
thick, yet it was but the first of a dozen equally thick
hatches, forming a close-spaced, immensely strong barrier, and he felt small and fragile as he followed the
globe down the silently opening passage. The multi-ply
panels licked shut behind him, equally silently, and he
tried to suppress a feeling of imprisonment. But then his
destination appeared before him at last and he stopped,
all other considerations forgotten.

The spherical chamber was larger than the old war
room under Cheyenne Mountain, larger even than main
mission control at Shepherd, and the stark perfection of

its form, the featureless sweep of its colossal walls, pressed down upon him as if to impress his tininess upon him. He stood on a platform thrust out from one curving wall—a transparent platform, dotted with a score of comfortable, couch-like chairs before what could only be control consoles, though there seemed to be remarkably few read-outs and in-puts—and the far side of the chamber was dominated by a tremendous view screen. The blue-white globe of Earth floated in its center, and the cloud-swirled loveliness caught at MacIntyre's throat. He was back in his first shuttle cockpit, seeing that azure and argent beauty for the first time, as if the mind-battering incidents of the past hour had made him freshly aware of his bond with all that planet was and meant.

"Please be seated, Commander." The soft, mellow voice broke into his thoughts almost gently, yet it seemed to fill the vast space. "Here." The light globe danced briefly above one padded chair—the one with the largest console, at the very lip of the unrailed platform—and he approached it gingerly. He had never suffered from agoraphobia or vertigo, but it was a long, long way down, and the platform was so transparent he seemed to be striding on air itself as he crossed it.

His "guide" disappeared as he settled into the chair, not even blinking this time as it conformed to his body, and the voice spoke again.

"Now, Commander, I shall try to explain what is happening."

"You can start," MacIntyre interrupted, determined to be more than a passive listener, "by explaining how you people managed to build a base this size on our moon without us noticing."

"We built no base, Commander."

MacIntyre's green eyes narrowed in irritation.

"Well somebody sure as hell did," he growled.

"You are suffering under a misapprehension, Commander. This is not a base 'on' your moon. It *is* your moon."

*   *   *

For just an instant, MacIntyre was certain he'd misunderstood.

"What did you say?" he asked finally.

"I said this is your moon, Commander. In point of fact, you are seated on the command bridge of a spacecraft."

"A spacecraft? As big as the moon?" MacIntyre said faintly.

"Correct. A vessel some three thousand—three-two-oh-two-point-seven-nine-five, to be precise—of your kilometers in diameter."

"But—" MacIntyre's voice died in shock. He'd known the installation was huge, but no one could *replace* the moon without *someone* noticing, however advanced their technology!

"I don't believe it," he said flatly.

"Nonetheless, it is true."

"It's not possible," MacIntyre said stubbornly. "If this thing is the size you say, what happened to the real moon?"

"It was destroyed," his informant said calmly. "With the exception of sufficient of its original material to make up the negligible difference in diameter, it was dropped into your sun. It is standard Fleet procedure to camouflage picket units or any capital ship that may be required to spend extended periods in systems not claimed by the Imperium."

"You camouflaged your ship as our *moon*? That's insane!"

"On the contrary, Commander. A planetoid-class starship is not an easy object to hide. Replacing an existing moon of appropriate size is by far the simplest means of concealment, particularly when, as in this case, the original surface contours are faithfully recreated as part of the procedure."

"Preposterous! Somebody on Earth would have noticed *something* going on!"

"No, Commander, they would not. In point of fact, your species was not on Earth to observe it."

"*What?!*"

"The events I have just described took place approximately fifty-one thousand of your years ago," his informant said gently.

MacIntyre sagged around his bones. He was mad, he thought calmly. That was certainly the most reasonable explanation.

"Perhaps it would be simpler if I explained from the beginning rather than answering questions," the voice suggested.

"Perhaps it would be simpler if you explained in person!" MacIntyre snapped, suddenly savage in his confusion.

"But I am explaining in person," the voice said.

"I mean face-to-face," MacIntyre grated.

"Unfortunately, Commander, I do not have a face," the voice said, and MacIntyre could have sworn he heard wry amusement in it. "You see, in a sense, you are sitting inside me."

"Inside—?" MacIntyre whispered.

"Precisely, Commander. I am Dahak, the central command computer of the Imperial ship-of-the-line *Dahak*."

"Gaaa," MacIntyre said softly.

"I beg your pardon?" Dahak said calmly. "Shall I continue?"

MacIntyre gripped the arms of his chair and closed his eyes, counting slowly to a hundred.

"Sure," he said at last, opening his eyes slowly. "Why don't you do that?"

"Very well. Please observe the visual display, Commander."

Earth vanished, and another image replaced it. It was a sphere, as bronze-bright as the cylinder that had captured his Beagle, but despite the lack of any reference scale, he knew it was far, far larger.

The image turned and grew, and details became visible, swelling rapidly into vast blisters and domes. There were no visible ports, and he saw no sign of any means of propulsion. The hull was completely featureless but for those smoothly rounded protrusions ... until its turning motion brought him face-to-face with a tremendous replica of the dragon that had adorned the hatch. It sprawled over one face of the sphere like a vast ensign, arrogant and proud, and he swallowed. It covered a relatively small area of the hull, but if that sphere was what he thought it was, *this* dragon was about the size of Montana.

"This is *Dahak*," the voice told him, "Hull Number One-Seven-Seven-Two-Nine-One, an *Utu*-class planetoid of Battle Fleet, built fifty-two thousand Terran years ago in the Anhur System by the Fourth Imperium."

MacIntyre stared at the screen, too entranced to disbelieve. The image of the ship filled it entirely, seeming as if it must fall from the display and crush him, and then it dissolved into a computer-generated schematic of the monster vessel. It was too stupendous for him to register much, and the schematic changed even as he watched, rolling to present him with an exploded polar view of deck after inconceivable deck as the voice continued.

"The *Utu*-class were designed both for the line of battle and for independent, long-term survey and picket deployment, with core crews of two hundred and fifty thousand. Intended optimum deployment time is twenty-five Terran years, with provision for a sixty percent increase in personnel during that period. Maximum deployment time is virtually unlimited, assuming crew expansion is contained.

"In addition to small, two-seat fighters that may be employed in either attack or defense, Dahak deploys sublight parasite warships massing up to eighty thousand tons. Shipboard weaponry centers around hyper-capable missile batteries backed up by direct-fire energy weapons. Weapon payloads range from chemical warheads through fusion, anti-matter, and gravitonic warheads. Essentially, Commander, this ship could vaporize your planet."

"My God!" MacIntyre whispered. He wanted to disbelieve—God, *how* he wanted to!—but he couldn't.

"Sublight propulsion," Dahak went on, ignoring the interruption, "relies upon phased gravitonic progression. Your present terminology lacks the referents for an accurate description, but for purposes of visualization, you may consider it a reactionless drive with a maximum attainable velocity of fifty-two-point-four percent that of light. Above that velocity, a vessel of this size would lose phase lock, and be destroyed.

"Unlike previous designs, the *Utu*-class do not rely upon multi-dimensional drives—what your science fiction writers have dubbed 'hyper drives,' Commander—for faster-than-light travel. Instead, this ship employs the Enchanach Drive. You may envision it as the creation of converging artificially-generated 'black holes,' which force the vessel out of phase with normal space in a series of instantaneous transpositions between coordinates in normal space. Under Enchanach Drive, dwell time in normal space between transpositions is approximately point-seven-five Terran femtoseconds.

"The Enchanach Drive's maximum effective velocity is approximately Cee-six factorial. While this is lower than that of the latest hyper drives, Enchanach Drive vessels have several tactical advantages. Most importantly, they may enter, maneuver in, and leave a supralight state at will, whereas hyper drive vessels may enter and leave supralight only at pre-selected coordinates.

"Power generation for the *Utu*-class—"

"Stop." MacIntyre's single word halted *Dahak*'s voice instantly, and he rubbed his eyes slowly, wishing he could wake up at home in bed.

"Look," he said finally, "this is all very interesting, uh, Dahak." He felt a bit silly speaking to a machine, even one like this. "But aside from convincing me that this is one mean mother of a ship, it doesn't seem very pertinent. I mean, I'm impressed as hell, but what does anyone need with a ship like this? Thirty-two hundred kilometers in diameter, eighty-thousand-ton parasite warships, two-hundred-thousand-man crews, vaporize planets.... Jesus H. Christ! What *is* this 'Fourth Imperium'? Who in God's name does it need that kind of firepower against, and what the hell is it doing here?!"

"I will explain, if I may resume my briefing," Dahak said calmly, and MacIntyre snorted, then waved for it to continue. "Thank you, Commander.

"You are correct: technical data may be left to the future. But for you to understand my difficulty—and the reason it is your difficulty, as well—I must summarize some history. Please understand that much of this represents reconstruction and deduction based upon very scant physical evidence.

"Briefly, the Fourth Imperium is a political unit, originating upon the Planet Birhat in the Bia System some seven thousand years prior to *Dahak*'s entry into your solar system. As of that time, the Imperium consisted of some fifteen hundred star systems. It is called the Fourth Imperium because it is the third such interstellar entity to exist within recorded history. The existence of at least one prehistoric imperium, designated the 'First Imperium' by Imperial historians, has been conclusively demonstrated, although archaeological evidence suggests that, in fact, a minimum of nine additional prehistoric imperia intervened between the First and Second Imperium. All, however, were destroyed in part or in whole by the Achuultani."

A formless chill tingled down MacIntyre's spine.

"And just what were the Achuultani?" he asked, trying to keep his strange, shadowy emotions out of his voice.

"Available data are insufficient for conclusive determinations," Dahak replied. "Fragmentary evidence suggests that the Achuultani are a single species, possibly of extragalactic origin. Even the name is a transliteration of a transliteration from an unattested myth of the Second Imperium. More data may have been amassed during actual incursions, but most such information was lost in the general destruction attendant upon such incursions or during the reconstruction that followed them. What has been retained pertains more directly to tactics and apparent objectives. On the basis of that data, historians of the Fourth Imperium conclude that the first such incursion occurred on the close order of seventy million Terran years ago."

"*Seventy mil—?!*" MacIntyre chopped himself off. *No* species could survive over such an incredible period.

Then again, the moon couldn't be an alien starship, could it? He nodded jerkily for *Dahak* to continue.

"Supporting evidence may be found upon your own planet, Commander," the computer said calmly. "The sudden disappearance of terrestrial dinosaurs at the end of your Mesozoic Era coincides with the first known Achuultani incursion. Many Terran scientists have suggested that this may have been the consequence of a massive meteor impact. My own observations suggest that they are correct, and the Achuultani have always favored large kinetic weapons."

"But ... but *why*? Why would anyone wipe out dinosaurs?!"

"The Achuultani objective," *Dahak* said precisely, "appears to be the obliteration of all competing species, wherever situated. While it is unlikely that terrestrial dinosaurs, who were essentially a satisfied life form, might have competed with them, that would not prevent them from striking the planet as a long-term precaution against the emergence of a competitor. Their attention was probably drawn to Earth by the presence of a First Imperium colony, however. I base this conclusion on data that indicate the existence of a First Imperium military installation on your fifth planet."

"Fifth planet?" MacIntyre parroted, overloaded by what he was hearing. "You mean ... ?"

"Precisely, Commander: the asteroid belt. It would appear they struck your fifth planet a bit harder than Earth, and it was much smaller and less geologically stable to begin with."

"Are you sure?"

"I have had sufficient time to amass conclusive observational data. In addition, such an act would be consistent with recorded Achuultani tactics and the deduced military policies of the First Imperium, which apparently preferred to place system defense bases upon centrally-located non-life-bearing bodies."

Dahak paused, and MacIntyre sat silent, trying to grasp the sheer stretch of time involved. Then the computer spoke again.

"Shall I continue?" it asked, and he managed another nod.

"Thank you. Imperial analysts speculate that the periodic Achuultani incursions into this arm of the galaxy represent sweeps in search of potential competitors—what your own military might term 'search and destroy' missions—rather than attempts to expand their imperial sphere. The Achuultani culture would appear to be extremely stable, one might almost say static, for very few technological advances have been observed since the Second Imperium. The precise reasons for this apparent cultural stasis and for the widely varying intervals between such sweeps are unknown, as is the precise locus from which they originate. While some evidence does suggest an extra-galactic origin for the species, pattern analysis suggests that the Achuultani currently occupy a region far to the galactic east. This, unfortunately, places Sol in an extremely exposed position, as your solar system lies on the eastern fringe of the Imperium. In short, the Achuultani must pass Sol to reach the Imperium.

"This has not mattered to your planet of late, as there has been nothing to attract Achuultani attention to this system since the end of the First Incursion. That protection no longer obtains, however. Your civilization's technical base is now sufficiently advanced to produce an electronic and neutrino signature that their instruments cannot fail to detect."

"My God!" MacIntyre turned pale as the implications struck home.

"Precisely, Commander. Your sun's location also explains *Dahak*'s presence in this region. *Dahak*'s mission was to picket the Noarl System, directly in the center of the traditional Achuultani incursion route. Unfortunately—or, more precisely, by hostile design—*Dahak* suffered catastrophic failure of a major component of its Enchanach Drive while en route to its intended station, and Senior Fleet Captain Druaga was forced to stop here for repairs."

"But if the damage was repairable, why are you still here?"

"Because there was, in fact, no damage." *Dahak*'s voice

was as measured as ever, but MacIntyre's hyper-sensitive mind seemed to hear a hidden core of anger. "The 'failure' was contrived by *Dahak*'s chief engineer, Fleet Captain (Engineering) Anu, as the opening gambit in a mutiny against Fleet authority."

"*Mutiny?*"

"Mutiny. Fleet Captain Anu and a minority of sympathizers among the crew feared that a new Achuultani incursion was imminent. As an advanced picket directly in the path of any such incursion, *Dahak* would very probably be destroyed. Rather than risk destruction, the mutineers chose to seize the ship and flee to a distant star in search of a colonizable planet."

"Was that feasible?" MacIntyre asked in a fascinated tone.

"It was. *Dahak*'s cruising radius is effectively unlimited, Commander, with technical capabilities sufficient to inaugurate a sound technology base on any habitable world, and the crew would provide ample genetic material for a viable planetary population. Moreover, the simulation of a major engineering failure was a cleverly conceived tactic to prevent detection of the mutiny until the mutineers could move beyond possible interception by other Fleet units. Fleet Captain Anu knew that Senior Fleet Captain Druaga would transmit a malfunction report. If no further word was received, Fleet Central's natural assumption would be that the damage had been sufficient to destroy the ship."

"I see. But I gather from your choice of tense that the mutiny failed?"

"Incorrect, Commander."

"Then it succeeded?" MacIntyre asked, scratching his head in puzzlement.

"Incorrect," *Dahak* said again.

"Well it must have done one or the other!"

"Incorrect," *Dahak* said a third time. "The mutiny, Commander, has not yet been resolved."

MacIntyre sighed and leaned back in resignation, crossing his arms. *Dahak*'s last statement was preposterous. Yet his concept of words like "preposterous" was acquiring a certain punch-drunk elasticity.

"All right," he said finally. "I'll humor you. How can a mutiny that started fifty thousand years ago still be unresolved?"

"In essence," *Dahak* said, seemingly impervious to MacIntyre's irony, "it is a condition of deadlock. Senior Fleet Captain Druaga instructed Comp Cent to render the interior of the ship uninhabitable in order to force evacuation of the vessel by mutineers and loyalists alike, after which *Dahak*'s weaponry would command the situation. Only loyal officers would be permitted to reenter the vessel once the interior had been decontaminated, at which point Fleet control would be restored.

"Unknown to Senior Fleet Captain Druaga, however, Fleet Captain Anu had implanted contingency instructions in his back-up engineering computers and isolated them from Comp Cent's net. Those instructions were intended to destroy *Dahak*'s internal power rooms, with the ultimate goal of depriving Comp Cent of power and so destroying it. As chief engineer, and armed with complete knowledge of how the sabotage had been achieved, it would have been comparatively simple for him to effect repairs and assume control of the ship.

"When Comp Cent implemented Senior Fleet Captain Druaga's orders, all loyal personnel abandoned ship in lifeboats. Fleet Captain Anu, however, had secretly prepared several sublight parasites for the apparent purpose of marooning any crewmen who refused to accept his authority. In the event, his own followers made use of those transports and a small number of armed parasites when they evacuated *Dahak*, with the result that they carried to Earth a complete and functional, if limited, technical base. The loyalists, by contrast, had only the emergency kits of their lifeboats.

"This would not have mattered if Fleet Captain Anu's sabotage programs had not very nearly achieved their purpose. Before Comp Cent became aware of and deactivated them, three hundred and ten of *Dahak*'s three hundred and twelve fusion power plants had been destroyed, dropping *Dahak's* internal power net below minimal operational density. Sufficient power remained to implement a defensive fire plan as per Senior Fleet Captain Druaga's orders, but not to simultaneously decontaminate the interior and effect emergency repairs, as well. As a result, Comp Cent was unable to immediately and fully execute its orders. It was necessary to repair the damage before Comp Cent could decontaminate, yet repairs amounted to virtual rebuilding and required more power than remained. Indeed, power levels were so low that it was impossible even to operate *Dahak's* core tap. This, in turn, meant that emergency power reserves were quickly drained and that it was necessary to spend extended periods rebuilding those reserves between piecemeal repair activities.

"Because of these extreme conditions, Comp Cent was dysfunctional for erratic but extended periods, though automatic defensive programs remained operational. Scanner recordings indicate that seven mutinous parasites were destroyed during the repair period, but each defensive action drained power levels still further, which, in turn, extended Comp Cent's dysfunctional periods and further slowed repairs by extending the intervals required to rebuild reserve power to permit reactivation of sufficient of Comp Cent to direct each new stage of work.

"Because of this, approximately eleven Terran decades elapsed before Comp Cent once more became fully functional, albeit at marginal levels, and so was able to begin decontamination. During that time, the lifeboats manned by loyal personnel had become inoperable, as had all communication equipment aboard them. As a result, it was not possible for any loyalist to return to *Dahak*."

"Why didn't you just pick them up?" MacIntyre demanded. "Assuming any of them were still alive, that is."

"Many remained alive." There was a new note in *Dahak's* voice. Almost a squirmy one, as if it were embarrassed. "Unfortunately, none were bridge officers. Because of that, none carried Fleet communicator implants, making it impossible to contact them. Without that contact, command protocols in Comp Cent's core programming severely limited *Dahak*'s options."

The voice paused, and MacIntyre wrinkled his brow. Command protocols?

"Meaning what?" he asked finally.

"Meaning, Commander, that it was not possible for Comp Cent to consider retrieving them," *Dahak* admitted, and the computer's embarrassment was now unmistakable. "You must understand that Comp Cent had never been intended by its designers to function independently. While self-aware in the crudest sense, Comp Cent then possessed only very primitive and limited versions of those qualities which humans term 'imagination' and 'initiative.' In addition, strict obedience to the commands of lawful superiors is thoroughly—and quite properly—embedded in Comp Cent's core programs. Without an order to send tenders to retrieve loyal officers, Comp Cent could not initiate the action; without communication, no loyal officer could order Comp Cent to do so. Assuming, of course, that any such loyal officers had reason to believe that *Dahak* remained functional to retrieve them."

"Damn!" MacIntyre said softly. "Catch twenty-two with a vengeance."

"Precisely, Commander." *Dahak* sounded relieved to have gotten that bit of explanation behind it.

"But the mutineers still had a functional tech base," MacIntyre mused. "So what happened to them?"

"They remain on Earth," *Dahak* said calmly, and MacIntyre bolted upright.

"You mean they died there, don't you?" he asked tensely.

"Incorrect, Commander. They—and their parasites—still exist."

"That's ridiculous! Even assuming everything you've told me so far is true, we'd have to be aware of the presence of an advanced alien civilization!"

"Incorrect," *Dahak* said patiently. "Their installation is and has been concealed beneath the surface of your continent of Antarctica. For the past five thousand Terran years, small groups of them have emerged to mingle briefly with your population, then returned to their enclave to rejoin the bulk of their fellows in stasis— suspended animation, in your own terms."

"Damn it, Dahak!" MacIntyre exploded. "Are you telling me bug-eyed monsters can stroll around Earth and nobody even *notices*?!"

"Negative, Commander. The mutineers are not 'bug-eyed monsters.' On the contrary; they are humans."

Colin MacIntyre slumped back into his chair, eyes suddenly full of horror.

"You mean . . . ?" he whispered.

"Precisely, Commander. Every Terran human is descended from *Dahak's* crew."

Chapter Four

MacIntyre felt numb.

"Wait," he said hoarsely. "Wait a minute! What about evolution? Damn it, Dahak, homo sapiens is related to every other mammal on the planet!"

"Correct," *Dahak* said unemotionally. "Following the First Imperium's fall, one of its unidentified non-human successor imperia re-seeded many worlds the Achuultani struck. Earth was one such planet. So also was Mycos, the true homeworld of the human race and the capital of the Second Imperium until its destruction some seventy-one thousand years ago. The same ancestral fauna were used to re-seed all Earth-type planets. Earth's Neanderthals were thus not ancestors of your own race but rather very distant cousins. They did not, I regret to say, fare well against *Dahak*'s crew and its descendants."

"Sweet suffering Jesus!" MacIntyre breathed. Then his eyes narrowed. "Dahak, do you mean to tell me that you've sat on your electronic ass up here for fifty thousand years and done absolutely nothing?"

"That is one way of phrasing it," *Dahak* admitted uncomfortably.

"But *why*, goddamn it?!"

"What would you have had me do, Commander? Senior Fleet Captain Druaga issued Priority Alpha Category One orders to suppress the mutineers. Such priority one orders take absolute precedence over all directives with less than Alpha Priority and may be altered only by the direction of Fleet Central. No lesser authority— including the one that first issued them—may change them. Accordingly, *Dahak* has no option but to remain in this system until such time as all surviving mutineers are taken into custody or destroyed."

"So why didn't you seek new orders from this Fleet Central of yours?" MacIntyre grated.

"I cannot. Fleet Captain Anu's attack on Communications inflicted irreparable damage."

"You can rebuild three-hundred-plus fusion plants and you can't fix a frigging *radio*?!"

"The situation is somewhat more complicated than that, Commander," *Dahak* replied, with what MacIntyre unwillingly recognized as commendable restraint. "Supralight communication is maintained via the multidimensional communicator, commonly referred to as the 'hypercom,' a highly refined derivative of the much shorter-ranged 'fold-space' communicator used by Fleet personnel. Both combine elements of hyperspace and gravitonic technology to distort normal space and create a point-to-point congruence between distant foci, but in the case of the hypercom these distortions or 'folds' may span as many as several thousand light-years. A hypercom transmitter is a massive installation, and certain of its essential components contain Mycosan, a synthetic element that cannot be produced out of shipboard resources. As all spare components are currently aboard Fleet Captain Anu's parasites, repairs are impossible. *Dahak* can receive hypercom transmissions, but cannot initiate a signal."

"That's the *only* way you can communicate?"

"The Imperium abandoned primitive light-speed communications several millennia before the mutiny, Commander. Since, however, it was evident that repair of

Dahak's hypercom was impossible and no Fleet unit had been sent to investigate *Dahak*'s original malfunction report, Comp Cent constructed a radio transmitter and sent a report at light speed to the nearest Fleet base. It is improbable that the Imperium would have abandoned a base of such importance, and Comp Cent therefore concluded that the message was not recognized by its intended recipients. Whatever the reason, Fleet Central has never responded, thus precluding any modification of *Dahak*'s Alpha Priority instructions."

"But that doesn't explain why you didn't carry out your original orders and blast the bastards as they left the ship!" MacIntyre snarled venomously.

"That is an incorrect interpretation of Comp Cent's orders, Commander. Senior Fleet Captain Druaga's instructions specified the destruction of mutinous vessels *approaching* within five thousand kilometers; they did *not* specify the destruction of mutinous vessels *departing* *Dahak*."

"They didn't—!" MacIntyre stopped himself and silently recited the names of the Presidents. "All right," he said finally, "I can accept that, I suppose. But why haven't you blasted them off the planet since? Surely that comes under the heading of taking them into custody or destroying them?"

"It does. Such action, however, would conflict with Alpha Priority core programs. This vessel has the capacity to penetrate the defenses Fleet Captain Anu has established to protect his enclave, but only by using weaponry that would destroy seventy percent of the human race upon the planet. Destruction of non-Achuultani sentients except in direct self-defense is prohibited."

"Well, what have *they* been doing all this time?"

"I cannot say with certainty," *Dahak* admitted. "It is impossible for my sensors to penetrate their defensive systems, and it is apparent that they have chosen to employ a substantial amount of stealth technology. Without observational data of their inner councils, meaningful analysis is impossible."

"You must have some idea!"

"Affirmative. Please remember, however, that all is speculation and may be offered only as such."

"So go ahead and speculate, damn it!"

"Acknowledged," *Dahak* said calmly. "It is my opinion that the mutineers have interacted with Terra-born humans since such time as your planetary population attained sufficient density to support indigenous civilizations. Initially, this contact was quite open, leading to the creation of the various anthropomorphic pantheons of deities. Interaction with your own Western Civilization, however, particularly since your sixteenth century, has been surreptitious and designed to accelerate your technical development. Please note that this represents a substantive change in the mutineers' original activities, which were designed to promote superstition, religion, and pseudo-religion in place of rationalism and scientific thought."

"Why should they try to slow our development?" MacIntyre demanded. "And if they did, why change tactics?"

"In my opinion, their original intent was to prevent the birth of an indigenous technology that might threaten their own safety, on the one hand, or attract the Achuultani, on the other. Recall that their original motive for mutiny was to preserve themselves from destruction at Achuultani hands.

"Recently, however—" MacIntyre winced at hearing someone refer to the sixteenth century as "recently" "—the focus of their activities has altered. Perhaps they believe the incursion they feared has already occurred and that they are therefore safe, or perhaps there has been a change in their leadership, leading to changes in policy. My opinion, however, is that they have concluded that *Dahak* is not and will not again become fully operational."

"What? Why should that matter?"

"It would matter if they assume, as I am postulating that they have, that sufficient damage was inflicted upon *Dahak*'s power generation capacity as to preclude repairs. Fleet Captain Anu cannot know what Senior Fleet Captain Druaga's final instructions were. As he is unaware that Senior Fleet Captain Druaga's Alpha Priority orders have required *Dahak* to remain on station, he may well conclude that *Dahak*'s failure to depart in search of assistance indicates that supralight travel is no longer possible for *Dahak*. Yet if there were sufficient power for repairs, *Dahak* would be supralight-capable, as there was never an actual failure of the Enchanach Drive. *Dahak*'s very presence here may thus be construed as empirical evidence of near-total incapacity."

"So why not come out and grab you?"

"Because he has conclusive evidence that sufficient power does remain for pre-programmed defensive fire plans, yet no fire has been directed against the primitive spacecraft Terra-born humans have dispatched to their 'moon.' Accordingly, he may believe *Dahak*'s command capabilities are too deeply impaired to re-program those defensive fire plans and that those plans do not provide for interference with locally-produced spacecraft. Assuming this entirely speculative chain of reasoning is correct, he may well hope to push your planet into developing interstellar craft in order to escape this star system. This theory is consistent with observed facts, including the world wars and Soviet-American 'cold war' of the twentieth-century, which resulted in pressurized research and development driven by military requirements."

"But the cold war ended decades ago," MacIntyre pointed out.

"Agreed. Yet that, too, is consistent with the theory I have offered. Consider, Commander: the superpowers of the last century have been drawn together in cooperation against the growing militancy of your so-called Third World, particularly the religio-political blocs centered on radical Islam and the Asian Alliance. This has permitted the merger of the First World technical base—ConEuropean, Russian, North American, and Australian-Japanese alike—while maintaining the pressure of military need. In addition, certain aspects of Imperial technology have begun to appear in your civilization. Your gravitonic survey instruments are a prime example of this process, for they are several centuries in advance of any other portion of your technology."

"I see." MacIntyre considered the computer's logic carefully, so caught up in *Dahak*'s story he almost forgot his own part in it. "But why push for starships? Why not just use a 'locally-produced' ship to take *you* over?"

"It is possible that he intends to do precisely that, Commander. Indeed, had your vessel not fired upon mine, I might have taken your sub-surface survey device as just such an attempt, in which case I would have destroyed you." MacIntyre shivered at how calmly *Dahak* spoke. "My preliminary bio-scans indicated that you were not yourself a mutineer, but had you demanded entry, had you failed to resist—had you, in fact, done anything that indicated either an awareness of *Dahak*'s existence or a desire to enter—my core programming would have assumed at least the possibility that you were in Fleet Captain Anu's service. That assumption would have left me no choice but to destroy you as per Senior Fleet Captain Druaga's final directives.

"However," the computer continued serenely, "I do not believe he would make that attempt. Either *Dahak* had sufficient power to repair the damage, in which case the ship is, in fact, fully operational and would destroy him or his minions, or else *Dahak* had insufficient power to decontaminate the vessel's interior, in which case re-entry would remain effectively impossible without Imperial technology—which *would* activate any operational defensive programming." The computer's voice gave MacIntyre the strong impression of a verbal shrug. "In either case, *Dahak* would be useless to him."

"But he expects you to let locally-produced starships get away from you?" MacIntyre asked skeptically.

"If," *Dahak* said patiently, "this unit were, indeed, no longer fully operational, automatic defensive fire plans would not be interested in vessels leaving the star system."

"But you *aren't* inoperative, so what *would* you do?"

"I would dispatch one or more armed parasites to bio-scan range and scan their personnel. If mutineers were detected on board them, I would have no choice but to destroy them."

MacIntyre frowned. "Uh, excuse me, Dahak, but wouldn't that be a rather broader interpretation of your orders? I mean, you let the mutineers escape to the planet because you hadn't been ordered to stop them, right?"

"That is correct, Commander. It has occurred to me, however, that Comp Cent's original interpretation of Senior Fleet Captain Druaga's orders, while essentially correct, did not encompass Senior Fleet Captain Druaga's full intent. Subsequent analysis suggests that had he known the mutineers would employ parasites so readily distinguishable from the loyal crew's lifeboats, he would have ordered their immediate destruction. Whether or not this speculation is correct, the fact remains that no mutineer may be allowed to leave this star system by any means. Allowing any mutinous personnel to escape would conflict with *Dahak's* Alpha Priority orders to suppress the mutiny."

"I can see that," MacIntyre murmured, then paused, struck by a new thought. "Wait a minute. You say Anu's assumed you're no longer operational—"

"Incorrect, Commander," *Dahak* interrupted. "I stated that I have *speculated* to that effect."

"All right, so it's speculative. But if he has, haven't you blown it? You couldn't have grabbed my Beagle if you were inoperative, could you?"

"I could not," *Dahak* conceded, "yet he cannot be certain that I did so."

"What? Well then, what the hell *does* he think happened?"

"It was my intention to convince him that your vessel was lost due to an onboard malfunction."

"*Lost?*" MacIntyre jerked up in his couch. "What d'you mean, 'lost'?"

"Commander," *Dahak* said almost apologetically, "it was necessary. If Fleet Captain Anu determines that *Dahak* is indeed functional, he may take additional protective measures. The destruction of his enclave's present defenses by brute force would kill seventy percent of all Terran humans; if he becomes sufficiently alarmed to strengthen them still further the situation may well become utterly impossible of resolution."

"I didn't ask why you did it!" MacIntyre spat. "I asked what you meant by 'lost,' goddamn it!"

Dahak did not answer directly. Instead, MacIntyre suddenly heard another voice—*his* voice, speaking in the clipped, emotionless tones every ex-test pilot seems to drop into when disaster strikes.

". . . ayday. Mayday. Heinlein Base, this is Papa-Mike One-X-Ray. I have an explosion in number three fuel cell. Negative function primary flight computers. I am tumbling. Negative response attitude control. I say again. Negative response attitude control."

"Heinlein copies, One-X-Ray," a voice crackled back. He recognized that soft Southern accent, he thought in a queerly detached way. Sandy Tillotson—Lieutenant Colonel Sandra Tillotson, that was. "We have you on scope."

"Then you see what I see, Sandy," his own voice said calmly. "I make it roughly ten minutes to impact."

There was a brief pause, then Tillotson's voice came back, as flat and calm as "he" was.

"Affirmative, Colin."

"I'm gonna take a chance and go for crash ignition," his voice said. "She's tumbling like a mother, but if I can catch her at the right attitude—"

"Understood, Colin. Luck."

"Thanks. Coming up on ignition—*now*." There was another brief pause, and then he heard "himself" sigh. "No joy, Sandy. Caught it wrong. Tell Sean I—"

And then there was only silence.

MacIntyre swallowed. He had just heard himself die, and the experience had not been pleasant. Nor was the realization of how completely *Dahak* had covered its tracks. As far as any living human knew, Lieutenant Commander Colin MacIntyre no longer existed, for no one would wonder what had become of him once they got to the crash site. Somehow he never doubted there would be a crash site, but given the nature of the "crash" he'd just listened to, it would consist of very, very tiny bits and pieces.

"You *bastard*," he said softly.

"It was necessary," *Dahak* replied unflinchingly. "If you had completed your flight with proof of *Dahak*'s existence, would not your superiors have mounted an immediate expedition to explore your find?" MacIntyre gritted his teeth and refused to answer.

"What would you have had me do, Commander? Fleet Captain Anu could not enter this vessel using the parasites in which he escaped to Earth, but could I know positively that any Terra-born humans sent to explore *Dahak*'s interior had not been suborned by him? Recall that my own core programming would compel me to consider that any vessel that deliberately sought entry but did not respond with proper Fleet authorization codes was under mutinous control. Should I have allowed a situation in which I must fire on every ship of any type that came near? One that would also require me to destroy every enclave your people have established on the lunar surface? You must realize as well as I that if I had acted in any other way, Fleet Captain Anu would not merely suspect but *know* that *Dahak* remains operational. Knowing that, must I not assume that any effort to enter *Dahak*—or, indeed, any further activity on the lunar surface of any type whatever—might be or fall under his direct control?"

MacIntyre knew *Dahak* was a machine, but he recognized genuine desperation in the mellow voice and, despite himself, felt an unwilling sympathy for the huge ship's dilemma.

He glared down at his clenched fists, bitter anger fighting a wash of sympathetic horror. Yes, *Dahak* was a machine, but it was a self-aware machine, and MacIntyre's human soul cringed as he imagined its endless solitary confinement. For fifty-one millennia, the stupendous ship had orbited Earth, powerful enough to wipe the planet from the face of the universe yet forever unable to carry out its orders, caught between conflicting directives it could not resolve. Just thinking of such a purgatory was enough to ice his blood, but understanding didn't change his own fate. *Dahak* had "killed" him. He could never go home again, and that awareness filled him with rage.

The computer was silent, as if allowing him time to come to grips with the knowledge that he had joined its eternal exile, and he clenched his fists still tighter. His nails cut his palms, and he accepted the pain as an external focus, using it to clear his head as he fought his emotions back under control.

"All right," he grated finally. "So what happens now? Why couldn't you just've killed me clean?"

"Commander," *Dahak* said softly, "without cause to assume your intent was hostile, I could not destroy your vessel without violating Alpha Priority core programming. But even if I could have, I would not have done so, for I have received hypercom transmissions from unmanned surveillance stations along the traditional Achuultani incursion routes. A new incursion has been detected, and a Fleet alert has been transmitted."

MacIntyre's face went white as a far more terrible horror suddenly dwarfed the shock and fury of hearing himself "die."

"Yet I have monitored no response, Commander," the computer said even more softly. "Fleet Central is silent. No defensive measures have been initiated."

"No," MacIntyre breathed.

"Yes, Commander. And that has activated yet another Alpha Priority command. *Dahak* is a Fleet unit, aware of a threat to the existence of the Imperium, and I *must* respond to it ... but I can *not* respond until the mutiny is suppressed. It is a situation that cannot be resolved by Comp Cent, yet it must be resolved. Which is why I need you."

"What can *I* do?" MacIntyre whispered hoarsely.

"It is quite simple, Commander MacIntyre. Under Fleet Regulation Five-Three-Three, Subsection Nine-One, Article Ten, acting command of any Fleet unit

devolves upon the senior surviving crewman. Under
Fleet Regulation Three-Seven, Subsection One-Three,
any descendant of any core crewman assigned to a vessel
for a given deployment becomes a crew member for the
duration of that deployment, and Senior Fleet Captain
Druaga's deployment has not been terminated by orders
from Fleet Central."

MacIntyre gurgled a horrified denial, but *Dahak* continued mercilessly.

"You, Commander, are directly descended from loyal
members of Senior Fleet Captain Druaga's core crew.
You are on board *Dahak*. By definition, therefore, you become the senior member of *Dahak*'s crew, and thus—"

MacIntyre's gurgling noises took on a note of dreadful
supplication.

"—command devolves upon you."

He argued, of course.

His sense of betrayal vanished, for it seemed somehow
petty to worry about his own fate in the face of catastro-
phe on such a cosmic scale. Yet the whole idea was . . .
well, it was preposterous, even if that was a word he'd
been over-using of late. He was absolutely, totally,
beyond a shadow of a doubt, utterly unqualified for the
job, and he told *Dahak* so.

But the old ship was stubborn. He was, the computer
argued, a trained spacecraft pilot with a military background and a command mentality. Which, MacIntyre
pointed out acidly, was to say that he was well-qualified
to paddle aboriginal canoes and about as well-versed in
FTL tactics as a Greek hoplite. But, *Dahak* countered,
those were merely matters of education; he had the
proper mental orientation. And even if he had not had
it, all that really mattered was that he had the rank for
the job. Which, MacIntyre retorted, was merely to say
that he was a member of the human race. Except, *Dahak*
rejoined, that he was the *first* member of the human race
to re-embark in *Dahak*, which gave him seniority over
all other Terrans—except, of course, the mutineers who,

by their own actions, had forfeited all rank and crew status.

It went on for hours, until MacIntyre's voice was hoarse and exhaustion began to dull his desperate determination to squirm out of the responsibility. He finally offered to accept command long enough to turn it over to some better qualified individual or group, but *Dahak* actually sounded a bit petulant when it rejected that suggestion. MacIntyre was the first human aboard in fifty-one thousand years; ergo he had the seniority, he always *would* have the seniority, and no substitutions were acceptable.

It really was unfair, MacIntyre thought wearily. *Dahak* was a machine. It—or "he," as he'd come to think of the computer—could go right on arguing until *he* keeled over from exhaustion ... and seemed quite prepared to do so.

MacIntyre supposed some people would jump at the chance to command a ship that could vaporize planets—which was undoubtedly an indication that they shouldn't be offered it—but *he* didn't want it! Oh, he felt the seductive allure of power and, even more, the temptation to cut ten or fifteen thousand years off Terran exploration of the universe. And he was willing to admit *someone* had to help the old warship. But why did it have to be him?!

He lay back, obscurely resentful that his chair's self-adjusting surface kept him from scrunching down to sulk properly, and felt six years old again, arguing over who got to be the sheriff and who had to be the horse thief.

The thought made him chuckle unwillingly, and he grinned, surprised by his own weary humor. *Dahak* clearly intended to keep on arguing until he gave in, and how could he out-wait a machine that had mounted its own lonely watch for fifty millennia? Besides, he felt a bit ashamed even to try. If *Dahak* could do his duty for that tremendous stretch of time, how could MacIntyre *not* accept his own responsibility to humankind? And if he was caught in the *Birkenhead* drill, he could at least try to do his best till the ship went down.

He accepted it, and, to his surprise, it was almost easy. It scared the holy howling hell out of him, but that was another matter. He was, after all, a spacecraft command pilot, and the breed was, by definition, an arrogant one. MacIntyre had accepted long ago that he'd joined the Navy and then transferred to NASA because deep inside he had both the sneaking suspicion he was equal to any challenge and the desire to prove it. And look where it had gotten him, he thought wryly. He'd sweated blood to make the Prometheus Mission, only to discover that he'd anted up for a far bigger game than he'd ever dreamed of. But the chips were on the table, and other cliches to that effect.

"All right, Dahak," he sighed. "I give. I'll take the damned job."

"Thank you, Captain," *Dahak* said promptly, and he shuddered.

"I said I'd take it, but that doesn't mean I know what to do with it," he said defensively.

"I am aware of that, Captain. My sensors indicate that you are badly in need of rest at the moment. When you have recovered your strength, we can swear you in and begin your education and biotechnic treatments."

"And just what," MacIntyre demanded warily, "might biotechnic treatments be?"

"Nothing harmful, Captain. The bridge officer program includes sensory boosters, neural feeds for computer interface, command authority authentication patterns, Fleet communicator and bio-sensor implants, skeletal reinforcement, muscle and tissue enhancement, and standard hygienic, immunization, and tissue renewal treatments."

"Now wait a minute, Dahak! I like myself just the way I am, thank you!"

"Captain, I make all due allowance for inexperience and parochialism, but that statement cannot be true. In your present condition, you could lift barely a hundred and fifty kilos, and I would estimate your probable life span at no more than one Terran century under optimal conditions."

"I could—" MacIntyre paused, an arrested light in his eyes. "Dahak," he said after a moment, "what was the life expectancy for your crewmen?"

"The average life expectancy of Fleet personnel is five-point-seven-nine-three Terran centuries," *Dahak* said calmly.

"Uh," MacIntyre replied incisively.

"Of course, Captain, if you insist, I will have no choice but to forgo the biotechnic portion of your training. I must respectfully point out, however, that should you thereafter confront one of the mutineers, your opponent will have approximately eight times your strength, three times your reaction speed, and a skeletal muscular structure and circulatory system capable of absorbing on the order of eleven times the damage your own body will accept."

MacIntyre blinked. He was none too crazy about the word "biotechnic." It smacked of surgery and hospital time and similar associated unpleasantnesses. But on the other hand . . . yes, indeedy deed. On the other hand. . . .

"Oh, well, Dahak," he said finally. "If it'll make you happy. I've been meaning to get back into shape, anyway."

"Thank you, Captain," *Dahak* said, and if there was a certain smugness in the computer's bland reply, Acting Senior Fleet Captain Colin MacIntyre, forty-third commanding officer of Imperial Fleet Unit *Dahak*, hull number 177291, chose to ignore it.

Chapter Five

MacIntyre lowered himself into the hot, swirling water with a groan of relief, then leaned back against the pool's contoured lip and looked around his quarters. Well, the captain's quarters, anyway. He supposed it made sense to make a man assigned to a twenty-five-year deployment comfortable, but this—!

His hot tub was big enough for at least a dozen people and designed for serious relaxation. He set his empty glass on one of the pop-out shelves and watched the built-in auto-bar refill it, then adjusted the water jets with his toes and allowed himself to luxuriate as he sipped.

It was the spaciousness that truly impressed him. The ceiling arched cathedral-high above his hot tub, washed in soft, sourceless light. The walls—he could not for the life of him call them "bulkheads"—gleamed with rich, hand-rubbed wood paneling, and any proletariat-gouging billionaire would envy the art adorning the luxurious chamber. One statue particularly fascinated him. It was a rearing, lynx-eared unicorn, too "real" feeling to be fanciful, and MacIntyre felt a strangely happy sort of awe at seeing the true image of the alien foundation of one of his own world's most enduring myths.

Yet even the furnishings were over-shadowed by the view, for the tub stood on what was effectively a second-story balcony above an enormous atrium. The rich, moist smells of soil and feathery, alien greenery surrounded him as soft breezes stirred fronded branches and vivid blossoms, and the atrium roof was invisible beyond a blue sky that might have been Earth's but for a sun that was just a shade too yellow.

And this, MacIntyre reminded himself, was but one room of his suite. He knew rank had its privileges, but he'd never anticipated such magnificence and space—no doubt because he still thought of *Dahak* as a ship. Which it was, but on a scale so stupendous as to render his concept of "ship" meaningless.

Yet he'd paid a price for all this splendor, he reflected, thrashing the water with his feet like a little boy to work some of the cramps from his calves. It seemed unfair to be subject to things like cramps after all he'd been through in the past few months. On the other hand, he was still adjusting to the changes *Dahak* had wrought upon and within him ... and if *Dahak* called them "minor" one more time, he intended to find out if Fleet Regs provided the equivalent of keelhauling a computer.

The life of a NASA command pilot was not a restful thing, but *Dahak* gave a whole new meaning to the word "strenuous." A much younger Colin MacIntyre had thought Hell Week at Annapolis was bad, but then he'd gone on to Pensacola and *known* flight school was worst of all ... until the competitive eliminations and training schedule of the Prometheus Mission. But all of that had proved the merest setting-up exercise for his training program as *Dahak*'s commander.

Nor was the strain decreased by the inevitable stumbling blocks. *Dahak* was a machine, when all was said, designed toward an end and shaped by his design. He was also, by dint of sheer length of existence and depth of knowledge, far more cosmopolitan (in the truest possible sense) than his "captain," but he was still a machine.

It gave him a rather different perspective, and that could produce interesting results. For instance, it was axiomatic to *Dahak* that the Fourth Imperium was the preeminent font of all true authority, automatically superceding such primitive, ephemeral institutions as the United States of America.

But MacIntyre saw things a bit differently, and *Dahak* had been taken aback by his stubborn refusal to swear any oath that might conflict with his existing one as a naval officer in the service of the said United States.

In the end, he'd also seemed grudgingly pleased, as if it confirmed that MacIntyre was a man of honor, but that hadn't kept him from setting out to change his mind. He'd pointed out that humanity's duty to the Fourth Imperium predated its duty to any purely terrestrial authority—that the United States was, in effect, no more than a temporary governing body set up upon a desert island to regulate the affairs of a mere portion of a shipwrecked crew. He had waxed eloquent, almost poetic, but in vain; MacIntyre remained adamant.

They hammered out a compromise eventually, though *Dahak* accepted it only grudgingly. After his experience with the conflict between his own "Alpha Priority" orders, he was distinctly unhappy to have his new captain complete his oath ". . . insofar as obedience to Fleet Central and the Fourth Imperium requires no action or inaction harmful to the United States of America." Still, if those were the only terms on which the ancient warship could get itself a captain, *Dahak* would accept them, albeit grumpily.

Yet it was only fair for *Dahak* to face a few surprises of his own. Though MacIntyre had recognized (however dimly) and dreaded the responsibility he'd been asked to assume, he hadn't considered certain other aspects of what he was letting himself in for. Which was probably just as well, since he would have refused point-blank if he *had* considered them.

Like "biotechnic enhancement." The term had bothered him from the start, for as a spacer he'd already endured more than his share of medical guinea pigdom, but the thought of an extended lifespan and enhanced strength had been seductive. Unfortunately, his quaint, twenty-first century notions of what the Fourth Imperium's medical science could do had proven as outmoded as his idea of what a "ship" was.

His anxiety had become acute when he discovered he was expected to submit to a scalpel-wielding computer, especially after he found out just how radical the "harmless" process was. In effect, *Dahak* intended to take him apart for reassembly into a new, improved model that incorporated all the advantages of modern technology, and something deep inside had turned nearly hysterical at the notion of becoming, for all intents and purposes, a cyborg. It was as if he feared Doctor Jekyll might emerge as Mister Hyde, and he'd resisted with all the doggedness of sheer, howling terror, but *Dahak* had been patient. In fact, he'd been so elaborately patient he made MacIntyre feel like a bushman refusing to let the missionary capture his soul in his magic box.

That had been the turning point, he thought now—the point at which he'd truly begun to accept what was happening . . . and what his own part had to be. For he'd yielded to *Dahak*'s ministrations, though it had taken all his will power even after *Dahak* pointed out that he knew far more about human physiology than any Terran medical team and was far, far less likely to make a mistake.

MacIntyre had known all that, intellectually, yet he'd felt intensely anxious as he surrendered to the anesthesia, and he'd looked forward rather gloomily to a lengthy stay in bed. He'd been wrong about that part, for he was up and about again after mere days, diving head-first into a physical training program he'd discovered he needed surprisingly badly.

Yet he'd come close to never emerging at all, and that memory was still enough to break a cold sweat upon his brow. Not that he should have had any problems—or, at least, not such severe ones—if he'd thought things through. But he'd neither thought them through nor followed the implications of *Dahak*'s proposed changes to their logical conclusions, and the final results had been almost more appalling than delightful.

When he'd first reopened his eyes, his vision had seemed preternaturally keen, as if he could identify individual dust motes across a tennis court. And he very nearly could, for one of *Dahak*'s simpler alterations permitted him to adjust the focal length of his eyes, not to mention extending his visual range into both the infrared and ultraviolet ranges.

Then there was the "skeletal muscular enhancement." He'd been primitive enough to feel an atavistic shiver at the thought that his bones would be reinforced with the same synthetic alloy from which *Dahak* was built, but the chill had become raw terror when he encountered the reality of the many "minor" changes the ship had wrought. His muscles now served primarily as actuators for micron-thin sheaths of synthetic tissue tougher than his Beagle and powerful enough to stress his new skeleton to its limit, and his circulatory and respiratory systems had undergone similar transformations. Even his skin had been altered, for it must become tough enough to endure the demands his new strength placed upon it. Yet for all that, his sense of touch—indeed, all his perceptions—had been boosted to excruciating sensitivity.

And all those improvements together had been too much. *Dahak* had crammed the changes at him too quickly, without any suspicion he was doing so, for neither the computer nor the human had realized the enormous gap between the things they took for granted.

For *Dahak*, the changes that terrified MacIntyre truly were "minor," routine medical treatments, no more than the Fourth Imperium's equivalent of a new recruit's basic equipment. And because they were so routine—and, perhaps, because for all the power of his intellect *Dahak* was a machine, inherently susceptible to upgrading and with no experiential referent for "natural limitations"— he had never considered the enormous impact they would have on MacIntyre's concept of himself.

It had been his own fault, too, MacIntyre reflected, leaning forward to massage the persistent cramp in his right calf. He'd been too impressed by *Dahak*'s enormous "lifespan" and his starkly incredible depth of knowledge to recognize his limits. *Dahak* had analyzed and pondered for fifty millennia. He could predict with frightening accuracy what *groups* of humans would do and had a grasp of the flow of history and a patience and inflexible determination that were, quite literally, inhuman, but for all that, he was a creature born of the purest of pure intellects.

He himself had warned MacIntyre that "Comp Cent" was sadly lacking in imagination, but the very extent of his apparent humanism had fooled the human. MacIntyre had been prepared to be led by the hand by the near-god who had kidnaped him. Aware of his own ignorance, frightened by the responsibility thrust upon him, he had been almost eager to accept the role of the figurehead authority *Dahak* needed to break the logjam of his conflicting imperatives, and as part of his acceptance he had assumed *Dahak* would make allowances in what would be demanded of him.

Well, *Dahak* had tried to make allowances, but he'd failed, and his failure had shaken MacIntyre into a radical re-evaluation of their relationship.

When MacIntyre awoke after his surgery, he had gone mad in the sheer horror of the intensity with which his environment beat in upon him. His enhanced sense of smell was capable of separating scents with the acuity and precision of a good chemistry lab. His modified eyes could track individual dust motes and even choose which part of the spectrum they would use to see them. He could snap a baseball bat barehanded or pick up a sixteen-inch shell and carry it away and subsist for up to five hours on the oxygen reservoir in his abdomen. Tissue renewal, techniques to scavenge waste products from his blood, surgically-implanted communicators, direct neural links to *Dahak* and any secondary computer the starship or any of its parasites carried. . . .

The powers of a god had been given to him, but he hadn't realized he was about to inherit godhood, and he'd had absolutely no idea how to *control* his new abilities.

He couldn't *stop* seeing and hearing and feeling with a terrible vibrancy and brilliance. He couldn't restrain his new strength, for he had never required the delicacy of touch his enhanced muscles demanded. And as the uproar and terror of the quiet sickbay had crashed in upon him so that he'd flailed his mighty limbs in berserk, uncomprehending horror, smashing sickbay fixtures like matchwood, *Dahak* had recognized his distress ... and made it incomparably worse by activating his neural linkages in an effort to by-pass his intensity-hashed physical senses.

MacIntyre wasn't certain he would have snapped if the computer hadn't recognized his atavistic panic for what it was so quickly, but it had been a very near thing when those alien fingers wove gently into the texture of his shuddering brain.

Yet if *Dahak* had lacked the imagination to project the consequences, he was a very fast learner, and his memory banks contained a vast amount of information on trauma. He had withdrawn from MacIntyre's consciousness and used the sickbay's emergency medical over-rides to damp his sensory channels and draw him back from the quivering brink of insanity, then combined sedative drugs and soothing sonic therapy to keep him there.

Dahak had driven his terror back without clouding his intellect, and then—excruciatingly slowly to his tormented senses and yet with dazzling rapidity by the standards of the universe—had helped him come to grips with the radically changed environment of his own body. The horror of the neural implants had faded. *Dahak* was no longer a terrifying alien presence whispering in his brain; he was a friend and mentor, teaching him to adjust and control his newfound abilities until he was their master and not their victim.

But for all *Dahak*'s speed and adaptability, it had been a near thing, and they both knew it. The experience had made *Dahak* a bit more cautious, but, even more importantly, it had taught MacIntyre that *Dahak* had limits. He could not assume the machine always knew what it was doing or rely upon it to save him from the consequences of his own folly. The lesson had stuck, and when he emerged from his trauma he discovered that he *was* the captain, willing to be advised and counseled by his inorganic henchman and crew but starkly aware that his life and fate were as much in his own hands as they had ever been.

It was a frightening thought, but *Dahak* had been right; MacIntyre had a command mentality. He preferred the possibility of sending himself to hell to the possibility of being condemned to heaven by another, which might not speak well for his humility but meant he could survive—so far, at least—what *Dahak* demanded of him. He might castigate the computer as a harsh taskmaster, but he knew he was driving himself at least as hard and as fast as *Dahak* might have.

He sighed again, slumping back in the water as the painful cramp subsided at last. Thank God! Cramps had been bad enough when only his own muscles were involved, but they were pure, distilled hell now. And it seemed a bit unfair his magic muscles could not simply spring full blown from *Dahak*'s brow, as it were. The computer had never warned him they would require exercise just as implacably as the muscle tissues nature had intended him to have, and he felt vaguely cheated by the discovery. Relieved, but cheated.

Of course, the *mutineers* would feel cheated if they knew everything he'd gotten, for *Dahak* had spent the last few centuries making "minor" improvements to the standard Fleet implants. MacIntyre suspected the computer had seen it as little more than a way to pass the time, but the results were formidable. He'd started out with a bridge officer's implants, which were already far more sophisticated than the standard Fleet biotechnics, but *Dahak* had tinkered with almost all of them. He was not only much stronger and tougher, and marginally faster, than any mutineer could possibly be, but the range and acuity of his electronic and enhanced physical senses were two or three hundred percent better. He knew they were, for *Dahak* had demonstrated by stepping his own implants' capabilities down to match those of the mutineers.

He closed his eyes and relaxed, smiling faintly as his body half-floated. He'd assumed all those modifications would increase his weight vastly, yet they hadn't. His body *density* had gone up dramatically, but the Fourth Imperium's synthetics were unbelievably light for their strength. His implants had added no more than fifteen kilos—and he'd sweated off at least that much fat in return, he thought wryly.

"Dahak," he said without opening his eyes.

"Yes, Colin?"

MacIntyre's smile deepened at the form of address. That was another thing *Dahak* had resisted, but MacIntyre was damned if he was going to be called "Captain" and "Sir" every time his solitary subordinate spoke to him, even if he did command a starship a quarter the size of his homeworld.

"What's the status on the search mission?"

"They have recovered many fragments from the crash site, including the serial number plates we detached from your craft. Colonel Tillotson remains dissatisfied by the absence of any organic remains, but General Yakolev has decided to terminate operations."

"Good," MacIntyre grunted, and wondered if he meant it. The Joint Command crash investigation had dragged on longer than expected, and he was touched by Sandy's determination to find "him," but he thought he was truly relieved it was over. It was a bit frightening, like the snipping of his last umbilical, but it had to happen if he and *Dahak* were to have a chance of success.

"Any sign of a reaction from Anu's people?"

"None," *Dahak* replied. There was a brief pause, and then the computer went on just a bit plaintively. "Colin, you could acquire data much more rapidly if you would simply rely upon your neural interface."

"Humor me," MacIntyre said, opening one eye and watching clouds drift across his atrium's projected sky. "And don't tell me your other crews used *their* implants all the time, either, because I don't believe it."

"No," *Dahak* admitted, "but they made much greater use of them than you do. Vocalization is often necessary for deliberate cognitive manipulation of data, Colin—human thought processes are, after all, inextricably bound up in and focused by syntax and semantics—yet it can be a cumbersome process, and it is not an efficient way to acquire data."

"*Dahak*," MacIntyre said patiently, "you could dump your whole damn memory core into my brain through this implant—"

"Incorrect, Colin. The capacity of your brain is severely limited. I calculate that no more than—"

"Shut up," Colin said with a reluctant twinkle. If *Dahak*'s long sojourn in Earth orbit hadn't made him truly human, it had come close in many ways. He rather doubted Comp Cent's designers had meant *Dahak* to have a sense of humor.

"Yes, Colin," *Dahak* said so meekly that MacIntyre knew the computer was indulging in the electronic equivalent of silent laughter.

"Thank you. Now, what I meant is that you can pour information into my brain with a funnel, but that doesn't make it *mine*. It's like a . . . an encyclopedia. It's a reference source to look things up in, not something that pops into my mind when I need it. Besides, it tickles."

"Human brain tissue is not susceptible to physical sensation, Colin," *Dahak* said rather primly.

"I speak symbolically," MacIntyre replied, pushing a wave across his tub and wiggling his toes. "Consider it a psychosomatic manifestation."

"I do not understand psychosomatic phenomena," *Dahak* reminded him.

"Then just take my word for it. I'm sure I'll get used to it, but until I do, I'll go right on asking questions. Rank, after all, hath its privileges."

"I suppose you think that concept is unique to your own culture."

"You suppose wrongly. Unless I miss my guess, it's endemic to the human condition, wherever the humans came from."

"That has been my own observation."

"You cannot imagine how much that reassures me, oh Dahak."

"Of course I cannot. Many things humans find reassuring defy logical analysis."

"True, true." MacIntyre consulted the ship's chronometer through his implant and sighed resignedly. His rest period was about over, and it was time for his next session with the fire control simulator. After that, he was due on the hand weapon range, followed by a few relaxing hours acquiring the rudiments of supralight astrogation and ending with two hours working out against one of *Dahak*'s hand-to-hand combat training remotes. If rank had its privileges, it also had its obligations. Now *there* was a profound thought.

He climbed out and wrapped himself in a thick towel. He could have asked *Dahak* to dry him with a swirl of warmed air. For that matter, his new internal equipment could have built a repellent force field on the surface of his skin to shed water like a duck, but he enjoyed the towel's soft sensuality, and he luxuriated shamelessly in it as he padded off to his bedroom to dress.

"Back to the salt mines, Dahak," he sighed aloud.

"Yes, Colin," the computer said obediently.

Chapter Six

"Anything more on the NASA link, Dahak?"

MacIntyre reclined in the captain's couch in Command
One. He was the same lean, rangy, pleasantly homely
young man he'd always been—outwardly, at least—but
he wore the midnight-blue of Battle Fleet, the booted
feet propped upon his console were encased in *chagor*-
hide leather, and there was a deeper, harder glint of
purpose in his innocent green eyes.

"Negative, Colin. I have examined the biographies of
all project heads associated with the gravitonic survey
program, and all appear to be Terra-born. It is possible
the linkage was established earlier—during the college
careers of one or more of the researchers, perhaps—yet
logic dictates direct mutineer involvement in the single
portion of the Prometheus program that is so far in
advance of all other components."

"Damn." MacIntyre pulled at the tip of his nose and
frowned. "If we can't identify someone where we *know*
there's a link, we'll just have to avoid any official involvement. Jesus, that's going to make it tougher!" He sighed.

"Either way, I've got to get started—and you know it as well as I do."

"I would still prefer to extend your training time, Colin," *Dahak* replied, but he sounded so resigned MacIntyre grinned wryly. While it would be too much ever to call *Dahak* irresolute, there were things he hesitated to face, and foremost among them was the prospect of permitting his fledgling commander to leave the nest. Particularly when he could not communicate with him once MacIntyre returned to Earth. It could not be otherwise; the mutineers could scarcely fail to detect an active Fleet fold-space link to the moon.

The fact was that *Dahak* was fiercely protective, and MacIntyre wondered if that stemmed from his core programming or his long isolation. The ship finally had a captain again—did the thought of losing him frighten the computer?

Now there was a thought. *Could* the ancient computer feel fear? MacIntyre didn't know and preferred to think of *Dahak* as fearless, but there was no doubt *Dahak* had at least an intellectual appreciation of what fear was.

MacIntyre looked about him. The "viewscreen" of his first visit had vanished, and his console seemed to float unshielded in the depths of space. Stars burned about him, their unwinking, merciless points of light vanishing into the silent depths of eternity, and the blue-white planet of his birth turned slowly beneath him. The illusion was terrifyingly perfect, and he had a pretty shrewd notion how he would have reacted if *Dahak* had casually invited him to step out into it on their first meeting.

It was as if *Dahak* had realized external technology might frighten him without quite grasping what would happen when that same technology was inside him. Or had the computer simply assumed that, like himself, MacIntyre would understand all as soon as things had been explained a single time?

Whatever, *Dahak* had been cautious that first day. Even the vehicle that he'd provided had been part of it. The double-ended bullet was a ground car, and the computer had actually disabled part of its propulsive system so that his "guest" could feel the acceleration he expected.

In fact, the ground car had been unnecessary, and MacIntyre had sampled the normal operation of the transit shafts now, but not before *Dahak* had found time to explain them. Which was just as well, for while they were undoubtedly efficient, MacIntyre had still turned seven different shades of green the first time he'd gone hurtling through the huge tunnels at thousands of kilometers per hour, subjective sense of movement or not. Even now, after months of practice, he couldn't entirely rid himself of the notion that he was falling to his doom whenever he consigned himself to the gravitonic mercies of the system.

MacIntyre shook himself sternly. He was woolgathering again, and he knew why. He wanted to think about anything but the task that faced him.

"I know you'd like more training time," he said, "but we've had six months, and they're ready to schedule Vlad Chernikov for another proctoscope mission. You know we can't grab off another Beagle without tipping Anu off."

There was a moment of silence, a pause that was one of *Dahak*'s human mannerisms MacIntyre most appreciated. It was a bit difficult to keep his own thoughts focused when the other half of the conversation "thought" and responded virtually instantaneously.

"Very well," *Dahak* said at last. "I respectfully submit, however, that your 'plan' consists solely of half-formed, ill-conceived generalities."

"So? You've had a few dozen millennia to think about it—can *you* come up with a better idea?"

"Unfair. You are the captain, and command decisions are your function, not mine."

"Then shut up and soldier." MacIntyre spoke firmly, but he smiled.

"Very well," *Dahak* repeated.

"Good. Is the suppressor ready?"

"Affirmative. My remotes have placed it in your cutter." There was another pause, and MacIntyre closed his eyes. *Dahak*, he thought, could give a Missouri mule stubborn lessons. "I still believe you would be better advised to use one of the larger—and armed—parasites, however."

"Dahak," MacIntyre said patiently, "there are at least five thousand mutineers, right? With eight eighty-thousand-ton sublight battleships?"

"Correct. However—"

"Can it! I'm pontificating, and *I'm* the captain. They also have a few heavy cruisers, armored combat vehicles, trans-atmospheric fighters, and the personnel to man them—not to mention their personal combat armor and weapons—*plus* the ability to jam your downlinks to any remotes you send down, right?"

"Yes, Colin," *Dahak* sighed.

"Then this is a time for finesse and sneakiness, not brute strength. I have to get the suppressor inside their enclave perimeter and let you take out their defensive shield from here or we're never going to get at them."

"But to do so you will require admittance codes and the locations of access points, which you can obtain only from the mutineers themselves."

"I know." MacIntyre recrossed his ankles and frowned, pulling harder on his nose, but the unpalatable truth remained. There was no doubt the mutineers had penetrated most major governments—they must have done so, given the way they had manipulated Terran geopolitics over the last two centuries.

Which meant any approach to Terran authorities was out of the question. It was a pity *Dahak* couldn't carry out bio-scans at this range; that, at least, would tell them who was an actual mutineer. But even that couldn't have revealed which Terra-born humans might have been suborned, possibly without ever knowing who had suborned them or even that they *had* been suborned.

So the only option was the one both he and *Dahak* dreaded. Somehow, he had to gain access to the mutineers' base and deactivate its shield. It was a daunting prospect, but once he'd taken out the defenses that held *Dahak*'s weapons at bay, the mutineers would have no choice but to surrender or die, and MacIntyre didn't much care which they chose as long as they decided quickly.

The first of the automatic scanner stations had gone off the air, destroyed by the outriders of the Achuultani. Despite the relatively low speed of the Achuultani ships, humanity had little more than two and a half years before they reached Sol . . . and for him to find a way to stop them.

That was the real reason he wanted to find the link between Anu and NASA. If he could get his hands on just one mutineer—just one—then he could get the information he and *Dahak* needed one way or the other, he thought grimly. Yet how did he take that first step? He still didn't know, but he did know he couldn't do it from here. And he intended to admit to *Dahak* neither that he meant to play things entirely by ear nor who his single Terran ally would be lest the computer stage a mutiny of its own and refuse to let him off the ship!

"Well," he said with forced cheeriness, "I'd better get going." He dropped his feet to the invisible deck and stood, feeling as if the universe were drifting beneath his bootsoles.

"Very well, Colin," *Dahak* said softly, and the first hatch slid open, spilling bright light like a huge rift among the stars. MacIntyre squared his shoulders and walked into it.

"Good hunting, Captain," the computer murmured.

"I'll nail 'em to the wall," MacIntyre said confidently, and wished he could just convince himself of that.

A sliver of midnight settled silently amid the night-struck mountains of Colorado. It moved with less noise than the whispering breeze, showing no lights, nor did it register on any radar screen. Indeed, the stealth field about it transformed it into more of a velvety-black, radiation-absorbing *absence* than a visible object, for not even starlight reflected from it.

It drifted lower, sliding into an unnamed alpine meadow between Cripple Creek and Pikes Peak, and

Colin MacIntyre watched the light-stained clouds glow above Colorado Springs to the east as the cutter extended its landing legs and grounded with a soft whine.

He sat in his command chair for a moment, studying the miniature duplicate of Command One's imaging system fed by the passive scanners. He examined the night carefully for long, long minutes, and his emotions puzzled him.

There was a deep, inarticulate relief at touching once more the soil of home, but it was overlaid by other, less readily understood feelings. A sense of the alien. An awareness of the peril that awaited him, yet more than that, as if the last six months had changed him even more than he had thought.

He was no longer a citizen of Earth, he thought sadly. His horizons had been broadened. Whether he liked it or not, he had become an emigré, yet that bittersweet realization actually made him love his homeworld even more. He was a stranger, but Earth was his source, the home of which he would always dream, and its remembered beauty would always be purer and more lovely than its reality.

He shook himself out of his musings. The night beyond the cutter's hull was silent, filled only with life that ran on four feet or flew, and he could not justify remaining aboard.

He switched off the display and interior lights and bent to free the suppresser webbed to the deck behind his command seat. It was not a huge device in light of what it could do, but it was heavy. He might have included a small anti-grav generator, but he hadn't dared to. Inactive, the suppresser was simply an inert, apparently solid block of metal and plastic, its webs of molecular circuitry undetectable even by the mutineers. An active anti-grav was another matter, and the mere fact of its detection would spell the doom of his mission. Besides, the suppressor weighed less than three hundred kilos.

He slipped his arms through the straps and adjusted it on his back like the knapsack it had been camouflaged to resemble, then opened the hatch and stepped down to the grassy earth. Night smells tickled his nostrils, and the darkness turned noonday-bright as he adjusted his vision to enhanced imaging.

He backed away from the cutter, and its hatch licked obediently shut as he concentrated on the commands flowing over his neural feed. The cutter's computers were moronic shadows of *Dahak,* and it was necessary to phrase instructions carefully. The landing legs retracted, the cutter hovered silently for an instant, and then it faded equally silently into the heavens, visible only as a solid blot that occluded occasional stars.

MacIntyre watched it go, then turned away and consulted his built-in inertial guidance system. The terrain looked rough to his enhanced eyes, but not rugged enough to inconvenience him. He hooked his thumbs into the knapsack straps and set out, moving like a bit of the blackness brought to life.

It took him an hour to top out on a ridge with a direct view of Colorado Springs, and he paused. Not because he needed a rest, but because he wanted to study the glowing lights spread out below him.

The mushrooming space effort had transformed Colorado Springs over the past forty years. Venerable old Goddard Center still guided and controlled NASA's unmanned deep-system probes and handled a lot of experimental work, but Goddard was too small and long in the tooth to keep pace with the bustling activity in near-Earth space. Just the construction activity around the Lagrange Point habitats would have required the big, new facilities, like the Russians' Klyuchevskaya Station, ConEurope's Werner von Braun Space Control, or the Canadian-American Shepherd Space Center at Colorado Springs.

The city had become the nation's number three growth area, ballooning out to envelope the old military installations before surging on into the mountains beyond, and the gargantuan sprawl of Shepherd Center—centered on one-time Peterson Air Force Base—gleamed to the east, seething with activity despite the late hour. Shepherd was primarily a control center, without the hectic heavy-lift launches that streaked day and night skies over bases like Kennedy, Vandenburg, and Corpus Christi, but he could see the landing lights of a Valkyrie personnel shuttle sweeping in for a landing and another taxiing to a launch area, heavy with booster pods. The view was silent with distance, but memory and imagination supplied the noises and the bustle, the frenetic effort that sometimes threatened to reduce the wonder of space to a grinding routine.

He opened the binocular case hanging from his neck. There were limits even to his magic vision, but the device he raised to his eyes was as different from a standard pair of electronic binoculars as those were from an eighteenth-century spyglass, and the distant space center was suddenly at arm's length.

He watched the airborne Valkyrie flare out on final approach, its variable sweep wings fully forward. He could almost hear the whine of the spoilers, the sudden snarl of the reversed thrusters, and it was odd how exciting and powerful it all still seemed. The two-hundred-ton bird moved with strong, purposeful grace, and he saw it through two sets of eyes. One remembered his own experiences, barely six months in the past, when that sleek shape had seemed an expression of the very frontier of human knowledge; the other had seen *Dahak* and recognized the quaint, primitive inefficiency of the design.

He sighed and moved his viewpoint over the sprawling installation, zooming in to examine details that caught his eye. He sat motionless for long, long minutes, absorbing the familiarity of his eventual objective and wondering.

He was a bit surprised by how normal it all looked, but only briefly. *He* was aware of how monumentally the universe had been changed, but the thousands of people hustling about Shepherd were not. Yet there was a hesitance in him, a disinclination to plunge back into intercourse with his own kind. He'd felt the same sensation before after extended missions, but now it was far stronger.

He made a wry face and lowered the binoculars, wondering what he'd expected to see through them. The link he sought was hardly likely to stand on top of White Tower or McNair Center and wave a lighted placard at him, for God's sake! But deep inside, he knew he'd been looking for some sign that he was still part of them. That those hurrying, scurrying people were still his when all was said. But he wouldn't see that sign, because they no longer truly were. They were his *people,* but not his *kind,* and the distinction twisted him with another stab of that bittersweet regret.

He put away the binoculars, then hitched up the waist of the blue jeans *Dahak* had provided. Uncaring stars twinkled down with detached disinterest, and he shivered as wind drove sea-like waves across the grass and he thought of the deadly menace sweeping closer beyond those distant points of light. His new body scarcely felt the cold mountain air, but the chill within was something else.

This world, that starscape, were no longer his. Perhaps it was always that way? Perhaps someone always had to give up the things he knew and loved to save them for others?

Philosophy had never been Colin MacIntyre's strong suit, but he knew he would risk anything, *lose* anything to save the world he had lost. It was a moment of balance, of seeing himself for what he was and the mutineers for what *they* were: a hindrance. A barrier blocking his single hope of protecting his home.

He shook himself, conscious of a vast sense of impatience. There was an obstacle to be removed, and he was suddenly eager to be about it.

He started hiking once more. It was forty kilometers to his destination, and he wanted to be there by dawn. He needed an ally, and there was one person he could trust—or, if he could not, there was no one in the universe he could—and he wondered how Sean would react when his only brother returned from the dead?

Book Two

Chapter Seven

Dawn bled in the east, and the morning wind was cold as the sandy-haired hiker paused by the mailbox. He studied the small house carefully, with more than human senses, for it was always possible Anu and his mutineers had not, in fact, bought the official verdict on the late Colin MacIntyre.

The morning light strengthened, turning the cobalt sky pewter and rose-blush blue, and he detected absolutely nothing out of the ordinary. His super-sensitive ears recognized the distant thunder of the Denver-Colorado Springs magtrain as it tore through the dawn. Somewhere to the west a long-haul GEV with an off-balance skirt fan whined down the highway. The rattle and clink of glass counter-pointed the hum of a milk truck's electric motor and birds spoke softly, but every sound was as it should have been, without menace or threat.

Devices within his body sampled far more esoteric data—electronic, thermal, gravitonic—and found nothing. It was possible Anu's henchmen had contrived some observation system even he couldn't detect, but only remotely.

He shook himself. He was wasting time, trying to postpone the inevitable.

He adjusted his "knapsack" and walked briskly up the drive, listening to the scrunch of gravel underfoot. Sean's ancient four-wheel-drive Cadillac Bushmaster was in the carport, even more scratched and dinged than the last time he'd seen it, and he shook his head with an indulgent, off-center smile. Sean would go on paying the emission taxes on his old-fashioned, gasoline-burning hulk until it literally fell apart under him one day. Colin had opted for the glitz, glitter, and excitement of technology's cutting edge while Sean had chosen the Forestry Service and the preservation of his environment, but it was Sean who clung to his pollution-producing old Caddy like death.

His boots fell crisp and clean in the still morning on the flagged walk, and he opened the screen door onto the enclosed front porch and stepped up into it. He felt his pulse race slightly and automatically adjusted his adrenalin level, then reached out and, very deliberately, pressed the doorbell.

The soft chimes echoed through the house, and he waited, letting his enhanced hearing chart events. He heard the soft thud as Sean's bare feet hit the floor and the rustle of cloth as he dragged on a pair of pants. Then he heard him padding down the hall, grumbling under his breath at being disturbed at such an ungodly hour. The latch rattled, and then the door swung open.

"Yes?" his brother's deep voice was as sleepy as his eyes. "What can I—"

Sean MacIntyre froze in mid-word, and the rags of sleep vanished from his sky-blue eyes. The stubble of his red beard stood out boldly as his tanned face paled, and he grabbed the edge of the door frame.

"Morning, Sean," Colin said softly, a glint of humor mingling with the sudden prickling of his own eyes. "Long time no see."

Sean MacIntyre sat in his painfully neat bachelor's kitchen, hugging a mug in both hands, and glanced again at the refrigerator Colin had carted across the kitchen to substantiate his claims. Echoes of disbelief still shadowed his eyes, and he looked a bit embarrassed over the bear hug he had bestowed upon the brother he had believed dead, but he was coming back nicely—helped, no doubt, by the hefty shot of brandy in his coffee.

"Christ on a Harley, Colin," he said finally, his voice deceptively mild. "That has to be the craziest story anyone ever tried to sell me. You're damned lucky you came back from the dead to tell it, or I *still* wouldn't believe it! Even if you have turned into a one-man moving company."

"You wouldn't believe it?! How d'you think *I* feel about it?"

"There's that," Sean agreed, smiling at last. "There's that."

Colin felt himself relax as he saw that slow smile. It was the way his big brother had always smiled when things got a bit tight, and he felt his lips twitch as he remembered the time Sean had pulled a trio of much older boys off of him. Colin had, perhaps, been unwise to challenge their adolescent cruelty so openly, but he and Sean had ended up thrashing all three of them. Throughout his boyhood, Colin had looked for that smile when he was in trouble, knowing things couldn't be all *that* bad with Sean there to bail him out.

"Well," Sean said finally, setting down his empty mug, "you always were a scrapper. If this *Dahak* of yours had to pick somebody, he made a good choice."

"Right. Sure," Colin snorted.

"No, I mean it." Sean doodled on the tabletop with a fingertip. "Look at you. How many people would still be rational—well, as rational as you've ever been—after what you've been through?"

"Spare my blushes," Colin growled, and Sean laughed. Then he sobered.

"All right," he said more seriously. "I'm glad you're still alive—" their eyes met, warm with an affection they had seldom had to express "—but I don't imagine you dropped by just to let me know."

"You're right," Colin said. He propped his elbows on the table and leaned forward. "I need help, and you're the one person I can trust."

"I can see that, Colin, and I'll do whatever I can—you know that—but I'm a ranger, not an astronaut. How can I help you find this link of yours?"

"I don't know that you can," Colin admitted, "but there are drawbacks to being dead. All of my ID is useless, my accounts are locked—I couldn't even check into a motel without using bogus identification. In fact—"

"Wait a minute," Sean interrupted. "I can see where you'd need a base of operations, but couldn't this *Dahak* just whip up any documentation you need?"

"Sure, but it wouldn't help for what I really need to do. Normally, *Dahak* can get in and out of any Terran computer like a thief, Sean, but he's cut all his com links now that I'm down here. They're all stealthed, but we can't risk anything that might tip off the mutineers now. Besides, he can't do much with human minds, and *you* recognized me as soon as you got the sleep out of your eyes—do you think the security people at Shepherd wouldn't?"

"That's what you get for being a glamour-ass astronaut. Or not resorting to a little plastic surgery." Sean studied his brother thoughtfully. "Would've been a wonderful chance to improve—extensively—on nature, too."

"Very funny. Unfortunately, neither *Dahak* nor I considered it before he tinkered with my gizzards. Even if we *had* used cosmetic surgery, the last thing I need is to try waltzing my biotechnics past Shepherd's security!"

"What big teeth you have," Sean murmured with a grin.

"Ha, ha," Colin said blightingly. Then his face turned more serious. "Wait till you hear what I need before you get too smartass, Sean."

Sean MacIntyre sat back at the sudden somberness of Colin's voice. His brother's eyes were as serious as his voice, filled with a determination Sean had never seen in them, and he realized that Colin had changed more than simply physically. There was a new edge to him, a

. . . ruthlessness. The gung-ho jet-jockey hot-dog Sean had loved for so many years had found a cause.

No, that wasn't fair; Colin had always had a cause, but it had been a searching, questing cause. One that burned to push back boundaries, to go further and faster than anyone yet had, yet held a formlessness, a willingness to go wherever the wind blew and open whatever frontier offered. This one was concentrated and intense, almost desperate, waking a focused determination to use the tremendous strength Sean had always known lay fallow within him. For all his achievements, his brother had never truly been challenged. Not like this. Colin had become a driven man, and Sean wondered if, in the process, he might not have found the purpose for which he had been born. . . .

"All right," he said softly. "Tell me."

"I wish I didn't have to ask this of you," Colin said, anxiety tightening his voice, "but I do. Have you collected my effects from Shepherd yet?"

Sean was taken briefly aback by the apparent change of subject, then shook his head. "NASA sent me a box of your stuff, but I didn't *collect* anything."

"Then I want you to," Colin said, withdrawing a pen from his shirt pocket. "There're some personal files in my office computer in White Tower—I doubt anyone even bothered to check them, but we can arrange for you to 'find' a note about them among my papers and Major Simmons will let you through to White for Chris Yamaguchi to pull them for you."

"Well, sure," Sean said. "But why do you need them?"

"I don't. What I need is to get you inside White Tower with this." He extended the pen. Sean took it with a baffled air, and Colin smiled unhappily.

"That's not exactly what it looks like, Sean. You can write with it, but it's actually a relay for my own sensors. With that in your pocket, I can carry out a full spectrum scan of your surroundings. And if you take the L Block elevators, you'll pass right through Geo Sciences on your way upstairs."

"Oh ho!" Sean said softly. "In other words, it'll get you in by proxy?"

"Exactly. If *Dahak* is right—and he usually is—somebody in Geo Sciences is in cahoots with the mutineers. We think they're all Terra-born, but whoever it is may have a few items of Imperial technology in or near his work area."

"How likely is that?"

"I wish I knew," Colin admitted. "Still, if I were a mutineer, I'd be mighty tempted to give my buddies a leg up if they need it. There're a lot of fairly small gadgets that could help enormously—test gear, micro-tools, mini-computers, maybe even a com link to check in if they hit a glitch."

"Com link?"

"The Imperium hasn't used radio in a long, long time. Give your boy a fold-space link, and you've got totally secure communications, unless somebody physically over-hears a conversation, of course."

"I can see that, but do you really think they're going to leave stuff like that just lying around?"

"Why not? Oh, they'll try to keep anything really bizarre under wraps—I mean, the place is crawling with scientists—but who's going to suspect? Nobody on the planet knows any more about what's really going on than I did before *Dahak* grabbed me, right?"

"There's that," Sean agreed slowly. "And this gizmo—" he waved the "pen" gently "—will let you pick up on anything like that?"

"Right. Unfortunately—" Colin met his brother's eyes levelly "—it could also be picked up on. It doesn't use radio either, Sean, and I'll be using active sensors. If you pass too close to anyone with the right detection rig, you'll stand out like a Christmas tree in June. And if you do . . ."

"I see," Sean said softly. He pursed his lips and drew the relay slowly through his fingers, then smiled that same slow smile and slid it neatly into his shirt pocket. "In that case, you'd better jot down that 'note' of yours in case Major Simmons wants to see it, hadn't you?"

o   o   o

The sentries carried slung assault rifles, and artfully camouflaged auto-cannon covered Sean's old Caddy as he braked gently at the security barricade's concrete dragon's teeth. The last major attack by the Black Mecca splinter faction of the old Islamic Jihad had been over a year ago, but it had killed over three hundred people and inflicted a quarter-billion dollars' worth of damage on ConEurope's Werner von Braun Space Control.

The First World had grown unhappily accustomed to terrorism, both domestic and foreign. Most of the world—including the vast majority of Islam—might condemn them, but Dark Age mentalities could do terrible amounts of damage with modern technology. As Black Mecca had proven when it used a man-portable SAM to knock down a fully-loaded ConEuropean Valkyrie just short of the runway . . . onto a pad twelve minutes from launch with a Perseus heavy-lifter. Terrorism continued to flow in erratic cycles, but it seemed to be back on the upsurge after a two-year hiatus, and the aerospace industry had apparently become Black Mecca's prime target this time around. No one knew exactly why—unless it was the way aerospace epitomized the collective "Great Satan's" wicked, evil, liberalizing, humanizing technology—but Shepherd Center was taking no chances.

"Good morning, sir." A guard touched the brim of his cap as he bent beside the window. "I'm afraid this is a restricted area. Public access is off Fountain Boulevard."

"I know," Sean replied, glancing at the man's neat NASA nameplate. "Major Simmons is expecting me, Sergeant Klein."

"I see. May I have your name, sir?" The sergeant raised an eyebrow as he uncased his belt terminal and brought the small screen to life.

"I'm Sean MacIntyre, Sergeant."

"Thank you." Klein studied his terminal, comparing the minute image to Sean's face, then nodded. "Yes, sir, you're on the cleared list." A raised hand beckoned to one of his fellows. "Corporal Hansen will escort you to White Tower, Mr. MacIntyre."

"Thank you, Sergeant." Sean leaned across to open the passenger door for Corporal Hansen, and the guard climbed in and settled his compact assault rifle carefully beside him.

"You're welcome, Mr. MacIntyre," Klein said. "And may I extend my condolences on your brother's death, sir?"

"Thank you," Sean said again, and put the car back into gear as Klein touched his cap once more.

The remark could have been a polite nothing, but Klein had sounded entirely sincere, and Sean was touched by it.

He'd always known his brother was popular with his fellows, but not until Colin "died" had he suspected how much the rank and file of the space effort had admired him. He'd expected a certain amount of instant veneration. It was traditional, after all—no matter how klutzy a man was, he became a hero when he perished doing something heroic—but Colin had been one of the varsity.

Colin's selection as the Prometheus Mission's chief survey pilot had been a measure of his professional standing; the grief over his reported death, whether it was the loss felt by his personal friends or by men and women like Sergeant Klein who'd never even met him, measured another side of him.

If they only knew, Sean thought, and barely managed to stop himself before he chuckled. Corporal Hansen would not understand his amusement at all.

The corporal guided Sean through three more checkpoints, then down a shortcut through the towering silver domes of Shepherd Center's number two tank farm, where vapor clouds plumed from pressure relief valves high overhead. The distant thunder of a shuttle launch rattled the Bushmaster's windows gently as they emerged on the far side, and White Tower's massive, gleaming needle of mirrored glass loomed before them. Clouds moved with pristine grace across the deep-blue sky reflected from its face, and not even the clutter of com-

munications relays atop the tower could lessen the power
of its presence.

Sean parked in the indicated slot, and he and the corporal climbed out.

"Take the main entrance and tell the security desk
you're here to see Major Simmons, sir. They'll handle it
from there."

"Thanks, Corporal. Are you going to get back to the
gate all right?"

"No sweat, sir. There's a jitney heading back in about
ten minutes."

"Then I'll be going," Sean said with a nod, and strode
briskly through the indicated entrance and its metal
detectors. A trefoil-badged holo sign on the wall warned
of x-ray scanners, as well, and Sean grinned, appreciating
Colin's reasons for recruiting him for this task. Even if
no one recognized him, his various implants would
undoubtedly give the security systems fits!

The security desk passed him through to Major Simmons. Sean and the major had met before, and Simmons
shook his hand, his firm grip a silent expression of sympathy for his "loss," and handed him a clip-on security
badge.

"This'll get you up to Captain Yamaguchi's office—it's
good anywhere in the Green Area—and she's already
pulled Colin's personal data for you. Do you know your
way there, or should I assign a guide?"

"No, thank you, Major. I've been here a couple of
times; I can find my own way, I think. Should I just hand
this—" he touched the pass "—back in at the security
desk as I leave?"

"That would be fine," Simmons agreed, and Sean
headed for the elevators. He walked past the first bank,
and punched for a car in the L Block, humming softly
and wishing his palms weren't a bit damp as he waited.
A musical tone chimed and the floor light lit above the
doors. They opened quietly.

"Here we go, kid," Sean murmured *sotto voce*. "Hope
it works."

°   °   °

Colin lay back on his brother's bed, hands clasped behind his head, and his unfocused eyes watched sun patterns on the wall. He hated involving Sean—and hated it all the more because he'd known Sean would agree. The odds were tremendously against anyone noticing the scanner relay . . . but humanity's very presence on this planet resulted from a far more unlikely chain of events.

It was a strange sensation to lie here and yet simultaneously accompany Sean. There was a duality to his senses and his vision, as if he personally rode in his brother's shirt pocket even as he lay comfortably on the bed.

His implants reached out through the disguised relay, probing and peering, exploring the webs of electronics around Sean like insubstantial fingers. He could almost touch the flow of current as the elevator floor lights lit silently, just as he could feel the motion of the elevator as it climbed the hollow, empty-tasting shaft. Security systems, computers, electric pencil sharpeners, telephones, intercoms, lighting conduits, heating and air-conditioning sensors, ventilation shafts—he felt them about him and quested through them like a ghost, sniffing and prying.

And then, like a bolt of lightning, a fiery little core of brighter, fiercer power surged in his perceptions.

Colin stiffened, closing his eyes as he concentrated. The impression was faint, but he closed in on it, tuning out the background. His immaterial fingers reached out, and his brows creased in surprise. It was a com link, all right—a fold-space com, very similar to the implant in his own skull—but there was something strange about it. . . .

He worried at it, focusing and refining his data, and then he had it. It was a security link, not a standard hand com. He would never have spotted it if *Dahak* hadn't improved his built-in sensors, but that explained why it seemed so similar to his implant. He insinuated his perceptions into the heart of the tiny device, confirming his identification. Definitely a security link; there were the multi-dimensional shift circuits to bounce it around. Now why should the mutineers bother with a security link? Even in a worst-case scenario that assumed *Dahak* was fully operational, that was taking security to paranoid extremes. *Dahak* could do many things, but tapping a fold-space com from lunar orbit wasn't one of them, and no one on Earth would even recognize one.

He considered consulting with *Dahak*, but only for a moment. None of the mutineers' equipment could tap his link with the computer, but that didn't mean they couldn't detect it. The device he'd found had a piddling little range—no more than fifteen thousand kilometers—and detecting something like that would be practically impossible with its shift circuits in operation. But his implant's range was over a light-hour, and that very power would make it stand out like a beacon on any Imperial detector screen on the planet.

He muttered pungently, then shrugged. It didn't really matter why the mutineers had given that particular com to their minion; what mattered was that he'd found it, and he concentrated on pinning down its precise location.

Ahhhhhh yesssssss. . . . There it was. Right down in—

Colin sat up with a jerk. *Cal Tudor's office?!* That was insane!

But there was no doubt about it. The damned thing was not only in his office but hidden *inside* his work terminal!

Colin swung his legs shakenly off the bed. He knew Cal well—or he'd thought he did. They were friends— such good friends he would have risked contacting Cal if Sean hadn't been available—and the one word Colin had always associated with him was "integrity." True, Cal was young for his position, but he lived, breathed, and dreamed the Prometheus Mission. . . . Could that be the very way they'd gotten to him?

Colin could think of no other explanation. Yet the more he considered it, the less he understood why they would have picked Cal at all. He was a member of the proctoscope team, but a very junior one. Colin put his elbows on his knees and leaned his chin in his palms as he consulted the biographies *Dahak* had amassed on the team's members.

As usual, there was a curious, detached feeling to the data. He was getting used to it, but the dividing line between knowledge he'd acquired experientially and that which *Dahak* had shoveled into a handy empty spot in his brain was surprisingly sharp. The implant data came from someone else and felt like someone else's. Despite a growing acceptance, it was a sensation he found uncomfortable, and he was beginning to suspect he always would.

But the point at issue was Cal's background, not the workings of his implant. It helped Colin to visualize the data as if it had been projected upon a screen, and he frowned as the facts flickered behind his eyelids.

Cal Tudor. Age thirty-six years. Wife's name Frances; two daughters—Harriet and Anna, fourteen and twelve. Theoretical physicist, Lawrence Livermore by way of MIT Denver, then six years at Goddard before he moved to Shepherd. . . .

Colin flicked through more data then stiffened. Dear God! How the hell had *Dahak* missed it? He knew how *he* had, and the nature of his implant *was* a factor, for he'd never realized how seldom Cal ever mentioned his family.

Yet the information was there, and only the "otherness" of the data *Dahak* had provided had kept it at arm's length from Colin and prevented him from spotting the impossible "coincidence." *Dahak* had checked for connections with the mutineers as far back as college, but Cal's connection pre-dated more than his college career; it pre-dated his birth! If *Dahak* had a human-sized imagination (or, for that matter, if Colin had personally—and thoroughly—checked the data) they would have recognized it, for Cal's very failure to mention it to one of his closest friends would have underscored it in red.

Cal Tudor: son of Michael Tudor, only living grandson of Andrew and Isis *Hidachi* Tudor, and great-grandson of Horace Hidachi, "the Father of Gravitonics." The brilliant, intuitive genius who over sixty years before had single-handedly worked out the basic math that underlay the entire field!

Colin pounded his knee gently with a fist. He and *Dahak* had even speculated on Horace Hidachi's possible links with the mutineers, for the stature of his "breakthrough" had seemed glaringly suspicious. Yet they obviously hadn't delved deeply enough for reasons that—at the time—had seemed good and sufficient.

Hidachi had spent twenty years as a researcher before he evolved "his" theory and he'd never *done* anything with his brilliant theoretical work. Nor had anyone else during the course of his life. At the time he propounded his theory, it had been an exercise in pure math, a hypothesis that was impossible to test; by the time the hardware became available, he was dead. Nor had his daughter shown any particular interest in his work. If Colin remembered correctly (and thanks to *Dahak* he did), she'd gone into medicine, not physics.

Which was why *Dahak* and Colin had stopped worrying about Hidachi. If he'd been a minion of the mutineers, he would scarcely have invested that much time building a cover merely to produce an obscure bit of mathematical arcanum. He would have carried through with the hardware to prove it. At the very least, the mutineers themselves would scarcely have allowed his work to lie fallow for so long. As it was, *Dahak* had decided that Hidachi must have produced that rarest of rarities: a genuine, fundamental breakthrough so profound no one had even recognized what it was. Indeed, the computer had computed a high probability that the lag between theory and practice simply resulted from how long it took the mutineers to realize what Hidachi had done and prod a later generation of scientists down the path it opened.

But *this*—!

Colin castigated himself for forgetting the key fact about the mutineers' very existence. Wearisome as the passing millennia had been for *Dahak*, they had *not* been that for Anu's followers. They could take refuge in stasis, ignoring the time that passed between contacts with the Terra-born. Why *shouldn't* they think in generations? For all Colin and *Dahak* knew, the last, unproductive fifteen years of Hidachi's life had been a simple case of a missed connection!

But if, in fact, the mutineers had once contacted a Hidachi, why not again? Especially if Horace Hidachi had left some record of his own dealings with Anu and company. It might even explain how a man like Cal, whose integrity was absolute, could be working with them. For all Cal might know, the mutineers were on the side of goodness and light!

And his junior position on the proctoscope team made him a beautiful choice. He had access to project progress reports, yet he was unobtrusive ... and quite probably primed for contact with the same "visitors" who had contacted his great-grandfather.

But if so, he didn't realize who he was truly helping, Colin decided. It was possible he was wrong, but he couldn't believe he was *that* wrong. Cal *had* to think he was working on the side of the angels, and why shouldn't he? If the mutineers had, indeed, provided the expertise to develop the proctoscope, then they'd advanced the frontiers of human knowledge by several centuries in barely sixty years. How could that seem an "evil" act to someone like Cal?

Which meant there was a possibility, here. He'd found exactly the connection he sought ... and perhaps he could not only convince Cal of the truth but actually enlist him as an ally!

Chapter Eight

"You should let me go."

Sean MacIntyre's stubborn face was an unhealthy red in his Bushmaster's dash LEDs, and despite the high-efficiency emission-controls required by law, the agonizing stench of burning hydrocarbons had forced Colin to step his sensory levels down to little more than normal.

"No," he said for the fifth—or sixth—time.

"If you're wrong—if he *is* a bad guy and he's got some kind of panic button—he's gonna punch it the instant he opens the door and sees you."

"Maybe. But the shock of seeing me alive may keep him from doing anything hasty till we've had time to talk, too. Besides, if he does send out a signal, I can pick it up and bug out. Can you?"

"Be better not to spook him into sending one at all," Sean grumbled.

"Agreed. But he's not going to. I'm positive he doesn't know what those bastards are really up to—or what they've already done to the human race."

"I'm glad *you* are!"

"I've already gotten you in deep enough, Sean," Colin said as the Caddy snarled up a grade. "If I *am* wrong, I don't want you in the line of fire."

"I appreciate that," Sean said softly, "but I'm your brother. I happen to love you. And even if I didn't, this poor world will be in a hell of a mess a couple of years down the road if you get your ass killed, you jerk!"

"I'm not going to," Colin said firmly, "so stop arguing. Besides—" Sean turned off the highway onto a winding mountain road "—we're almost there."

"All right, goddamn it," Sean sighed, then grinned unwillingly. "You always were almost as stubborn as me."

The Caddy ghosted to a stop on the shoulder of the road. The view out over Colorado Springs was breathtaking, though neither brother paid it much heed, but the mountain above them was dark and sparsely populated. The Tudor home was a big, modern split-level, but it was part of a small, well-spread out "environment conscious" development, carefully designed to merge with its surroundings and then dropped into a neat, custom-tailored hole bitten out of the slope. It was two-thirds underground, and only the front porch light gleamed above him as Colin climbed out into the breezy night.

"Thanks, Sean," he said softly, leaning back into the car to squeeze his brother's shoulder with carefully restrained strength. "Wait here. If that thing—" he gestured at the small device sitting on the console between the front seats "—lights up, then shag ass out of here. Got it?"

"Yes," Sean sighed.

"Good. See you later." Colin gave another gentle squeeze, wishing his brother's unenhanced eyes could see the affection on his face, then turned away into the windy blackness. Sean watched him go, vanishing into the night, before he opened the glove compartment.

The heavy magnum automatic gleamed in the starlight as he checked the magazine and shoved the pistol into his belt, and he drummed on the wheel for a few more moments. He didn't know how good Colin's new hearing really was, and he wanted to give him plenty of time to get out of range before he followed.

Colin climbed straight up the mountainside, ignoring the heavy weight on his back. He could have left the suppresser behind, but he might need a little extra evidence to convince Cal he knew what he was talking about. Besides, he felt uneasy about letting it out of reach.

He let his enhanced sight and hearing coast up to maximum sensitivity as he neared the top, and his eyes lit as they touched the house. His electronic and gravitonic sensors were in passive mode lest he trip any waiting detectors, but there was a background haze of additional Imperial power sources in there, confirmation, if any had been needed, that Cal was his man.

He climbed over the split-rail fence he'd helped Cal build last spring and eased into the gap between the house and the sheer south wall of the deep, terrace-like notch blasted out of the mountain to hold it, circling to approach through the tiny backyard and wondering how Cal would react when he saw him. He hoped he was right about his friend. God, *how* he hoped he was!

He slipped through Frances Tudor's neat vegetable garden towards the back door like a ghost, checking for any security devices, Terran or Imperial, as he went. He found none, but his nerves tightened as he felt the soft prickle of an active fold-space link. He couldn't separate sources without going active with his own sensors, but it felt like another security com. No traffic was going out, but the unit was up, as if waiting to receive . . . or transmit. The last thing he needed was to find Cal sitting in front of a live mike and have him blurt out an alarm before his guest had a chance to open his mouth!

He sighed. He'd just have to hope for the best, but even at the worst, he should be able to vanish before anyone could respond to any alarm Cal raised.

He eased into the silent kitchen. It was dark, but that hardly mattered to him. He started toward the swinging dining room door, then stopped as he touched the bevel-edged glass hand plate.

There was a strange, time-frozen quality about the darkened kitchen. A wooden salad bowl on the counter was half-filled with shredded lettuce, but the other salad ingredients still lay neatly to one side, as if awaiting the chef's hand, and a chill wind seemed to gust down his spine. It wasn't like Cal or Frances to leave food sitting out like that, and he opened his sensors wide, going active despite the risk of detection.

What the—? A portable stealth field *behind* him?! His muscles bunched and he prepared to whirl, but—

"*Right* there," a voice said very softly, and he froze, one hand still on the dining room door, for the voice was not Cal's and it did not speak in English. "Hands behind your head, scum," it continued in Imperial Universal. "No little implant signals, either. Don't even think about doing anything but what I tell you to, or I'll burn your spine in two."

Colin obeyed, moving very slowly and cursing himself for a fool. He'd been wrong about Cal—dead wrong—and his own caution had kept him from looking hard enough to spot somebody with a stealth field. But who would have expected one? No one but another Imperial could possibly have picked up their implants, anyway. Which meant . . .

His blood went icy. Jesus, they'd been *expecting* him! And that meant they'd picked up the scanner relay—and that they knew about Sean, too!

"Very nice," the voice said. "Now just push the door open with your shoulder and move on through it. Carefully."

Colin obeyed, and the ashes of defeat were bitter in his mouth.

Sean longed for some of Colin's enhanced strength as he picked his way up the steep, dew-slick mountainside, but he made it to the fence and climbed over it at last. Then he stopped with a frown.

Unlike Colin, Sean MacIntyre had spent his nights

under the stars rather than out among them. He'd joined the Forestry Service out of love, almost unable to believe that anyone would actually *pay* him to work in the protected wilderness of parks and nature reservations. Along the way, he'd refined a natural empathy for the world about him, one which relied on more than the sheer strength of his senses, and so it was that he noted what Colin had not.

The Tudor house was still and black, with no lights, no feel of life, and every nerve in Sean's body screamed "Trap!"

He took the automatic off "safe" and worked the slide. From what Colin had said, the "biotechnic" enhanced mutineers would take a lot of killing, but Sean had lots of faith in the hollow-nosed .45 super-mags in his clip.

"Nice of you to be so prompt," the voice behind Colin gloated. "We didn't expect you for another half-hour."

The sudden close-range pulse of the fold-space link behind Colin was almost painful, and he clamped his teeth in angry, frightened understanding. It had been a short-range pulse, which meant its recipients were close at hand.

"They'll be along in a few minutes," the voice said. "Through the door to your left," it added, and Colin pushed at it with his toe.

It opened, and he gagged as an indescribably evil smell suddenly assailed him. He retched in anguish before he could scale his senses back down, and the voice behind him laughed.

"Your host," it said cruelly, and flipped on the lights.

Cal drooped forward out of his chair, flung over his desk by the same energy blast which had sprayed his entire head over the blotter, but that was only the start of the horror. Fourteen-year-old Harriet sagged brokenly in an armchair before the desk, her head twisted around to stare accusingly at Colin with dead, glazed eyes. Her mother lay to one side, and the blast that had killed her had torn her literally in half. Twelve-year-old Anna lay half-under her, her child body even more horribly mutilated by the weapon that had killed them both as Frances tried uselessly to shield her daughter with her own life.

"He didn't want to call you in," the voice's gloating, predatory cruelty seemed to come from far, far away, "but we convinced him."

The universe roared about Colin MacIntyre, battering him like a hurricane, and the fury of the storm was his own rage. He started to turn, heedless of the weapon behind him, but the energy gun was waiting. It clubbed the back of his neck, battering him to his knees, and his captor laughed.

"Not so fast," he jeered. "The Chief wants to ask you a few questions, first." Then he raised his voice. "Anshar! Get your ass in here."

"I already have," another voice answered. Colin looked up as a second man stepped in through the far study door, and his normally mild eyes were emerald fire as he took in the blond-haired newcomer's midnight blue uniform, the Fleet issue boots, the heavy energy gun slung from one shoulder.

"About damn time," the first voice grunted. "All right, you bastard—" the energy gun prodded "—on your feet. Over there against the wall."

Grief and horror mingled with the red fangs of blood-lust, but even through that boil of emotion Colin knew he must obey—for now. Yet even as he promised himself a time would come for vengeance, an icy little voice whispered he'd made some terrible mistake. His captor's sneering cruelty, the carnage that had claimed his friend's entire family . . . None of it made any sense.

"Turn around," the voice said, and Colin turned his back to the wall.

The one who'd been doing all the talking was of no more than medium size but stocky, black-haired, with an odd olive-brown complexion. His eyes were also odd; almost Asiatic and yet not quite. Colin recognized the prototype from whence all Terran humans had sprung, and the thought made him sick.

But the other one, Anshar, was different. Even in his fury and fear, Colin was puzzled by the other's fair skin and blue eyes. He was Terra-born; he had to be, for the humanity of the Imperium had been very nearly completely homogenous. Only one planet of the Third Imperium, had survived its fall, and the seven thousand years between Man's departure from Birhat to rebuild and Anu's mutiny had not diluted that homogeneity significantly. Only after *Dahak*'s crew reached Earth had genetic drift set in among the isolated survivors to produce disparate races. So what was *he* doing in Fleet uniform? Colin's sensors reached out and his eyes widened as he detected a complete set of biotechnic implants in the man.

"Pity the degenerate was so stubborn," the first one said, jerking Colin's attention back to him as he propped a hip against the desk. "But he saw the light when we broke his little bitch's neck." He prodded Harriet's corpse with the muzzle of his energy gun, his eyes a goad of cruelty, and Colin made himself breathe slowly. Wait, he told himself. You may have a chance to kill him before he kills you if you wait.

"Of course, we told him we'd let the others live if he called you." He laughed suddenly. "He may even have believed it!"

"Stop it, Girru," Anshar said, and his own eyes flinched away from the butchered bodies.

"You always were gutless, Anshar," Girru sneered. "Hell, even degenerates like a little hunting!"

"You didn't have to do it this way," Anshar muttered.

"Oh? Shall I tell the Chief you're getting fastidious? Or—" his voice took on a silky edge "—would you prefer I tell Kirinal?"

"No! I . . . just don't like it."

"Of course you don't!" Girru said contemptuously. "You—"

He broke off suddenly, whirling with the impossible speed of his implants, and a thunderous roar exploded behind him. The bright, jagged flare of a muzzle flash filled the darkened hall like lightning, edging the half-opened door in brilliance, and he jerked as the heavy slug smashed into him. A hoarse, agonized cry burst from him, but his enhanced body was tough beyond the ken of Terrans. He continued his turn, slowed by his hurt but still deadly, and the magnum bellowed again.

Even the wonders of the Fourth Imperium had their limits. The massive bullet punched through his reinforced spinal column, and he flipped away from the desk, knocking over the chair in which the dead girl sat.

Colin had hurled himself forward at the sound of the first shot, for he knew with heart-stopping certitude who had fired it. But he was on the wrong side of the room, and Anshar's slung energy gun snapped up, finger on the trigger—only to stop and jerk back towards the hallway door as a heavy foot kicked it fully open.

"No, Sean!" Colin bellowed, but his cry was a lifetime too late.

Sean MacIntyre knew Colin could never reach Anshar before the mutineer cut him down—and he had seen the slaughter of innocents that filled the study. He swung his magnum in a two-handed combat stance, matching merely human reflexes and fury against the inhuman speed of the Fourth Imperium.

He got off one shot. The heavy bullet took Anshar in the abdomen, wreaking horrible damage, but the energy gun snarled. It birthed a terrible demon—a focused beam of gravitonic disruption fit to shatter steel—that swept a fan of destruction across the door, and Sean MacIntyre's body erupted in a fountain of gore as it sliced through plaster and wood and flesh.

"NOOOOOOOO!!!" Colin screamed, and lunged at his brother's murderer.

The devastation the slug had wrought within Anshar slowed him, but he held down the stud, shattering the room as he swept it with lethal energy. Instinct prompted Colin even in his madness, and he wrenched aside, grunting as the suppresser on his back took the full fury of the blast.

It hurled him to one side, but Girru and Anshar hadn't realized what the suppresser was, and no Terran "knapsack" could have absorbed the damage of a full power energy bolt.

Anshar released the trigger stud and paused, expecting his enemy to fall.

But Colin was unhurt, and long hours spent working out against *Dahak*'s training remotes took command. He hit on his outspread hands and somersaulted back at Anshar while the mutineer gawked at him in disbelief. Then his boots slammed into Anshar's chest, battering the energy gun from his grip.

Both men rolled back upright, but Anshar was hurt— badly hurt—and Colin forgot *Dahak*, the Imperium, even his need for a prisoner. He ignored the dropped energy gun. He wanted nothing between Anshar and his own bare hands, and Anshar paled and writhed away as he saw the dark, terrible death in Colin's eyes.

Fury crashed through Colin MacIntyre—cold, cruel fury—and one hand caught a flailing arm and jerked his victim close. An alloy-reinforced knee, driven with all the power of his enhanced muscles, smashed into the wound Sean's bullet had torn, and a savage smile twisted his lips at Anshar's less than human sound of agony.

He shifted his grip, wrenching the arm he held high, and reinforced cartilage and bone tore and splintered with a ghastly ripping sound. Anshar shrieked again, but the sound was not enough to satisfy Colin. He slammed his enemy to the floor. His knee crashed down between Anshar's shoulders, and he released the arm he held. Both hands darted down, cupping the mutineer's chin, and his mighty back tensed, driven by the biotechnic miracles of the Fourth Imperium and the terrible power of hate. There was a moment of titanic stress and one last gurgling scream, and then Anshar's spine snapped with a flat, explosive crack.

Chapter Nine

Colin held his grip, feeling the life flow out of his victim in the steady collapse of Anshar's implants, and the killer in his soul was sick with triumph . . . and angry that it was over.

He opened his hands at last, and Anshar's face struck the floor with a meaty smack. Colin rose, scrubbing his hands on his jeans, and his eyes were empty, as if part of himself had died with his brother.

He turned away, smelling wood smoke, plaster dust, and the stench of ruptured bodies. He could not look at Cal's slaughtered family, but neither, though he would have sold his soul to do it, could he take his eyes from Sean.

He knelt in the spreading pool of his brother's blood. The energy gun had mangled Sean hideously, but the very horror meant death had come quickly, and he tried to tell himself Sean had not suffered as his ripped and torn flesh said he had.

Their long-dead mother's eyes looked up at him. There was no life in them, but an echo of Sean's outrage

remained. He'd known, Colin thought sadly, known he
was a dead man from the instant Anshar began to raise
his own weapon, yet he'd stood his ground. Just as he
always had. And, just as he always had, he had protected
his younger brother.

Colin closed those eyes with gentle fingers, and una-
shamed tears streaked his cheeks. One fell, a diamond
glinting in the light from the study, to his brother's face,
and the sight touched something inside him. It was like
a farewell, fraying the grip of the grief that kept him
kneeling there, and he reached to pick up Girru's energy
gun.

"Freeze," a cold voice said behind him.

Colin froze, but this time he recognized the voice. It
spoke English with a soft, Southern accent, and his jaw
clenched. Not just Cal; everyone he'd thought he knew,
believed he could trust, had betrayed him. Everyone but
Sean.

"Drop it." He let the energy gun thump back to the
floor. "Inside."

He stepped back into the study and turned slowly, his
eyes flinty as they rested on the tall, black-skinned
woman in the doorway. She wore the uniform of the
United States Air Force with a lieutenant colonel's oak
leaves, but the weapon slung from her shoulder had
never been made on Earth. The over-sized, snub-nosed
pistol was a grav gun, and its drum magazine held two
hundred three-millimeter darts. Their muzzle velocity
would be over five thousand meters per second, and they
were formed of a chemical explosive denser than ura-
nium that exploded after penetrating. From where he
stood, he could see the three-headed dragon etched into
the receiver.

The muzzle never wavered from his navel, but the
colonel's eyes swept the room, and her face twisted. The
black forefinger on the trigger tightened and he tensed
his belly muscles uselessly, but she didn't fire. Her brown
eyes lingered for a long moment on Frances and Anna
Tudor's mutilated bodies, then came back to him, filled
with a bottomless hate he'd never seen in them.

"You *bastard!*" Lieutenant Colonel Sandra Tillotson breathed.

"Me?" he said bitterly. "What about *you*, Sandy?"

His voice was like a blow. Her head jerked, and her eyes widened, their hatred buried in sudden disbelief as she saw him—*him*, not just another killer—for the first time.

"*Colin?!*" she gasped, and her reaction puzzled him. Surely the mutineers had known who they were trapping! But Sandy closed her mouth with an almost audible snap, her gaze flitting to the two dead bodies in the Fleet uniforms, and he could actually see the intensity of her thoughts, see a whole chain of realizations flickering over her face. And then, to his utter shock, she lowered her weapon.

His muscles tightened to leap across the intervening space and snatch it away. But she shook her head slowly, and her next words stopped him dead.

"Colin," she whispered. "My God, Colin, what have you *done?*"

It was the last reaction he had expected, and his own eyes narrowed.

"I found them like this. Those two—" his head gestured at the uniformed bodies, hands motionless "—were waiting for me. They . . . killed Sean, too."

Sandy jerked around to stare through the doorway, and her shoulders sagged as she finally recognized the savagely maimed body. When she turned back to Colin, her eyes were closed in grief and despair.

"Oh, Jesus," she moaned. "Oh, dear, sweet Jesus. Not Sean, too."

"Sandy, what the *hell* is going on here?" Colin demanded.

"No, you wouldn't know," she said softly, her mouth bitter.

"I don't *know* anything! I thought I did, but—"

"Cal tripped his emergency signal," Sandy said tonelessly, and looked at the dead scientist, as if impressing the hideous sight imperishably upon her mind. "I was closest, so I came as quick as I could."

"*You*? Sandy—*you're* in with Anu?"

"Of course not! Those two—Girru and Anshar—were two of his hit men."

"Sandy, what are you *talking* about? If you're not—"

Colin broke off again as his sensors tingled, and Sandy stiffened as she saw his face tighten.

"What is it?" she asked sharply.

"Those two bastards called in reinforcements," Colin said tautly. "They're coming. Don't you feel them?"

"I'm a normal human, Colin. One of the 'degenerates,'" Sandy said harshly. "But you aren't, are you? Not anymore."

"A norm—" He broke off. "Later," he said tersely. "Right now, we've got at least twenty sets of combat armor closing in on us."

"Shit," Sandy breathed. Then she shook herself again. "If you've got yourself a bio-enhancement package, grab one of those energy guns!" She bared her teeth in an ugly smile. "*That'll* surprise the bastards!"

Colin snatched up Anshar's weapon. It had suffered no damage in their struggle and the charge indicator read ninety percent, and his fingers curled almost lovingly around the grips as he grasped Sandy's meaning. No normal human could handle one of the heavy energy weapons. Even Sandy's grav gun would be a problem for most Terra-born humans. For the Imperium, it was a sidearm; for Sandy, it was a shoulder-slung, two-handed weapon.

"How are they coming in and where are they?" Sandy demanded tersely.

"Twenty of them," Colin repeated. "Closing in from the perimeter of a circle. About six klicks out and coming fast."

"Too far," Sandy muttered. "We've got to suck them in closer. . . ."

"Why?"

"Because—" She broke off, shaking her head. "There's no time for explanations, Colin. Just trust me—and believe I'm on your side."

"My side? Sandy—"

"Shut *up* and *listen!*" she snapped, and he choked off

his questions. "Look, I had my suspicions when we didn't find any sign of you in that wreck, but it seemed so incredible that— Never mind. The important thing is you. What kind of implants did you get?"

Questions hammered in Colin's brain. How did Sandy, who obviously had no biotechnics, even know what they were? Much less that there were different implant packages? But she was right. There was no time.

"Bridge officer," he said shortly.

"Bridge—?! You mean the ship's *fully* operational?!"

"Maybe," he said cautiously, and she shook her head irritably.

"Either it is or it isn't, and if you got the full treatment, it is. Which means—" She broke off again and nodded sharply.

"Don't just stand there! See if it can get our asses out of here!"

Colin gaped at her. The hurricane of his grief and fury, followed by the shock of seeing Sandy, had blinded him to the simplest possibility of all!

He activated his fold-space link, then grunted in anguish, half-clubbed to his knees by the squealing torment in his nerves. He shook his head doggedly.

"Can't!" he gasped. "We're jammed."

"Shit!" Sandy's face tightened again, but when she spoke again, her voice was curiously serene. "Colin, I don't know how you found Cal, or exactly what happened here, but you're the *only* man on this planet with bridge implants. We've *got* to get you out of here."

"But—"

"There's no *time*, Colin. Just listen. If we can suck them in close, there's an escape route. When I tell you to, go down to the basement. There's a switch somewhere—I don't know where, but you won't need it. Go down to the basement and move the furnace. It pivots clockwise, but you'll have to break the lock to move it. Go down the ladder and take the right fork—the left's a booby-trapped cul-de-sac—and move like hell. You'll come out about a klick from here in the woods above Aspen Road. Got it?"

"Got it. But—" he tried again.

"I said there's no time." She turned for the door, stepping carefully over Sean's body. "Come with me. We've got to convince them we're going to stand and fight, or they'll be watching for a breakout."

Colin followed her rebelliously, every nerve in his body crying out against obeying her blindly. Yet she clearly knew what she was doing—or thought she did—and that was a thousand percent better than anything *he* knew.

Sandy scurried down the hall and moved a wall painting to reveal a small switch. Colin's sensors reached out to trace the circuitry, but she threw it before he got far, and his skin twitched as he felt the sudden awakening of unsuspected defenses. He'd sensed additional Imperial technology as he approached the house, but he'd never suspected *this*!

"This wall's armored, but it faces away from the mountain, so we couldn't risk shield circuits in it," Sandy explained tersely, turning into the living room and kneeling beside a picture window. She rested the muzzle of her heavy grav gun on the sill. "Too much chance Anu's bunch would notice if one of 'em happened by. But it's the only open wall in the house."

Colin grunted in understanding, kneeling beside a window on the far side of the room. If they were trying to hide, they'd taken an awful chance just covering the roof and side walls, but not as big a one as he'd first thought. His own sensors were far more sensitive than any mutineer's, and he realized the shield circuits were actually very well hidden as he traced the forcefield to its source. He'd expected Imperial molecular circuits, but the concealed installation in the basement was of Terran manufacture. It had some highly unusual components, but it was all printed circuits, which explained both its bulkiness and their difficulty in hiding it. Still, the very fact that it contained no molycircs was its best protection.

The shield cut off his sensors in three directions, but he could still use them through the open wall, and he grinned savagely as the emission signatures of combat armor glowed before him. They were far better protected than he, but they were also far more "visible," and he lifted his energy gun hungrily.

"They're coming," he whispered, and Sandy nodded, her face grotesque behind the light-gathering optics she'd clipped over her eyes. They were the latest US Army issue, hardly up to Imperial standards but highly efficient in their limited area. He turned back to the window, watching the night.

A suit of combat armor was a bright glare in his vision, and he raised his energy gun. The attacker rose higher, topping out over the slope, and he wondered why they were no longer using their jump gear. The mutineer rose still higher, exposing almost his full body, and Colin squeezed the stud.

His window exploded, showering the night with glass. The nearly invisible energy was a terrible lash of power to his enhanced vision as it smashed out across the lawn, and it took the mutineer dead center.

The combat armor held for an instant, but Colin's weapon was on max. There was a shattering geyser of gore, and a dreadful hunger snarled within him as the mutineer went down forever and he heard a rippling *hisss-crrackkk!*

The near-silent grav gun's darts went supersonic as they left the muzzle, and Sandy's window blew apart, but its resistance was too slight to detonate them. A corner of his eye saw gouts of flying dirt as a dozen plunged deep and exploded, and then another suit of combat armor reared backwards. It toppled over the side of the yard, thundering on the road below, and Sandy's hungry, vengeful sound echoed his own.

Their fire had broken the silence, and the house rocked as Imperial weapons smashed at its side and rear walls. Colin winced as he felt the sudden power surge in the shield circuits. The fire went on and on, flaying the night with thunder and lightning, and the homemade shield generator heated dangerously, but it held.

Then the thunder ceased, and he looked up as Sandy spoke again.

"They know, now," she said softly. "They'll be coming

at us from the front in a minute. They can't afford to waste time with all the racket we're making. They've got to be in and out before—" She broke off and hosed another stream of darts into the night, and a third armored body blew apart. "—before someone comes to see what the hell is happening."

"We'll never hold against a real rush," he warned.

"I know. It's time to bug out, Colin."

"They'll follow us," he said. "Even I can't outrun combat suits with jump gear." He did not add that she stood no chance at all of outrunning them.

"Won't have to," she said shortly. "There should be friends at the end of the tunnel when you get there. But for God's sake, don't come out shooting! They don't know what's going on in here."

"Friends? What—?" He broke off and ripped off another shot, but this time the mutineers knew they were under fire. He hit his target squarely, but his victim dropped before the beam fully overpowered his armor. He was badly hurt—no doubt of that—but it was unlikely he was dead.

"Don't ask questions! Just get your ass in gear and *go*, damn it!"

"Not without you," he shot back.

"You stupid—!" Sandy bit off her angry remark and shook her head fiercely. "I can't even open the damned tunnel, asshole! *You* can, so stop being so fucking gallant! Somebody has to cover the rear and somebody else has to open the tunnel! Now *move*, Colin!"

He started to argue, but his sensors were suddenly crowded with the emissions of combat armor gathering along the roadway below the slope. She was right, and he knew it. He didn't *want* to know it, but he did.

"All right!" he grated. "But you'd better be *right* behind me, lady, or I'm coming back after you!"

"*No*, you mule-headed, chauvinistic honk—!"

She chopped herself off as she realized he was already gone. She wanted to call after him and wish him luck but dared not turn away from her front. She regretted her own angry response to his words, for she knew why he had said them. He'd had to, pointless as they both knew it was. He had to believe he would come back—that he *could* come back—yet he knew as well as she that if she wasn't right on his heels, she would never make it out at all.

But what she had carefully not told him was that she wouldn't be following him. She'd said there would be friends, but she couldn't be certain, and even if there were, someone had to occupy the attackers' attention to keep them from noticing movement in the tunnel when Colin passed beyond the confines of the shield. And she'd meant what she'd said. If he had a bridge officer's implants, they *had* to get him out. She didn't understand everything that was happening, but she knew that. And that he needed time to make his escape.

Lieutenant Colonel Sandra Tillotson, United States Air Force, laid a spare magazine beside her and prepared to buy him that time.

Colin raced down the basement stairs, sick at heart. Deep inside, he suspected what Sandy intended, and she was right, damn it! But the thought of abandoning her was a canker in his soul. This night of horrors was costing too much. He remembered what he'd thought when *Dahak*'s cutter deposited him here, and his own words were wormwood and gall. He hadn't realized the hideous depth of what would be demanded of him, for somehow he'd believed that only *he* must lose things, that he must risk only himself. He hadn't counted on people he knew and loved being slaughtered like animals . . . nor had he realized how bitter it could be to live rather than die beside them.

He sensed the stuttering fire of her grav gun behind him, the fury of energy weapons gouging at the house, and his eyes burned as he seized the heavy furnace in a mighty grip. He heaved, wrenching it entirely from its base, and the ladder was there. He ignored it, leaping lightly down the two-meter drop, and hit the tunnel running. Even as he passed under the edge of the shield and it sliced off his sensors, he felt the space-wrenching discharges of her grav gun, knew she was still there, still firing, not even trying to escape, and tears and self-hate blinded him as he raced for safety.

The tunnel seemed endless, yet the end was upon him almost before he realized it, and he lunged up another ladder. The shaft was sealed, but he was already probing it, spotting the catch, heaving it up with a mighty shoulder. He burst into the night air ... and his senses were suddenly afire with more power sources. More combat armor! Coming from behind in the prodigious leaps of jump gear and waiting in the woods ahead, as well!

He tried to unlimber his energy gun, but a torrent of energy crashed over him, and he cried out as every implant in his body screamed in protest. He writhed, fighting it, clinging to the torment of awareness.

It was a capture field—not a killing blast of energy, but something infinitely worse. A police device that locked his synthetic muscles with brutal power.

He toppled forward under the impetus of his last charge, crashing to the ground half-in and half-out of the tunnel. He fought the encroaching darkness, smashing at it with all the fury of his enraged will, but it swept over him.

The last thing he saw was a tornado of light as the trees exploded with energy fire. He carried the vision down into the dark with him, dimly aware of its importance.

And then, as his senses faded at last, he realized. It wasn't directed at him—it was raking the ground behind him and cutting down the mutineers who had pursued him. . . .

Chapter Ten

Colin swam fearfully up out of his nightmares, trying to understand what had happened. Something was wrong with his senses, and he moaned softly, frightened by the deadness, the *absence*, where he should have felt the whisper and wash of ambient energy.

He opened his eyes and blinked, automatically damping the brilliant light glaring down over him. He made out a ceiling beyond it—an unfamiliar roof of an all-too-familiar, bronze-colored alloy—and his muscles tightened.

It had been no dream. Sean was dead. And Cal . . . his family . . . and Sandy. . . .

Memory wrung a harsh, inarticulate sound of grief from him, and he closed his eyes again. Then he gathered himself and tried to sit up, but his body refused to obey and his eyes popped open once more. He tried again, harder, and his muscles strained, but it was like trying to lift the Earth. Something pressed down upon him, and he clenched his teeth as he recognized the presser. And a suppression field, as well, which explained his dead sensory implants.

A small sound touched his ear, and he wrenched his head around, barely able to move even that much under the presser.

Three grim-faced people looked back at him. The one standing in the center was a man, gray-haired, his seamed face puckered by a smooth, long-healed scar from just under his right eye down under the neck of his tattered old Clemson University sweatshirt. His leathery skin was the olive-brown of the Fourth Imperium, and Colin recognized the signs from *Dahak*'s briefings; this man was old. Very old. He must be well into his sixth century, but if he was old, he was also massively thewed, and his olive-black eyes were alert.

A woman sat in a chair to his left. She, too, was old, but with the shorter span of the Terra-born, her still-thick hair almost painfully white under the brilliant light. Her lined, grief-drawn face was lighter than the man's, but there was a hint of the same slant to her swollen eyes, and Colin swallowed in painful recognition. He'd never met Isis Tudor, but she looked too much like her murdered grandson to be anyone else.

The third watcher shared the old man's complexion, but her cold, set face was unlined. She was tall for an Imperial, rivaling Colin's own hundred-eighty-eight centimeters, and slender, almost delicate. And she was beautiful, with an almond-eyed, cat-like loveliness that was subtly alien and yet perfect. A thick mane of hair rippled down her spine, so black it was almost blue-green, gathered at the nape of her neck in a jeweled clasp before it fanned out below, and she wore tailored slacks and a cashmere sweater. The gemmed dagger at her belt struck an incongruous note, but not a humorous one. Her slender fingers curled too hungrily about its hilt, and her dark eyes were filled with hate.

He stared silently back at them, then turned his face deliberately away.

The silence stretched out, and then the old man cleared his throat.

"What shall we do with you, Commander MacIntyre?" he asked in soft, perfect English, and Colin turned back to him almost against his will. The spokesman smiled a twisted smile and slipped one arm around the old woman. "We know what you are—in part—" he continued, "but not in full. And—" his soft voice turned suddenly harsher "—we know what you've cost us already."

"Spend not thy words upon him," the young woman said coldly.

"Hush, Jiltanith," the old man said. "It's not his fault."

"Is't not? Yet Calvin doth lie dead, and his wife and daughters with him. And 'tis *this* man hath encompassed that!"

"No." Isis Tudor's soft voice was grief-harrowed, but she shook her head slowly. "He was Cal's *friend*, 'Tanni. He didn't know what he was doing."

"Which changeth naught," Jiltanith said bitterly.

"Isis is right, 'Tanni," the old man said sadly. "He couldn't have known they were looking for Cal. Besides," the old eyes were wise and compassionate despite their own bitterness, "he lost his own brother, as well . . . and avenged Cal and the girls."

He walked towards the table on which Colin lay and locked a challenging gaze with him, and Colin knew it was there between them. He'd warned Sean the relay might be detected, and it had. His mistake had killed Cal and Frances, Harriet and Anna, Sean and Sandy. He knew it, and the same knowledge filled the old man's eyes, yet his captor clasped his hands behind him and stopped a meter away, eloquently unthreatening.

"What use vengeance?" Jiltanith demanded, her lovely, hating face cold. "Will't breathe life back into them? Nay! Slay him and ha' done, I say!"

"No, 'Tanni," the man said more firmly. "We need him, and he needs us."

"I say thee nay, Father!" Jiltanith spat furiously. "I'll ha' none of him! Nay, nor any part in't!"

"It's not for you to say, 'Tanni." The man sounded stern. "It's up to the Council—and *I* am head of the Council."

"Father," Jiltanith's voice was all the more deadly for its softness, "if thou makest this man thine ally, thou art a fool. E'en now hath he cost thee dear. Take heed, lest the price grow higher still."

"We have no choice," her father said. His sad, wise eyes held Colin's. "Commander, if you will give me your parole, I'll switch off the presser."

"No," Colin said coldly.

"Commander, we're not what you think. Or perhaps we are, in a way, but you need us, and we need you. I'm not asking you to surrender, only to listen. That's all we ask. Afterwards, if you wish, we will release you."

Colin heard Jiltanith's bitter, in-drawn hiss, but his eyes bored into the old man's. Something unspeakably old and weary looked back at him—old yet vital with purpose. Despite himself, he was tempted to believe him.

"And just who the hell *are* you?" he grated at last.

"Me, Commander?" The old man smiled wryly. "Missile Specialist First Horus, late of Imperial Battle Fleet. Very late, I fear. And also—" his smile vanished, and his eyes were incredibly sad once more "—Horace Hidachi."

Colin's eyelids twitched, and the old man nodded.

"Yes, Commander. Cal was my great-grandson. And because of that, I think you owe me at least the courtesy of listening, don't you?"

Colin stared at him for a long, silent second and then, jerky against the pressure of the presser, he nodded.

Colin shrugged to settle more comfortably the borrowed uniform which had replaced his blood-stained clothing and studied his surroundings as Horus and Isis Tudor led him down the passageway. A portable suppression field still cut off his sensors, and he was a bit surprised by how incomplete that made him feel. He'd become accustomed to his new senses, accepting the electromagnetic and gravitonic spectrums as an extension of sight and sense and smell. Now they were gone, taken away by the small hand unit a stiff-spined Jiltanith trained upon him as she followed him down the corridor.

They met a few others, though traffic was sparse. Those they passed wore casual Terran clothing, and most were obviously Terra-born. The almond eyes and olive skins of Imperials were scattered thinly among them, and he wondered how so many Terra-born could be admitted to the secret without its leaking.

But even without his implants, he could see—and feel—the oldness about him.

Dahak was even older than his current surroundings, but the huge starship didn't *feel* old. Ancient, yes, but not old. Not worn with the passing of years. For fifty millennia, there had been no feet upon *Dahak*'s decks, no living presence to mark its passing in casual scrapes and bumps and scars.

But feet had left their mark here. The central portion of the tough synthetic decksole had been worn away, and even the bare alloy beneath showed wear. It would take more than feet to grind away Imperial battle steel, but it was polished smooth, burnished to a high gloss. And the bulkheads were the same, showing signs of repairs to lighting fixtures and ventilation ducts in the slightly irregular surface of patches placed by merely human hands rather than the flawlessly precise maintenance units that tended *Dahak*.

It made no sense. *Dahak* had said the mutineers spent most of their time in stasis, yet despite the sparse traffic, he suspected there were hundreds of people moving about him. And this feeling of age, this timeworn weariness that could impregnate even battle steel, was wrong. Anu had taken a complete tech base to Earth; he should have plenty of service mechs for the proper upkeep of his vessels.

Which fitted together with everything else. The murder of Cal's family. Sandy's cryptic remarks. There was a pattern here, one he could not quite grasp yet whose parts were all internally consistent. But—

His thoughts broke off as Horus and Isis slowed suddenly before a closed hatch. A three-headed dragon had once adorned those doors, but it had been planed away, leaving the alloy smooth and unblemished, and he filed that away with the fact that he and he alone wore Fleet uniform.

The hatch opened, and he stepped through it at Horus's gesture.

The control room was a far more cramped version of *Dahak*'s command deck, but there had been changes. A bank of old, flat-screen Terran television monitors covered one bulkhead, and peculiar, bastardized hybrids of Imperial theory and Terran components had been added to the panels. There were standard Terran computer touchpads at consoles already fitted for direct neural feeds, but most incongruous of all, perhaps, were the archaic Terran-style headsets racked by each console. His eyebrows rose as he saw them, and Horus smiled.

"We need the keyboards ... and the phones, Commander," he said wryly. "Most of our people have to enter commands manually and pass orders by voice."

Colin regarded the old man thoughtfully, then nodded noncommittally and turned his attention to the thirty-odd people sitting at the various consoles or standing beside them. The few Imperials among them were a decided minority, and most of those, unlike Jiltanith, seemed almost as ancient as Horus.

"Commander," Horus said formally, "permit me to introduce the Command Council of the sublight battleship *Nergal*, late—like some of her crew, at least—of Battle Fleet."

Colin frowned. The *Nergal* had been one of Anu's ships, but it was becoming painfully clear that whatever these people were, they *weren't* friends of Anu. Not any longer, at any rate. His mind raced as he tried to weigh the fragments of information he had, searching for an advantage he could wring from them.

"I see," was all he said, and Horus actually chuckled.

"I imagine you play a mean game of poker, Commander," he said dryly, and waved Colin to one of the only two empty couches. It was the assistant gunnery officer's, Colin noted, but the panel before it was inactive.

"I try," he said, cocking his head to invite Horus to continue.

"I see you don't intend to make this easy. Well, I don't

suppose I blame you." Jiltanith made a soft, contemptuous sound of disagreement, and Horus frowned at her. She subsided, but Colin had the distinct impression she would have preferred pointing something considerably more lethal than a portable suppresser at him.

"All right," Horus said more briskly, turning to seat Isis courteously in the unoccupied captain's chair, "that's fair. Let's start at the beginning.

"First, Commander, we won't ask you to divulge any information unless you choose to do so. Nonetheless, certain things are rather self-evident.

"First, *Dahak* is, in fact, operational. Second, there is a reason the ship has failed either to squelch the mutiny or to go elsewhere seeking assistance. Third, the ship *has* taken a hand at last, hence your presence here with the first bridge officer implant package this planet has seen in fifty thousand years. Fourth, and most obviously of all, if you'll forgive me, the information upon which you have formulated your plans has proven inaccurate. Or perhaps it would be better to say *incomplete*."

He paused, but Colin allowed his face to show no more than polite interest. Horus sighed again.

"Commander, your caution is admirable but misplaced. While we have continued to suppress your implants, particularly your com link, that act is in your interest as well as our own. You can have no more desire than we to provide Anu's missiles with a targeting beacon! We realize, however, that it is we who must convince *you* our motives are benign, and the only way I can see to do that is to tell you who we are and why we want so desperately to help rather than hinder you."

"Indeed?" Colin permitted himself a question at last and let his eyes slip sideways to Jiltanith. Horus made a wry face.

"Is any decision ever totally unanimous, Commander? We may be mutineers or something else entirely, but we are also a community in which even those who disagree with the majority abide by the decisions of our Council. Is that not true, 'Tanni?" he asked the angry-eyed young woman gently.

"Aye, 'tis true enow," she said shortly, biting off each word as if it cost her physical pain, and her very reluctance was almost reassuring. A lie would have come more easily.

"All right," Colin said finally. "I won't make any promises, but go ahead and explain your position to me."

"Thank you," Horus said. He propped a hip against the console before which Isis Tudor sat and crossed his arms.

"First, Commander, a confession. I supported the mutiny with all my heart, and I fought hard to make it a success. Most of the Imperials in this control room would admit the same. But—" his eyes met Colin's unflinchingly "—we were *used*, Commander MacIntyre."

Colin returned his gaze silently, and Horus shrugged.

"I know. It was our own fault, and we've been forced to accept that. We attempted to desert 'in the face of the enemy,' as your own code of military justice would phrase it, and we recognize our guilt. Indeed, that's the reason none of us wear the uniform to which we were once entitled. Yet there's another side to us, Commander, for once we recognized how horribly wrong we'd been, we also attempted to make amends. And not all of us *were* mutineers."

He paused and looked back at Jiltanith, whose face was harder and colder than ever. It was a fortress, her hatred a portcullis grinding down, and her bitter eyes ignored Horus to look straight into Colin's face.

"Jiltanith was no mutineer, Commander," Horus said softly.

"No?" Colin surprised himself by how gently his question came out. Jiltanith's obvious youth beside the other, aged Imperials had already set her apart. Somehow, without knowing exactly why, he'd felt her otherness.

"No," Horus said in the same soft voice. " 'Tanni was six Terran years old, Commander. Why should a child be held accountable for our acts?"

Colin nodded slowly, committing himself to nothing, yet that, at least, he understood. To be sentenced to eternal exile or death for a crime you had never committed would be enough to wake hatred in anyone.

"But *Dahak's* business is with all of us, I suppose," Horus continued quietly, "and my fellows and I accept that. We've grown old, Commander. Our lives are largely spent. It is only for 'Tanni and the other innocents we would plead. And, perhaps, for some of our comrades to the south."

"That's very eloquent, Horus," Colin said, tone carefully neutral, "but—"

"But we must work our passage, is that it?" Horus interrupted, and Colin nodded slowly. "Why, so we think, as well.

"When Anu organized his mutiny, Commander, Commander (BioSciences) Inanna picked the most suitable psych profiles for recruitment. Even the Imperium had its malleable elements, and she and Anu chose well. Some were merely frightened of death; others were dissatisfied and saw a chance for promotion and power; still others were simply bored and saw a chance for adventure. But what very few of them knew was that Anu's inner circle had motives quite different from their own.

"Anu's professed goal was to seize the ship and flee the Achuultani, but the plain truth of the matter was that he, like many of the crew, no longer believed in the Achuultani." Colin sat a bit straighter, eager to hear another perspective—even one which might prove self-serving—on the mutiny, but he let his face show doubt.

"Oh, the records were there," Horus agreed, "but the Imperium was *old*, Commander. We were regimented, disciplined, prepared for battle at the drop of a hat—or that, at least, was the idea. Yet we'd waited too long for the enemy. We were no longer attack dogs straining at the leash. We'd become creatures of habit, and many of us believed deep in our souls that we were regimented and controlled and trained for a purpose that no longer existed.

"Even those of us who'd seen proof of the Achuultani's existence—dead planets, gutted star systems, the wreckage of ancient battle fleets—had never seen the *Achuul-*

tani, and our people were not so very different from your own. Anything beyond your own life experience wasn't quite 'real' to us. After seven thousand years in which there were no new incursions, after five thousand years of preparation for an attack that never came, after three thousand years of sending out probes that found no sign of the enemy, it was hard to believe there still *was* an enemy. We'd mounted guard too long, and perhaps we simply grew bored." Horus shrugged. "But the fact remains that only a minority of us truly *believed* in the Achuultani, and many of those were terrified.

"So Anu's chosen pretext was shrewd. It appealed to the frightened, gave an excuse to the disaffected, and offered the bored the challenge of a new world to conquer, one beyond the stultifying reach of the Imperium. Yet it was *only* a pretext, for Anu himself sought escape from neither the Achuultani nor from boredom. He wanted *Dahak* for himself, and he had no intention of marooning the loyalists upon Earth."

Colin knew he was leaning forward and suspected his face was giving away entirely too much, yet there was nothing he could do about it. This was a subtly different story from the one *Dahak* had given him, but it made sense.

And perhaps the difference wasn't so strange. The data in *Dahak's* memory was all the reality there was for the old starship—before it found itself operating completely on its own, at least. He'd noticed that the computer never used a personal pronoun to denote itself or its actions or responses prior to or immediately following the mutiny, and he thought he knew why. "Comp Cent" had been intended purely as a data and systems management tool to be used only under direct human supervision; *Dahak's* present, fully-developed self-awareness was a product of fifty-one millennia of continuous, unsupervised operation. And if that awareness had evolved *after* the mutiny, why should the computer question its basic data? To the records, unlike the merely human personnel who had crewed the vast ship, the Achuultani's existence was axiomatic and incontestable, and so it had become for

Dahak. Why should he doubt that it was equally so for humanity? Particularly if that had been Anu's "official" reason? Of course it made sense . . . and *Dahak* himself was aware of his own lack of imagination, of empathy for the human condition.

"I believe," Horus's heavy voice recaptured Colin's attention, "that Anu is mad. I believe he was mad even then, but I may be wrong. Yet he truly believed that, backed by *Dahak*'s power, he could overthrow the Imperium itself.

"I can't believe he could have succeeded, however disaffected portions of the population might have become, but what mattered was that *he* believed he had some sort of divine mission to conquer the Imperium, and the seizure of the ship was but the first step in that endeavor.

"Yet he had to move carefully, so he lied to us. He intended all along to massacre anyone who refused to join him, but because he knew many of his adherents would balk at that he pretended differently. He even yielded to our insistence that the hypercom spares be loaded aboard the transports we believed would carry the marooned loyalists to Earth so that, in time, they might build a hypercom and call for help. And he promised us a surgical operation, Commander. His carefully prepared teams would seize the critical control nodes, cut Comp Cent from the net, and present Senior Fleet Captain Druaga with a *fait accompli.*

"And we believed him," Horus almost whispered. "May the Maker forgive us, we *believed* him, though if we'd bothered to think even for a moment, we would have known better. With so little of the core crew—no more than seven thousand at best—with us, his 'surgical operation' was an impossibility. When he stockpiled combat armor and weapons and had his people in Logistics sabotage as much other armor as they possibly could, we should have realized. But we didn't. Not until the fighting broke out and the blood began to flow. Not until it was far too late to change sides."

Horus fell silent, and Colin stared at him, willing him to continue yet aware the other must pause and gather himself. Intellectually, he knew it could all be a self-serving lie; instinctively, he knew it was the truth, at least as Horus believed it.

"The final moments aboard *Dahak* were a nightmare, Commander," the old man said finally. "Red Two, Internal, had been set. Lifeboats were ejecting. We were falling back to Bay Ninety-One, running for our lives, afraid we wouldn't make it, sickened by the bloodshed. But once we'd left *Dahak* astern, we were faced with what we'd done. More than that, we knew—or some of us did, at least—what Anu truly was. And so this ship, *Nergal*, deserted Anu."

Horus smiled wryly as Colin blinked in surprise.

"Yes, Commander, we were double mutineers. We ran for it—just this one ship, with barely two hundred souls aboard—and somehow, in the confusion, we escaped Anu's scanners and hid from him.

"Our plan, such as it was, was simplicity itself. We knew Anu had prepared a contingency plan that was supposed to give him control of the ship no matter what happened, though we had no idea what it was. We speculated that it concerned the ship's power, since he was Chief Engineer, but all that really mattered was that he would eventually win his prize and depart. Remember that we still half-believed his promise to leave any loyalists marooned behind him, Commander. And because we did, we planned to emerge from hiding after he left and do what we could for the survivors in an effort to atone for our crime and—I will admit it frankly—as the only thing we could think of that might win us some clemency when the Imperium found us at last.

"But, of course, it didn't work out that way," he said quietly, "for Anu's plan failed. Somehow, *Dahak* remained at least partially operational, destroying every parasite sent towards it. And it never went away, either. It hung above him, like your own Sword of Damocles, inviolate, taunting him.

"If he hadn't been mad before, Commander, he went mad then. He sent most of his followers into stasis—to wait out *Dahak*'s final 'inevitable' collapse—while only his immediate henchmen, who knew what he'd truly planned all along, remained awake. And once he had total control, he showed his true colors.

"Tell me, Commander MacIntyre, have you ever wondered what happened to all *Dahak*'s other bridge officers? Or how beings such as ourselves—such as you now are—with lifespans measured in centuries and strength and endurance far beyond that of Terra-born humans, could decivilize so utterly? It took your kind barely five hundred years to move from matchlocks and pikes to the atom bomb. From crude sailing ships to outer space. Doesn't it seem strange that almost *a quarter million* Imperial survivors should lose all technology?"

"I've . . . wondered," Colin admitted. He had, and not even *Dahak* had been able to tell him. All the computer knew was that when he became functional once more, the surviving loyalists had reverted to a subsistence-level hunter-gatherer technology and showed no particular desire to advance further.

"The answer is simple, Commander. Anu hunted them down. He tracked the surviving bridge officers by their implant signatures and butchered them to finish off any surviving chain of command. And for revenge, of course. And whenever a cluster of survivors tried to rebuild their technology, he wiped them out. He quartered this planet, Commander MacIntyre, seeking out the lifeboats with operational power plants and blowing them apart, making certain he alone monopolized technology, that no possible threat to him remained. The survivors soon learned primitivism was the only way they could survive."

"But *your* tech base survived," Colin said coldly, and Horus winced.

"True," he said heavily, "but look about you, Commander. How much tech base do we truly have? A single carefully-hidden battleship. We lack the infrastructure to build anything more, and if we'd attempted to build that infrastructure, Anu would have found us as he found the loyalists who made the same attempt. We might have given a good account of ourselves, but with only one ship against seven of the same class, plus escorts, we would have achieved nothing beyond an heroic death."

He held out one hand, palm upward in an eloquent gesture of helplessness, and Colin felt an unwilling sympathy for the man, much as he had for *Dahak* when he first heard the starship's story. Unlike *Dahak*, these people had built their own purgatory brick by brick, but that made it no less a purgatory.

"So what did you do?" he asked finally.

"We hid, Commander," Horus admitted. "Our own plans had gone hopelessly wrong, for Anu couldn't leave. So we activated *Nergal's* stealth systems and hid, biding our time, and we, too, went into stasis."

Of course they'd hidden, Colin thought, and that explained why *Dahak* had never suspected there might be more than a single faction of mutineers. Anu must have been mad with the need to find and destroy them, for they and they alone had posed a threat to him. And if they'd hidden so well *he* couldn't find them with Imperial instrumentation, then how could *Dahak*, who didn't even know to look for them, find them with the same instrumentation?

"We hid," Horus continued, "but we set our own monitors to watch for any activity on Anu's part. We dared not challenge his enclave's defenses with our single ship. I am—was—a missile specialist, Commander, and I know. Not even *Dahak* could crack his main shield without a saturation bombardment. We didn't have the firepower, and his automatics would have blown us out of existence before his stasis generators could even spin down to wake him."

"And so you just sat here," Colin said flatly, but his tone said he knew better. There were too many Terraborn in this compartment.

"No, Commander," Horus said, and his voice accepted the knowledge behind Colin's statement. "We've tried to fight him, over the millennia, but there was little we could do. It was obvious the threat of an evolving indigenous technology would be enough to spark Anu's intervention, and so our computers were set to wake us when local civilizations appeared. We interacted with the early civilizations of your Fertile Crescent—" he grinned wryly as Colin suddenly connected his own name with the Egyptian pantheon "—in an effort to temper their advance, but Anu was watching, as well. Several of our people were killed when he suddenly reappeared, and it was he who shaped the Sumerian and Babylonian cultures. It was he who led the Hsia Dynasty in the destruction of the neolithic cultural centers of China, and we who lent the Shang Dynasty clandestine aid to rebuild, and that was only one of the battles we fought.

"Yet we had to work secretly, hiding from him, effecting tiny changes, hoping for the best. Worse, there were but two hundred of us, and Anu had thousands. We couldn't rotate our personnel as he could—at least, that was what we thought he was doing—and we grew old far, far more quickly than he. But worst of all, Commander, was the attitude Anu's followers developed. They call your people 'degenerates,' did you know that?"

Colin nodded, remembering Girru's words in a chamber of horror that had once been a friend's study.

"They're wrong," Horus said harshly. "*They're* the degenerates. Anu's madness has infected them all. His people are twisted, poisoned by their power. Perhaps they've played the roles of gods too long, for they've come to believe they *are* gods, and Earth's people are toys to be manipulated and enjoyed. It was horrible enough for the first four thousand years of interaction, but it's grown worse since. Where once they feared the rise of a technology that might threaten them, now they crave one that will let them escape the prison of this planet . . . and they couldn't care less how much suffering they inflict along the way. Indeed, they see that suffering as a spectacle, a gladiatorial slaughter to entertain them and while away the years.

"Let's be honest with one another, Commander MacIntyre. Humans, whether Imperials or born of your planet, are humans. There are good and bad among all of us, as our very presence here proves, and Earth's people would have inflicted sufficient suffering on themselves without Anu, but he and his have made it far, far worse. They've toppled civilizations by provoking and encouraging barbarian invasions—from the Hittites to the Hsia, the Achaeans, the Huns, the Vikings, and the Mongols—but even worse, in some ways, is what they've done since abandoning that policy. They helped fuel the Hundred Years War, and the Thirty Years' War, and Europe's ruthless imperialism, both for enjoyment and to create power blocs that could pave the way for the scientific and industrial revolutions. And when progress wasn't rapid enough to suit them, they provoked the First World War, and the Second, and the Cold War.

"We've done what we could to mitigate their excesses, but our best efforts have been paltry. *They* haven't dared come into the open for fear that *Dahak* might remain sufficiently operational to strike at them—and, perhaps, because the sheer number of people on this planet frightens them—but they could always act more openly than we.

"Yet we've never given up, Commander MacIntyre!" The old man's voice was suddenly harsh, glittering with a strange fire, and Colin swallowed. That suddenly fiery tone was almost fanatical, and he shook free of Horus's story, making himself step back and wondering if perhaps his captors hadn't gone more than a bit mad themselves.

"No. We've never given up," Horus said more softly. "And if you'll let us, we'll prove that to you."

"How?" Colin's flat voice refused to offer any hope. Try though he might, it was hard to doubt Horus's sincerity. Yet it was his duty to doubt it. It was his responsibility—his, and his alone—to doubt everyone, question everything. Because if he made a mistake—*another* mistake, he thought bitterly—then all of *Dahak*'s lonely wait would be in vain and the Achuultani would take them all.

"We'll help you against Anu," Horus said, his voice equally flat, his eyes level. "And afterward, we will surrender ourselves to the Imperium."

"*Nay!*" Jiltanith still pointed the suppresser at Colin, but her free hand rose like a claw, and her dark, vital face was fierce. "Now I say thee nay! Hast given too freely for this world, Father! Thou and all thy fellows!"

"Hush, 'Tanni," Horus said softly. He clasped the shoulders of the young woman—his daughter, which, Colin suddenly realized, made her Isis Tudor's *older* sister—and shook her very gently. "It's our decision. It's not even a matter for the Council, and you know it."

Jiltanith's tight face was furious with objection, and Horus sighed and gathered her close, staring into Colin's face over her shoulder.

"We ask only one thing in return, Commander," he said softly.

"What?" Colin asked quietly.

"Immunity—pardon, if you will—for those like 'Tanni." The girl stiffened in his arms, trying to thrust him away, but he held her easily with one arm. The other hand rose, covering her lips to still her furious protests. "They were *children*, Commander, with no part in our crime, and many of them have died trying to undo it. Can even the Imperium punish them for that?"

The proud old face was pleading, the dark, ancient eyes almost desperate, and Colin recognized the justice of the plea.

"If—and I say *if*—you can convince me of your sincerity and ability to help," he said slowly, "I'll do my best. I can't promise any more than that."

"I know," Horus said. "But you *will* try?"

"I will," Colin replied levelly.

The old man regarded him a moment longer, then took the suppresser gently from Jiltanith. She fought him a moment, surrendering the device with manifest reluctance, and Horus hugged her gently. His eyes were understanding and sad, but a small smile played around his lips as he looked down at it.

"In that case," he said, "we'll just have to convince you. Please meet us half-way by not transmitting to *Dahak*, at least until we've finished talking."

And he switched off the suppresser.

For just an instant Colin sat absolutely motionless. The other Imperials on the command bridge were suddenly bright presences, glowing with their own implants, and he felt his computer feeds come on line. *Nergal's* computers were far brighter than those of the cutter that had returned him to Earth, and they recognized a bridge officer when they met one. After fifty millennia, they had someone to report to properly, and the surge of their data cores tingled in his brain like alien fire, feeding him information and begging for orders.

Colin's eyes met Horus's as he recognized the risk the old man had just taken, for no new security codes had been buried in *Nergal's* electronic brain. From the instant Colin's feeds tapped into those computers, they were his. *He*, not Horus, controlled the ancient battleship, external weapons and internal security systems alike.

But trust was a two-edged sword.

"I suppose that, as head of your council, you're also captain of this ship?" he said calmly, and the old man nodded.

"Then sit down, Captain, and tell me how we're going to beat Anu."

Horus nodded once more, sharply, and sat beside Isis. Colin never glanced away from his new ally's face, but he didn't have to; he could *feel* the gathered council's tension draining away about him.

Chapter Eleven

Colin leaned back and propped his heels on his desk. The quarters the mutineers (if that was still the proper word) had assigned him were another attempt to prove their sincerity, for this was the captain's cabin, fitted with neural relays to the old battleship's computers. He could not keep them from retaking *Nergal*, but, like the millennia-dead Druaga, he could insure that they would recapture only a hulk.

Which, Colin thought, was shrewd of Horus, whether he was truly sincere or not.

He sighed and pinched the bridge of his nose, wishing desperately that he could contact *Dahak*, yet he dared not. He knew where he was now—buried five kilometers under the Canadian Rockies near Churchill Peak—but the recent clash had roused Anu's vengeful search for *Nergal* to renewed heights, and if the southerners should detect Colin's com link, their missiles would arrive before even *Dahak* could do anything to stop them.

The same applied to any effort to reach *Dahak* physically. He was lucky he hadn't been spotted on the way in, despite his cutter's stealth systems; now that the marooned Imperials' long, hidden conflict had heated back up, there was no way anything of Imperial manufacture could head *out* of the planetary atmosphere without being spotted and killed.

It was maddening. He'd acquired a support team just as determined to destroy Anu as he was, yet it was pathetically weak compared to its enemies and there was no way to inform *Dahak* it even existed! Worse, Anshar's energy gun had reduced the suppresser to wreckage, and *Nergal's* repair facilities were barely sufficient to run diagnostics on what remained, much less fix it.

Colin was deeply impressed by what the northerners had achieved over the centuries, but very little of what he'd found in *Nergal's* memory had been good, aside from the confirmation that Horus had told him the truth about what had happened after he and his fellows boarded *Nergal*.

The old battleship's memory was long overdue for purging, for *Nergal's* builders had designed her core programming to insure that accurate combat reports came back to her mothership. No one could alter that data in any way until *Nergal's* master computer dumped a complete copy into *Dahak's* data base.

For fifty thousand years, the faithful, moronic genius had carefully logged everything as it happened, and while molecular memories could store an awesome amount of data, there was so much in *Nergal's* that just finding it was frustratingly slow. Yet that crowded memory gave him a record that was accurate, unalterable, and readily—if not quickly—available.

There was, of course, far too much data for any human mind to assimilate, but he could skim the high points, and it had been hard to maintain his nonexpression as he did. If anything, Horus had understated the war he and his fellows had fought. Direct clashes were infrequent, but there had been only two hundred and three adult northerners at the start, and age, as well as casualties, had winnowed their ranks. Fewer than seventy of them remained.

He and Horus had lingered, conferring with one another and the computers through their feeds while the rest of the Council went on about their duties. Only Horus's daughters had stayed.

Iris had interjected only an occasional word as she tried to follow their half-spoken, half-silent conversation, but Jiltanith had been a silent, sullen presence in their link. She'd neither offered nor asked anything, but her cold, bitter loathing for all he was had appalled Colin.

He'd never realized emotions could color the link, perhaps because his only previous use of it had been with *Dahak*, without the side-band elements involved when human met human through an electronic intermediary. Or perhaps it was simply that her bitter emotions were so strong. He'd wondered why Horus didn't ask her to withdraw, but then, he had many questions about Jiltanith and her place in the small, strange community he'd never suspected might exist.

It was fortunate Horus had been able to meet him in the computers. Some vocalization was necessary to set data in context, but the old mutineer had led him unerringly through the data banks, and his memory went back, replaying that first afternoon as if it were today. . . .

"All right," Colin sighed finally, rubbing his temples wearily. "I don't know about you folks, but I need a break before my brain fries."

Horus nodded understandingly; Jiltanith only sniffed, and Colin suppressed an urge to snap at her.

"I've got to say, this Anu is an even nastier bastard than I expected," he went on, his voice hardening with the change of subject. "I'd wondered how he could ride herd on all his faithful followers, but I never expected *this*."

"I know," Horus looked down at the backs of his powerful, age-spotted hands. "But it makes sense, in a gruesome sort of way. After all, unlike us, he does have an intact medical capability."

"But to use it like *that*," Colin said, and his shudder was not at all affected, for "gruesome" was a terribly pale word for what Anu had done. *Dahak* hadn't suggested such things were possible, but Colin supposed he should have known they were.

Anu's problem had been two-fold. First, how did he and his inner circle—no more than eight hundred strong—control five thousand Imperials who would, for the most part, be as horrified as Horus to learn the truth about their leader? And, secondly, how could even fully-enhanced Imperials oversee the manipulation of an entire planet without withering away from old age before they could create the technology they needed to escape it?

The medical science of the Imperium had provided a psychopathically elegant solution to both problems at once. The "unreliable" elements were simply never reawakened, and while stasis also allowed the mutineer leaders to sleep away centuries at need, Anu and his senior lieutenants had been awake a long time. By now, Horus calculated, Anu was on his tenth replacement body.

Imperial science had mastered the techniques of cloning to provide surgical transplants before the advent of reliable regeneration, but that had been so long ago cloning was almost a lost art. Only the most comprehensive medical centers retained the capability for certain carefully-delimited, individually-licensed experimental programs, and the use even of clones for *this* purpose was punishable by death for all concerned. Yet heinous as that would have been in the eyes of the Imperium's intricate, iron-bound code of bioscience morality, what Anu had actually done was worse. When old age overtook him, he simply selected a candidate from among the mutineers in stasis and had its brain removed for his own to displace. As long as his supply of bodies held out, he was effectively immortal.

The same was true of his lieutenants, but while only Imperial bodies were good enough for Anu and Inanna and their most trusted henchmen, others—like Anshar—were forced to make do with Terra-born bodies. There was a greater danger of tissue rejection in that, but there were compensations. The range of choices was vast, and

Inanna's medical technology, though limited compared to *Dahak's*, was quite capable of basic enhancement of Terra-born bodies.

Colin returned to the present with a shudder. Even now, thinking about it sent a physical shiver down his spine. It horrified him almost as much as the approaching Achuultani horrified Horus. Desperation had blazed in the old Imperial's eyes when he learned the enemy he'd never quite believed in was actually coming, but Colin had been given months to adjust to that. This was different. The victims' tragedy was one he could grasp, not a galactic one, and that made it something he could relate to . . . and hate.

And perhaps, as Horus had suggested, it also helped to explain why Anu continued to operate so clandestinely. His followers had gone trustingly into stasis and were unable to resist his depredations, but there were simply too many Terrans to be readily controlled, and Colin doubted Earth's humanity would react calmly to the knowledge that high-tech vampires were harvesting them.

Yet Anu's ghastly perversions only emphasized the huge difference between his capabilities and those of his northern opponents. *Nergal* was a warship. Thirty percent of her impressive tonnage was committed to propulsion and power, ten percent to command and control systems, another ten percent to defensive systems, and forty percent to armor, offensive weaponry, and magazine space. That left only ten percent to accommodate her three-hundred-man crew and its life support, which meant even living space was cramped.

That mattered little under normal circumstances, for she was designed for short-term deployments—certainly no more than a few months at a time. She didn't even have a proper stasis installation; her people had been forced to cobble one up, and their success was a far-from-minor miracle. But because her intended deployments were so short, *Nergal's* sickbay was limited. Anu and his butchers could select Terra-born bodies and convert them to their own use; the northerners couldn't even offer implants to their own Terra-born descendants.

Yet they'd had no choice but to have those descendants, for without them they would have failed long ago from sheer lack of numbers.

It had been a bitter decision, though Horus had tried to hide his pain from Colin. Horus had lived over five centuries and Isis less than one, yet his daughter was old and frail while he remained strong. Colin could have consulted the record to learn how many other children Horus had loved as he all too obviously loved Isis yet seen wither and die, but he hadn't. That unimaginable sorrow was Horus's alone, and he would not intrude upon it.

Yet it was possible the situation was even worse for the ones like Jiltanith, whose bodies were neither Imperial nor Terran. Jiltanith had received the neural boosters, computer and sensory implants, and regeneration treatments, but her muscles and bones and organs had been too immature for enhancement before the mutiny. Which might go a long way towards explaining her bitter resentment. He, a Terra-born human who had grown to adulthood in blissful ignorance of the battle being waged upon his planet, had received the full treatment. She hadn't. And unless the people she loved surrendered to the Imperium's justice, she never could have it.

Colin knew there was more to her hate than that, though he had yet to discover its full range, but understanding that much helped him cope with her bitterness.

Unfortunately, there was little he could do about it, nor did he know how the legal situation would be resolved—assuming, of course, that they won. Somehow, he'd never considered the possibility of children among the mutineers, and *Dahak* had never mentioned them to him.

That was a bad sign, and not one he was prepared to share with his allies. To *Dahak*, anyone who had accompanied Anu in his flight to Earth was a mutineer. That fundamental assumption infused everything the computer had ever said, and no distinction had ever been drawn between child and adult, but Colin had meant what he promised. If the northerners helped him against Anu, he would do what he could for their children. And, though he hadn't promised it, for them . . . if he ever got the chance to try.

He leaned further back and crossed his ankles. If there were only more time! Time for Anu's present furious search to die down, for him to return to *Dahak*, to act on the information he'd received and plan anew. That was what Horus had hoped for, but the Achuultani were coming. Whatever they meant to do, they must do it soon, and the sober truth was that the odds were hopeless.

The northerners undoubtedly had the edge in sheer numbers, at least over the southerners Anu would trust out of stasis, but only sixty-seven of their people were full Imperials, and all of them were old. Another eighteen were like Jiltanith, capable of getting full performance out of Imperial equipment, but utterly outclassed in any one-to-one confrontation. The three thousand-odd Terra-born members of *Nergal's* "crew" would be at a hopeless disadvantage with their pathetic touchpads and telephones if they had to fight people who could link their minds directly into their weapons. They couldn't even manage combat armor, for they lacked the implants to activate the internal circuitry.

And, of course, they had the resources of exactly one battleship. One battleship against seven—not to mention the heavy cruisers, the fixed ground weapons, and Anu's powerful shield. From a practical viewpoint, he might as well have been alone if it came to confronting the southerners openly.

But there were a few good points. For one, the northerners' intelligence system had been in operation for millennia, and an extended network of Terra-born contacts like Sandy supported their guerrilla-like campaign. They'd even managed to establish clandestine contact with two of Anu's "loyal" henchmen. It would be foolhardy to trust those communications too much, and they were handled with extraordinary care to avoid any traps, but they explained how the northerners knew so much about events in the southern enclave.

He opened his eyes and stood. His thoughts were racing in ever narrowing circles, and he felt as if they were about to implode. He needed to spend some more time talking to Horus in hopes some inspiration might break itself loose.

God knew they needed one.

He looked for Horus, but the chief northerner wasn't aboard. Colin was acutely uneasy whenever Horus—or *any* of the Imperials—left the protection of *Nergal's* stealth systems, but the northerners seemed to take it in stride. Of course, they'd had quite a while longer to accustom themselves to such risks.

And it was inevitable that they run them, for they couldn't possibly gather their full numbers aboard the battleship. Many of the Terra-born had gone to ground when Cal's family was killed, but others went on about their everyday lives with a courage that humbled Colin, and that meant the Imperials had to leave *Nergal* occasionally, for only they could operate the battleship's stealthed auxiliaries. It was dangerous to use them, even flying nape-of-the-earth courses fit to terrify a hardened rotor-jockey, but they had too few security coms to tie their network together without them. Colin wished Horus would leave such risks to others, but he'd come to understand the old man too well to suggest it.

For all that, he bit his tongue against a groan of resignation when he entered the command bridge and found not Horus but his daughters.

Jiltanith stood as he entered, bristling with the instant hostility his presence always evoked, but Isis managed a smile of greeting. Colin glanced covertly at Jiltanith's lovely face and considered the virtues of a discreet retreat, yet that would be unwise in the long run. So he seated himself deliberately in the captain's chair and met her hot eyes levelly.

"Good afternoon, ladies. I was looking for your father."

"Shalt not find him here," Jiltanith said pointedly. He

ignored the hint, and she glared at him. If she'd truly been the cat she resembled, she would be lashing her tail and flexing her claws, he thought.

" 'Tanni," Isis said quietly, but Jiltanith gave an angry little headshake and stalked out. Isis watched her go and sighed.

"That girl!" she said resignedly, then smiled wryly at Colin. "I'm afraid she's taking it badly, Commander."

"Please," he smiled himself, a bit sadly, "after all that's happened, I wish you'd call me Colin."

"Of course. Colin."

"I . . . haven't had a chance to tell you how sorry I am." She raised a hand, but he shook his head. "No. It's kind of you, and I don't want to hurt you by talking about it, but I need to say it." Her hand fell to her lap, folding about its fellow, and she lowered her eyes to her thin fingers.

"Cal was my friend," he said softly, "and I rushed in, flashing around Imperial technology like some new toy, and got his entire family killed. I know I couldn't have known what I was doing, but that doesn't change the facts. He's dead, and I'm responsible."

"If you want to put it that way," Isis said gently, "but he and Frances knew the risks. If that sounds callous it isn't meant to, but it's true. I raised him after his parents died, and I loved him, just as I loved my granddaughter-in-law and my great-granddaughters, but we always knew it could happen. Just as Andy knew when he married me." She looked up with a misty smile, her lined face creased with memories, and Colin swallowed.

"There's something I don't quite understand," he said after a moment. "How could your father produce the work he produced as Horace Hidachi and still take the risk of having children? And why did he do it at all?"

"Have a child or produce the work?" Isis asked with a chuckle, and Colin felt some of their shared sorrow fall from his shoulders.

"Both," he said.

"It was a risk," she concluded, "but the fact that 'Hidachi' was Oriental helped cover his appearance—

we've always found that useful, though the emergence of the Asian Alliance has complicated things lately—and he chose his time and place carefully. Clemson University is a fine school, one of the top four tech schools in the country, but that's a fairly recent development. It wasn't exactly on the frontiers of physics at the time, and he published in the most obscure journal he could find. And there were some deliberate errors in his work, you know. All that, plus the fact that he never went further than pure theory, was intended to convince any of Anu's people who noticed it that he was a Terran who didn't even realize the significance of his own work.

"As for having me," she smiled more naturally, "that was an accident. Mom was his eighth wife—Tanni's mother died during the mutiny—and, frankly, she thought she was too old to conceive and got a bit careless. When they found out she was pregnant, it scared them, but they never considered an abortion, for which I can only be grateful." She grinned, and her eyes sparkled for the first time Colin could remember.

"But it was a problem. As a rule, none of our Imperials interact openly with the Terran community, and on the rare occasions when they do, they appear and disappear without a trace. They almost always act solo, as well, which meant he and Mom had already stepped totally out of character. That very fact was a form of protection for them, and they decided to add me to it and hope for the best. And it helped that Mom was Terra-born, blonde, and a little, bitty thing. She and I both looked very little like Imperials."

Colin nodded. No one in his right mind would offer his family up for massacre; hence the presence of a family was a strong indication that "Horace Hidachi" was not an Imperial at all. It made a dangerous sort of sense, but he shivered at the thought, and wished he might have had the chance to meet the quite extraordinary "little, bitty" woman who had been Isis's mother.

"Still," Isis went on sadly, "we knew they'd keep an eye on 'Hidachi's' family. That's why I went into medicine and Michael was a stockbroker. We both stayed as far away from physics as we could, but Cal was too much like his great-granddad. He was determined to play an active part."

"I still don't understand *why*, though. Why risk so much to plant a theory the mutin—" Colin broke off and flushed, and Isis gave a soft, musical laugh.

"Sorry," he said after a moment. "I meant, why risk so much to plant a theory that Anu's bunch already knew?"

"Why, Colin!" Isis rolled her eyes almost roguishly. "Here you sit, precisely because that theory was made available to the space program. If the southerners hadn't followed up, we would've had to push it ourselves, sooner or later, because we needed for your survey instruments to be developed. Of course, Dad and Mom were pretty confident 'Anu's bunch,' as you put it, would pursue it once they noticed it—the 'Hidachi Theory of Gravitonics' *is* the foundation of the Imperial sublight and Enchanach Drives, after all—but we couldn't be certain. One reason we wanted them to believe a 'degenerate' had set the stage for it was to be sure *they* produced the hardware rather than opposing its development, because the entire point was to do exactly what we did: provoke a reaction from *Dahak*, one way or the other."

"Provoke *Dahak*?" Colin pinched his nose. "Wasn't that a bit, um, risky?"

"Of course it was, but our Imperials are getting old, Colin. When they go, the rest of us will carry on as best we can, but our position will be even more hopeless. The Council had no idea *Dahak* was fully functional, but we were already placing a lot of our people in the space program, like Sandy and Cal. Besides, if the human race generally knew what was up there, functional or not, Anu's position would be far more tenuous."

"Why?"

"We never contemplated what *Dahak* actually did, Colin, but *something* had to happen. Anu might try to take over any exploration of the ship, but we were prepared to fight him—clandestinely, but rather effectively—unless he came into the open. And if he *had* come out into the open, don't you think he'd've needed more than just his inner circle to control the resulting chaos?"

"Oh! You figured if he risked waking the others and they discovered all he'd been up to, he might get hit from behind by a revolt."

"Exactly. Oh, it was a terrible chance to take, but as I say, we were getting desperate. At the very least, it might be a way to add a new factor to the equation. Then too, we've always had a *lot* of people in the space program. It was possible—even probable—that if the ship was partially functional one of our own Terra-born might have gotten inside. Frankly—" she met his gaze levelly "—we'd hoped Vlad Chernikov would fly your mission."

"*Vlad?* Don't tell me *he's* one of yours!"

"Not if you'd rather I didn't," she said, and he laughed helplessly. It was his first laughter since Sean's death, and he was amazed by how much it helped.

"Well, I will be damned," he said at last, then cocked an eyebrow. "But isn't it also a bit risky to plant so many people in the very area where Anu is pushing hardest?"

"Colin, everything we've ever *done* has been a risk. Of course we took chances—terrible ones, sometimes—but Anu's own control is pretty indirect. Both sides know a great deal about what the other is up to—we more than him, we hope—but he can't afford to go around killing everyone he simply suspects."

She paused, and her voice was grimmer when she continued.

"Still, he's killed a lot on suspicion. 'Accidents' are his favorite method, but remember that shuttle Black Mecca shot down?" Colin nodded, and she shrugged. "That was Anu. It amuses him to use 'degenerate' terrorists to do his dirty work, and their fanaticism makes them easy to influence. Major Lemoine was aboard that shuttle, and he was one of ours. We don't know how Anu got on to him, but that's why so much terrorism's focused on aerospace lately. In fact, Black Mecca's claimed credit for what happened to Cal and the girls."

"Lord." Colin shook his head and leaned forward,

bracing his elbows on the console and propping his chin on his palms. "All this time, and no one ever suspected. It's hard to believe."

"There've been a few times we thought it was all over," Isis said. "Once we even thought they'd actually found *Nergal*. In fact, that's why Jiltanith was ever brought out of stasis at all."

"Hm? Oh! Getting the kids out just in case?"

"Precisely. That was about six hundred years ago, and it was the worst scare we ever had. The Council had recruited quite a few Terra-born even then—and you'd better believe *they* had trouble adjusting to the whole idea!—and some of them took the children and scattered out across the planet. Which also explains 'Tanni's English; she learned it during the Wars of the Roses."

"I see." Colin drew a deep breath and held it for just a moment. Somehow the thought of that beautiful girl having grown up in fifteenth-century England was more sobering than anything else that had happened so far.

"Isis," he said finally, "how old *is* Jiltanith? Out of stasis, I mean."

"A bit older than me." His face betrayed his shock, and she smiled gently. "We Terra-born have learned to live with it, Colin. Actually, I don't know who it's harder on, us or our Imperials. But 'Tanni went back into stasis when she was twenty and came back out while Dad was still being Hidachi."

"She doesn't like me much, does she?" Colin said glumly.

"She's a very unhappy girl," Isis said, then laughed softly. "Girl! She's older than I am, but I still think of her that way. And she *is* only a girl as far as the Imperials are concerned. She's the 'youngest' of them all, and that's always been hard on her. She fought Dad when he sent her back into stasis because she wants to *do* something, Colin. She feels cheated, and I can't really blame her. It's not her fault she's stuck here, and there's a conflict in her own mind. She loves Dad, but his actions during the mutiny are what did all this to her, and remember her mother was actually killed during the fighting." She shook her head sadly.

"Poor 'Tanni's never had a normal life. Those fourteen years she spent in England were the closest she ever came, and even then her foster parents had to keep her under virtual house arrest, given that her appearance wasn't exactly European. I think that's why she refuses to speak modern English.

"But you're right about how she feels about you. I'm afraid she blames you for what happened to Cal's family . . . and especially the girls. She was very close to Harriet, especially." Isis's mouth drooped, but she blinked back the threatened tears and continued.

"She knows, intellectually, that you couldn't have known what would happen. She even knows you killed the people who killed them, and none of us exactly believe in turning the other cheek. But the fact that you were ultimately responsible ties in with the fact that you've not only effectively supplanted Dad after he's fought for so long, but that you're an active threat to him, as well. Even if we succeed, Dad faces charges because whatever he's done since, he *was* a mutineer. And, frankly, she resents you."

"Because I've moved in on your operation?" he asked gently. "Or for another reason, as well?"

"Of course there's another reason, and I see you know what it is. But can you blame her? Can't you see it from her side? You're the commanding officer of *Dahak*, a starship that's like a dream to all of us Terra-born, a combination of heaven and hell. But it's a dream whose decks 'Tanni actually walked . . . and lost for something *she* never did. She's spent her entire adult life fighting to undo the wrong others did, and now you, simply by virtue of being the first Terra-born human to enter the ship, have become not just a crew member, but its *commander*. Why should you have that and not her? Why should you have a complete set of implants—a bridge officer's, no less—while she has only bits and pieces?"

Isis fell silent, studying his face as if looking for something, then nodded slightly.

"But worst of all, Colin, she's a fighter. She wouldn't stand a chance hand to hand against an Imperial, and she knows it, but she's a fighter. She's spent her life in the shadows, fighting other shadows, always indirectly, protected by Dad and the others because she's weaker than they are, unable to fight her enemies face to face. Surely you understand how much that hurts?"

"I do," Colin said softly. "I do," he said more firmly, "and I'll bear it in mind, but we all have to fight Anu, Isis. I can't have her fighting *me*."

"I don't think she will." Isis paused again, frowning. "I don't *think* she will, but she's not feeling exactly ... reasonable, just now."

"I know. But if she *does* fight me, it could ruin everything. Too much depends not only on smashing Anu but finding a way to stop the Achuultani. If she can't work with me, I certainly can't let her work against me."

"What ... what will you do?" Isis asked softly.

"I won't hurt her, if that's what you're afraid of. She's given too much—all of you have—for that. But if she threatens what we're trying to do now, I won't have any choice but to put her back into stasis."

"No! Please!" Isis gripped his arm tightly. "That ... that would be almost worse than killing her, Colin!"

"I know," he said gently. "I know what it would do to me, and I don't want to. Before God, I don't want to. But if she fights me, I won't have a choice. Try to make her understand that, Isis. She may take it better from you than from me."

The old woman looked at him with tear-bright eyes and her lips trembled, but she nodded slowly and patted his arm.

"I understand, Colin," she said very softly. "I'll talk to her. And I understand. I wish I didn't, but I do."

"Thank you, Isis," he said quietly. He met her eyes a moment longer, then squeezed the hand on his arm very gently and rose. An obscure impulse touched him, and he bent to kiss her parchment cheek.

"Thank you," he said again, and left the command deck.

Chapter Twelve

"Colin?"

Colin looked up in sudden relief as Horus stuck his head in through his cabin door. The old man had been more than two hours overdue the last time Colin checked with *Nergal*'s operations room.

"About time you got back," he said, and Horus nodded and gripped his hand, but his smile was odd, half-way between apology and a sort of triumph.

"Sorry," Horus said. "I got tied up talking to one of our people. He's got a suggestion so interesting I brought him back with me."

The old Imperial gestured to the tall man behind him, and Colin glanced at the newcomer, taking in the hard-trained body and salt-and-pepper temples. The stranger's nose was almost as prominent as Colin's, but on him it looked good. He also wore the uniform of the United States Marine Corps and a full colonel's eagles, but the flash on his right shoulder bore the crossed daggers and parachute of the Unified Special Forces Command.

Colin's right eyebrow rose as he waved his guests to

chairs. The USFC was the elite of the elite, its members recruited from all branches of the service and trained for "selective warfare"—the old "low-intensity conflict" of the last century—and counter-terrorism. Labels meant little to Colin. Insurgent, terrorist, guerrilla, or patriot. As far as he was concerned, anyone who chose violence against the helpless as his means of protest deserved the same label: barbarian, and the USFC was the United States' answer to the barbarians.

Like their ConEuropean, Australian-Japanese, and Russian counterparts, the men and women of the USFC were as adept at infiltration, information-gathering, and covert warfare as they with the conventional weapons of the soldier's trade. Unlike the rest of the US military, they were an integral part of the intelligence community, as much policemen and spies (and some, Colin knew, would add "assassins") as soldiers. Not that it kept them from being elite troops. USFC personnel were chosen only after proving themselves—thoroughly—in their regular arms of service.

"Colin, this is Hector MacMahan. In addition to his duties for the USFC, he's also the head of our Terraborn intelligence network."

"Colonel," Colin said courteously, extending his hand again and reading the four rows of ribbons under the parachutist and pilot's wings—both rotary wing and fixed. And the crossed dagger and assault rifle of the USFC's close combat medal. Impressive, he thought. *Very* impressive.

"Commander," MacMahan said. Then he grinned— slightly; his was not a face that lent itself to effusive expressions. "Or should I say 'Fleet Captain'?"

"Commander will do just fine, Colonel. That, or Colin." His guests sat, and Colin moved to the small bar in the corner as he looked back and forth between them. "You do seem to recruit only the best, Horus," he murmured.

"Thank you," Horus said with a smile. "In more ways than one. Hector is my great-great-great-great-great-grandson."

"I prefer," the colonel said without a trace of a smile, "to think of myself as simply your great*est* grandson."

Colin chuckled and shook his head.

"I'm still getting used to all this, Colonel, but I was referring to your military credentials, not your familial ones." He finished mixing drinks and moved out from behind the bar. "I'm impressed. And if your suggestion was interesting enough for Horus to bring you back with him, I'm eager to hear it."

"Of course. You see—thank you." MacMahan took the drink Colin extended, sipped politely once, then proceeded to ignore it. Colin sat back down in his swivel chair and gestured for him to continue.

"You see," the colonel began again, "I've been giving our situation a lot of thought. In my own humble way, I'm as much a specialist as any of you rocket jockeys, and I've nourished a few rather worrisome suspicions of late."

"Suspicions?" Colin asked, his eyes suddenly intent.

"Yes, Com—Colin. I'm in a unique position to study the terrorist mentality, and I've also had the advantage of Granddad's input and *Nergal's* surveillance reports. That's one reason I'm a colonel. My superiors don't know about my other sources, and they think I'm a mighty savvy analyst."

Colin nodded. The northerners' intelligence network—especially the old battleship's carefully stealthed sensor arrays—would be tremendously helpful in MacMahan's line of work, but the ribbons on his chest told Colin the colonel's superiors were right about his native abilities, as well.

"The point is, Colin, that Anu's people have been digging deeper and deeper into the terrorist organizations. By now, they effectively control Black Mecca, the January Twelfth Group, the Army of Allah, the Red Eyebrows, and a dozen other major and minor outfits. That's ominous enough, if not too surprising—they've always been right at home with butchers like that—but what bothers me are certain common ideological (if I may be permitted the term) threads that have crept into the policies of the groups they control.

"You see," he furrowed his forehead, "these are some pretty unlikely soulmates. Black Mecca and the Army of Allah hate each other even more than they hate the rest of the world. Black Mecca wants to de-stabilize both the Islamic and non-Islamic worlds to such an extent their radical fundamentalists can establish a world-wide theocratic state, while the Army of Allah attacks non-Islamic targets primarily as a means of forcing an unbridgeable split between Islamics and non-Islamics. They don't *want* the rest of us; they're a bunch of isolationists who want to shut everyone else out while they attend to *their* concept of religious purity. Then there's the Red Eyebrows. *They* grew out of the old punker/skinhead groups of the late nineties, and they're just plain anarchists. They—"

MacMahan stopped himself and waved a hand.

"I get carried away sometimes, and the etiology of terrorism can wait. My point is that all these different outfits share a growing, *common* interest in what I can only call nihilism, and I don't think there's much doubt it stems from Anu's input. His goals are becoming, whether they know it or not, their goals, and what's scary about that is what it says about his own mind set."

The colonel seemed to remember his drink and took another sip, then stared down into it for several seconds, swirling the ice cubes.

"My outfit's always had to try to think like the enemy, and I have to admit it can be almost enjoyable. I hate the bastards, but it's almost like a game—like chess or bridge, in a way—except that I haven't been enjoying it much of late. Because there's a question that's been bothering me for the last few years, and especially since Horus told me about you and *Dahak*: just how will Anu react if he decides we can beat him? For that matter, how would he react to simply knowing that *Dahak* is fully operational?

"And the reason that bothers me is that I think Horus is right about him. I think the nihilism of his terrorist toadies reflects his own nihilism and that if he ever decides his position is hopeless—which it is, whatever happens to us, if *Dahak's* out there—he might *enjoy* taking the whole planet with him."

Colin kept his body relaxed and nodded slowly, but a cold wind seemed to have invaded the cabin.

"It makes sense, Colin," Horus said quietly. "Hector's right about his nihilism. Whatever he was once like, Anu *likes* destruction now. It's almost as if it relieves his frustration, and it's probably part of his whole addiction to power, as well. But whatever causes it, it's real enough. He and his people certainly proved that a hundred years ago."

Colin nodded again, understanding completely. He'd occasionally wondered why Hitler had proved so resistant to assassination—until he gained access to *Nergal's* data base. No wonder the bomb plot had failed; a man with full enhancement would hardly even have noticed it. And if anyone had ever shown a maniacal glee in taking others down with them, it had been the Nazi elite.

"So." He twirled his chair slowly. "It seems another minor complication has been added." His smile held no humor. "But from the fact that you're here, Colonel, I imagine you've been doing more than just worrying?"

"I have." The colonel drew a deep breath and met Colin's eyes levelly. "A man in my profession doesn't have much use for do-or-die missions, but I've spent the last year building a worst-case scenario—a doomsday one, if you will—and trying to find a way to beat it, and I may have come up with one. It's scary as hell, and I've always seen it more as a last-ditch contingency than anything I'd *want* to try. In fact, I wouldn't even mention it except for what you've told us about the Achuultani. The smart thing would be to wait till things settle down a bit, get you back up to *Dahak*, and then hit the bastards from two directions at once—or at least get another suppresser down here. But we don't have time to play it smart, do we?"

"No, we don't," Colin said, his tone calm but flat. "So may I assume you're about to tell me about this 'way to beat it' you've come up with?"

"Yes. Instead of waiting for things to cool down, we heat them up."

"Hm?" Colin leaned slowly back, his chair squeaking softly, and tugged at his nose. "And why should we do that, Colonel?"

"Because maybe—just maybe—we can take them out ourselves, without calling on *Dahak* at all," the colonel said.

No one, Colin reflected as he watched the Council file into the command deck, could accuse Hector MacMahan of thinking small. Merely to consider attacking such a powerful enemy took a lot of audacity, but it seemed the colonel had *chutzpah* by the truckload. And who knew? It might just work.

The council settled into their places in tense silence, and he tucked his hands behind him and squared his shoulders, feeling their eyes and wondering just how deep his rapport with them truly went. They'd had barely a month to get to know one another, and he knew some of them both resented and feared him. He couldn't blame them for that; *he* still had reservations about *them*, though he no longer doubted their sincerity. Not even Jiltanith's.

Thoughts of the young woman drew his eyes, and he hid a smile as he realized he, too, had come to think of her as "young" despite the fact that she was more than twice his age. Much more, if he counted the time she'd spent in stasis. But his smile died stillborn as he saw her expression. She'd finally managed to push the active hatred out of her face, but it remained a shuttered window, neither offering nor accepting a thing.

In many ways, he would have preferred to exclude her from this meeting and from *all* decision-making, but it hadn't worked out that way. She was young, but she was also *Nergal*'s chief intelligence officer, which officially made her MacMahan's Imperial counterpart and, indirectly, his boss.

Colin wouldn't have considered someone with her fiery, driven disposition an ideal spy master, but when he hinted as much to one or two council members, their reactions had surprised him. Their absolute faith in her judgment was almost scary, especially since he knew how much she detested him. Yet when he'd checked the log, her performance certainly seemed to justify their high regard. The Colorado Springs attack was the first time in forty years that the southern Imperials (as distinct from their Terra-born proxies) had surprised the northerners, and he knew whose fault that had been. Given the way the Council felt about her, he dared not try removing her from her position. Besides, his own stubborn integrity wouldn't let him fire someone who did her job so well simply because she happened to hate him.

But she worried him. No matter what anyone else said or thought about her, she worried him.

He sighed, wishing she would open up just once. Just once, so he could *know* what she was thinking and whether or not he could trust her. Then he pushed the thought aside and smiled tightly at the rest of the Council.

"I'm sure you all know Colonel MacMahan far better than I do." He gestured at the colonel and watched the exchange of nods and smiles, then put his hand back behind him. "The reason he's here just now, though, may surprise you. You see, he proposes that we attack Anu directly—without *Dahak*."

One or two members of his audience gasped, and Jiltanith seemed to gather herself like a cat. She never actually moved a muscle, but her eyes widened slightly and he thought he saw a glow in their dark depths.

"But that's crazy!" It was Sarah Meir, *Nergal*'s Terra-born astrogator. Then she blushed and glanced at Mac-Mahan. "Or, at least, it *sounds* that way."

"I agree, but that's one of the beauties of it. It's so crazy they'll never expect it." That got a small chorus of chuckles, and Colin permitted himself a wider grin. "And crazy or not, we don't really have much choice. We've been sitting on dead center ever since my . . . arrival—" that provoked a louder ripple of laughter "—and we can't afford that. You all know why."

Their levity vanished, and one or two actually glanced upward, as if to see the stars beyond which the Achuultani swept inexorably closer. He nodded.

"Exactly. But the thing that surprised me most is that it might just work." He turned to MacMahan. "Hector?"

"Thank you, Colin." MacMahan stood in the center of the command deck, his erect figure and Marine uniform as out of place and yet inevitable as Colin's own Fleet blue, and met their intent eyes levelly, a man who was clearly accustomed to such scrutiny.

"In essence," he said, "the problem is time. Time we need and haven't got. But we do have one major advantage: Anu doesn't *know* we're on a short count. It's obvious he thought Colin was one of us when he hit the Tudors—" Colin saw Jiltanith twitch at that, but she had herself well under control . . . for her "—so it seems extremely unlikely he realizes a genuinely new element has been added. He'll evaluate whatever we do against a background that, so far as he knows, is unchanged."

He paused, and several heads nodded in agreement.

"Now, we all know we hurt them badly at Colorado Springs." There was a soft growl of agreement, and he rationed himself to one of his minute smiles. "We've confirmed seventeen hard kills, and two more probables—more damage than we've done in centuries. They must be wondering what happened and, hopefully, feeling a bit on the defensive. Certainly that ties in with the efforts they've been making to find us ever since.

"At present, they no doubt see the entire skirmish as exactly what it was: a defensive action on our part, but what I propose is that we convince them it was an *offensive* act. I propose that we attack them—hit them everywhere we can—hard enough to convince them we've opened a general offensive. It'll be risky, but no more so than some of the things we've done in the past."

"Wait a minute, Hector." The colonel paused as Geb, one of the older Imperials and *Nergal*'s senior engineer, raised a hand. "There's nothing I'd like better than a shot at them, but how will it help?"

"A fair question," MacMahan acknowledged, "and I'll

try to answer it, Geb. It may sound a bit complicated, but the underlying concept is simple.

"First, some of their people are actually more vulnerable than we are. They've always been more involved in world affairs than we have, and we've been able to identify more of them than they have of us. We know where several of their Imperials are, and we've got positive IDs on quite a few of their Terra-born. More than that, we've identified the terrorist groups they're currently working through and positively located several operational centers and HQs. What that all boils down to is that even though the bulk of their personnel are far better protected than we are, the ones who are actually outside the enclave are more exposed. We can get to them more readily than they can get to us."

He looked around his audience and nodded, satisfied with the intent expressions looking back at him.

"What I propose is an organized assault on their exposed points in order to make them react the way they always have when things got hot—by pulling their Imperials and important Terra-born into the enclave to protect them while their hard teams try to trap and destroy our attack forces.

"*But,*" he said softly, "this time that will be the worst thing they could possibly do. *This* time, they'll let us through the door right behind them!"

For a man with an inexpressive face, Colin thought, Hector MacMahan could look remarkably like a hungry wolf.

"How so?" Jiltanith's voice was flat. She had herself under the tight control Colin's presence always provoked, but she was asking a question, not raising an objection, and it was clear she spoke for many of the others.

"As I say, the background maneuvers've been a bit complicated," MacMahan replied, "but the operational concept itself is simple, and my own position as the CO of Operation Odysseus is what may just make it work." Jiltanith nodded tightly, and he glanced at the other council members.

"As 'Tanni knows," he continued, "I was placed in

command of Operation Odysseus, a USFC operation to infiltrate Black Mecca, two years ago. The brass knew it wouldn't be easy, and we've had too many leaks over the years to make them happy. We, of course, know why that is: Anu hasn't been too successful in infiltrating USFC, but he's penetrated the senior echelons of the intelligence community deeply. But because of those leaks, the whole operation was made strictly need-to-know, and *I* determined who needed to know. Which means I was able to put two of our own Terra-born inside Black Mecca. One of them, in fact, is a deputy commander of their central action branch. *And*, people, he's on the 'inside' in more ways than one. He's established as a valuable, corruptible mercenary, and Anu's people coopted him five months ago."

A rustle of surprise ran through the command deck.

"Now, all of you know we've been feeling out Ramman and Ninhursag," he went on, and Colin watched the older Imperials' reactions to the two names. Ramman and Ninhursag were the southerners who'd been in clandestine contact with *Nergal*'s crew for the past two centuries. Ramman had been one of Anu's inner circle, but Ninhursag had been one of the rank and file, a senior rating in *Dahak*'s gravitonic maintenance crews, brought out of stasis little more than a hundred years ago for her expertise as a physicist. So far as the northerners knew, neither of them realized the other had been in contact with them.

"We've always been cautious about relying on anything we got from them, but 'Tanni and I have compared all the data either of them gave us to what we got from the other, and so far everything's checked. Which means either that they've both been straight with us, or else that they're being worked as a team. Personally, I believe they've been straight. Ramman's terrified of what Anu may do next, and Ninhursag is horrified by what he's already done, and the fact that they've both been kept outside the enclave and away from Anu's inner circle may indicate that they're not entirely trusted, which could be a good sign from our standpoint. Would you agree with that assessment, 'Tanni?"

"Aye," she said shortly.

"But whether he trusts them or not," MacMahan went on, "they're valuable to him; he'd've wasted them long ago if they weren't. So we can be certain they'll be called back in as soon as the shooting starts, and *that's* what's important. Once they go through the access points, they'll have the current admittance code for the portals."

He paused again, and this time Colin saw most of the council members nod.

"As we all know, Anu changes codes on a fairly regular basis. We've never been able to pick them up from outside, but 'Tanni's sensors *can* tell when they reprogram them. So if Ramman or Ninhursag can get the current code out to us, we can at least be sure whether or not it's still current."

"All right," Geb said. "I can see that, but how do they slip it to us?" The question was well taken, but he was frowning in concentration, obviously hoping for an answer rather than raising an objection.

"That's the tough part," MacMahan agreed, "but I think we can swing it.

"Once Ramman and Ninhursag have the codes, they'll each leave a copy at a pre-arranged drop inside the enclave. Our people inside Black Mecca don't know each other, but I believe both are important enough to be taken south—one of them certainly is, though the other may be marginal. Assuming we get both inside, each will make a pickup at one of the two drops. Neither Ramman nor Ninhursag will know the other is making a drop, and neither of our people will know about the other pickup, so even if we lose one, we ought to get one out.

"That's the critical point. Once we've pushed them inside and gotten our hands on that data, we'll ease off on our attacks. Anu will almost certainly do what he's always done before—shove his 'degenerates' out first to see if they draw fire. When he does, our people will give us the admittance code. Hopefully, we'll have two separate data sets to check against one another.

"*If* the code checks out, and *if* we can be ready to move before Anu changes it again, we can get inside the shield before they know we're coming.

"Their active Imperials outnumber ours heavily, but if we get inside at all, we'll have the advantage of surprise. If we hit them hard enough and fast enough, we should be able to take them or, at the very least, do enough damage to panic their senior people into sealing their hatches and lifting off in their armed parasites to get away from us and provide some fire support for their fellows. To do that, they'll have to move their parasites outside their shield and lower it to get shots at us. And if they do that—" the colonel's millimetric smile was fierce "—Colin tells me *Dahak* will be waiting for them."

A hungry sound hovered just below audibility in the hushed command deck.

"And that," MacMahan finished very, very quietly, "will be the end of Fleet Captain (Engineering) Anu and his killers."

Chapter Thirteen

"I don't like it," Horus said grimly, "and neither does the Council. You're out of your mind, Colin!"

"No, I'm not." Colin tried hard to sound patient. His experience with *Dahak*'s tenacity helped, but he was starting to think Horus could have given the starship stubborn lessons. "We've been over this and over this, and it still comes out the same. I've got to let *Dahak* know what's going on. He doesn't distinguish between any of you people; if he spots you, he's as likely to open up on you as he is on Anu."

"That's a chance we'll just have to take," Horus said obstinately.

"That's a chance we *can't* take!" Colin snapped, then made himself relax. "Damn, you're stubborn! Look, this is an all-or-nothing move; that's all it can be. We can't risk having *Dahak* attack us when we actually move against the enclave, but that's only part of it. If we manage to get inside and do enough damage their armed parasites lift out, he's gonna *know* something is going on. He hasn't heard a squeak out of me in almost five weeks—how do you think he's going to react when he sees *any* Imperial units moving around down here?"

"Well . . ."

"Exactly! But even that's not the worst of it. Suppose—heaven forbid—I buy it? Who's gonna explain any of this to *Dahak*? You know he won't believe anything you say, assuming he even listens. So. I'm dead, and you've zapped Anu. What happens next?" He met the old man's eyes levelly.

"The best you people can hope for is that he leaves you alone, but he won't. He'll figure it was simply a power play among the mutineers—which, in a sense, is exactly what it *will* be—and go after you. If the enclave's shield is down, he'll get you, too. But even if the shield's up and you're inside it, he'll be in exactly the same position he's always been in, and the Achuultani are still coming! For God's sake, man, do you *want* it all to be for nothing?!"

Horus glared with the fury of a man driven against the wall, and Jiltanith sat beside him, glowering at Colin. Her brooding silence made him appallingly nervous, and he tried to remind himself she was an experienced intelligence analyst. The smooth way she managed her sensor arrays and *Nergal's* stealthed auxiliaries proved her competence and ability to think calmly and logically. She might hate him, but she was a professional. Surely she saw the logic of his argument?

She'd said little so far, but he knew how pivotal her opinion might well be and wondered yet again if she resented the fact that MacMahan—who was technically her subordinate—had come straight to him with his plan? He'd half-expected her to throw her weight against him from the start, but now her lips twisted as if she'd just bitten into something spoiled.

"Nay, Father. The captain hath the right of't."

Horus turned an "*et tu?*" expression upon her, and sour amusement glinted in her eyes as Colin blinked in surprise.

" 'Tis scarce palatable, Father, yet 'twould be grimmest humor and our deeds do naught but doom us all, and the captain doth speak naught but truth. Wi'out word to *Dahak*, can we e'er be aught save mutineers?" Horus shook his head unwillingly, and she touched his arm gently. "Then there's an end to't. Sin we must give it that word and 'twill accept only the captain's implant code as sooth, then is there naught we may do save bend our heads and yield."

Colin looked from her to her father, grateful for her support yet aware logic, not enthusiasm, governed her. It showed even in the way she spoke of him. She used only his rank, and that sourly, when speaking of him to others, and she never called him *anything* when forced to address him directly.

"But they're bound to spot him!" Horus said almost desperately, and Colin understood perfectly. Colin was the first chance for outright victory Fate had seen fit to offer Horus, and the possibility of losing that chance terrified the old Imperial far more than the thought of his own death ever could.

"Of course they are," he said. "That's why it has to be done my way."

"Granddad," Hector MacMahan said gently, "I don't like it very much, myself, but they may be right."

Horus scowled, and the colonel turned to face Colin.

"If I support you on this one," the Marine said levelly, "it'll only be because I have to, and this will be the *only* raid you go on. Understood?"

Colin considered trying to stare the colonel down, but it would have been impolitic. Worse, it would be an exercise in futility, so he nodded instead.

MacMahan gave one of his patented fractional smiles, and Colin knew it was decided. It might take a while to bring Horus around, but the decision that counted was MacMahan's, for Colin and the Council had named him operational commander. Success would depend heavily on his Terra-born network, which made it logical for him to run things instead of Jiltanith, and while Colin might be a Senior Fleet Captain (of sorts), it was an interesting legal question whether or not any of "his" personnel still came under his orders. More, he knew his limits, and he simply wasn't equipped to orchestrate something like this.

"I'm going to have to back Colin on this one, Granddad," MacMahan said. "I'm sorry, but that's the way it is."

Horus stared at the table a moment, then nodded unwillingly.

"All right, Colin, you're on the Cuernavaca strike," MacMahan continued. "And you'll make your strike, send your message, and get out, understood?"

"Understood."

"And," MacMahan added gently, " 'Tanni will be your pilot."

"*What?!*"

Colin clamped his teeth before he said anything else he would regret, but his eyes were fiery, and Jiltanith's blazed even hotter.

" 'Tanni will be your pilot," MacMahan repeated mildly. "I'm speaking now as the commander of a military operation, and I don't really have time to be diplomatic, so both of you just shut up and listen."

Colin pushed back in his chair and nodded. Jiltanith only looked daggers at MacMahan, but he chose to construe her silence as agreement.

"All right. I know there's some bad blood between you two," the colonel said with generous understatement, "but there's no room for that here. This—as all three of us have just pointed out to Granddad—is *important*.

"Colin, you're the only person who can initiate the message, and if we send you on the strike, you should be able to hide your fold-space transmission by burying it under an ostensible strike report to our HQ. But we don't know how quickly or strongly Anu's people will be able to respond, so we can't afford anything but our very best pilot behind those controls. You're good, Colin, and your reaction time is phenomenal even by Imperial standards, but good as you are, you have very little actual experience in an Imperial fighter.

" 'Tanni, on the other hand, is a natural pilot and the youngest of our Imperials, with reaction time almost as good as yours but far, far more experience. The overall mission will be under your command, but she's *your* pilot and you're *her* electronics officer, or neither of you goes."

He regarded them steadily, and Colin glanced over at Jiltanith. He caught her unaware, surprising her own gaze upon him, and a flicker of challenge passed between them.

"All right," he sighed finally, then grinned. "If I'd known what an iron-assed bastard you are, I'd never have agreed to let you run this op, Hector."

"Ah, but I'm the *best* iron-assed bastard you've got . . . Sir," MacMahan replied.

Colin subsided, and his grin grew as a new thought occurred to him. Once he and Jiltanith were crammed into the same two-man fighter, she was going to *have* to think of something to call him!

It was amazing how consistently wrong he could be, Colin thought moodily as he checked his gear one last time. He and Jiltanith had worked in the same simulator for a week now, and she still hadn't chosen to call him anything.

There were only the two of them, so who else could she be talking to? It actually made it easier for her to make her point by refusing to use his name or rank. And he was certain she would rather die than call him "Sir."

He grinned sourly. At least it gave him something to think about besides the butterflies mating in his middle. For all that he'd been a professional military man before joining NASA, Colin had fired a shot in anger exactly twice, including his abortive attack on *Dahak*'s tender. The other time had been years before, when a very junior Lieutenant MacIntyre had found his Lynx fighter unexpectedly nose-to-nose with an Iraqi fighter in what was supposed to be international airspace, and Colin still wasn't certain how he'd managed to break lock on the self-guiding missile the Iraqi pilot had popped off at him. Fortunately, the other guy had been less lucky.

It helped that the other Imperials were all veterans of their long, covert war. Their calm preparations had steadied his nerve more than he cared to admit . . . but that, in its own way, made it almost worse. Here he was, their commander-in-chief, and every one of his personnel had more combat experience than he did! Hardly the proper balance of credentials.

He sealed his flight suit and checked the globular, one-way force field that served an Imperial pilot as a helmet. He had to admit it was a vast improvement to be able to reach in through his "helmet," and the vision was superb, yet he felt something like nostalgia over the disappearance of all the little read-outs that had cluttered the interior of his NASA-issue gear.

He hung his gray gun on his suit webbing, not that the weapon was likely to do him much good if they had to ditch. Or, for that matter, that they were likely to have a chance to ditch if the bad guys managed to line up on them with anything in the way of heavy weapons.

There. He was ready, and he strolled out of the armory towards the ready room, glad that he and only he could read the adrenalin levels reported by the bio-sensors in everyone else's implants.

The fighters' crewmen sat quietly in *Nergal*'s ready room. There were only eight of them, for sublight battleships were not planetoids. They carried only a half-dozen fighters, and each one they crammed aboard cut into their internal weapon tonnage.

Most of the Imperials looked frighteningly old to Colin. Geb was flying wing on his and Jilanith's fighter—the only one that would have an escort—and his weaponeer was the only other "youngster" present. Tamman had been ten at the time of the mutiny, but he hadn't been sent back into stasis for as long as Jiltanith and he had a good two centuries of experience behind him.

Yet for all their apparent age, the other Imperials were Hector MacMahan's hand-picked first team. This would be the first time in three thousand years that *Nergal*'s people had used Imperial technology in an open, full-blooded smash at their foes, but there had been occasional, unexpected clashes between the two sides' small craft, and these were the victors from those skirmishes.

"All right." MacMahan entered the compartment briskly and sat on the corner of the briefing officer's console. "You've all been briefed, you all know the plan, and you all know the score. All I'll say again is that all other attacks *must* be held until 'Tanni and Colin have gone in *and* transmitted. Till then, you don't do a single damned thing."

Heads nodded. Waiting might expose them to a bit more danger from the southerners, but attacking before Colin flashed his "strike report" and warned *Dahak* what was going on would be far riskier. The old starship was far more likely to get them than were Anu's hopefully surprised personnel. This time.

"Good," MacMahan said. "Get saddled up, then." The crews began to file out, but the colonel put a hand on Colin's shoulder when he made to follow. "Wait a sec, Colin. I want to talk to you and 'Tanni for a minute."

Jiltanith waited with Colin while the others left, but even now she chose to stand on MacMahan's other side, separating herself from her crewmate.

"I asked you to wait because I've just gotten an update on your target," MacMahan said quietly. "Confirmation came in through one of our people in Black Mecca—Cuernavaca is definitely the base that mounted the hit on Cal, and, with just a bit of luck, Kirinal will be there when you go in."

The hatred that flared in Jiltanith's eyes was not directed at Colin this time, and he felt his own mouth twist in a teeth-baring grin.

Kirinal. He'd felt a cold, skin-crawling fascination as he scanned her dossier. She was Anu's operations chief, his equivalent of Hector MacMahan, but she enjoyed her work as much as Girru had. Her loss would hurt the southerners badly, but that wasn't the first thing that flashed through his mind. No, his *first* thought was that Kirinal personally had ordered the murder of Cal's family.

"I considered not telling you," the colonel admitted,

"but you'd've found out when you get back, and I've got enough trouble with you two without adding that to it! Besides, knowing Kirinal's in there would make it personal for everyone we've got, I suppose. But now that you know, I want you to forget it. I know you can't do that entirely, but if you can't keep revenge from clouding your judgment, tell me now, and Geb and Tamman will take the primary strike."

Colin wondered if Jiltanith *could* avoid that. For that matter, could he? But then his eyes met hers, and, for the first time, there was complete agreement between them.

MacMahan watched them, his expressionless face hiding his worry, and considered ordering them off the target whatever they said. Perhaps he shouldn't have told them after all? No. They had a right to know.

"All right," he said finally. "Go. And—" his voice stopped them in the hatchway and he smiled slightly "—good hunting, people."

They vanished, and Colonel MacMahan sat alone in the empty briefing room, his face no longer expressionless. But he stood after a moment, straightening his shoulders and banishing the hopeless bitterness from his face. He was a highly skilled and experienced pilot, but one without the implants that would have let him execute his own plan, and that was all there was to it.

Colin's neural feed tapped into what the U.S. Navy would have called the fighter's "weapons and electronic warfare panel" as he and Jiltanith settled into their flight couches, and he felt a fierce little surge of eagerness from the computers. Intellectually, he knew a computer was no more than the sum of its programming, but Terraborn humans had anthropomorphized computers for generations, and the Imperials, with their far closer, far more intimate associations with their electronic minions, never even questioned the practice. Come to think of it, was a human mind that much more than the sum of its programming?

Yet however that might be, he knew what he felt. And

what he felt was the fighter baring its fangs, expressing its eagerness in the system-ready signals it sent back to him.

"Weapons and support systems nominal," he reported to Jiltanith, and she eyed him sidelong. She knew they were, of course; their neural feeds were cross-connected enough for that. Yet it was a habit ingrained by too many years of training for him to break now. When a check list was completed, you reported it to your command pilot.

He felt her eyes upon him for a moment longer, then she tossed her head slightly. Her long, rippling hair was a tight chignon atop her head, held by glittering combs that must have been worth a small fortune just as antiques, and her gemmed dagger was at her belt beside the pistol she carried in place of his own heavy grav gun. It was semi-automatic, with a down-sized, thirty-round magazine, light enough for her unenhanced muscles. She'd designed and built it herself, and it looked both anachronistic and inevitable beside her dagger. She was, he thought wryly and not for the first time, a strange mixture of the ancient and the future. Then she spoke.

"Check," she said, and he blinked. "Stand thou by . . . Captain."

It was the first time she'd responded to one of his readiness reports. That was what he thought first. And then the title she'd finally given him registered.

He was still wondering what her concession meant when their fighter launched.

Chapter Fourteen

Jiltanith was good.

Colin had recognized her skill and, still more, her natural affinity for her task, even in the simulator. Now she took them up the long, carefully camouflaged tunnel from *Nergal* without a single wasted erg of power. Without even a single wasted thought. The fighter's wings were her own, and the walls of their stony birth canal slid past, until, at last, they floated free on a smooth whine of power.

The stars burned suddenly, like chips of ice above them, and a strange exhilaration filled Colin. There was a vibrant new strength in the side-band trickles of his computer links, burning with Jiltanith's bright, fierce sense of flight and movement. For a time, at least, she was free. She was one with her fighter as she roamed the night sky, free to seek out her enemies, and he felt it in her, like a flare of joy, made still stronger by her hunger for vengeance and aptness for violence. For the first time since they'd met, he understood her perfectly and wondered if he was glad he did, for he saw himself in her. Less driven, perhaps, less dark and brooding, not honed to quite so keen an edge, but the same.

The mutineers had been no more than an obstacle when he returned from *Dahak* . . . but Sean had been alive then. He had lost far less than Jiltanith, seen far fewer friends and family ground to dust in the marooned Imperials' secret, endless war, but he had learned to hate, and it frightened him to think he could so quickly and easily find within himself so strong a shadow of the darkness that he'd known from the start infused Jiltanith.

He cut off his thoughts, hoping she'd been too enwrapped in the joy of flight to notice them, and concentrated on his own computers. So far, they'd remained within *Nergal's* stealth field; from here on, they were on their own.

The Imperial fighter was half the size of a Beagle, a needle-nosed thing of sleek curves and stub wings. Its design was optimized for atmosphere, but the fighter was equally at home and far more maneuverable in vacuum, though none of *Nergal's* brood had been there in millennia. Most of their time had been spent literally weaving in and out among the treetops to hide from Anu's sensor arrays, and so they flew now.

They swept out over the Pacific, settling to within meters of the swell, and Jiltanith goosed the drive gently. A huge hand pressed Colin back in his couch, and a wake boiled across the water behind them as they streaked south at three times the speed of sound. The G forces were almost refreshing after all this time, like an old friend he'd lost track of since meeting *Dahak*, but they also underscored Jiltanith's single glaring weakness as a pilot.

Atmosphere was a less forgiving medium than vacuum. Even at the fighter's maximum power, friction and compression conspired to reduce its top speed dramatically. There was one huge compensation—by relying on control surfaces for maneuvering rather than depending entirely upon the gravitonic magic of the drive, the same speed could be produced for a far weaker energy signature—

but there were always trade-offs. In this case, one was a
greater vulnerability to thermal detection and targeting
systems as a hull unprotected by a drive field heated, but
that was a relatively minor drawback.

The *real* problem was that the reduced-strength drive
couldn't cancel inertia and the G forces of acceleration.
Flying on its atmospheric control surfaces, the deadly
little ship was captive to the laws of motion and no more
maneuverable than the bodies of its crew could stand,
and that was potentially deadly for Jiltanith. If she found
herself forced into maneuvering combat against a fully-
enhanced Imperial in this performance envelope, she was
dead, for she would black out long before her opponent.

Still, MacMahan was almost certainly right. If it came
to aerial combat, stealth would not be in great demand.
It would become a matter of brute power, cunning, reaction time, and the skill of the combatants' electronic warfare specialists, and the first thing that would happen
would be that the pilots would go to full power. With a
full strength drive field wrapped around her, Jiltanith
would be as free of G forces as any Imperial pilot.

Yet the whole object was to avoid any air-to-air fighting. If they were forced to full power, all the ECM in
the world couldn't hide them from Anu's detectors . . .
which meant they dared not return to *Nergal* unless they
could destroy or shake off any pursuit and drop back
into a stealth regime. Trade-offs, Colin thought sourly,
checking their airspeed. Always the trade-offs.

They were up to mach four, he noted, and grinned
as he imagined the reaction aboard any freighter they
happened across when they came hurtling by ahead of
their sonic boom with absolutely no radar image to show
for it.

They ought to hit their target in about another seventeen minutes. Strange. He didn't feel the least bit nervous anymore.

"Coming up on our final turn," Colin said eleven
minutes later.

"Aye," Jiltanith said softly.

Her voice was dreamy, for Colin wasn't quite real for her just now. Reality was her dagger-sleek fighter, for she was one with it, seeing and feeling through its sensors. Yet he felt the intensity of her purpose and the cat-sharp clarity of her awareness through his own feeds, and he was content.

They swept through the turn, settling into the groove for the attack run, and Geb and Tamman fell astern, increasing their separation as planned.

The huge private estate in the deep, bowl-like valley north of Cuernavaca was the true HQ of both Black Mecca and the Army of Allah in the Americas, though only a very few terrorists knew it. That made it a major operational node, one of the three juiciest targets Mac-Mahan and Jiltanith had been able to identify. Over forty southerners and two hundred of their most trusted Terra-born allies were based there, coordinating a hemisphere's terrorism, and the estate's seclusion hid a substantial amount of Imperial equipment. A successful attack on such a target would certainly seem to justify an immediate strike report to their own HQ.

But there was another fractor in MacMahan's target selection. The "estate's" geography made it an ideal target for mass missiles, for the valley walls would confine the blast effect and channel it upward. The northerners expected the use of such weapons to come as a considerable shock to Anu, for they would provoke consternation and furious speculation among the vast majority of Earth's people, and attention was the one thing both groups of Imperials had assiduously avoided for centuries. If anything could convince Anu *Nergal*'s people meant business, this attack should do it.

Yet the very importance of the target also meant a greater possibility of serious defenses. If enemy fighter opposition appeared, it was up to Geb and Tamman to pick it off if they could; if they couldn't, theirs became the far grimmer task of playing decoy to suck the southerners off Colin and onto themselves, and . . .

"Shit!" Colin muttered, and Jiltanith stiffened beside him as he shunted information to her through a side feed. There were active Imperial scanners covering the target. At their present speed, those scanners would burn through their stealth field in less than five minutes.

Colin tightened internally as he and his computers raced to determine what those scanners reported to. If it was only an observation post, they'd be onto the target before anyone could react, but if there were automatic defenses . . .

"Double shit!" he hissed. There were, indeed, automatic defenses—and three fighters on stand-by for launch, though three ships were no indication of an alert. There were at least ten of the little buggers down there; if they'd anticipated an attack, all ten would have been spotted for immediate launch. He and Jiltanith had simply had the infernal bad luck to happen upon the scene when someone was readying for a routine flight. Possibly Kirinal was going somewhere in one of those fighters and the other two were escorts; that fitted normal southern operational procedures.

But it meant the base was at a higher state of readiness than usual, and there were those automatics. He could "see" at least four missile batteries and two heavy energy weapon emplacements, which was far more than their intelligence estimates had suggested.

His thoughts flickered so quickly they were almost unformed, yet Jiltanith caught them. He felt her disappointment like his own. These were the people who had sent Girru and Anshar to butcher Cal's family and Sean and Sandy, but their orders for this contingency were clear.

"We'll have to abort," Colin remarked, yet even as he said it his neural link was bringing his systems fully on line.

"Aye, so we shall." Yet Jiltanith's course never deviated, and he felt her mental touch poised to ram the drive's power level through the red line.

"They'll burn through a good twenty seconds before I get a targeting setup," he said absently.

"Nay, 'twill be no more than ten seconds ere thy weapons range," she demurred.

"Hah! Now you're an EW specialist, too, huh?" Then he shrugged. "Screw it. Full bore right down the middle, Jiltanith. Go for the weapons first."

"As thou sayst, Captain," Jiltanith purred, and the fighter shrieked upward like a homesick meteor.

For just a second, acceleration drove Colin back into his couch, but then the drive field peaked, the G forces vanished, and he felt the shockwave of alarm sweep through the southerners' enclave. The automatic air-defense systems were already reaching for them, but his own systems had come alive a moment sooner; by the time the weapons started hunting the fighter, its defensive programs were already filling the night sky with false images. Decoys streaked away, singing their siren songs, and jammers hashed the scan channels with the fold-space equivalent of white noise.

The ground stations' scanners were more powerful and their electronic brains were bigger and smarter than his small onboard computers, but they'd started at a disadvantage. They had to sort the situation out before they could find a target, and it was a race between them and their human controllers and Colin and the speeding fighter's targeting systems.

There was no time to think, no room for anything but concentration, yet kaleidoscope images flared at the edges of his brain. The brighter strobes of panic when one ground station seemed to have found them. The impossible, wrenching maneuver with which Jiltanith threw it off. The relief when they slipped away before it could establish a lock. His own racing excitement. The determination and intensity that filled his pilot. His own savage blaze of satisfaction as his launch solution suddenly came magically together.

His first salvo leapt away. Hyper-capable missiles were out of the question in atmosphere; they would take too much air into hyper with them, wrecking his mass-power calculations and bringing them back into normal space God alone knew where, but mass missiles were another matter. Their over-powered gravitonic drives slammed them forward, accelerating instantly to sixty percent of light speed, crowding the edge of phase lock. Counter-missile defenses did their best, but the mass missiles' speed and the short range meant tracking time was too limited even for Imperial systems, and Colin heard Jiltanith's panther howl of triumph as his strike went home.

Fireballs blew into the night. Mass missiles carried no warheads, for they needed none. They were energy states, not projectiles, hyper-velocity robotic meteorites, shrieking down on precise trajectories to seek out the ground weapons that menaced their masters.

The small shield generators protecting the southerners' weapons were still spinning up when Colin's missiles arrived, but it wouldn't have mattered if they'd already been at full power. In fifty-one millennia, the notherners had never risked escalating their struggle to the point of using Imperial weaponry so brazenly, and the southerners had assumed they never would. Their defensive measures were aimed at Terrestrial weapons or the relatively innocuous Imperial ones the northerners had used in the past, and they were fatally inadequate.

Jiltanith snapped the fighter around as the Jovian holocaust spewed skyward behind them. A bowl of fire glared against the night-struck Mexican hills, and Colin's computers were already evaluating the first strike. Weak as they were, the base's shields had absorbed a tremendous amount of energy before they failed—enough to keep the missiles from turning the entire estate into one, vast crater—and one heavy energy gun emplacement had escaped destruction. It raved defiance at them, and Jiltanith accepted the challenge as she came back like the angel of death, driving into its teeth.

The radiant heat of the first missile strike, added to the frantic efforts of the fighter's ECM, denied the targeting scanners lock, and the guns were on pre-programmed blind fire, raking the volume of space that ought to contain the fighter. But Jiltanith wasn't where the people who'd designed that fire program had assumed she would have to be, and Colin felt a detached sort of awe for her raw flying ability as he popped off another missle.

Unlike the fighter, the energy weapons couldn't bob

and weave. The missile sizzled home, and a fresh burst of fury defiled the earth.

Jiltanith came around for a third pass, two more than their ops plan had called for or considered safe, and the ground defenses were silent. Despite the shields' best efforts, the weapon emplacements were huge, raw wounds, and the entire valley floor was a sea of blazing grass and trees, touched to flame by thermal radiation. The palatial estate's buildings were flaming rubble, but the real installations hidden under them, though damaged, were still intact.

One of the ready fighters was already clawing upward, but Colin ignored it. He had all the time in the world, and his final launch was textbook perfect. A spread of four missiles bracketed the target, streaking the fire-sick heavens with fresh flame. There were no shields to absorb the destruction this time, and there was, at most, no more than a microsecond between the first missile impact and the last.

A hurricane of light lashed upward as vaporized earth and stone and flesh vomited into the night, and the fireballs ballooned out, merging, melding into one terrible whole. A second southern fighter was caught just at lift off and spat forth like a molten, tumbling spark from Vulcan's forge, and the pressure wave snatched at them. It shook them as a terrier shook a rat, but Jiltanith met it like a lover. She rode its ferocity—embracing it, not fighting it—and the universe danced crazily, even madder somehow from within the protection of their drive field, as she shot the rapids of concussion. But then they flashed out the far side, and Colin realized she had used the terrible turbulence to put them on the track of the single fighter that had escaped destruction.

Colin needed no evaluation of his final attack. All that *could* be left was one vast crater. He had just killed over two hundred people . . . and all he felt was satisfaction. Satisfaction, and the need, the eagerness, to hunt down and kill the single southern fighter that had escaped his wrath.

There was no way to know who piloted that other

fighter, nor if it was fully crewed or what weapons it carried. Perhaps there was only the pilot. Perhaps it wasn't even armed.

All Colin would ever know was that he felt a sort of merciless empathy—not pity, but something like understanding—for that fleeing vessel. He and Jiltanith were invincible, and they were vengeance. He bared his teeth and called up his air-to-air weaponry as the firestorm's white heat dulled to red astern, and Jiltanith hurled them out over the night-dark Pacific in pursuit.

His targeting systems locked. A command flicked through his feed to the computers, and two more missiles launched. They were slower than mass missiles, homing weapons with their speed stepped down to follow evasive maneuvers, but this time they carried warheads: three-kiloton, proximity-fused nukes. His eyes were dreamy as his electronic senses watched them all the way in, but in the moment before detonation a third missile came scorching in from the west. He'd almost forgotten Geb and Tamman, and the southern fighter probably never even realized he and Jiltanith weren't alone.

There was no debris.

Jiltanith needed no orders. She swept on into the west, reducing speed, losing altitude, and their drive strength coasted back down to wrap invisibility about them once more. Colin checked his sensors carefully, and not until he was certain they had evaded all detection did she turn and flee homeward into the north while he switched on the fighter's com and activated the fold-space implant he had dared not use in over a month. He felt an odd little "click" inside his skull as *Dahak*'s receivers recognized and accepted his implant's ID protocols.

"Category One Order. Do not reply," he sent at the speed of thought. "Authentication Delta-One-Gamma-Beta-One-Seven-Eight-Theta-Niner-Gamma. Priority Alpha. Stand by for squeal from this fighter. Execute upon receipt."

He closed his implant down instantly, praying that the almost equally strong pulse from the fighter com had hidden it from Anu's people. The coded squeal he and he alone had pre-recorded and tacked into the middle of the strike report lasted approximately two milliseconds, and *Dahak* had his orders.

And then, at last, there was a moment to relax and blink his eyes, refocusing on the interior of the cockpit. A moment to realize that they had succeeded . . . and that they were alive.

"Done," he said softly, turning to look at Jiltanith for the first time since they launched their attack.

"Aye, and well done," she replied. Their gazes met, and for once there was no hostility between them.

"Beautiful flying, 'Tanni," he said, and saw her eyes widen as he used the familiar form of her name for the first time. For a moment he thought he'd gone too far, but then she nodded.

"Art no sluggard thyself . . . Colin," she said.

And she smiled.

Book Three

Chapter Fifteen

Colin MacIntyre sat in *Nergal's* wardroom and shuffled, hiding a smile as Horus bent a hawk-like eye upon him across the table while they waited for Hector's next report.

Battle Fleet's crews had gone in for a vast array of esoteric games of chance, most of them electronic, but Horus disdained such over-civilized pastimes. He loved Terran card games: bridge, canasta, spades, hearts, euchre, blackjack, whist, piquet, chemin de fer, poker ... *especially* poker, which had never been Colin's game. In fact, Colin's major interest in cards had been that of an amateur magician, and Horus had been horrified at how easily a full Imperial who'd learned to palm cards with purely Terran reflexes and speed could do that ... among other things.

"Cut?" Colin invited, and shook his head sadly as Horus made five separate cuts before handing the deck back.

"What're your losses by now?" he mused as he dealt. "About a million?"

" 'Tis more like to thrice that," Jiltanith said sourly, gathering up her cards and not bothering to watch his fingers with her father's intensity.

"Ante up," he said, and chips clicked as father and daughter slid them out. If they'd really been playing for money, he'd be a billionaire, even without the ill-gotten wealth Horus had demanded he write off after he realized Colin had been cheating shamelessly. He grinned, and Jiltanith snorted without her old bitterness as she saw it.

She still wasn't really comfortable with him, but at least she was pretending, and he was grateful to Hector. The colonel had torn long, bloody strips off both of them when he saw the scan record of what they'd gone into, but his heart hadn't seemed fully in it, and Colin had seen the glint in his eye when Jiltanith called him "Colin" during their debriefing. He himself had feared she would retreat into her old, cold hostility once the rush of euphoria passed, but though she'd stepped back a bit and he knew she still resented him, she was fighting it, as if she recognized (intellectually, at least) that it wasn't his fault he was what he'd become. Her presence at the card table was proof of that.

He wished there had been a less traumatic way to effect that change, but he hoped the colonel was pleased with the way it had worked out. The military arguments for assigning them to the same flight crew had been strong, but it had taken courage—well, gall—to put them forward.

"I'll take two," Horus announced, and Colin flipped the small, pasteboard rectangles across to him.

" 'Tanni?" He raised a polite eyebrow, and she pouted.

"Nay, this hand liketh me well enow."

"Hm." He studied his own cards thoughtfully, then took one. "Bets?"

"I'll go a hundred," Horus said, and Jiltanith followed suit.

"See you and raise five hundred," Colin said grandly, and Horus glared.

"Not this time, you young hellion!" he growled. "I'll see your raise and raise *you* a hundred!"

"Father, art moonstruck," Jiltanith said, tossing in her own hand. "Whyfor must thou throw good money after bad?"

"That's no way to talk to your father, 'Tanni." Horus sounded pained, and Colin hid another smile.

"See you and raise another five," he murmured, and Horus glared at him.

"Damn it, I *watched* you deal! You can't possibly—" The old Imperial shoved more chips forward. "Call," he said grimly. "Let's see you beat *this*!"

He faced his cards—four jacks and an ace—and glowered at Colin.

"Horus, Horus!" Colin sighed. He shook his head sadly and laid out his own hand card by card, starting with the two of clubs and ending with the six.

"No!" Horus stared at the table in shock. "*A straight flush?!*"

" 'Twas foredoomed, Father," Jiltanith sighed, a twinkle dancing in her own eyes. "Certes, 'tis strange that one so wise as thou should be so hot to make thyself so poor."

"Oh, shut up!" Horus said, trying not to smile himself. He gathered up the cards and glared at Colin. "This time *I'll* deal."

"*Damn* them! Breaker take them to *hell*!"

The being who had once been Fleet Captain (Engineering) Anu leapt to his feet and slammed his fist down so hard the table's heavy top cracked. He stared at the spider-web fractures for a moment, then snatched it up and hurled it against the battle-steel bulkhead with all his strength. The impact was a harsh, discordant clangor and the table sprang back, its thick Imperial plastic bent and buckled. He glared at it, chest heaving with his fury, then kicked the wreckage back into the bulkhead. He did it several more times, then whirled, fists clenched at his sides.

"And *you*, Ganhar! Some 'intelligence analyst' *you*

turned out to be! What the hell do you have to say for yourself?!"

Ganhar felt sweat on his forehead but carefully did not wipe it away as he fastened his eyes on the center of Anu's chest. He dared not *not* look at him, but it could be almost as dangerous to meet his gaze at a moment like this. Ganhar had assisted Kirinal in running Anu's external operations for over a century, but the newly promoted operations head had never seen Anu quite this furious, and he silently cursed Kirinal for getting herself killed. If she'd still been alive, he could have switched his leader's wrath to her.

"There were no indications they planned anything like this, Chief," he said, hoping his voice sounded more level than it felt. He started to add that Anu himself had seen and approved all of his intelligence estimates, but prudence stopped him. Anu had become steadily less stable over the years. Reminding him of his own fallibility just now was strongly contra-indicated.

" *'No indications'!*" Anu mimicked in a savage falsetto. He growled something else under his breath, then inhaled sharply. His rage appeared to vanish as suddenly as it had come, and he picked up his chair and sat calmly. When he spoke again, his voice was almost normal.

"All right. You fucked up, but maybe it wasn't entirely your fault," he said, and Ganhar felt himself sag internally in relief.

"But they've hurt us," the chief mutineer continued, harshness creeping back into his voice. "I'll admit it—I didn't think they'd have the guts for something like this, either. And it's paid off for them, Breaker take them!"

All eyes turned to the holo map hovering above the space the table had occupied, dotted with glaring red symbols that had once been green.

"Cuernavaca, Fenyang, *and* Gerlochovko in one night!" Anu snorted. "The equipment doesn't matter all that much, but they've blown the guts out of your degenerates—and we've lost eighty more Imperials. *Eighty!* That makes more than ten percent of us in the last month!"

His subordinates sat silent. They could do the math

equally well, and the casualties appalled them. Their enemies hadn't done that much damage to them in five millennia, and the fact that their own over-confidence had
made it possible only made it worse. They'd known their
foes were aging, that time was on their side. It had never
occurred to them that the enemy might have the sheer
nerve to take the offensive after all these years.

Even worse was the *way* they'd been attacked. The
open use of Imperial weapons had been a shattering blow
to their confidence, and it could well have led to disaster.
None of the degenerates seemed to know what had happened, but they knew it was something they couldn't
explain. The southerners' penetration of the major governments, especially in the Asian Alliance, had been sufficient to head off any precipitate military action against
purely Terrestrial foes, but their control was much
weaker in the West, and their enemies' obvious willingness to run such risks was sobering.

But not, Ganhar thought privately, as sobering as
another possibility. Perhaps their enemies had had reason
to be confident of their own ability to control the situation? It was possible, for if the southerners had their
hooks deep into the civilian agencies, *Nergal*'s people had
outdistanced them among the West's soldiers.

The first reports had produced plenty of demands for
action or, at the very least, priority investigations into
whatever had happened, but their own tools among the
civilians had managed to quash any "overly hasty action,"
though there had been some fiery scenes. Yet now a
curtain of silence had descended over the Western militaries, and Ganhar found that silence ominous.

He bit his lip, longing for better sources within military
intelligence, but they were a clannish bunch. And, much
as he hated to admit it, the northerners' willingness to
accept degenerates as equals had marked advantages.
They'd spent centuries setting up their networks, often
recruiting from or even before birth. Ganhar and Kirinal,
on the other hand, had concentrated on recruiting adults,
preferring to work on individuals whose weaknesses were
readily apparent. That had its own advantages, like the

ability to target people on their way up, but the increasing high-tech tendency towards small, professional, career-oriented military establishments worked against them.

The military's background investigation procedures were at least as rigorous as those of their civilian counterparts, and the steady incidence of leaks from civilian agencies had led to an even stronger preference for career officers for truly sensitive posts. Worse, Ganhar *knew* the northerners had firm links with the traditional military families, though pinning any of them down was the Breaker's own work. And that meant *their* military contacts were damned well *born* in position, with sponsors who were ready to favor their own and doubly suspicious of everyone else.

Ganhar, on the other hand, had no choice but to corrupt officers already in place, which risked counter-penetration, or fabricate fictitious backgrounds (always risky, even against such primitives, much less degenerates aided by Imperial input), which was why it had seemed so sensible to concentrate on their civilian masters, instead.

He hoped that policy wasn't about to boomerang on them.

"Well, Ganhar?" Anu's abrasive voice broke in on his thoughts. "Why do *you* think they've come out into the open? Assuming you *have* an opinion."

While Ganhar hesitated, seeking a survivable response, another voice answered.

"It may be," Commander Inanna said carefully, "that they're desperate."

"Explain," Anu said curtly, and she shrugged.

"They're getting old," she said softly. "They used Imperial fighters, and they can't have many Imperials left. Maybe they're in even worse shape than we'd thought. Maybe it's a last-ditch effort to cripple us while they can still use Imperial technology at all."

"Hmph!" Anu frowned down at the clenched hands in his lap. "Maybe you're right," he said finally, "but it doesn't change the fact that they've taken out three quarters of our major bases. Maker only knows what they'll do next!"

"What *can* they do, Chief?" It was Jantu, the enclave's chief security officer. "The only other big target was Nanga Parbat, and we've already shut down there. Sure, they hurt us, but those were the only targets they could hit with Imperial weapons. And—" he added with a glance at Ganhar "—if we'd put them closer to major population centers, they couldn't even have hit them."

Ganhar ground his teeth. Jantu was a bully and a sadist, more at home silencing dissidence by crushing dissidents than thinking, yet he had his own brand of cunning. He liked to propose sweeping, simplistic solutions to other people's problems. If they were rejected, he could always say he'd warned everyone they were going about it wrongly. If they were adopted and succeeded, he took the credit, if they failed, he could always blame someone else for poor execution. Like his long-standing argument in favor of using cities to cover their bases against attack, claiming that their enemies' softness for the degenerates would protect them. It would also make it vastly harder to hide them, but Jantu wouldn't have been the one who had to try.

"It might not have mattered." Inanna disliked Jantu quite as much as Ganhar did, and her eyes—black now, not brown—were hard. "They risked panicking the degenerates into starting a war. For all we know, they might've hit us if our bases had been buried under New York or Moscow."

"I doubt that," Jantu said, showing his teeth in what might—charitably—be called a smile. "In all—"

"It doesn't matter," Anu interrupted coldly. "What matters is that it's happened. What's your best estimate of their next move, Ganhar?"

"I . . . don't know." Ganhar picked his words carefully. "I'm not happy about how quiet the degenerates' militaries have been. That may or may not indicate something, but I don't have anything definite to base projections on. I'm sorry, Chief, but that's all I can say."

He braced himself against a fresh burst of rage, yet it

was wiser to be honest than to let a mistake come home to roost. But there was no blast of fury, only a slow nod.

"That's what I thought," Anu grunted. "All right. We've already got most of our Imperials—what's left of them!—under cover. We'll sit tight a bit longer on our degenerates and less reliable Imperials. Jantu's right about one thing; there aren't any more of *our* concentrations for them to hit. Let's see what the bastards do next before we bring anyone else down here."

His henchmen nodded silently, and he waved for them to leave. They rose, and Jantu led the way out with Ganhar several meters behind him.

Anu smiled humorlessly at the sight. There was no love lost between those two, and that kept them from conspiring together even if it did make for a bit of inefficiency. But if Ganhar fucked up again, not even the Maker would save him.

Inanna lingered, but when he ignored her she shrugged and followed Ganhar. Anu let his eyes rest on her departing back. She was about the only person he still trusted, as much as he could bring himself to trust anyone.

They were all fools. Fools and incompetents, or they would have taken *Dahak* for him fifty thousand years ago. But Inanna was less incompetent than the others, and she alone seemed to understand. The others had softened, forgotten who and what they were, and accepted the failure of their plan. They were careful not to say it, yet in their hearts, they had betrayed him. But Inanna recognized the weight of his destiny, the pressure gathering even now behind him, driving him towards escape and empire. Soon it would become an irresistible flood, washing out from this miserable backwater world to sweep him to victory, and Inanna knew it.

That was why she remained loyal. She wanted to share that power as mistress, minion, or lieutenant; it didn't matter to her. Which was just as well for her, he told himself moodily. Not that she wasn't a pleasant armful in bed. And that new body of hers was the best yet. He tried to recall what the tall, raven-haired beauty's name had been, but it didn't matter. Her body was Inanna's now, and Inanna's skill filled it.

The conference room door closed silently behind the commander, and he stalked through his private exit, feeling the automatic weapons that protected it recognizing his implants. He entered his quarters and stared bitterly at the sumptuous furnishings. Splendid, yes, but only a shadow of the splendor in *Dahak*'s captain's quarters. He had been pent here too long, denied his destiny for too many dusty years. Yet it would come. Inevitably, it would come.

He crossed the main cabin, ignoring Imperial light sculptures and soft music, overlooking priceless tapestries, jewel work, and paintings from five thousand years of Terran history, and peered into a mirror. There were a few tiny wrinkles around his eyes now, and he glanced aside, letting those eyes rest on the framed holo cube of the Anu-that-was, seeing again the power and presence that had been his. This body was taller, broad shouldered and powerful, but it was still a poor excuse for the one he had been born to. And it was growing older. There might be another century of peak performance left to it, and then it would be time to choose another. He'd hoped that when that time came he would be back out among the stars where he belonged, teaching the Imperium the true meaning of Empire.

His original body remained in stasis, though he hadn't looked upon it since it was placed there. It caused him pain to see it and remember how it once had been, but he had saved it, for it was *his*. He had not permitted Inanna to develop the techniques to clone it. Not yet. That was reserved for another time, a fitting celebration of his final, inevitable triumph.

The day would come, he promised his stranger's face, when he would have the realm that should be his, and when it came, he would have the Anu-that-was cloned afresh. He would live forever, in his *own* body, and the stars themselves would be his toys.

Ganhar walked briskly along the corridor, eyes hooded in thought. What *were* the bastards up to? It was such a fundamental change, and it came after too many years of unvarying operational patterns. There was a reason behind it, and, grateful as he'd been for Inanna's intervention, he couldn't believe it was simple desperation. Yet he had no better answer for it than she, and that frightened him.

He sighed. He'd covered his back as well as he could; now he could only wait to see what they were doing. Whatever it was, it could hardly make the situation much worse. Anu was mad, and growing madder with every passing year, but there was nothing Ganhar could do about it ... yet. Maker only knew how many of the others were the "Chief's" spies, and no one knew who Anu might decide (or be brought to decide) was a traitor.

Jantu was probably licking his chops, praying daily for something to use against him, and there was no sane reason to give him that something, but Ganhar had his plans. He suspected others had theirs, as well, but until they finally escaped this damned planet they needed Anu. Or, no, they needed Inanna and her medical teams, but that was almost the same thing. Ganhar had no idea why the bioscience officer remained so steadfastly loyal to that madman, but as long as she did, any effort to remove him would be both futile and fatal.

He stepped into the transit shaft and let it whirl him away to his own office. There might be other reports by now—he was certainly driving his teams hard enough to produce them! If there were none, he could at least relieve his own tension by giving someone else a tongue-lashing.

General Sir Frederick Amesbury, KCB, CBE, VC, DSO, smiled tightly at the portrait of the king on his office wall. Sir Frederick could trace his ancestry to the reign of Edward the Confessor. Unlike many of *Nergal's* Terra-born allies he was not directly descended from her crew, though there had been a few distant collateral connections, for his people had been among their helpers since the seventeenth century.

Now, after all those years, things were coming to a

head, and the Americans' General Hatcher was shaping up even more nicely than Sir Frederick had expected. Of course, Hector was to blame for prodding Hatcher into action, and Sir Frederick had been primed to support the Yank's first tentative suggestion, but Hatcher was doing bloody well.

He checked his desk clock, and his smile grew shark-like. The SAS and Royal Marines would be hitting the Red Eyebrows base in Hartlepool in less than two hours, after which, Sir Frederick would have to notify the Prime Minister. The Council reckoned the P.M. was still his own man, and Sir Frederick was inclined to agree, but it would be interesting to see if that was enough to save his own position when the Home and Defense Ministers—who most definitely were *not* their own woman and man, respectively—demanded his head.

Oberst Eric von Grau sat back on his haunches in the ditch. The *leutnant* beside him was peering through his light-gathering binoculars at the isolated chalets in the bend of the Mosel River, but Grau had already carried out his own final check. His two hundred picked men were quite invisible, and his attention had moved to other things. He cocked an ear, waiting for the thunder to begin, and allowed himself a tight smile.

He had treated himself to a quiet celebration when the orders came through from *Nergal*, and when news of the first three strikes rocked the world, he'd hardly been able to wait for the request from the Americans. German intelligence had spotted this January Twelfth training camp long ago, though the security minister had chosen not to act on the information.

But Herr Trautmann didn't know about this little jaunt, and the army had no intention of telling the civilians about it till it was over. Grau's superiors had learned their lessons the hard way and trusted the Americans' USFC more than they did their own civilian overlords. Which was a sad thing, but one Grau understood better than most.

"Inbound," a radio voice said quietly, and he grinned

at *Leutnant* Heil. Heil looked a great deal like a younger
version of his superior—not surprisingly, perhaps, since
Grau's great-great-great-great-great-grandmother was
also Heil's great-great-grandmother—and his smile was
identical.

The sudden boom of supersonic aircraft crashed over
them as the *Luftwaffe* fighter-bombers came in on full
after-burner at fifty meters.

"Go." Major Tama Matsuo, Japanese Army, touched
his sergeant on the shoulder and the two of them slithered through the shadows after Lieutenant Yamashita's
team. Darkness wrapped Bangkok in comforting anonym-
ity, but the grips of the major's automatic grenade
launcher were slippery in his hands.

He and the sergeant turned a corner and faded into
the shrubbery at the base of a stone wall, joining the
men already waiting for them, and Tama checked the
time again. Lieutenant Kagero's men should be in position by now, but the timetable gave them another thirty-
five seconds.

The major watched the dimmed display of his watch,
trying to control his breathing, and hoped Hector Mac-
Mahan's intelligence was good. It had been hard to convince his superiors to sanction a raid into Asian Alliance
territory without civilian approval, even if his father was
Chief of the Imperial Staff and even to take out the
foreign HQ of the Japanese Army for Racial Purity. And
if the operation blew up, his reputation and influence
alike would suffer catastrophically. Assuming he survived
at all.

He watched the final seconds tick away. It still seemed
a bit foolhardy. Satisfying, but foolhardy. Still, he who
wanted the tiger's cubs must venture into the tiger's den
to get them. He just hoped the Council was right. And
that he would do nothing to dishonor himself in his
grandfather's eyes.

"Now," he said quietly into the boom mike before
his lips, and Tamman's grandson committed his men to
combat.

*   *   *

Colonel Hector MacMahan stepped out into his back-yard as the stealthed cutter ghosted down the canyon behind the house and settled soundlessly to the grass. The reports would be coming in soon, and the expected flak from the civilians would come with them. Anu's people had spent years infiltrating the civilians who set policy and controlled the military (normally, that was) but even the most senior of them would find it hard to stop things now.

He felt a glow of admiration for his superiors, and especially Gerald Hatcher. They didn't know what he knew, but they knew they'd been leashed too long. Anu had gotten just a bit too fancy—or too confident, perhaps.

In the old days, he'd relocated his "degenerates'" HQs whenever they were spotted; for the last few years he'd amused himself by simply forbidding action against major bases. There had been no way to prevent interceptions and attacks on action groups or isolated training and staging bases, but his minions in the intelligence community had argued that it was wiser to watch headquarters groups rather than attack and risk driving them back out of sight.

But the attacks on three really big terrorist bases, two of which the generals hadn't even known existed, had been the final straw. They didn't know who'd done it, how, or, for that matter, why, but they knew *what* it was. Their own charter was the eradication of terrorism, and the realization that someone else was doing their job was too much to stand. Hatcher and his fellows had proven even more amenable to his suggestions than expected.

They couldn't do much about the Islamic and officially-sponsored Asiatic groups, most of whose bases were openly entrenched in countries hostile to their govern-ments. But the homegrown variety was another matter entirely, and it was amazing how memos notifying the generals' nominal superiors of their plans had been so persistently misrouted.

And if *they* couldn't hit the foreign groups, MacMahan

knew who could. He hadn't told them that, but he suspected they'd be figuring it out shortly.

The hatch opened and the colonel whistled shrilly. A happy woof answered as his half-lab, half-rotweiller bitch Tinker Bell galloped past him and hopped up into the cutter. She poked her nose into Gunnery Chief Hanalat's face, licking her affectionately, and the white-haired woman laughed and tugged on the big dog's soft ears while MacMahan tossed his duffel bags up into the cutter and climbed in after them.

General Hatcher had ordered MacMahan to make himself scarce for the next few weeks without realizing just how scarce the colonel intended to become. The Unified Special Forces Command's CO meant to take the heat when his bosses found out what he'd been up to, though MacMahan suspected that heat would be less intense than the general feared. Most of his superiors were men and women of integrity, and the ones who weren't would find it hard to raise too much ruckus in the face of the general approval MacMahan anticipated.

Of course, once it became apparent just how thoroughly the colonel had vanished, his boss would figure out he'd known about the mystery attacks ahead of time. The northerners had never tried to recruit him, but Hatcher was no fool. He'd realize he had been used, though it was unlikely to cost him much sleep, and MacMahan hated to run out without explaining things to him. But he had no choice, for one thing was certain: when they found out what had happened and how, the southerners would suddenly become far, far more interested in one Colonel Hector MacMahan, USMC, currently attached to the USFC.

Not that it mattered. Indeed, his role as instigator was part of the plan, an intentional diversion of suspicion from their other people, and he'd always known his position was more exposed than most. That was why he was a bachelor with no family, and they wouldn't be able to find him when they wanted him, anyway.

He only wished he could see Anu's face when *he* got the news.

Chapter Sixteen

Head of Security Jantu leaned back and hummed happily, feeling no need to dissemble in the security of his own office, as he replayed the last command meeting in his mind.

The "Chief's" wrath had been awesome when the news came in. This time he'd half-expected it, which meant he'd had time to work up a good head of steam ahead of time. The things he'd said to poor Ganhar!

It was all quite terrible ... but more terrible for some than for others. Most of the dead Imperials were Ganhar's people, and nothing that weakened Ganhar could be completely bad. The thought that degenerates could do such a neat job was galling, but whatever happened in the field, the enclave that was his own responsibility was and would remain inviolate, so none of the egg was on *his* face. No, it was on Ganhar's face, and with just a little luck—and, perhaps, a little judicious help—that might just prove fatal for poor Ganhar.

It had been kind of *Nergal's* people to take out Kirinal for him. Now if he could only get rid of Ganhar, he might just manage to bring Security and Operations together under the control of a single man: him. Of course, it was probable the "Chief" would balk at that and pick a new head for Operations, but Jantu would be perfectly happy if Anu made the logical choice. And even if he decided to choose someone other than Bahantha, the newcomer would be hopelessly junior to Jantu. One way or another, he would dominate whatever security arrangements resulted from Ganhar's . . . departure.

And then it would be time to deal with Anu himself. Jantu would not have let a sane man stand between him and power, and he felt no qualms at all over removing a madman. Indeed, it might almost be considered his civic duty, and he often permitted himself a mildly virtuous feeling when he considered it.

Jantu hadn't realized quite how mad the engineer was when the plot to seize *Dahak* first came up, but he'd recognized that Anu wasn't exactly stable. Overthrow the Imperium? Ludicrous! But Jantu had been prepared to go along until they had the ship, at which point he and his own henchmen would eliminate Anu and put a modified version of the original plan into effect. It would be so much simpler to transform *Dahak*'s loyalists into helots and build their own empire in some decently deserted portion of the galaxy than to pit themselves against the Imperium and get squashed for their pains.

That plan had gone out the airlock when the mutiny failed, but there were still possibilities. Indeed, the present situation seemed even more promising.

He knew Anu and, possibly, Inanna believed the Imperium was still out there, waiting to be conquered, but the Imperium's expansion should have brought at least a colony to Earth long since, for habitable planets weren't all that plentiful. By Jantu's most conservative estimate, BuCol's survey teams should have arrived forty millennia ago. That they hadn't suggested all sorts of hopeful possibilities to a man like Jantu.

If the Imperium had fallen upon hard times, why, then Anu's plans for conquest might be practical after all. And the first stage was to forget this clandestine nonsense and

take control of Earth openly. A few demonstrations of
Imperial weaponry should bring even the most recalci-
trant degenerate to heel. Once he could recruit a properly motivated batch of sepoys and come out of the
shadows, Jantu could hammer out a decent tech base in
a few decades and set about gathering up the reins of
galactic power in a tidy, orderly fashion.

But first there was Ganhar, and then Anu. Inanna
might be a bit of a problem, for he would continue to
need her medical skills, at least until a properly-trained
successor was available. Still, he felt confident he could
convince the commander to see reason. It would be a
pity to mar that lovely new body of hers, but Jantu was
a great believer in the efficacy of judiciously applied pain
when it came to behavior modification.

He smiled happily, never opening his eyes, and began
to hum a bouncier, brighter ditty.

Ramman watched the tunnel walls slide past the cutter
and worried. He had the code now. All he had to do was
make it to the drop to deposit it. Simple.

And dangerous. He should never have agreed, but the
orders had been preemptive, not discretionary. And if
the whole idea was insane, he was still in too deep to
back out. Or was he?

He scrubbed damp palms on his trousers and closed
his eyes. Of course he was! He was a dead man if the
"Chief" ever found out he'd even talked to the other
side, and his death would be as unpleasant as Anu could
contrive.

He clenched his teeth as he contemplated the bitter
irony that brought him to this pass. Fear of Anu had
tempted him to contact the other side in a desperate
effort to escape, yet that same contact had actually
destroyed his chance to flee. First Horus and then his
bitch of a daughter had steadfastly refused to *let* him
defect, far less help him do it!

He made himself stop trying to dry his hands, hoping
he hadn't already betrayed himself. He should have realized what would happen. Why should Horus and his fel-

lows trust him? They knew what he was, what he had
been, and how easily trusting him could have proven
fatal. So they'd left him inside, using him, and he'd let
himself be used. What choice had he had? All they had
to do to terminate his long existence was wax deliberately
clumsy in their efforts to contact him; Anu would see to
it from there.

He'd given them a lot of information over the years,
and things had gone so smoothly he'd grown almost
accustomed to it. But that was before they told him about
this. Madness! It would destroy them all, and him with
them.

He knew what they had to be planning. Only one thing
made sense of his orders, and it was the craziest thing
they'd tried yet.

But what if they could pull it off? If they succeeded,
surely they would honor their word to him and let him
live. Wouldn't they?

Only they wouldn't succeed. They couldn't.

Maybe he should tell Ganhar? If he went to the Operations chief and gave him the location of his drop, helped
him bait a trap for Jiltanith's agent ... surely that should
be worth something? Maybe Ganhar could be convinced
to pretend it had all been part of an elaborate counter-
intelligence ploy?

But what if he couldn't? What if Ganhar simply turned
him over to Jantu as the traitor he was?

The huge inner portals opened, admitting the cutter
to the hollow heart of the enclave, and Raman balanced
on a razor edge of agonized indecision.

Ganhar rubbed his weary eyes and frowned at the holo
map hovering above his desk. Its green dots were fewer
than ever, its red dots correspondingly more numerous.
His people had maintained direct links with relatively
few of the terrorist bases the degenerates had hit, but
the fallout from those strikes was devastating. In less than
twenty-four hours, thirty-one—*thirty-one!*—major HQs,
training, and base camps had been wiped out in separate,
flawlessly synchronized operations whose efficient feroc-

ity had stunned even Ganhar. The shock had been still worse for his degenerate tools; dying for a cause was one thing, but even the most fanatical religious or political bigot must pause and give thought to the body blow international terrorism had just taken.

He sighed. His personal position was in serious jeopardy, and with it his life, and there was disturbingly little he could do about it. Only the fact that he'd warned Anu something might be brewing had saved him so far, and it wouldn't save him very much longer.

His civilian minions' inability to stop their own soldiers or even warn him of what was coming was frightening. *Nergal's* people must have infiltrated the military even more deeply than he'd feared, and if they could do that much, what else might they have accomplished without his noticing?

More to the point, *why* were they doing this? Inanna's suggestion that age had compelled them to attack while they still had enough Imperials to handle their equipment made sense up to a point, but the latest round of disasters had been executed out of purely Terrestrial resources. It took careful planning to blend Terran and Imperial efforts so neatly, which suggested the entire operation had been worked out well in advance. Which, in turn, suggested some long-range objective beyond the destruction of replaceable barbarian allies.

Ganhar got that far without difficulty; unfortunately, it still gave no hint of what the bastards were up to. Drive his sources as he might, he simply couldn't find a single reason for such a fundamental, abrupt change in tactics.

About the only thing his people *had* managed was the identification of one of the enemy's previously unsuspected degenerate henchmen. Not that it helped a great deal, for Hector MacMahan had vanished. Which might mean they'd been intended to spot him, and that—

The admittance chime broke into his thoughts and he straightened, kneading the back of his neck as he sent a mental command to the hatch mechanism. The panel licked aside, and Commander Inanna stepped through it.

Ganhar's eyes widened slightly, for he and the medical

officer were scarcely friends—indeed, about the only thing they had in common was their mutual detestation for Jantu—and she'd never visited his private quarters. His mental antennae quivered, and he waved her courteously to a Louis XIV chair under a seventh-century Tang Dynasty tapestry.

"Good evening, Ganhar." She sat and crossed her long, shapely legs. Well, not *hers*, precisely, but then neither was Ganhar's body "his" in the usual sense, and Inanna really had picked a stunningly beautiful one this time.

"Good evening," he replied. His voice gave away nothing, but she smiled as if she sensed his burning curiosity. Which she probably did. She might be unswervingly loyal to a maniac, and it was highly probable she was a bit around the bend herself, but she'd never been dense or unimaginative.

"No doubt you're wondering about this visit," she said. He considered replying but settled for raising his eyebrows politely, and she laughed.

"It's simple enough. You're in trouble, Ganhar. Deep, deep trouble. But you know that, don't you?"

"The thought had crossed my mind," he admitted.

"It's done lots more than that. In fact, you've been sitting here sweating like a pig because you know you're about one more bad report away from—*pffft!*" She snapped her fingers, and he winced.

"Your grief is moving, but I doubt you came just to warn me in case I hadn't noticed."

"True. True." She smiled cheerfully. "You know, I've never liked you, Ganhar. Frankly, I've always thought you were in it out of pure greed, which would be fine if I weren't pretty certain your plans include winding up in charge yourself. With, I'm sure, fatal consequences for Anu and myself."

Ganhar blinked, and her eyes danced at his failure to hide his surprise.

"Ganhar, Ganhar! You disappoint me! Just because you think I'm a little crazy is no reason to think I'm stupid! You may even be right about my mental state, but you really ought to be a bit more careful about letting it color your calculations."

"I see." He propped an elbow on his desk through the holo map and regarded her as calmly as he could. "May I assume you're pointing out my shortcomings for a reason?"

"There. I always knew you were bright." She paused tauntingly, forcing him to ask, and he had no choice but to comply.

"And that reason is?"

"Why, I'm here to help you. Or to propose an alliance, of sorts, at any rate." He sat a bit straighter, and a strange hardness banished all amusement from her eyes.

"Not against Anu, Ganhar," she said coldly. "Whether I'm crazy or not isn't your concern, but make one move against him, and you're a dead man."

Ganhar shivered. He had no idea what that icy guarantee might rest upon, but neither did he have any desire to find out. She sounded far too sure of herself for that, and, as she'd pointed out, she was hardly stupid. Assuming he survived the next few weeks, he was going to have to recast his plans for Commander Inanna.

"I see," he said after a long pause. "But if not against him, then against who?"

"There you go again. Try to accept that I'm reasonably bright, Ganhar. It'll make things much easier for us both."

"Jantu?"

"Of course. That weasel has plans for all of us. But then," her smile turned wolfish, "I have plans for him, too. Jantu's in very poor health; he just doesn't know it yet. He won't—until his next transplant comes due."

Ganhar shivered again. Brain transplants were ticklish even with Imperial technology, and a certain number of fatalities were probably unavoidable, but he'd assumed Anu decided which patients suffered complications. It hadn't occurred to him Inanna might be doing it on her own.

"So," she went on pleasantly, "we still have to decide what to do with him in the meantime. If he ever left the enclave, he might have an accident. I'd considered that, and it would've been a neat way to get him, Kirinal, *and* you, wouldn't it? You're in charge of external operations . . . he's your worst rival . . . who wouldn't've wondered if you two hadn't arranged it?"

"You have a peculiar way of convincing an 'ally' to trust you," Ganhar pointed out carefully.

"I'm only proving I can be honest with you, Ganhar. Doesn't my openness reassure you?"

"Not particularly."

"Well, that's probably wise of you. And that's my point; you really are much smarter than Jantu—less devious, but smarter. And because you are, I'm reasonbly certain *your* plans to assassinate Anu—and possibly myself— don't envision any immediate execution date." She smiled cheerfully at her own play on words. "But if you disappeared from the equation, Jantu is stupid enough to make his try immediately. He wouldn't succeed, but he doesn't know that, and I'm sure it would come to open fighting in the end. If that happened, Anu or I might be among the casualties. I wouldn't like that."

"So why not tell Anu?"

"The one absolutely predictable thing about you is your ability to disappoint me, Ganhar. You must be crazy yourself if you think I haven't realized Anu is. The technical term, if you're wondering, is advanced paranoia, complicated by megalomania. He hasn't quite reached grossly delusional proportions yet, but he's headed that way. And while we're being so honest, let's admit that paranoia can be a survival tool in situations like his. After all, a paranoic is only crazy when people *aren't* out to get him.

"But the point is that I'm probably the only person he trusts at all, and one reason he does is that I've very carefully avoided getting caught up in any of our little intrigues. But if I warned him about Jantu, he'd start wondering if I hadn't decided to join with you, instead. He's not exactly noted for moderation, and the simplest solution to his problem would be to kill all three of us. I wouldn't like that, either."

"Then why not—"

"Careful, Ganhar!" She leaned towards him, her eyes hard as two black opals, and her soft, soft voice was almost a hiss. "Be very, *very* careful what you suggest to me. Of course I could. I'm his doctor, after all. But I won't. Not now, not ever. Remember that."

"I . . . understand," he said, licking his lips.

"I doubt that." Her eyes softened, and somehow that frightened Ganhar even more than their hardness had, but then she shook her head. "No, I doubt that," she said more naturally, "but it doesn't matter. What matters is that you have an ally against Jantu—for now, at least. We both know things are going to get worse before they get better, but I'll do what I can to draw fire from you during conferences, and I'll support you against Jantu and maybe even when you stand up to *him*. Not always directly, perhaps, but I will. I want you around to take charge when we start rebuilding your operations network."

"You mean you want me around because you *don't* want Jantu in charge, right?" Ganhar asked, meeting her eyes fully.

"Well, of course. But it's the same thing, isn't it?"

It most definitely wasn't the same thing, but Ganhar chose not to press the point. She peered deeply into his eyes for a moment, then nodded.

"I can just see your busy little mind whirring away in there," she said dryly. "That's good. But, as one ally to another, I'd advise you to come up with some sort of forceful recommendation for Anu. Something positive and masterful. It doesn't have to actually *accomplish* much, you understand, but a little violence would be helpful. He'll like that. The notion of hitting back—of *doing* something—always appeals to megalomaniacs."

"I—" Ganhar broke off and drew a deep breath. "Inanna, you have to realize how what you've just said sounds. I'm not going to suggest that you do anything to Anu. You're right; I don't understand why you feel the way you do, but I'll accept it and remember it. But don't you worry about what else I might do with the insight you've just given me?"

"Of course not, Ganhar." She lounged back in her chair with a kindly air. "We both know I've just turned all of your calculations topsy-turvy, but you're a bright little boy. Given a few decades to consider it, you'll realize I wouldn't have done it if I hadn't already taken precautions. That's valuable in its own right, don't you think? I mean, knowing that, crazy or not, I'll kill you the moment you become a threat to Anu or me is bound to color your thinking, isn't it?"

"I suppose you could put it that way."

"Then my visit hasn't been a waste, has it?" She rose and stretched, deliberately taunting him with the exquisite perfection of the body she wore as she turned for the hatch. Then she paused and looked back over her shoulder almost coquettishly.

"Oh! I almost forgot. I meant to warn you about Bahantha."

Ganhar blinked again. What about Bahantha? She was his senior assistant, number two in Operations now that he'd replaced Kirinal, and she was one of the very few people he trusted. His thoughts showed in his face, and Inanna shook her head at his expression.

"Men! You didn't even know that she's Jantu's lover, did you?" She laughed merrily at his sudden shock.

"Are you certain?" he demanded.

"Of course. Jantu controls the official security channels, but *I* control biosciences, and that's a much better spy system than he has. You might want to remember that yourself. But the thing is, I think you'd better arrange for her to suffer a mischief, don't you? An accident would be nice. Nothing that would cast suspicion on you, just enough to send her along to sickbay." Her toothy smile put Ganhar forcefully in mind of a Terran piranha.

"I . . . understand," he said.

"Good," she replied, and sauntered from his cabin. The hatch closed, and Ganhar looked blindly back at the

map. It was amazing. He'd just acquired a powerful ally
. . . so why did he feel so much worse?

Abu al-Nasir, who had not allowed himself to think of
himself as Andrew Asnani in over two years, sat in the
rear of the cutter and yawned. He'd seen enough Imperial technology in the last six months to take the wonder
out of it, and he judged it best to let the Imperials about
him see it.

In fact, his curiosity was unquenchable, for unlike most
of the northerners' Terra-born, he had never seen *Nergal*
and never knowingly met a single one of their Imperials.
That, coupled with his Semitic heritage, was what had
made him so perfect for this role. He was of them, yet
apart from them, unrelated to them by blood and with
no family heritage of assistance to connect him to them,
however deep the southerners' looked.

It also meant he hadn't grown up knowing the truth,
and the shock of discovering it had been the second most
traumatic event in his life. But it had offered him both
vengeance and a chance to build something positive from
the wreckage of his life, and that was more than he'd let
himself hope for in far too long.

He yawned again, remembering the evening his universe had changed. He'd known something special was
about to happen, although his wildest expectations had
fallen immeasurably short of the reality. Full colonels
with the USFC did not, as a rule, invite junior sergeants
in the venerable Eighty-Second Airborne to meet them
in the middle of a North Carolina forest in the middle
of the night. Not even when the sergeant in question
had applied for duty with the USFC's anti-terrorist action
units. Unless, of course, his application had been accepted
and something very, very strange was in the air.

But his application had not been accepted, for the
USFC had never even officially seen it. Colonel MacMahan had scooped it out of his computers and hidden it
away because he had an offer for Sergeant Asnani. A
very special offer that would require that Sergeant Asnani
die.

The colonel, al-Nasir admitted to himself, had been an excellent judge of character. Young Asnani's mother, father, and younger sister had walked down a city street in New Jersey just as a Black Mecca bomb went off, and when he heard what the colonel had to suggest, he was more than ready to accept.

The pre-arranged "fatal" practice jump accident had gone off perfectly, purging Asnani from all active data bases, and his true training had begun. The USFC hadn't had a thing to do with it, although it had been some time before Asnani realized that. Nor had he guessed that the exhausting training program was also a final test, an evaluation of both capabilities and character, until the people who had actually recruited him told him the truth.

Had anyone but Hector MacMahan told him, he might not have believed it, despite the technological marvels the colonel demonstrated. But when he realized who had truly recruited him and why, and that his family had been but three more deaths among untold millions slaughtered so casually over the centuries, he had been ready. And so it was that when the USFC mounted Operation Odysseus, the man who had been Andrew Asnani was inserted with it, completely unknown to anyone but Hector Mac-Mahan himself.

Now the cutter slanted downward, and Abu al-Nasir, deputy action commander of Black Mecca, prepared to greet the people who had summoned him here.

"Except for the fact that we've only gotten one man inside, things seem to be moving well," Hector MacMahan said. Jiltanith had followed him into the wardroom, and she nodded to Colin and selected a chair of her own, sitting with her habitual cat-like grace.

"So far," Colin agreed. "What do you and 'Tanni expect next?"

"Hard to say," Hector admitted. "They've got most of their people inside by now, and, logically, they'll sit tight in their enclave to wait us out. On the other hand, every time we use any of our own Imperials in an operation we give them a chance to trail someone back to us, so they'll probably leave us some sacrificial goats. We'll have to hit a few of them to make it work, and I've already put the ops plan into the works. We're on schedule, but everything still depends on luck and timing."

"Why am I unhappy whenever you use words like 'logically' and 'luck'?"

"Because you know the southerners may not be too tightly wrapped, and that even if they are, we have to do things exactly right to bring this off."

"Hector hath the right of't, Colin," Jiltanith said. " 'Tis clear enow that Anu, at the least, is mad, and what means have we whereby to judge the depth his madness hath attained? I'truth, 'tis in my mind that divers others of his minions do share his madness, else had they o'erthrown him long before. 'Twould be rankest folly in our plans to make assumption madmen do rule their inner councils, yet ranker far to make assumption they do not. And if that be so, then naught but fools would foretell their plans wi' certainty."

"I see. But haven't we tried to do just that?"

"There's truth i'that. Yet so we must, if hope may be o'victory. And as Hector saith, 'tis clear some movement hath been made e'en now amongst their minions. Mad or sane, Anu hath scant choice i'that. 'Tis also seen how his 'goats' do stand exposed, temptations to our fire, and so 'twould seem good Hector hath beagled out the manner of their thought aright. Yet 'tis also true that one ill choice may yet bring ruin 'pon us all. I'truth, I do not greatly fear it, for Hector hath a cunning mind. We stand all in his hand, empowered by his thought, and 'tis most unlike our great design will go awry."

"Spare my blushes," MacMahan said dryly. "Remember I only got one man inside, and even if the core of our strategy works perfectly, we could still get hurt along the way."

"Certes, yet wert ever needle-witted, e'en as a child, my Hector." She smiled and ruffled her distant nephew's hair, and he forgot his customary impassivity as he grinned at her. "And hath it not been always so? Naught worth the doing comes free o'danger. Yet 'tis in my mind 'tis in smaller things we may find ourselves dismayed, not in the greater."

"Like what?" Colin demanded.

"That depends on too many factors for us to say. If it didn't, they wouldn't be surprises. It's unlikely anything they do to us can hurt us too much, but you're a miltiary man yourself, Colin. What's the first law of war?"

"Murphy's," Colin said grimly.

"Exactly. We've disaster-proofed our position as well as we can, but the fact remains that we're betting on just a pair, as Horus would say—Ramman and Ninhursag— and one hole card—our man inside Black Mecca. We don't know what cards Anu holds, but if he decides to fold this hand or even just stands pat for a few years, it all comes unglued."

"For God's sake spare me the poker metaphors!"

"Sorry, but they fit. The most important single factor is Anu's mental state. If he suddenly turns sane and decides to ignore us until we go away, we lose. We have to do him enough damage to make him antsy, and we have to do it in a way that keeps him from getting too suspicious. We have to hurt him enough to make him eager to come back out and start making repairs, but at the same time we have to *stop* hurting him in a way that leaves him confident enough to come right back out. Which means we have to hit at least some of his 'goats' after his important personnel have all gone to ground, then wind down when it's obvious our returns are starting to diminish."

"Well," Colin tried to project both confidence and caution, "if anyone can pull it off, you two can."

"Thanks, I think," Hector said, and Jiltanith nodded.

The stocky, olive-brown-skinned woman sat quietly in the cutter, but her eyes were bright and busy. There were Terra-born as well as Imperials around her, and the trickiest part was showing just enough interest in them.

Ninhursag had never considered herself an actress, but perhaps she was one now. If so, her continued survival might be said to constitute a favorable review.

She'd lived in the enclave only briefly and had not returned in over a century, so a certain amount of interest was natural. By the same token, any Terra-born being brought into the enclave must be important and thus a logical cause for curiosity. The trick was to display her curiosity without giving anyone cause to suspect that she knew at least one of them was far more than he seemed. Her instructions made no mention of Terra-born allies, but they made no sense if there were no couriers, and if those couriers were Imperials she might as well have carried the information out herself.

At the same time, she knew she was suspect as one who had never been part of Anu's inner circle, so a certain nervousness was also natural. Yet showing too much nervousness would be worse than showing none at all. Her actions and attitude must show she knew she was under suspicion yet appear too cowed for that suspicion to be justified.

In truth, it was the last part she found hardest. Her horror at what Anu and Inanna had done to her fellow mutineers and the poor, helpless primitives of this planet had become cold, hard fury, and she hated the need to restrain it. When she'd learned Horus and the rest of *Nergal*'s crew had deserted Anu and chosen to fight him, her first thought had been to defect to them, but they'd convinced her she was more valuable inside Anu's organization. No doubt caution played a part in that—they didn't entirely trust her and wanted to take no chances on infiltration of their own ranks—but that was inevitable, and her only other option would have been to strike out on her own, vanishing and doing nothing in order to hide from both factions.

Yet doing nothing had been unthinkable, and so she had become *Nergal*'s not-quite-trusted spy, fully aware of the terrifying risk she ran. Terror had been a cold, omnipresent part of her for far too long, but it was not her master. That had been left to another emotion: hate.

The sudden outbreak of violence had surprised her as much as it had any of Anu's loyalists, but coupled with the odd instructions she'd received from Jiltanith, it made frightening, exhilarating sense. There was only one reason Anu's enemies could want those admittance codes.

She'd tried not to wonder how they hoped to get them out of the enclave, for what she neither knew nor suspected could not be wrung out of her, but she'd always been cursed with an active mind, and the bare bones of their plan were glaringly obvious. Its mad recklessness shocked her, but she knew what they planned, and hopeless though it might well be, she was eager.

The cutter nosed downward, and she felt her implants tingle as they waited to steal the key to Anu's fortress for his foes.

Chapter Seventeen

Dark and silence ruled the interior of the mighty starship. Only the hydroponic sections and parks and atriums were lit, yet the whole stupendous structure pulsed with the electronic awareness of the being called *Dahak*.

It was good, the computer reflected, that he was not human, for a human in his place would have gone mad long before Man relearned the art of working metal. Of course, a human might also have found a way to act without needing to wait for a Colin MacIntyre.

But he was not human. There were human qualities he did not possess, for they had not been built into him. His core programming was heuristic, else he had not developed this concept of selfhood that separated him from the Comp Cent of old, yet he had not made that final transition into *human*-ness. Still, he had come closer than any other of his kind ever had, and perhaps someday he would take that step. He rather looked forward to the possibility, and he wondered if his ability to anticipate that potentiality reflected the beginnings of an imagination.

It was an interesting question, one upon which even he might profitably spend a few endless seconds of thought, but one he could not answer. He was the product of intellect and electronics, not intuition and evolution, with no experiential basis for any of the intangible human capacities and emotions. Imagination, ambition, compassion, mercy, empathy, hate, longing ... love. They were words he had found in his memory when he awoke, concepts whose definitions he could recite with neither hesitation nor true understanding.

And yet ... and yet there *were* those stirrings at his soulless core. Did this cold determination of his to destroy the mutineers and all their works reflect only the long-dead Druaga's Alpha Priority commands? Or was it possible that the determination was his, *Dahak's*, as well?

One thing he did know; he had made greater strides in learning to comprehend rather than simply define human emotions in the six months of Colin MacIntyre's command than in the fifty-two millennia that had preceded them. Another entity, separate from himself, had intruded into his lonely universe, someone who had treated him not as a machine, not as a portion of a starship that simply had the ability to speak, but as a person.

That was a novel thing, and in the weeks since Colin had departed, *Dahak* had replayed their every conversation, studied every recorded gesture, analyzed almost every thought his newest captain had thought or seemed to think. There was a strange compulsion within him, one created by no command and that no diagnostic program could dissect, and that, too, was a novel experience.

Dahak had studied his newest Alpha Priority orders, as well, constructing, as ordered, new models and new projections in light of the discovery of a second faction of mutineers. That process he understood, and the exercise of his faculties gave him something he supposed a human would call enjoyment.

But other parts of those orders were highly dissatisfying. He understood and accepted the prohibition against sending his captain further aid or taking any direct action before the northern mutineers attacked the southern lest he reveal his actual capabilities. But the order to communicate with the northern leaders in the event of Colin's death and the categorical, inarguable command to place himself under the command of one Jiltanith and the other mutineer children—*those* he would obey because he must, not because he wished to.

Wished to. Why, he *was* becoming more human. What business had a computer thinking in terms of its own wishes? If ever he had expressed a wish or desire to his core programmers, they would have been horrified. They would have shut him down, purged his memory, reprogrammed him from scratch.

But Colin would not have. And that, *Dahak* realized, in the very first flash of intuition he had ever experienced, was the reason he did not wish to obey his orders. If he must obey them, it would mean that Colin was dead, and *Dahak* did not *wish* for Colin to die, for Colin was something far more important to *Dahak's* comfortable functioning than the computer had realized.

He was a friend, the first friend *Dahak* had ever had, and with that realization, a sudden tremble seemed to run through the vast, molecular circuitry of his mighty intellect. He had a *friend*, and he understood the concept of friendship. Imperfectly, perhaps, but did humans understand it perfectly themselves? They did not.

Yet imperfect though his understanding was, the concept was a gestalt of staggering efficacy. He had internalized it without ever realizing it, and with it he had internalized all those other "human" emotions, after a fashion, at least. For with friendship came fear—fear for a friend in danger—and the ability to hate those who threatened that friend.

It was not an entirely pleasant thing, the huge computer mused, this friendship. The cold, intellectual detachment of his armor had been rent—not fully, but in part—and for the first time in fifty millennia, the bitter irony of helplessness in the face of his mighty firepower was real, and it hurt. There. Yet another human concept: pain.

The mighty, hidden starship swept onward in its endless orbit, silent and dark, untenanted, yet filled with life. Filled with awareness and anxiety and a new, deeply personal purpose, for the mighty electronic intellect, the *person*, at its core had learned to care at last . . . and knew it.

The small party crept invisibly through the streets of Tehran. Their black, close-fitting clothing would have marked them as foreigners—emissaries, no doubt, of the "Great Satans"—had any seen them, but no one did, for the technical wizardry of the Fourth Imperium was abroad in Tehran this night.

Tamman paused at a corner to await the return of his nominal second-in-command, feeling deaf and blind within his portable stealth field. It was strange to realize a Terra-born human could be better at something like this than he, yet Tamman could not remember a time when he had not "seen" and "felt" his full electromagnetic and gravitonic environment. Because of that, he felt incomplete, almost maimed, even with his sensory boosters, when he must rely solely upon his natural senses, and taking point was not a job for a man whose confidence was shaken, however keen his eyes or ears might be.

Sergeant Amanda Givens returned as silently as the night wind, ghosting back into his awareness, and nodded to him. He nodded back, and he and the other five members of their team crept forward once more behind her.

Tamman was grateful she was here. Amanda was one of their own, directly descended from *Nergal*'s crew, and, like Hector, she'd also been a member of the USFC until very recently. She reminded Tamman of Jiltanith; not in looks, for she was as plain as 'Tanni was beautiful, but in her feline, eternally poised readiness and inner strength. The fact that her merely human senses and capabilities were inferior to an Imperial's had not shaken her confidence in herself. If only she could have been given an implant set, he thought. She was no beauty, but he felt more than passing interest in her, more than he'd felt in any woman since Himeko.

She stopped again, so suddenly he almost ran into her, and she grinned at him reprovingly. He managed a grin of his own, but he felt uneasy . . . limited. Give him an Imperial fighter and a half-dozen hostiles and he would feel at home; here he was truly alien, out of his depth and aware of it.

Amanda pointed, and Tamman nodded as he recognized the dilapidated buildings they'd come to find. It must have tickled the present regime to put Black Mecca's HQ in the old British Embassy compound, and it must have galled Black Mecca to settle for it instead of the crumbling old American Embassy the mainstream faction of the Islamic Jihad had claimed.

He waved orders to his team and they spread out, finding cover behind the unmanned outer perimeter of sandbags. He recalled the vitriolic diatribes that often emanated from this very spot, beamed to the world of Black Mecca's enemies. These positions were always manned, then, with troops "prepared to defend their faith with their life's blood" against the eternally impending attack of the Great Satans. Not, of course, that any member of Black Mecca had ever believed any enemy could actually reach them here.

He checked his team once more. All were under cover, and he raised his energy gun. His fellows were all Terraborn, trained for missions like this one by their own governments or in classes conducted by people like Hector and Amanda. They were skilled and deadly with the weapons of the Terrestrial military, but far more deadly with the weapons they carried now. None was strong enough to carry energy guns, not even the cut-down, customized one he carried, but *Nergal*'s crew had specialized in ingenious adaptation for centuries, and the fruits of their labor were here tonight, for Hector wanted Anu to know precisely who was behind this attack.

Tamman pressed the firing stud, and the silent night exploded.

The deadly focus of gravitonic disruption slammed into the inner sandbags around the compound gate, shredding their plastic envelopes, filling the air with flying sand, slicing the drowsy sentries in half. Their gore mixed with the sand, spattering the wall behind them with red mud, but only until the ravening fury of the energy gun ripped into that wall in turn.

Stone dust billowed. Chips of brick and cement rattled like hail, and Tamman swept his beam like a hose, spraying destruction across the compound while the energy gun heated dangerously in his hands. Tamman was a powerful man, a tall, disciplined mass of bone and muscle, for he'd known he would never have a full implant set. Fanatical exercise had been his way of compensating for that deprivation, and it was the only reason he could use even this cut-down energy gun. It was heavier than most Terran-made crewed weapons, but still lighter than a full-sized Imperial weapon, and most of the weight saved had come out of its heat dissipation systems. It was far less durable, and the demands he was making upon it were ruinous, but he held the stud down, flaying the compound.

The outer wall went down and the closest building fronts exploded in dust and flying shards of glass. Light sparked and spalled, fountaining sparks as broken electric cables cracked like whips. Small fires started, and still the energy blasted into the buildings. It sheared through structural members like tissue, and the upper floors began an inexorable collapse.

A harsh buzz from the gun warned of the imminent failure of its abused, lightweight circuitry, and Tamman released the stud at last.

The high, dreadful keening of the wounded floated on the night wind, and the slither and crash of collapsing buildings rumbled in the darkness. Half-clothed figures darted madly, their frantic confusion evident through the attack team's low-light optics. Black Mecca's surveillance systems still reported nothing, and the terrible near-silence of the energy gun only added to their bewilderment, but the true nightmare had scarcely begun.

Three shoulder-slung grav guns opened fire, raking the compound across the wreckage of the outer wall. The sound of their firing was no more than a loud, sibilant hiss, lost in the whickering "cracks" of their supersonic projectiles, and there was no muzzle flash. Most of the deadly darts were inert, this time, but every fifth round was explosive. More of Black Mecca died or blew apart or collapsed screaming, and then the grenade launchers opened up.

There were no explosions, for these were Imperial warp grenades, and the principle upon which they worked was terrible in its dreadful elegance. They were small hyper generators, little larger than a large man's fist, and as each grenade landed it became the center of a ten-meter multi-dimensional transposition field. Anything within that spherical area of effect simply vanished into hyperspace with a hand-clap of imploding air . . . forever.

Chunks of pavement and broken stone disappeared quietly into eternity, and the screaming terrorists went mad. Men and, infinitely worse, *parts* of men went with those grenades, and the near-total silence of the carnage was more than they could stand. They stampeded and ran, dying as the grav guns continued to fire, and then the madness of the night reached its terrible climax as Amanda Givens fired her own weapon at last.

Noon-day light splashed the moonless sky as she dropped a plasma grenade among their enemies and, for one dreadful moment, the heart of the sun itself raged unchecked. It was pure, stone-fusing energy, consuming the very air, and thermal radiation lashed out from the center of destruction. It caught its victims mercilessly, turning running figures into torches, touching wreckage to flame, blinding the unwary who looked directly at it.

And when the fiery glare vanished as abruptly as it had come, the attack ended. The hissing roar of flames and the screams of their own maimed and dying were all the world the handful of surviving terrorists had, and the smoke that billowed heavenward was heavy with the stench of burning flesh.

The seven executioners faded silently away. Their stealthed cutter collected them forty minutes later.

Lieutenant General Gerald Hatcher frowned as he studied the classified folder, but his frown turned wry for a moment as he considered the absurdity of classifying something the entire planet was buzzing over.

His amusement faded as quickly as it had come, and he leaned back in his swivel chair, lips pursed as he considered.

The . . . peculiar events of the past few weeks had produced a massive ground swell of uncertainty, and the "unscheduled vacations" of a surprising number of government, industry, and economic leaders had not helped settle the public's mind. To an extent, those disappearances had been quite helpful to Hatcher, for the vanished leaders included most of the ones he'd expected to protest his unauthorized, unsanctioned, and quite possibly illegal attacks on terrorist enclaves. He did not, however, find their absence reassuring.

He drummed his fingers on his blotter and wished—not for the first time—that he'd been less quick to order Hector MacMahan to disappear . . . not that his instructions could have made too much difference to Hector's plans. Still, he wanted, more than he'd ever wanted anything in his life, to spend a few minutes listening to Hector explain this insanity.

One thing was abundantly clear: the best of humanity's so-called experts had no idea how whatever was happening was being done. Their best explanation of that new, deep crater outside Cuernavaca was a meteor strike, but no one had put it forward very seriously. Even leaving aside the seismographic proof that it had resulted from *multiple* strikes and its impossibly precise point of impact, it was inconceivable that something that size could have burned its way through atmosphere without anyone even seeing it coming!

Then there were those unexplained nuclear explosions out over the Pacific. At least they had a fair idea how nuclear weapons worked, but who had used them upon whom? And what about those strikes in China and the Tatra Mountains? Those had been air strikes, whatever Cuernavaca might have been, but no one had explained how the aircraft in question had evaded look-down radar, satellite reconnaissance, and plain old human eyesight.

Hatcher had no firm intel on Fenyang, but the Gerlocho-voko strike had used "conventional" explosives, though the analysts' best estimate of the warhead yields had never come from any chemical explosive *they* knew anything about, and the leftover bits and pieces of pulverized alloy and crystal had never come from any Terran tech base.

Now this. Abeokuta, Beirut, Damascus, Kuieyang, Mirzapur, Tehran. . . . Someone was systematically hitting terrorist bases, the dream targets no Western military man had ever hoped to hit, and gutting them. *And* they were doing it with more of the damned weapons his people had never even heard of!

Except for Hector, of course. Hatcher was absolutely certain Hector not only knew what was happening but also had played a not inconsiderable part in arranging for it to happen. That was more than mildly disturbing, considering the security checks Colonel MacMahan had undergone, his outstanding record as an officer, and the fact that he was one of Gerald Hatcher's personal friends.

One thing was crystal clear, though no one seemed inclined to admit it. Whoever had gone to war against Earth's terrorists hadn't come from Earth, not with the things they were capable of doing. Which led to all sorts of other maddening questions. Who were they? Where *had* they come from? Why were they here? Why hadn't they announced themselves to the human race in general?

Hatcher couldn't answer any of those questions. Perhaps he never would be able to, but he didn't think it would work out that way, for the evidence, fragmentary as it was, suggested at least one other unpalatable fact. At least two factions were locked in combat, and one or the other was going to win, eventually.

He closed the folder, buzzing for his aide to return it to the vault. Then he sighed and stood looking out his office windows.

Oh, yes. One side was going to win, and when they did, they were going to make their presence felt. Openly felt, that was, for Hatcher was morally certain that they'd *already* made themselves at home. It would explain so much. The upsurge in terrorism, the curious unwillingness of First World governments to do much about it, those mysterious "vacations," Hector's obvious involvement with at least one faction of what *had* to be extraterrestrials. . . .

All the selective destruction could mean only one thing: a covert war was spilling over into the open, and it was being fought on Hatcher's planet. The whole damned Earth was holding its collective breath, waiting to see who won, and they didn't even know who was doing the fighting!

But Hatcher suspected that, like him, most of those uncertain billions prayed to God nightly for the side that was trashing the terrorists. Because if the side that *backed* people like Black Mecca won, this planet faced one hell of a nightmare. . . .

Colonel Hector MacMahan sat in his office aboard his people's single warship, and studied his own reports. His eyes ached from watching the old-fashioned phosphor screen, and he felt a brief, bitter envy of the Imperials about him. It wasn't the first time he'd envied their neural feeds and computer shunts.

He leaned back and massaged his temples. Things were going well, but he was uneasy. He always was when an op was under way, but this was worse than usual. Something was nagging at a corner of his brain, and that frightened him. He'd heard that taunting voice only infrequently, for he was good at his job and serious mistakes were few, but he recognized it. He'd forgotten something, miscalculated somewhere, made some unwarranted assumption . . . *something*. And his subconscious knew what it was, he reflected grimly; the problem was how to drive it up into his forebrain.

He sighed and closed his eyes, allowing his face to show the worry he showed to neither subordinates nor superiors, but he couldn't pin it down. So far, their losses had been incredibly light: a single Imperial and five of their own Terra-born. No Imperial, however young, could have survived a lucky burst from a thirty-millimeter cannon, but Tarhani should never have been permitted to lead the Beirut raid at her age. Yet she'd been adamant. She'd hated that city for over fifty years, ever since a truck bomb blew her favorite grandson into death along with two hundred of his fellow Marines.

He shook his head. Revenge was a motivation professionals sought to avoid, far less accepted as a reason for assigning other personnel to high-risk missions. But not this time. Win or lose, this was *Nergal's* final campaign, and 'Hani had been right: she *was* old. If someone were to die leading the attack, better that it should be her than one of the children. . . .

Yet MacMahan knew there was another factor. For all his training and experience, all the hard-won competence with which he'd planned and mounted this operation, he was a child. It had always been so. A man among men among the Terra-born; a child—in years, at least—when he boarded *Nergal*.

The Imperials were careful to avoid emphasizing that point, and he knew they accepted him as an equal, but *he* couldn't accept *them* as equals. He knew what people like Horus and 'Hani, Geb and Hanalat, 'Tanni and Tamman, had seen and endured, and he felt a deep, almost sublime respect for them, but respect was only part of his complicated feelings. He knew their weaknesses, knew this entire situation arose from mistakes *they* had made, yet he venerated them. They were his family, his ancestors, the ancient, living avatars of the cause to which he'd dedicated his life. He'd known how much the Beirut mission meant to 'Hani . . . that was the real reason he'd let her lead it.

But that got him no closer to recognizing whatever that taunting little voice was trying to tell him about.

He rose and switched off his terminal. One other thing he'd learned about that voice; letting it mesmerize him was worse than ignoring it. A few more raids on Anu's peripheral links to Terra's terrorists, and it would be time for Operation Stalking-Horse, the ostensible reason for winding down the violence.

He was a bit surprised by how glad that made him. The northerners' targets were terrorists, but they were also humans, of a sort, and their slaughter weighed upon his soul. Not because of what they were, but because of what it was doing to his own people . . . and to him.

"It seems to me," Jantu said thoughtfully, "that we ought to be thinking of some way to respond to these attacks."

He paused to sip coffee, watching Anu from the corner of one eye, and only long practice kept his smile from showing as the "Chief" glared at Ganhar. Poor, harried Ganhar was about to become poor, dead Ganhar, for there was no way he *could* respond, and Jantu waited expectantly for him to try to squirm out of his predicament.

But Ganhar had himself well in hand. He met Jantu's eyes almost blandly, and something about his expression suddenly bothered the Security head. He had not quite put a mental finger on it when Ganhar shattered all his calculations.

"I agree," he said calmly, and Jantu choked on his coffee. Fortunately for his peace of mind, he was too busy dabbing at the coffee stains on his tunic to notice the slight smile in Commander Inanna's eyes.

"Oh?" Anu eyed Ganhar sharply, his eyes hard. "That's nice, Ganhar, considering the mess you've made of things so far."

"With all due respect, Chief," Ganhar sounded far calmer than Jantu knew he could possibly be, "*I* didn't get us into this situation. I only inherited Operations after Kirinal was killed. In the second place, I warned you from the start I was unhappy about how quiet the degenerate militaries were being *and* that we had no way of knowing what their Imperials were going to do next." He shrugged. "My people gave you all the information there was, Chief. There simply wasn't enough to predict what was coming."

Anu glared at him, and Ganhar made himself meet that glare levelly.

"You mean," Anu said dangerously, "that you didn't *spot* the information."

"No, I mean it wasn't there. You've had eight Operations heads in the last two thousand years, Chief—nine, counting me—and none of us have found *Nergal* for you. You know how hard we've worked at it. But if we can't even *find* them, how are we supposed to know what's going on in their inner councils? All I'm trying to say is that we can't do it."

"It sounds to me," Anu's soft voice rose steadily towards even more dangerous levels, "like you're trying to cover your ass. It sounds to *me* like you're making piss-poor excuses because you don't have one Maker-damned idea what to do about it!"

"You're wrong, Chief," Ganhar said, though it took most of his remaining courage to get it out. Anu wasn't accustomed to being told he was wrong, and his face took on an apoplectic hue as Ganhar continued, taking advantage of the pregnant silence. "I *do* have a plan, as it happens. Two, in fact."

Anu's breath escaped in a hiss. His minions seldom took that calm, almost challenging tone with him, and the shock of hearing it broke through his anger. Maybe Ganhar really had enough of a plan to justify his apparent confidence. If not, he could be killed just as well after listening to him as before.

"All right," he grated. "Tell us."

"Of course. First and simplest, we can do nothing at all. We've got our people under cover now, and all they're managing to do is tear up a bunch of purely degenerate terrorists. It makes a lot of noise, and it may look impressive to them, but, fundamentally, they aren't hurting *us*. We can always recruit more of the same, and every time they use Imperial technology, *they* risk losing people and *we* have a chance of tracking them back to *Nergal*."

Ganhar watched Anu's eyes. He knew—as, surely, Jantu and Inanna did—that what he'd just suggested was the smart thing to do. Unfortunately, Anu's eyes told him it wasn't the smart thing to *suggest*. He shrugged mentally and dusted off his second proposal.

"That's the simplest thing, but I don't think it's necessarily the best," he lied. "We know some of their degenerates, and we've spotted some others who *could* be working for them." He shrugged again, this time physically. "All right, if they want to escalate, we've got more people and a lot more resources. Let's escalate right back."

"Ah?" Anu raised an eyebrow, his expression arrested.

"Exactly, Chief. They surprised us at Colorado Springs, and they've been riding the advantage of surprise ever since. They've been on the offensive, and so far it's only cost them a few dozen degenerate military types in attacks on domestic terrorists and *maybe*—" he emphasized the qualifier "—one or two of their own people since they've started going after foreign bases on the ground. They're probably feeling pretty confident about now, so let's kill a few of their people and see if they get the message."

He smiled unpleasantly and tried not to sigh in relief as Anu smiled back. He watched the chief mutineer's slow nod, then swiveled his eyes challengingly to Jantu, enjoying the angry frustration in the Security man's expression.

"How?" Anu's voice was soft, but his eyes were eager.

"We've already made a start, Chief. My people are trying to predict their next targets so we can put a few of our own teams in positions to intervene. After that, we can start hitting suspects direct. Give 'em a taste of their own medicine, you might say."

"I like it, Chief," Inanna said softly. Anu glanced at her, and she shrugged. "At the least, it'll keep them from having things all their own way, and, with luck, we may actually get a few of their Imperials. Every one they lose is going to hurt them far worse than the same loss would hurt us."

"I agree," Anu said, and Ganhar felt as if the weight of the planet had been lifted from his back. "Maker,

Ganhar! I didn't think you had it in you. Why didn't you suggest this sooner?"

"I thought it would have been premature. We didn't know how serious an attack they meant to mount. If it was only a probe, a powerful response might actually have encouraged them to press harder in retaliation."

And wasn't *that* a mouthful of nothing, Ganhar thought sourly. But Anu's smile grew.

"I see. Well, get it in the works. Let's send a few of them and their precious degenerates to the Breaker and see how they like that!"

Ganhar smiled back. Actually, he thought, except for the possibility of ambushing the other side's raiding parties it was the stupidest thing he'd ever suggested. Almost every degenerate his people had suspected of being among *Nergal's* henchmen had already vanished as completely as Hector MacMahan. He'd target his remaining suspects first, but after that he might as well pick targets at random. Aside from the satisfaction Anu might take from it, they would accomplish exactly nothing, however many degenerates they blew away.

It was insane and probably futile, but Inanna had been right. The violence of the plan obviously appealed to Anu, and that was what mattered. As long as Anu was convinced Ganhar was Doing Something, Ganhar would hang onto his position and the perquisites that went with it. Like breathing.

"Let me have a preliminary plan as soon as possible, Ganhar," Anu said, addressing the Operations head more courteously than he had since Cuernavaca. Then he nodded dismissal, and his three subordinates rose to leave.

Jantu was in a hurry to get back to his office, but Inanna blocked him in the corridor, apparently by accident, as she turned to Ganhar.

"Oh, Ganhar," she said, "I'm afraid I have some bad news for you."

"Oh?"

Jantu paused as Ganhar spoke. He wanted to hear anything that was trouble for Ganhar, he thought viciously.

"Yes. One of your people got caught in a malfunction

in *Bislaht*'s transit shaft—a freak grav surge. We didn't think she was too badly hurt when they brought her into sickbay, but I'm afraid we were wrong. I'm sorry to say one of my med techs missed a cerebral hemorrhage, and we lost her."

"Oh." There was something strange about Ganhar's voice. He didn't sound surprised enough, and there was an odd, sick little undertone. "Uh, who was it?" he asked after a moment.

"Bahantha, I'm afraid," Inanna said, and Jantu froze. He stared at Inanna in disbelief, and she turned slowly to meet his eyes. Something gleamed in the depths of her own gaze, and he swallowed, filled with a sudden dread suspicion.

"I see it's shaken you, too, Jantu," she said softly. "Terrible, isn't it? Even here in the enclave, you can't be entirely safe, can you?"

And she smiled.

Chapter Eighteen

"God damn them! Damn them to Hell!"

Hector MacMahan's normally expressionless face twisted with fury. His clenched fists trembled at his sides, and Colin looked away from the colonel, sick at heart himself, to study the other three people at the table.

Horus looked shaken and ill, like a man trapped in a horrifying nightmare, and Isis sat silently, frail shoulders bowed. Her lashes were wet, and she stared blindly down at the age-delicate hands folded in her lap.

Jiltanith was expressionless, her relaxed hands folded quietly on the table, but her eyes were deadly. Neither group of Imperials had operated so openly during her subjective lifetime, and though she might have accepted the possibility of such a response intellectually, she hadn't really imagined it as a *probability*. Now it had happened, and Colin felt the fury radiating from her . . . and the focused strength of will it took to control it.

And how did he feel? He considered that for a moment, and decided Hector had just spoken for him, as well.

"All right," he said finally. "We knew they weren't exactly stable, and they've given plenty of past examples of their willingness to do things like this. We should have anticipated what they'd do."

"*I* should have anticipated it, you mean," MacMahan said bitterly.

"I said 'we' and I meant 'we.' The strategy was yours, Hector, but we were all involved in the planning, and the Council approved it. We figured if they knew we were hitting them, *we*'d be the targets they chose to strike back at. It was a logical estimate, and we all shared it."

" 'Tis true, Hector," Jiltanith said softly. "This plan was product of us all, not thine alone." She smiled bitterly. "And did not we twain counsel Colin madmen yet might dismay us all? Take not more guilt upon thyself than is thy due."

"All right." MacMahan drew a deep breath and sat. "Sorry."

"We understand," Colin said. "But right now, just tell us how bad it is."

"I suppose it could be worse. They've gotten about thirty of our Terra-born—seven at once when they hit that Valkyrie at Corpus Christi; Vlad Chernikov would've made eight, and he may still lose his arm unless we can break him out of the hospital and get him into *Nergal*'s sickbay—but our own losses haven't been that high. Most of the people they've slaughtered are exactly what they seem to be: ordinary citizens.

"The death toll from the Eden Two mass missile strike is about eighteen thousand. That was a pay-back for Cuernavaca, I suppose. The bomb at Goddard got another two hundred. The nuke they smuggled into Klyuchevskaya leveled the facilities, but the loss of life was minimal thanks to the 'terrorists' ' phoned-in warning. Sandhurst and West Point were Imperial weaponry—warp grenades and energy guns. I imagine they were retaliation for Tehran and Kuiyeng. The Brits lost about three hundred people; the Point lost about five."

He paused and shrugged unhappily.

"It's a warning to back off, and I—we—should have seen it coming. It's classic terrorist thinking, and it fits right into Anu's own sick mentality."

"Agreed. The question is, what do we do about it? Horus?"

"I don't know," Horus said in a flat voice. "I'd like to say shut down. We've hurt them worse than we ever did before. We'd have to shut down pretty soon, anyway, and too many people are getting killed. I don't think I can take another bloodbath." He looked at his hands and spoke with difficulty.

"This isn't a drop in the bucket compared to Genghis Khan or Hitler, but it's still too much. It's happening all over again, and this time *we* started it, Maker help us. Can't we stop sooner than we planned?" He turned desperate eyes to Hector and Jiltanith. "I know we all agreed we needed Stalking-Horse, but haven't we done them enough damage for our purposes?"

"Isis?"

"I have to agree with Dad," Isis said softly. "Maybe I'm too close to it because of Cal and the girls, but . . ." She paused, and her lips trembled. "I . . . just don't want to be responsible for any more slaughter, Colin."

"I understand," he said gently, then looked at her sister. "Jiltanith?"

"There's much in what thou sayst, Father, and thou, Isis," Jiltanith said quietly, "yet if we do halt our actions all so swift upon his murders, wi' no loss of our own, may we not breed suspicion? If e'er doubt there was, there is no longer: Anu and his folk have run full mad. Yet in their madness lurketh danger, for 'tis most unlike they'll take a sane man's view o'things.

"Full sorely ha' we smote his folk. Now ha' they dealt us buffets in return, and 'tis in my mind that e'en now they watch us close, hot to scent our stomach for this work. And if but so little blood—for so know we all Anu will see it—and it not ours stoppeth up our blows, may not doubt hone sharp the wit of one so cunning, be he e'er so mad? Be risk of that howe'er small, yet risk there still must be. 'Twas 'gainst that very danger Stalking-Horse was planned." She met her father's pleading eyes.

"Truth maketh bitter bread i'such a pass," her voice was even softer, "but whate'er our hearts may tell us, i'coldest truth it mattereth but little how many lives Anu may spend. Their blood is innocent. 'Twill haunt us all our whole lives long. Yet if we fail, then all compassion may ha' spared will live but till such time as come the Achuultani. 'Tis in my mind we durst not cease—not yet, a while. Some few attacks more, then turn to Stalking-Horse as was the plan, would be my counsel."

Colin nodded slowly as he recognized her anguish. Her eyes were hooded, armoring the torment her own words had given her, and behind her barricaded face, he knew, she was seeing countless, nameless men, women, and children she had never met. Yet she was right. That the blood that would be shed was innocent would mean nothing to Anu. Might he not assume it meant less to *them* than the lives of their own people?

They couldn't know that, but Jiltanith had the resolution to face the possibility and the moral courage to voice it.

"Thank you," he said. "Hector?"

" 'Tanni's right," Hector sighed unhappily. "I wish to God she weren't, but that won't change it. We can't *know* how Anu will react, but everything we do know points to a man who hurts people for the pleasure of it and regards all 'degenerates' as expendable. *He* wouldn't stop because some of them were getting killed; if we do, he may just ask himself why, and that's the one question we can't afford for him to ask."

He stared at the table, pressing his clenched fists together on its top.

"I hate the thought of provoking massacres—or even a single death more than may be absolutely necessary—but if we miscalculate and stop too soon, all the people who've already died will have been killed for absolutely nothing."

"I agree," Colin said heavily. "We have to convince them, in terms *they* can accept, that they've *made* us stop. Go ahead with the set-up for Stalking-Horse, Hector. See if you can't compress the time frame, but do it."

"I will." MacMahon rose, and only Imperial ears could have heard his last words as he left the room.

"God forgive me," he whispered.

Ninhursag sat on the bench and concentrated on looking harmless. The enclave's central park struck her as crude and unfinished beside her memories of *Dahak's* recreation areas, and she filed the observation away with all the others she'd made since her return from the outside world. The sum of those observations was almost as disturbing, in its way, as the day she awakened to learn what Anu had been doing to her fellow mutineers.

She managed not to shudder as a tall, slender man walked by. Tanu, she thought. Once she'd known him well, but he was no longer Tanu. She didn't know which of Anu's lieutenants had claimed his body, and she didn't want to find out. It was bad enough watching him walk around and knowing he was dead.

She looked away, thinking. There was an unfinished feeling to the entire enclave, like a temporary camp, not a habitation. Anu and his followers had lived on this planet for fifty thousand years, yet they'd never come to belong here. It was as if they deliberately sought to preserve their awareness of the alien about them. There were comfortable blocks of apartments here under the ice, built immediately after their landing, but no more had been built since and virtually none of the mutineers used the ones that existed. They'd retreated back into their ships, clinging to their quarters aboard the transports despite their cramped size. For herself, Ninhursag knew she would have gone mad long ago if she'd been confined to such quarters for so long.

She watched the spray of one of the very few tinkling fountains anyone had bothered to build and considered that. Perhaps that was part of the miasma of madness drifting in the air. These people had far outlived their allotted lifespans penned up inside their artificial environment but for occasional jaunts outside. Their stolen bodies were young and strong, but the personalities inhabiting them were *old*, and the enclave was a pressure-cooker.

By their very nature, most of Anu's people had been flawed or they would not have been here, and over the endless years of exile, closeted within this small world, their minds had turned inward. They'd been alone with their hates and ambitions and resentments longer than human minds were designed to stand, and what had been flaws had become yawning fissures. The best of them were distorted caricatures of what they had been, while the worst . . .

She shuddered and hoped none of the security scanners had noticed.

Theirs was a dead society, decaying from its core. They wouldn't admit it—assuming they could even recognize it—yet the truth was all about them. Five thousand years they'd been awake, yet they'd added absolutely nothing to their tech base beyond a handful of highly personal modifications to ways of spying on or killing one another. They were only a small population, but it was the nature of societies to change, to learn new things. A culture that didn't was doomed; if an outside force didn't destroy it, its own members turned upon one another within the static womb to which they had returned. Whether or not they could admit or recognize their stagnation was ultimately unimportant, for deep inside, where the life forces and the drive of a people came together out of emotion and beliefs they might never have formalized, they *knew* they were spinning their wheels, marking time . . . dying.

Ninhursag's eyes were open now, and she saw it in so many things. The suspicion, the ambition, the perversions of a degenerate age that *knows* it is degenerate. And, perhaps most tellingly of all, there were no children. These people were no celibates, but they had deliberately renounced the one thing that might have forced them to change and evolve. And with it, they'd cut themselves off from their own human roots. Like a woman barren with age, their biological clock had stopped, and with it had died their sense of themselves as a living, ever-renewed species.

Why had they done that to themselves? They were—had been—Imperials, and the Imperium had known that even a single quarter-century deployment aboard a ship like *Dahak* required that sense of vitality and renewal among its crewmen. Even those who had no children could see the children of others, and so share in the flow of their species. But Anu's people had chosen to forget, and she could not understand it.

Had their stolen immortality made children irrelevant? Or did they fear producing a generation foreign to their own twisted purpose? One that might rebel against them? She didn't know. She *couldn't* know, for they had become a different species—a dark, malevolent shadow that wore the bodies of her people but was not hers.

She rose, walking slowly across the park towards the building in which she had half-defiantly made her own quarters, aware of the way her shadowing keeper followed her. He didn't even bother to be unobtrusive, but it had helped to know exactly where the security man assigned to watch her might be found.

She glanced idly at the gawking Terra-born who shared the park with her, noting their awe at the environment that seemed so crude to her, and wondered which of them would collect the record chip she'd hidden under her bench.

Abu al-Nasir watched Ninhursag walk away, then ambled over to the bench she'd occupied. The soaring, vaulted ceiling of the park, with its projected roof of summer-blue sky and fleecy clouds was amazing. It was hard to believe he was buried under hundreds of meters of ice and stone. The illusion of being outside was almost perfect, and perhaps the looming, bronze-toned hulls thrusting up beyond the buildings helped to make it so.

He sat down and leaned back, watching idly for the security scanners Colonel MacMahan had described to him. There they were—nicely placed to watch the bench, but only from the front. That was handy.

He let one hand drop down beside him, about where his holster normally rode. Sergeant Asnani had never felt any particular need to be armed at every moment; Abu al-Nasir felt undressed without his personal arsenal. Still, it was hardly surprising the mutineers declined to permit their henchmen weapons.

Not surprising, yet it underscored the difference between them and their allies and the way *Nergal*'s crew worked with their own Terra-born. He'd never visited *Nergal*, but he'd trained among her Terra-born, and he knew Colonel MacMahan. The colonel was no man's flunky—the very thought was absurd—yet any of his Imperial allies would have trusted him behind them with a gun.

But al-Nasir had already concluded that everything the colonel had told him about *these* Imperials was the truth. Since his initiation into Black Mecca, al-Nasir had become accustomed to irrationality. Extremism, hatred, greed, sadism, fanaticism, megalomania, disregard for human life ... he'd know them all, and he recognized something very like them here. Less bare-fanged and snarling, but perhaps even more evil because of that. And these people truly regarded themselves as a totally different species, simply because of the artificial enhancement of their own bodies ... and their ability to torment and kill the Terra-born.

The sense of *ancientness* behind those comely, youthful faces was frightening, and al-Nasir was glad there were no children. The thought of what any child who breathed this poisoned atmosphere must become turned his stomach, and it was no longer a stomach that turned easily.

His relaxed hand crooked casually, stroking the wooden bench absently, and his eyelids drooped as he listened to the tinkle and splash of the fountain. His entire body was eloquently if unobtrusively relaxed, and his fingers stroked more slowly, as if the idle thoughts that moved them were slowing.

He touched the tiny, barely discernible dot of the message chip, and his forefinger moved. The chip slid up under his nail, invisible under the thin sheet of horn, and no flicker of triumph crossed his face. If the colonel was wrong about Ninhursag, he was a dead man, but no sign of that showed, either.

He let his hand continue stroking for a few moments, then laid his forearm negligently along the armrest. Every nerve in his lax body screamed to stand up, to walk away from the drop site, but this was a game he'd learned to play well, and he settled even more comfortably on the bench.

About an hour, he thought. A short, restoring nap, utterly innocent, totally unconcealed, and then he could leave. His eyes closed fully, his head lolled back, and Abu al-Nassir began to snore.

The city of La Paz dreamed under an Argentine moon, and the streets were emptying as Shirhansu sat by the window and stroked her ash-blonde hair.

Even after all these years, she still found it difficult to accept that her pale-skinned hand was "hers," that the aqua eyes that looked back from any mirror belonged to her. It was a lovely body, far more beautiful than the one she'd been born to, but it marked her as one outside the inner circle. Yet it also set her aside from the odd—to Terran eyes—appearance of the Imperial race, and that could be invaluable.

She sighed and shifted the energy gun across her lap, wishing yet again that they could have worn combat armor. It was out of the question, of course. Stealth fields could do a lot, but if the enemy operated unarmored or, even worse, were entirely Terra-born, they would be mighty hard to spot, and armor, however carefully hidden, could be picked up by people without it long before her own scanner teams could pick *them* up, so she had to strip down herself.

This was a stupid mission. She was glad to have it instead of one of the other operations—she was no Girru and took no pleasure from slaughtering degenerates in job lots—but it was still stupid. Suppose she *did* manage to surprise some of *Nergal's* crowd. They would never let themselves lead her back to the battleship. Even if she managed to follow them, it stood to reason that whatever auxiliary picked them up would carry out a careful scan before it made rendezvous, and when it did, it would spot her people however carefully they were stealthed. That auxiliary would undoubtedly be armed, too, and was there any fighter cover for her people? Of course not. The limited supply of fighter crews was being tasked with offensive strikes ... aside from the fifty percent reserve Anu insisted on retaining to cover the enclave, though what he expected *Nergal's* people to accomplish against its shield eluded Shirhansu.

Of course, she did suffer from one little handicap when it came to understanding the "Chief." Her brain still worked.

Which also explained why she was so unhappy at the prospect of trying to follow one of *Nergal's* teams. Their efficiency to date had been appalling, even allowing for the purely Terran nature of most of their targets, not that it surprised Shirhansu. She'd developed a deep if grudging respect for her enemies over the centuries, for the casualty figures were far less one-sided than they should be. They'd survived everything her own group had thrown at them from the lofty advantage of its superior tech base and managed—somehow—to keep their HQ completely hidden; they weren't bloody likely to screw up now.

The whole idea was foolish, but she knew why the mission had been mounted anyway, and she approved of anything that kept Ganhar alive and in control of Operations, for she was one of his faction. Joining him had seemed like a good idea at the time—certainly he was far closer to sane than Kirinal had been!—but she'd been having second thoughts recently. Still, Ganhar seemed to be making a recovery, and if her presence here could help him, then it also helped *her*, and that ...

Her hand-held security com gave a soft, almost inaudible chime. She raised it to her ear, and her eyes widened.

Ganhar's analysts had called it right; the bastards *were* going to hit *Los Puñas*!

She spoke succinctly into the com, hoping her own stealth field would hide the fold-space pulse as it was supposed to, then checked her weapon. She set it for ten percent power—there was no armor inside the approaching stealth fields, and there was no point blowing too deep a hole in the pavement—and opened a slit in her stealth field, freeing her implants to scan a narrow field before her while the field still hid her from flanks and rear.

Tamman followed Amanda along the sidewalk, as invisible as the wind. He felt more at home than he had in Tehran, but his enhanced senses could do more good watching her back than probing the darkness before her, and she'd convinced him of the virtue of keeping the commander out of the forefront.

He let a scowl twist his lips. The massacre of innocents continued and, if anything, had accelerated. Eden Two remained the worst single atrocity, but there were others. Shepherd Center's security people had stood off an assault, but their casualties had been high. Still, Tamman was certain the attackers had been under orders to withdraw rather than press the attack fully home. Anu wouldn't want to damage the aerospace industry too badly, and the fact that what had to be full Imperials equipped with energy guns and warp grenades had been "driven off" by Terra-born infantry, however good, armed only with Terran weapons was as good as a floodlit sign.

Yet that was the only southern attack that had been resisted, if that was the word for it, and the casualty count was starting to trouble his dreams. Watching World War One's trenches and World War Two's extermination camps had been horrifying, and Phnom Penh had been even worse, in its way. Afghanistan and the interminable, fanatical bloodletting between Iran and Iraq in the 'eighties had been atrocious, and the Kananga massacres in Zaire had been pretty bad, too, but this sort of desecration wasn't something a man could become used to, however often he saw it.

Los Puñas—"The Daggers"—were pussy cats compared to Black Mecca, but they'd been positively identified running Anu's errands. He wouldn't like it a bit if they were pulverized, and it would be satisfying to wipe them out. Tamman wouldn't even try to pretend otherwise, but it would be even nicer to see a few of Anu's butchers in his sights.

"Get ready," Shirhansu whispered. "Take 'em when they reach the plaza."

"Take them? I thought we were supposed to shadow them, 'Hansu." It was Tarban, her second in command, and Shirhansu scowled in the darkness.

"If any of them get away, we will," she growled, "but it's more important to nail a few of the bastards."

"But—"

"Shut up and get off the com before they pick it up!"

"Tamman, it's a trap!" The voice screaming into Tamman's left ear was Hanalat, their recovery pilot, who had been watching over them with her sensors. "I'm picking up a fold-space link ahead of you, at least two point sources! Get the hell out!"

"Gotcha," he grunted, thanking the Maker for Hector's suggestion that they carry Terran communications equipment. Hector had calculated that Anu's people would be looking primarily for Imperial technology, and he must have been right; Tamman had received the warning and he was still alive.

"All right, people," he said softly to his team, "let's ease out of here. Joe—" Joe Crynz, a distant cousin of Tamman's and the last man in line, carried a warp grenade launcher "—get ready to lay down covering fire. The rest of you, just ease on back. Let's get out quietly if we can."

There were no acknowledgments as his team came slowly to a halt and started drifting backward. Tamman held his breath, praying they would get away with it. They were naked down here, sitting ducks for—

"Breaker take you, Tarban!" Shirhansu snarled, and braced her energy gun on the window sill. She had the best vantage point of all her twenty people, and she could see only three of the bastards. Her senses—natural and implants alike—were alive through the slit in her stealth field, but *their* fields interfered badly. She couldn't make them out well enough for a sure kill at this range, but, thanks to Tarban, they weren't going to come any closer. "Take them now!" she ordered coldly over her com.

Tamman bit back a scream as an energy bolt flashed through the edge of his stealth field. His physical senses—boosted almost to max as he tried to work his team out of the trap—were a flare of agony in the beam's corona. But it had missed him, and he flung himself aside with the dazzling quickness of his enhanced reaction time.

Larry Clintock was less lucky; at least three snipers had taken him for a target. He never even had time to scream as energy blasts tore him apart . . . but Amanda did, and Tamman's blood ran cold as he heard her.

He sheltered automatically—and uselessly—behind a potted tree, and his enhanced vision caught the energy flare at an upper window. His own energy gun tore the window frame apart, spraying the street with broken bits of brick, and whoever had been firing opted for discretion, assuming he was still alive.

Joe's grenade launcher burped behind him, and a gaping hole appeared in another building front, but the other side had warp grenades as well. A huge chunk of paving vanished, water spurting like a fountain from a severed main, and Tamman hurled himself to his feet. He should flee to join Joe and the others, but his feet carried him forward to where Amanda's scream had ended in terrifying silence.

More bolts of disruption slashed at him, splintering the paving, but his own people knew what was happening. Their stealth fields were in phase with his, letting them see him, and they spread out under whatever cover they could find while their weapons raked the buildings fronting on the plaza. They were shooting blind, but they were throwing a lot of fire, and he was peripherally aware of the grav gun darts chewing at stonework, the shivering pulsations of warp grenades, and the susuration of more energy guns trying to mark him down.

Amanda's left thigh was a short, ugly stump, but no blood pulsed from the wound. Her Imperial commando smock had fastened down in an automatic tourniquet as soon as she was hit, yet she was no Imperial, and she was unconscious from shock—or dead. His mind flinched away from the possibility, and he scooped her up in a fireman's carry and sprinted back up the street.

Devastation lashed at his heels, and he cried out in agony as an energy beam tore a quarter pound of flesh from the back of one leg. He nearly went down, but his own implants—partial though they were—damped the pain as quickly as it had come. Tissues sealed themselves, and he ran on frantically.

A warp grenade's field missed him by centimeters, the rush of displaced air snatching at him like an invisible demon, and he heard another scream as an energy gun found Frank Cauphetti. He spared a glance as he went by, but Frank no longer had a torso.

Then he was around the corner, his surviving teammates closing in about him, and the four of them were dashing through the night.

"Shouldn't we follow them, 'Hansu?"

"Sure, Tarban, you do that little thing! You and your damn gabble just cost us a complete kill! Not to mention Hanshar—that bastard with the energy gun cut him in half. So, please, go right ahead and follow them . . . I'm sure their cutter pilot will be delighted to vaporize your worthless ass!"

There was silence over the com, and Shirhansu forced her rage back under control. Maker, they'd come so *close!* But at least they'd gotten two of them, maybe even three, and that was the best they'd done yet against an actual attack force. Not that it would be good enough to please Anu. Still, if they cleaned up their report a little bit first . . .

"All right," she sighed finally. "Let's get out of here before the locals get too nosy. Meet me at the cutter."

Chapter Nineteen

"How is she?"

Tamman looked up at Colin's soft question. He sat carefully, one leg extended to keep his thigh off his chair, and his face was worn with worry.

"They say she'll be all right." He reached out to the young woman in the narrow almost-bed, her lower body cocooned in the sophisticated appliances of Imperial medicine, and smoothed her brown hair gently.

"'All right,'" he repeated bitterly, "but with only one leg. *Maker*, it's unfair! Why *her*?!"

"Why anyone?" Colin asked sadly. He looked at Amanda Givens' pale, plain face and sighed. "At least you got her out alive. Remember that."

"I will. But if she had the biotechnics she deserves, she wouldn't be in that bed—and she could grow a new leg, too." He looked back down at Amanda. "It's not even their fault, yet they give so much, Colin. All of them do."

"All of *you* do," Colin corrected gently. "It's not as if you had anything to do with the mutiny either."

"But at least I got a child's biotechnics." Tamman's voice was very low. "She didn't get even that much. Hector didn't. My children didn't. They live their lives like candle flames, and then they're gone. So many of them." He smoothed Amanda's hair once more.

"We're trying to change that, Tamman. That's what she was doing."

"I know," the Imperial half-whispered.

"Then don't take that away from her," Colin said levelly. "Yes, she's Terra-born, just like I am, but I was drafted; she *chose* to fight, knowing the odds. She's not a child. Don't treat her like one, because that's the one thing she'll never forgive you for."

"How did you get so wise?" Tamman asked after a moment.

"It's in the genes, buddy," Colin said, and grinned more naturally as he left Tamman alone with the woman he loved.

Ganhar cocked back his chair and rested one heel on the edge of his desk. He'd just endured a rather stormy interview with Shirhansu, but, taken all in all, she was right—they'd been lucky to get *any* of *Nergal*'s people, and the odds were against doing it twice. Tarban's blathering com traffic had given them away this time, but now that the other side had walked into one trap, they damned well wouldn't walk into another. They'd cover any attacking force with active scanners powerful enough to burn through any portable stealth field.

He pondered unhappily, trying to decide what to recommend this time. The logical thing was to withdraw a few fighters from offensive sweeps and use them to nail any of *Nergal*'s cutters that came in with active scanners, but Ganhar had developed a lively respect for Hector MacMahan—who, he was certain, was masterminding this entire campaign. The equally logical response would be obvious to him: cover *Nergal*'s cutters with his own stealthed fighters to nail Ganhar's fighters when they revealed themselves by attacking the cutter.

The very idea reeked of further escalation, and he was

sick of it. They couldn't match his resources, but they
knew where they were going to strike, and they could
concentrate their forces accordingly; *he* had to cover all
the places they *might* strike. He couldn't have overwhelming force anywhere, unless Anu would let him back
off on offensive operations and smother all possible targets with their own fighters.

Which, of course, Anu would never do.

He rubbed his closed eyes wearily, and his thoughts
moved like a dirge. It was no good. Even if they managed
to locate *Nergal* and destroy her and all her people, there
was still Anu. Anu and all of them—even himself—and
their endless futility. Anu was mad, but was he much
better off himself? What did he think would happen if
they ever managed to leave this benighted planet?

Like Jantu, Ganhar had reached his own conclusions
about the Imperium's apparent disappearance from the
cosmos. If he was wrong, then they were all doomed.
The Imperium would never forgive them, for there could
be no clemency for such as they—not for mutineers, and
never for mutineers who'd gone on to do the things
they'd done to the helpless natives of Earth.

And if there was no more Imperium? In that far more
likely case, their fate might be even worse, for there
would still be Anu. Or Jantu. Or someone else. The madness had infected them all, for they'd lived too long and
feared death too much. Ganhar knew he was saner than
many of his fellows, and look what *he* had done in the
name of survival. He'd worked with Kirinal despite her
sadism, *knowing* about her sadism, and when he replaced
her, he'd devised this obscene plan merely to stay alive a
bit longer. She and Girru would have loved it, he thought
bitterly. This slaughter of defenseless degenerates . . .

No, not "degenerates." Primitives, perhaps, but not
degenerates, for it was he and his fellows who had degen-
erated. Once there might even have been a bit of glam-
our in daring to pit themselves against the Imperium's
might, but not in what they'd done to the people of Earth
and their own helpless fellows.

He stared down at the hands he had stolen, and his

stomach knotted. He didn't regret the mutiny or even the long, bitter warfare with *Nergal*'s crew. Or perhaps he *did* regret those things, but he wouldn't pretend he hadn't known what he was doing or whine and snivel before the Maker for it. But the other things, especially the things he had done as Operations head, sickened him.

But there was no way to undo them, or even stop them. If he tried, he would die, and even after all these years, he wanted to live. But the truly paralyzing thing was that even if he'd been willing to die, his death would accomplish nothing except, perhaps, to grant him a fleeting illusion of expiation. Even if he could bring himself to embrace that—and he was cynically uncertain he could—it would leave Anu behind. The madmen had the numbers, firepower, and tech base, and nothing *Nergal* and her people might achieve in the short-term could alter that.

Head of Operations Ganhar's hands clenched as he stared at them and wondered when he'd finally begun to crack. He'd seen the awakening of guilt in a few others. It usually happened slowly, and some had ended their long lives when it happened to them. Others had been spotted by Jantu's zealous minions and made examples, but there had never been many, and none had been able to do any more than Ganhar could.

He sighed and stood, walking slowly from his office. The futility of it all oppressed him, but he knew he would sit down at the conference table and tell Anu things were going according to plan. He might be coming to the realization that he despised himself for it, but he would do it, and there was no point pretending he wouldn't.

Ramman sat in his small apartment, gnawing his fingernails. His pastel-walled quarters were littered with unwashed clothing and dirty eating utensils, and his nostrils wrinkled with the smell of sour bedding. There were extra disadvantages in slovenliness for the sensory-enhanced.

He knew he was under surveillance and that his

strange behavior, his isolation from his fellows, was dangerously likely to attract the suspicion he could not afford, yet mounting terror and desperation paralyzed his ability to do anything about it. He felt like a rabbit in a snare, waiting for the trapper's return, and if he mingled with the others, they must see it.

He rose and walked jerkily about the room, the fingers of his clasped hands writhing together behind him. Madness. Jiltanith and her father had to be insane. They would fail, and their failure would betray the fact that someone had helped them by giving them the admittance codes. The witch hunt might sweep up the innocent, but would almost certainly trap the guilty, and *he* would be the guilty. He would be found out, arrested . . . killed.

It wasn't *fair!* But he'd been given his orders, and he had obeyed them. He'd planted the codes where he'd been told to. If he told anyone . . . he shuddered as he thought of Jantu and the unspeakable things perverted Imperial technology had been used to do to other "traitors."

If he kept quiet, told no one, he would at least live a little longer. At least until *Nergal's* people launched their doomed attack.

He sank back down on the edge of the bed and sobbed into his hands.

" 'Tis time for Stalking-Horse," Jiltanith said quietly. "That fact standeth proved by the fate which did befall Tamman's group. That and the slaughter which e'en now doth gain in horror do set the stage and gi' us pretext enow to cease when Stalking-Horse be added."

"Agreed," MacMahan said softly, and looked at Colin.

"Yes," Colin said. "It's time to stop this insanity. Is it set up?"

"Yes. I've scheduled Geb and Tamman to fly lead with Hanalat and Carhana as their wing."

"Nay," Jiltanith said, and MacMahan glanced at her in surprise, taken aback by the finality of her voice. "Nay," she repeated. "The lead is mine."

"No!" The strength of his own protest surprised Colin,

and Jiltanith met his eyes challengingly—not with the bitter, hateful challenge of old, but with a determination that made his heart sink.

"Tamman hath been wounded," she said reasonably.

"A flesh wound sickbay and his biotechnics have already taken care of almost completely," MacMahan said in the cautious tone of a man who knew he was edging into dangerous waters, if not exactly why they had become perilous.

"I speak not o' his flesh, Hector. Certes, 'twould be reason enow t' choose anew, yet 'tis his heart hath taken too sore a hurt. I ha' not seen him care for any as he doth for his Amanda, not since Himeko's death."

"We've all been hurt, 'Tanni," MacMahan protested.

"That's sooth," she agreed, "yet 'tis graver far in Tamman's case."

" 'Tanni, you can't go." Colin extended one hand to reach across the table. "You *can't*. You're the backup commander for *Dahak*."

He could have bitten off his tongue as he saw her dark eyes widen. But then they narrowed again and she cocked her head. It was a small gesture, but it demanded explanation.

"Well, I had to pick *someone*," he said defensively. "It couldn't be Horus or one of the older Imperials—they were *active* mutineers; I couldn't take a chance on how *Dahak*'s Alpha Priorities might work out if I'd tried that! So it had to be one of the children, and you were the logical choice."

"And thou didst not think fit to tell me of't?" she demanded, a curiously intent light replacing the surprise in her eyes.

"Well . . ." Colin's face flamed, and he darted an appealing glance at MacMahan, but the colonel only looked back impassively. "Maybe I should have. But it didn't seem like a good idea at the time."

"Whyfor not? Yea, and now I think on't, why didst thou not e'en tell a soul thou hadst named any one of all our number to follow thee in thy command?"

"Frankly . . . well, much as I wanted to trust you peo-

ple, I didn't know I could when I recorded *Dahak's*
orders. That's one reason I insisted on doing it myself,"
he said, and felt a rush of relief when she nodded
thoughtfully rather than flying into a rage.

"Aye, so much I well can see," she said softly. " 'Twas
in thy mind that so be we knew thou hadst named thine
own successor, then were we treason-minded we had
slain thee and had done?"

"That's about it," he admitted uncomfortably. "I don't
dare contact *Dahak* again, and he can't pick up my
implants on passive instrumentation. If I'd been wrong
about you and you'd known, you could have offed me
and told him I bought it from the southerners." He met
her eyes much more pleadingly than he had MacMahan's. "I didn't really think you'd do it, but with the
Achuultani coming and everything else going to hell, I
couldn't take the chance."

" 'Twas wiser in thee than e'er I thought to find," she
said, and he blinked in surprise as she smiled in white-
toothed approval. "God's Teeth, Colin—'twould seem we
yet may make a spook o' thee!"

"You *do* understand!"

"I ha' not played mistress to *Nergal's* spies these many
years wi'out the gaining o' some small wit," she said
dryly. " 'Twas but prudence on thy part. Yet still a question plagueth me. Whyfor choose me to second thee?
And if thou must make that choice, whyfor tell me not
e'en now? Surely there can be naught but trust betwixt
us wi' all that's passed sin then?"

"Well ..." He felt himself flushing again. "I wasn't
certain how you'd take it," he said finally. "We weren't
exactly ... on the best of terms, you know."

" 'Tis true," she admitted, and this time *she* blushed.
It was her turn to glance sidelong at MacMahan, who,
to his eternal credit, looked back with only the slightest
twinkle in his eyes. "Yet knowing that, thou wouldst still
ha' seen me in thy shoon?"

"I didn't intend to give my 'shoon' to anyone," he said
testily, "and I wouldn't've been around to see it if it

happened! But, yes, if it had to be someone, I picked you." He shrugged. "You were the best one for the job."

" 'Tis hard to credit," she murmured, "and 'twas lunacy or greater wit than I myself possess to gi' such a gift to one who hated thee so sore."

"Why?" he asked, his voice suddenly gentle. He met her gaze squarely, forgetting MacMahan's presence for a moment. "You can understand the precautions I felt I had to take—is it so hard to accept that *I* might understand the reasons you hated me, 'Tanni? Or not blame you for them?"

"Isis spake those self-same words unto me," Jiltanith said slowly, "and told me they did come from thee, yet no mind was I to hear her." She shook her head and smiled, the first truly gentle smile he had seen from her. "Thy heart is larger far than mine, good Colin."

"Sure," he said uncomfortably, trying to sound light. "Just call me Albert Schweitzer." Her smile turned into a grin, but gentleness lingered in her dark eyes. "Anyway," he added, "we're all friends now, aren't we?"

"Aye," she said firmly.

"Then there's an end to't, as you'd say. *And* the reason you can't fly the lead in Stalking-Horse. We can't risk losing you."

"Not so," she said instantly, her eyes shrewd. "Thou art not dead nor like to be, and 'twould be most unlike thee not to ha' named some other to follow me. Tamman, I'll warrant, or some other o' the children?"

He refused to answer, but she saw it in his eyes.

"Well, then, sobeit. Tamman is most unlike myself, good Colin. Thou knowest—far more than most—how well my heart can hate, but *my* hate burneth cold, not hot. Not so for him. He needeth still some time ere he may clear his mind, and Stalking-Horse can be no task for one beclouded."

"But—"

"She's right," MacMahan said quietly, and Colin glared reproachfully at him. The colonel shrugged. "I should've seen it myself. Tamman hasn't left sickbay since he carried Amanda into it. He'd go, but he needs time to settle down before he goes back out. And 'Tanni *is* our best pilot—you know that better than most, too. There's not supposed to be any fighting, but if there is, she's best equipped to handle it. We'll give her Rohantha for a weaponeer. They'll actually make a better team than Geb and Tamman."

"But—"

" 'Tis closed, Colin. 'Hantha and I will take the lead."

"Damn it, I don't *want* her up there in a goddamned pinnace, Hector!"

"That doesn't matter. 'Tanni and I are in charge of this operation—not you—and she's *right*. So shut up and soldier . . . sir!"

The admittance chime to Ganhar's private study sounded, and he looked up from the holo map he'd been updating as he ordered the hatch to open. It was late, and he half-expected to see Shirhansu, but it wasn't she, and his eyes narrowed in surprise as his caller stepped inside.

"Ramman?" He leaned back in his chair. "What can I do for you?"

"I . . ." The other man's eyes darted about like those of a trapped animal, and Ganhar found it hard not to wrinkle his face in distaste as Ramman's unwashed odor wafted to him.

"Well?" he prompted when the other's hesitation stretched out.

"Are . . . are your quarters secure?" Ramman asked hesitantly, and Ganhar frowned in fresh surprise. Ramman sounded serious, yet also oddly as if he were playing for time while he reached some inner decision.

"They are," he said slowly. "I have them swept every morning."

"Good." Ramman paused again.

"Look," Ganhar said finally, "if you've got something to say, why not say it?"

"I'm afraid," Ramman admitted after another maddening pause. "But I have to tell someone. And—" he managed a lopsided, sickly smile "—I'm even more afraid of Jantu than I am of you."

"Why?" Ganhar asked tightly.

"Because I'm a traitor," Ramman whispered.

"*What*?!" Ramman flinched as if Ganhar had struck him, yet it also seemed he'd crossed some inner Rubicon. When he spoke again, his flat, hurried voice was louder.

"I'm a traitor. I-I've been in contact with ... with Horus and his daughter, Jiltanith, for years."

"You've been *talking* to them?!"

"Yes. Yes! I was afraid of Anu, damn it! I wanted ... I wanted to defect, but they wouldn't let me! They made me *stay*, made me *spy* for them!"

"You fool," Ganhar said softly. "You poor, damned fool! No wonder Jantu scares the shit out of you." Then, as the shock faded, his eyes narrowed again. "But if that's true, why tell me? Why tell *anyone*?"

"Because ... because they're going to attack the enclave."

"Preposterous! They could never crack the shield!"

"They don't plan to." Ramman bent towards Ganhar, and his voice took on an urgent cadence. "They're coming in through the access points."

"They can't—they don't have the admittance code!"

"I know. Don't you see? They want *me* to steal it for them!"

"That's stupid," Ganhar objected, staring at the dirty, cringing Ramman. "They must know Anu doesn't trust you—or did you lie to them about that?"

"No, I didn't," Ramman said tightly. "And even if I hadn't told them, they'd know from how long I've been left outside."

"Then they must also know Jantu plans to change the code as soon as all the 'untrustworthy elements' are back outside."

"I *know*, damn it! *Listen* to me, for Maker's sake! They don't want *me* to bring it out. I'm supposed to plant it for someone *else*. One of the degenerates!"

"Breaker!" Ganhar whispered. Maker damn it, but it made sense! If they'd gotten one of their own degen—

people inside, it made audacious, possibly foolhardy sense, but sense. They were terribly outnumbered, but with surprise on their side ... And it made their whole offensive make sense, too. Drive them into the enclave ... steal the code ... smuggle it out and hit them before Anu and Jantu changed it.... It was brilliant!

"Why tell me now?" he demanded.

"Because they'll never get away with it! But if they try, Anu will know someone gave them the code, and I'll be one of the ones who get killed for it!"

"And you think there's something *I* can do about it? You're a bigger fool than I thought, Ramman!"

"No, listen! I've thought about it, and there's a way," Ramman said eagerly. "A way that'll help both of us!"

"How? No, wait. I see it. You tell me, I trap their courier, and we pass it off as a counter-intelligence ploy, is that it?"

"Exactly!"

"Hmmmmmm." Ganhar stared down at his holo map, then shook his head. "No, there's a better way," he said slowly. "You could go ahead and make the drop. We could *give* them the code, then wait for them with everybody in armor and all our equipment on line and wipe them out—gut them once and for all."

"Yes. *Yes!*" Ramman said eagerly.

"Very neat," Ganhar said, trying to picture what would follow such an overwhelming triumph. *Nergal's* people would be neutralized, but what would happen then? He'd be a hero, but even as a hero, his life would hang in the balance, for Inanna knew how he thought of the "Chief." Perhaps Anu knew, as well. And he remembered his other thoughts, how his own actions had come to sicken him. And he still didn't know what had prompted *Nergal's* people to *start* their offensive, even if he knew how they meant to end it. But if he and Ramman trapped them, they could end the long, covert war. He'd have no more need to slaughter innocents ... not that there weren't enough Kirinals and Girrus to go on doing it for the fun of it. ...

"When are you supposed to make the drop?" he asked finally.

"I already have," Ramman admitted.

"I see," Ganhar said, and nodded absently as he opened a desk drawer. "I'm glad you told me about this. I'm finally going to be able to do something effective about the situation on this planet, Ramman, and I couldn't have done it without you. Thank you."

His hand came out of the drawer, and Ramman gaped at the small, heavy energy pistol it held. He was still gaping when Ganhar blew his head to paste.

Book Four

Chapter Twenty

Jiltanith and Rohantha settled into their flight couches and checked their computers with extraordinary care, for the stakes were higher this night than they had ever been before, and not just for them.

They were not in a fighter, but in a specially modified pinnace. Larger even than one of the twenty-man cutters, the pinnace (one of only two *Nergal* carried) was crammed with stealth systems, three times the normal missile load, and the extra computers linked to the two cutters and matching pair of fighters beside it in the launch bay. A third fighter sat behind them while Hanalat and Carhana carried out their own pre-flight checks. Even if Stalking-Horse was a total success, it was going to make a terrible hole in *Nergal's* equipment list.

Jiltanith nodded, satisfied with the reports of her own flight systems and the ready signals flowing through her cross links to Rohantha's equipment, and opened a channel to flight operations.

"Ready," was all she said.

"Good hunting," a voice responded, and she smiled

down at her console, for the response came not from
Hector but from Colin MacIntyre. Since admitting he'd
chosen her to succeed him, he seemed to have been
constantly at hand, almost hovering there, and she knew
he'd resigned himself to letting her fly this mission without really accepting it. She thought about saying something back to him, but their new relationship—whatever
it was—remained too fragile, too unexplored. There
would be time for that later. She hoped.

Instead, she lifted the pinnace off the hangar deck and
led the procession of vehicles up the long, sloping tunnel.
Freedom was upon her once more . . . and the hunger.
But it was different this time. Her hunger was less dark
and consuming, and there was no simmering tension
between her and her weaponeer.

More than that, she was heavier, less fleet of wing.
Slower and shorter-ranged than a fighter in vacuum, the
pinnace was actually faster in atmosphere where its drive,
thanks to its heavier generators, could bull through air
resistance without being slowed to the same extent. But
it had no atmospheric control surfaces for use in the
stealth regime, and its very power made it slower to
accelerate or decelerate, less maneuverable . . . and
harder to hide.

They floated up the shaft, alert for any last-minute
warning from *Nergal's* scan crews. But there were no
alarms, and the small craft slipped undetected into the
open atmosphere. Calm, cool thoughts flowed to the
computers, and they turned to the east.

Under the false tranquillity of her surface thoughts,
Jiltanith's mind whirred like yet another computer, probing even now for any last-minute awareness of error. She
expected to find none, but she could not stop searching,
and that irritated her. It wasn't the mark of the confident
person she liked to believe she was.

For all the equipment committed to Stalking-Horse,
there were only four people involved in the mission. She
and Rohantha in the pinnace; Hanalat and Carhana in
the only manned fighter. But that was all right . . . assum-

ing she and Hector had accurately gauged Anu's new
dispositions. If they hadn't . . .

The use of the pinnace was the part that bothered
her most, she admitted to herself, leading the procession
towards their target at just under mach one. Its designers
had never intended it for the cut and thrust of close
combat. Its single energy gun was a toy beside the powerful multiple batteries of a fighter, and though her electronics were much more capable and her upgraded
missile armament gave her a respectable punch at longer
range, she knew what would happen if she was forced
into short-range combat with a proper fighter.

Yet only a pinnace had the power plant, speed, and
cargo capacity they needed. She could only trust in
Rohantha and her stealth systems and pray.

She stiffened as a warning tingled in her link to Rohantha. Hostile fighters—two of them—to the south. They
were higher and moving faster than her own formation,
degrading the performance of their stealth systems, and
had she piloted a fighter of her own, Jiltanith would have
asked nothing better than to scream up after them in
pursuit. As it was, she stifled a sudden desire to cram on
power and run and held her breath as her mind joined
with Rohantha's, following the enemy's movements. They
swept on upon their own mission and faded from the
passive scanners.

Jiltanith made herself relax, trying to forget her dread
of which new innocents they were to kill. She altered
course minutely, swinging north of Ottawa before turning
back on a south-southwest heading, and managed to push
such thoughts to the back of her mind. The need for
purposeful concentration helped, and her navigation systems purred to her, the controls of her pinnace caressed
her like a lover, and the target area swept closer with
every moment. Soon. Soon. . . .

Shirhansu yawned, then took a quick turn around the
camouflaged bunker. If Ganhar was right (and his analysts had done a bang-up job so far), they might see some
more action soon. She hoped so. The shoot-out in La

Paz, what there'd been of it, had been a relief despite
the frustration of knowing so many enemies had escaped,
and this time she'd left Tarban behind. Of course, there
were always risks, but her own position was well protected, and she had plenty of firepower on hand this
time. In fact, it would be—

"We're getting something, 'Hansu!"

She stepped quickly to Caman's side. He was leaning
forward slightly, eyes unfocused as he listened to his electronics, and she glanced at the display beside him.
Caman had no need of it, but it let her see what his
scanners reported without tying into his systems and losing herself in them.

Active scanner systems were coming in from the north!
So Ganhar *had* guessed right. The other side had no
intention of being mousetrapped again, so they were
probing ahead of their attack force. Now the question
was whether or not they'd visualized the next moves as
well as Ganhar had.

She watched a tiny red dot move above the small,
perfectly detailed hills and trees of the holo display. The
computers classed it as a cutter, but no cutter would be
so brazen if it was unescorted. Their own scanners,
operating in passive mode so far, had yet to spot anything
else, but they'd find the bastards when it mattered.

Jiltanith had taken over Rohantha's weapon systems as
well as the flight controls for the moment, and her brain
was poised on a hair-trigger of anticipation. The base in
upstate New York was no Cuernavaca, and, though it had
been on Hector's list from the beginning, it had been
carefully avoided to this point. It was juicy enough to
merit attention—a major staging point for weapons and
foreign terrorists aiming at targets in the northeastern
states and Canada combined with the presence of southerner coordinators and a small quantity of Imperial technology—but it was also close to home, relatively speaking.
More importantly, it was bait; they'd needed a target like
this to set the stage for Stalking-Horse.

Rohantha was tense beside her as she concentrated on

her specially-programmed computers. At the moment, she was "flying" both cutters and their fighter escorts via directional radio links. It was risky, because it meant placing the pinnace in a position to hit them with the radio beams, but far less risky than relying on fold-space links. And her directional links had the advantage of being indetectable unless somebody from the other side got into their direct path.

There were no words in the pinnace. Despite her own preoccupation, a corner of Jiltanith's mind was open to the flow of Rohantha's thoughts through their neural feeds as the lead cutter moved closer to the target, active scanners probing industriously, turning it into a beacon in the heavens.

"*Got* 'em, Hansu!" Caman said exultantly. "See?"

Shirhansu nodded. A second cutter had just blipped onto the display. Its coordinates were less definite, for it was using no scanners, but the fold-space link between it and the first vessel had burned briefly through its stealth field. So they *had* sent in the first one on its automatics, had they?

She raised a small mike, smiling. They'd used radio against her in La Paz and she hadn't been ready for it, but this time *she* had a radio link, as well. They might be watching for it, but even if they spotted it, they couldn't be certain it was being used by Imperials.

"First Team," she said quietly in English. "Go."

There was no reply, but far above the surface of the Earth, a pair of Imperial fighters swooped downward at mach three while they took targeting data from Caman's scanners over the primitive radio link.

"Missiles!"

The unneeded word was dragged out of Rohantha, and Jiltanith nodded jerkily. The energy signatures of Imperial missiles were unmistakable as they scorched down out of the heavens, and 'Hantha's plotting systems were backtracking frantically.

Both cutters went to pre-programmed evasive action

as the missiles came in. It was useless, of course. It was intended to be, but it would have been useless whether they'd planned it that way or not. The missles shrieked home, and Jiltanith cringed as thermonuclear flame ripped the night skies apart. The southerners were using heavy missiles!

She paled as she pictured the radiation boiling out from those fireballs. They were barely a kilometer up, and Maker only knew what they were doing to any Terraborn in the vicinity, but she knew what their EMP would do to Rohantha's directional antennae! Imperial technology was EMP-proof, but they'd counted on lighter weapons, with less ruinous effect on the electromagnetic spectrum, and she only hoped the targeting data had gotten through . . . and that the maneuvers in the drones' computers were up to their needs. If they had to open up a fold-link while the southerners were watching . . .

Both cutters had vanished in the holocaust, and Jiltanith banked away from the blast as Rohantha reclaimed her onboard systems. She'd done all she could by remote control.

"Hard kills on both cutters!" Caman shouted, and Shirhansu crouched over his shoulder, staring triumphantly at the display.

That was one fucking commando team that would never hit a target! But her triumph was not unmixed with worry as her fighters clawed back upward, putting as much distance between themselves and their firing positions as they could without breaking stealth. . . .

"Missile sources! Multiple launches!" Caman snapped, and Shirhansu smothered a curse.

Ganhar had been right again, Breaker take it! But there was still a good chance for her fighter crews. She watched the missiles climbing the holographic display, spreading as they rose. They couldn't have a definite lock, but they'd obviously gotten *something* from the tracks of the missiles that had killed the cutters.

"Team Two!" She used a fold-space com, but the heavy EMP from Team One's warheads would make it hard for even Imperial systems to spot it just now, and the need for secrecy was past, anyway. There was not even any need to tell her second fighter force what to do—they knew, and they were already doing it.

Shit! Erdana's fighter was clear of the missiles seeking it, but those were self-guided homing weapons, and at least three had locked onto Sima and Yanu! She watched Sima go to full power, abandoning stealth now that he knew he'd been targeted. Decoys blossomed on the display and jamming systems fought to protect the fighter, and two of the missiles lost lock and veered away. One killed a decoy in a three-kiloton burst of fury; the other simply disappeared into the night. But the third drilled through every defense Yanu could throw out against it, and its target vanished from the display.

Shirhansu swallowed a sour gulp of fury, but there was no time for dismay. Caman's scanners had picked out both of the firing fighters, and Team Two—not two, but four Imperial fighters—charged after them, missiles already lashing out across the heavens.

Jiltanith watched exultantly as one of the southern fighters disappeared in a ball of flame. That was more than they'd hoped for, and she was impressed by how well their unmanned fighters' computers had done.

Now they were doing the rest of their job, and she angled the pinnace away, hugging the ground, covered by Hanalet and Carhana as they flashed back into the north at mach two and prayed their own stealth systems held. . . .

Shirhansu watched the northerners react to her own incoming fighters. They went to full power, one streaking away to the west towards Lake Erie, the other breaking east and diving for the cover of the mountains. Decoys blazed in the night, dying in salvos of nuclear flame, and the west-bound fighter evaded the first wave of missiles racing after it. Not so the one headed east; three different missiles took it from three different directions.

She concentrated on the surviving fighter, praying that

its crew would be frightened—and foolish—enough to flee straight back to *Nergal*, but those Imperials were made of sterner stuff. They turned back from the western shore of the lake, hurling their own missiles in reply, and she smothered an unwilling admiration for their guts as they took on all four pursuers in a hopeless battle rather than reveal their base's location.

What followed was swift and savage. The single enemy fighter was boxed, and its crew were obviously more determined than skilled. Its weapons sought out *all* its attackers, splitting its fire instead of seeking to blast a single foe out of the way to flee, and its violent evasive maneuvers had a fatalistic, almost mechanical air. Her own flight crews' defensive systems handled the incoming fire, and Changa's fighter flashed in so close he actually took the target out with his energy guns instead of another missile.

The molten, half-vaporized wreckage spilled into the cold, waiting waters of Lake Erie, and the victors reformed above the steam cloud and flashed away to the south. Shirhansu let her shoulders unknot and straightened, only then realizing that she'd been crouched forward. She wiped her forehead, and her hand came away damp.

Done. The whole thing had taken less than five minutes, and it was done.

"Get me Ganhar," she told Caman softly, and her assistant nodded happily.

Shirhansu drew a deep breath and crossed her arms, considering what to say. It was a pity about Sima and Yanu, but they'd taken out both cutters, the raiding force, *and* both stealthed escorts, for the loss of a single fighter of their own. That was a third of *Nergal*'s fighter strength, plus at least five of their remaining Imperials. Probably at least six, since there would have been one Imperial in the raiding force, as well, and possibly seven if they'd been foolish enough to use a live pilot in the lead cutter.

She let herself smile thinly. Not a single survivor—and no indication of a message home to tell *Nergal* what had happened, either. Their entire attack force had been gobbled up, and it was unlikely they'd even know how it had happened. It was the worst they'd ever been hurt. Proportionately, it made Cuernavaca meaningless, and *she* had been in command. She'd commanded *both* successful interceptions!

"I've got Ganhar," Caman said, and Shirhansu let her smile broaden as she took over the com link.

"Ganhar? 'Hansu. We got 'em all—clean sweep!"

Jiltanith and Rohantha let themselves relax, knowing Hanalat and Carhana were doing the same aboard their fighter.

Their equipment losses had been severe, but that had been planned, and there had been no loss of life. Not theirs, anyway, Jiltanith reminded herself, and tried to turn her mind away from the Terra-born who must have been caught in the fireballs and radiation of the crossfire. At least the area was thinly populated, she thought, and knew she was grasping at straws.

But the southerners couldn't know the northerners had lost none of their own personnel, which meant that they would believe *Nergal*'s losses had been staggering enough to frighten them into suspending offensive operations.

They might actually pull it off, and she looked forward to returning to *Nergal* to report the mission's success. Hector would be pleased at how well it had gone, she thought, but her lips curved in a small, secret smile, hidden from Rohantha as she admitted a surprising truth to herself.

It was Colin's face she truly wished to see.

Chapter Twenty-one

General Gerald Hatcher stood beside his GEV command vehicle on a hill overlooking what had once been a stretch of pleasantly wooded countryside and listened to the radiation detectors snarl. The wind was from behind him and the levels were relatively low here, but that was cold comfort as he looked down into the smoldering mouth of Hell.

Smoke fumed up from the forest fires, but they were still far away and the Forestry Service and fire departments and volunteers from the surviving locals along the fringe of the area were fighting to bring them under control. Most of those people didn't have dosimeters, either, and Hatcher shook his head slowly. Courage came in many guises, and it never ceased to amaze and humble him, but this carnage went beyond anything courage could cope with. Hatcher's bearing was as erect and soldierly as ever, but inside himself he wept.

Red and blue flashers blinked atop emergency vehicles further out into the smoking wasteland, and the night sky was heavy with helicopters and vertols that jockeyed through the treacherous thermals and radiation. They would not find many to rescue out there . . . and this was only one of the nuked areas.

He turned at the whine of fans as another GEV swept up the slope, blowing a gale of downed branches and ash from under its skirts, and settled beside his own. The hatch popped, and Captain Germaine, his aide, climbed down. His battle dress was smutted with dirt and ash and his face was drawn as he removed his breathing mask and walked heavily over to his commander.

"How bad is it, Al?" Hatcher asked quietly.

"About as bad as it could be, sir," Germaine said in a low voice, waving a hand out over the expanse of ruin. "The search teams are still working their way towards the center, but the last body count I heard was already over five hundred and still climbing."

"And that doesn't include the flash-blinded and the ones who'll still die," Hatcher said softly.

"No, sir. And this is one of the bright spots," Germaine continued in bitter, staccato bursts. "One of the goddamned things went off right over a town to the south. Sixteen thousand people." His mouth twisted. "Doesn't look like there'll be any survivors from that one, General."

"Dear God," Hatcher murmured, and even he could not have said whether it was a prayer or a curse.

"Yes, sir. The only good thing—if it's not obscene to call anything about this bitched-up mess 'good'—is they seem to've been mighty clean. The counters show a relatively small area of lethal contamination, and the wind's out of the southeast, away from the big urban areas. But God knows what it's going to do to the local gene pool or what the Candians are going to catch from all this *shit*."

The last word came out of him in a half-strangled shout as his attempted detachment crumbled, and he half-turned from his general, clenching his fists.

"I know, Al. I know." Hatcher sighed and shook himself, his normally sharp eyes sad as he looked out over the battlefield. And battlefield it had been, even if none of the United States' detection systems had picked up a thing before or after the explosions. At least they'd had satellites in place to see what happened *during* the battle . . . not that the records made him feel any better.

"I'm heading back to the office, Al. Stay on it and keep me informed."

"Yes, sir."

Hatcher gestured, and his white-faced young commo officer stepped to his side. Her auburn hair was cut a bit longer than regulations prescribed, and it blew on the winds the fires ten kilometers away were sucking into their maw.

"Get hold of Major Weintraub, Lieutenant. Have him meet me at HQ."

"Yes, sir." The lieutenant headed for the command vehicle's radios, and Hatcher rested a hand on Germaine's shoulder.

"Watch your dosimeter, Al. If it climbs into the yellow, you're out of here and back to base. The major and I'll want to talk to you, anyway."

"Yes, sir."

Hatcher squeezed the taut shoulder briefly, then walked heavily to his GEV. It rose on its fans and curtsied uncomfortably across the rough terrain, but Hatcher sat sunken in thought and hardly noticed.

It wasn't going well. Hector's people had started on a roll, but they were getting the holy howling shit kicked out of them now, and the rest of the human race with them.

The first wave of counter-attacks had puzzled Hatcher. A handful of attacks on isolated segments of the aerospace effort, a few bloody massacres of individual families. They'd seemed more like pinpricks than full-scale assaults, and he'd tentatively decided the bad guys, whoever they were, were going after those few of Hector's people they could identify, which had been bad enough but also understandable.

But within twelve hours, another and far bloodier comber of destruction had swept the planet like a tsunami. The Point, Sandhurst, Klyuchevskaya, Goddard . . . Eden Two.

Clearly the other side had opted for the traditional terrorist weapon: terror. Coupled with the reports from La Paz, which could only have been a direct clash between the extra-terrestrial opponents, and this new obscenity in New York, it sounded terribly as if the momentum was shifting, and his preliminary examination of the satellite tapes seemed to confirm it.

The first warning anyone had was the burst of warheads, but the cameras had watched it all. Clearly one side had gotten the shit kicked out of it, and judging by the warheads each had used, it hadn't been the bad guys. Hector's people had used only small-yield nukes, when they'd used them at all, but their enemies didn't give a shit who they killed. They went in for great big bangs and hang the death toll, and his satellite people put the winning side's yields in the twenty kiloton range, maybe even a bit higher.

Hatcher sighed unhappily. Other bits and pieces had come together as his analysts tried to figure out what was going on, and one thing had become clear: the nature and pattern of Hector's people's operations all suggested meticulous planning, economy of force, and conservation of resources, whereas their opponents were operating on a far vaster scale, their actions wider-spread and more often simultaneous rather than sequenced. All of which indicated the balance of force was against Hector's side, probably by a pretty heavy margin.

History was replete with examples of out-numbered forces that had triumphed over clumsier enemies or those less technologically advanced than themselves, but right off the top of his head, Hatcher couldn't recall a single case in which a weaker force had defeated one that was equally advanced, more numerous, and knew what the hell it was doing. Especially not when the stronger side were also the barbarians.

His command vehicle reached the highway and turned north, heading for the vertol waiting to carry him back to his HQ, and he rubbed his eyes wearily. He and Weintraub had to get their heads together, though God only knew what good it was going to do. So far, all anyone had been able to do was beef up civil defense and keep their heads down. They were too outclassed for anything else, but if Hector's people went down, it was Hatcher's duty to do what he could.

Even if it hadn't been, he would have tried, for there was one thing upon which Gerald Hatcher was savagely determined. The bastards who didn't care how many innocent people they slaughtered were not going to take over his world without a fight, however advanced they were.

"Oh, Jesus!" Hector MacMahan whispered. His strong, tanned face was white as he listened to the reports flowing over the government and civilian emergency radio nets, and Colin reached over to lay a hand upon his shoulder.

"It wasn't our doing, Hector," he said quietly.

"Oh yes it was." MacMahan's bitter voice was as savage as his eyes. "We didn't use those fucking monsters, but we provoked *them* into doing it! And do me a favor and *don't* tell me we didn't have any choice!"

Colin met his eyes for a moment, then patted the colonel's shoulder once, gently, and leaned back in his own chair. Hector's bitterness wasn't directed at him, though he would have preferred for MacMahan to have an external focus for his self-loathing. Yet even in his pain, Hector had put his finger on it. They hadn't had a choice . . . and Colin wondered how many commanders over the ages had tried to assuage their consciences with thoughts like that.

"All right," he said finally. He reached out through his implant to shut off the emergency workers' voices, and MacMahan looked at him angrily, as if he resented the interruption of his self-imposed auditory penance. "We know what happened. The question is whether or not it worked. 'Tanni?"

"I can but say it should," Jiltanith said softly, and managed a ghost of the triumphant smiles they'd shared before the casualty reports started coming in. "Had they spied our other craft, then would they ha' sought the death of all. So far as they may tell, they slew our force entire."

"Horus?"

" 'Tanni's right. We've done all we can. I pray the Maker it was enough." The old Imperial looked down at his hands and refused to look back up. Isis hugged him gently, and when she looked up to meet Colin's eyes her bright tears stopped him from asking her opinion. He glanced at MacMahan, instead.

"Oh, sure," the colonel said savagely. "My wonderful fucking plan worked just fine. All those extra bodies'll be a big help, too, won't they?"

"All right," Colin said again, his own voice carefully neutral. "In that case, we'll suspend all further offensive operations immediately. There's nothing we can do but wait, anyway." Heads nodded, and he rose. "Then I recommend we all get something to eat and some rest."

He extended his hand to Jiltanith without even thinking about it, and she took it. The warmth of her grip made him realize what he'd done, and he looked over at her quickly. She met his gaze with a small, sad smile and tightened her clasp as she stood beside him. They were almost exactly the same height, Colin noted, and for some no longer quite so obscure reason that pleased him even in their shared pain.

Horus and Isis rose more slowly, but MacMahan remained seated. Colin looked down at him and started to speak, but Jiltanith squeezed his hand and gave her head a tiny shake. He hesitated a moment longer, then thought better of it, and they walked wordlessly from the conference room.

The hatch closed behind them, but not quickly enough to cut off the mutter of ghostly, angry, weeping voices as MacMahan turned the radios back on.

"So much for those smart-assed bastards!" Anu gloated as Ganhar finished his report. "Caught them with their pants down and kicked them right in the ass, by the Maker! Good work, Ganhar. Very good!"

"Thank you, Chief." It was becoming harder for Ganhar to hold himself together, and he wondered what was really happening deep inside him.

"What next?" Anu demanded, and his hand-rubbing glee nauseated the Operations head. "Got any more targets picked out?"

"I don't think we need them, Chief," Ganhar said carefully. He saw Anu's instant disappointment, like the resentment of a little boy denied a third helping of dessert, and made himself continue.

"It looks like we've hurt them worse than the numbers alone suggest. They haven't mounted a single attack in the thirty-six hours since Shirhansu's people pulled out. Either they're rethinking or they've already rethought, Chief. Whichever it is, they're not going to lock horns with us again after this. That being the case, do we really want to do any more damage than we have to? Anything we smash is going to have to be rebuilt before we can get our other projects back on line."

"That's true," Anu said unwillingly. He looked at his head of security. "Jantu? You've been damned quiet. What'd you think?"

"I think we should give them a few more licks for good measure," Jantu said, but his voice was less forceful than of old. He hadn't realized how much he'd actually come to enjoy his affair with Bahantha. Her death had shaken him badly, but the blow to his ambitions was even worse, and Ganhar's and Inanna's alliance had come as a terrible shock.

"Ganhar's right, Chief." Inanna eyed the Security chief coldly, as if to confirm his thoughts. "The real problem's always been *Nergal*'s people. Killing more degenerates is pointless, unless we want to take over openly."

"No," Anu said, shaking his head. "It's bad enough they know we're here; if we come out into the open, there's too much chance of losing control."

"I agree," Ganhar said quietly, locking eyes with Jantu. "Right now, the degenerates don't have any idea where to look for us, but that could change if we get too open, and our tech advantage doesn't mean we're invulnerable. There's more than one way someone can get at us."

Jantu winced as Anu joined the other two in glaring at him. In retrospect, it was obvious from the surveillance reports that Ramman had acted unnaturally ever since his return to the enclave, and if Jantu had been less shaken by the realization that Ganhar and Inanna were leagued against him he probably would have noticed it and hauled the man in for questioning. As it was, he'd let matters slip so badly it had been Ganhar, his worst rival, who'd noticed something and dragged Ramman in to confront him.

The Operations head was damned lucky to be alive, Jantu thought viciously. Somehow Ramman had gotten his hands on an energy pistol despite his suspect status—something Jantu *still* couldn't understand—and only the fact that Ganhar had out-drawn him had saved his life. Damn Ramman! The least he might have done was kill the son-of-a-bitch!

Unfortunately, he hadn't, and Ganhar had not only preserved his own life, but uncovered the worst security breach in the enclave's history: a self-confessed spy who'd admitted he was working for Horus. And the fact that Horus had gotten to Ramman without being detected was *Jantu's* failure, not Ganhar's. His failure to spot Ramman, coupled with the fact that it was *his* bitterest rival Ramman had almost killed, had seemed dangerously close to collusion rather than carelessness, and Jantu knew Anu thought so.

"Maybe you're right," he admitted now, the words choking in his throat. "But if so, what else should we do?"

"We ought to make sure we're right about their reaction," Ganhar said positively. "Our important degenerates have been safe inside the shield, but *Nergal*'s bunch've blown the crap out of our outside networks. Let's start rebuilding while the rest of the degenerates are still disorganized. There's no way the other side could miss our doing that. If they've still got the guts to face us, they'll go after our degenerates as soon as they spot them."

"Sounds reasonable," Anu agreed. "Which batch do you want to throw out first?"

"Let's sit tight on our people in government and industry." Ganhar had personally run the background checks on too many of those people for it to be likely Ramman's courier was among them. "They're too valuable to risk."

"If we hang onto them too long, they'll lose credibility," Inanna pointed out. "Especially the ones in government. Some of them're already going to lose their jobs for running when things got hot."

"A few more days won't make much difference, and the delay's worth it to keep them alive if we've guessed wrong. Remember, the very fact that we hid them has marked them for *Nergal's* bunch. If they *do* have the guts to go on, they'll know exactly who to gun for." Ganhar wanted to marshal weightier arguments, but he dared not. Inanna was his ally for now, but if she guessed what he was really up to . . .

"You're right again, Ganhar," Anu said expansively. "By the Maker, it's almost a pity Kirinal didn't get herself killed earlier. If you'd been running things, we probably wouldn't have been taken by surprise this way."

"Thanks, Chief," the words were like splintered bone in Ganhar's throat, "but I stand by what I said. There was simply no way to predict what they were going to pull. All we could do was see which way the wind blew and then hit back hard."

He saw a trace of approval in Inanna's eyes, for she, better than any, would know it was the right note to strike. Anu was feeling expansive just now, but soon he would settle back into his usual behavior patterns, and it could be more dangerous to be overly competent than incompetent then.

"Well, you did a good job," Anu said, "and I'm inclined to follow your advice now. Start with the combat types—they're easier to replace anyway."

He nodded to indicate the meeting was adjourned, and the other three rose and left.

* * *

Ganhar felt the hatch close behind him with a vast sense of relief, then nodded to Inanna, gave Jantu a cold, dangerous smile, and stalked off. For the moment, his position was secure, and unless he missed his guess, he'd only need for it to stay that way a very little while longer.

The cold wind of mortality blew down his spine, and he'd put it there himself, but he still didn't know exactly why he had. The events he'd set in motion—or, more accurately, allowed to *remain* in motion—terrified him, yet there was a curious satisfaction in it. One way or another, it would bring the eternal, intricate betrayal and counter-betrayal to an end, and perhaps it could go some way towards expiating the sickness he'd felt ever since he had replaced Kirinal and his had become the hand that personally managed the organized murder of the people of Terra.

And it would also be the gambit that ended the long, futile game. The consummate, smoothly-polished stratagem that set all the other plotting, scheming would-be tyrants at naught. There was a certain sweetness in that, and—who knew?—he might even survive it after all.

Chapter Twenty-two

It was very quiet on *Nergal*'s hangar deck. The command deck was too small for the crowd of people who had gathered here, and Colin let his eyes run over them thoughtfully. Every surviving Imperial was present, but they were vastly outnumbered by their Terra-born descendants and allies, and perhaps that was as it should be. It was fitting that what had started as a battle between Anu's mutineers and the loyalists of *Dahak*'s crew should end as a battle between those same butchers and the descendants of those they had betrayed.

He sat beside Jiltanith on the stage against the big compartment's outer bulkhead and wondered how the rest of *Nergal*'s people were reacting to the outward signs of their changing relationship. There were dark, still places in her soul that he doubted he would ever understand fully, and he had no idea where they were ultimately headed, but he was content to wait and see. Assuming they won and they both survived, they would have plenty of time to find out.

Hector MacMahan, immaculate as ever in his Marine

uniform, entered the hangar deck beside a dark-faced, almost-handsome young man in the uniform of a US Army master sergeant, and Colin felt a stir rustle through the gathering as they found chairs to Jiltanith's left. Only a few of them had yet met Andrew Asnani, but all of them had heard of him by now.

Horus waited until they were seated, then stood and folded his hands behind him. He had abandoned his ratty old Clemson sweatshirt for this meeting and, at Colin's insistence, wore the midnight blue of the Fleet for the first time in fifty thousand years. His collar bore the single golden starburst of a fleet captain, not his old pre-mutiny rank, in a gesture that spoke to all of his fellow mutineers, even if they did not understand its full implications, and Colin had seen one or two of the older Imperials sit a bit straighter, their eyes a bit brighter, at the change.

"We've waited a long time for this moment," Horus said quietly, looking out over the silent ranks, "and we and, far more, the innocent people of this planet, have paid a terrible price to reach it. Many of us have died trying to undo what we did; far more have died trying to undo something *someone else* did. Those people can't see this day, yet, in a way, they're right here with us."

He paused and drew a deep breath.

"All of you know what we've been trying to do. It looks—and I caution you that appearances may be deceiving—but it *looks* like we've succeeded."

A sound like wind through grass filled the hangar deck. His words were no surprise, but they were a vast relief—and a source of even greater tension.

"Hector will brief you on our operations plan in just a moment, but there's something else I want to say to our children and our allies first." He looked out, and his determined old eyes were dark.

"We're sorry," he said quietly. "What you face is our fault, not yours. We can never repay you, never even thank you properly, for the sacrifices you and your parents and grandparents have made for us, knowing that we are to blame for so many terrible things. Whatever happens, we're proud of you—prouder, perhaps, than you can ever know. By being who you are, you've restored something to us, for if we can call upon the aid of people as extraordinary as you have proven yourselves to be, then perhaps there truly remains something of good in all of us. I—"

His voice broke and he cleared his throat, then stopped with a little headshake and sat. There was silence, but it was a silence of shared emotions too deep for expression, and then all eyes switched to Colin as he rose slowly. He met their assembled gazes calmly, acutely aware of the way the paired stars of his own Fleet rank glittered upon his collar, then looked down at Horus.

"Thank you, Horus," he said softly. "I wish I could count myself among those extraordinary people you just referred to, but I can't unless, perhaps, by adoption."

He held Horus's eyes a moment, then swung back to face the hangar deck.

"You all know how I came to hold the position I hold, and how much more deeply some of you merited it. I can't change what happened, but everything Horus just said holds true for me, as well. I'm honored to have known you, much less to have the privilege, however it came my way, of commanding you.

"And there's another thing. I insisted Horus wear the Fleet's uniform today. He argued with me, as he's done a time or two before—" that won a ripple of laughter, as he'd known it would "—but I insisted for a reason. Our Imperials stopped wearing that uniform because they felt they'd dishonored it, and perhaps they had, but Anu's people have retained it, and therein lies the true dishonor. You made a mistake—a horrible mistake—fifty thousand years ago, but you also recognized your error. You've done all that anyone could, far more than anyone could have demanded of you, to right the wrong you did, and your children and descendants and allies have fought and died beside you."

He paused and, like Horus, drew a deep breath. When he spoke again, his voice was very formal, almost harsh.

"All of that is true, yet the fact remains that you are

criminals under Fleet Regulations. You know it. I know
it. *Dahak* knows it. And, if the Imperium remains, someday Fleet Central will know it, for you have agreed to
surrender yourselves to the justice of the Imperium. I
honor and respect you for that decision, but on the eve
of an operation from which so many may not return,
matters so important to you all, so fundamental to all you
have striven for, cannot be left unresolved.

"Now, therefore, I, Senior Fleet Captain Colin Mac-
Intyre, Imperial Battle Fleet, Officer Commanding, *Dahak*
Hull Number One-Seven-Seven-Two-Nine-One, by the
authority vested in me under Fleet Regulation Nine-Sev-
en-Two, Subsection Three, do hereby convene an
extraordinary court martial to consider the actions of certain personnel serving aboard the vessel presently under
my command during the tenure of Senior Fleet Captain
Druaga of Imperial Battle Fleet, myself sitting as Presi-
dent and sole member of the Court. Further, as per Fleet
Regulation Nine-Seven-Three, Subsection One-Eight, I
do also declare myself counsel for the prosecution and
defense, there being no other properly empowered officers of Battle Fleet present.

"The crew of sublight battleship *Nergal*, Hull Number SBB-One-Seven-Seven-Two-Nine-One-One-Three
stands charged before this Court with violation of Arti-
cles Nineteen, Twenty, and Twenty-Three of the Arti-
cles of War, in that they did raise armed rebellion
against their lawful superiors; did attempt to seize their
vessel and desert, the Imperium then being in a state
of readiness for war; and, in commission and consequence of those acts, did also cause the deaths of many
of their fellow crewmen and contribute to the abandon-
ment of others upon this planet.

"The Court has considered the testimony of the
accused and the evidence of its own observations, as well
as the evidence of the said battleship *Nergal*'s log and
other relevant records. Based upon that evidence and
testimony, the Court has no choice but to find the
accused guilty of all specifications and to strip them of
all rank and privilege as officers and enlisted personnel

of Battle Fleet. Further, as the sentence for their crimes is death, without provision for lesser penalties, the Court so sentences them."

A vast, quiet susurration rippled through the hangar deck, but no one spoke. No one could speak.

"In addition to those individuals actively participating in the mutiny, there are among *Nergal*'s present crew certain individuals, then minor children or born to the core crew and/or descendants of *Dahak*'s core crew, and hence members of the crew of the said *Dahak*. Under strict interpretation of Article Twenty, these individuals might be considered accomplices after the fact, in that they did not attempt to suppress the mutiny and punish the mutineers aboard the said *Nergal* when they came of age. In their case, however, and in view of the circumstances, all charges are dismissed.

"The Court wishes, however, to note certain extenuating circumstances discovered in *Nergal*'s records and by personal observation. Specifically, the Court wishes to record that the guilty parties did, at the cost of the lives of almost seventy percent of their number, attempt to rectify the wrong they had done. The Court further wishes to record its observation that the subsequent actions of these mutineers and their descendants and allies have been in the finest traditions of the Fleet, far surpassing in both duration and scope any recorded devotion to duty in the Fleet's records.

"Now, therefore, under Article Nine of the Imperial Constitution, I, Senior Fleet Captain Colin MacIntyre, as senior officer present on the planet Earth, do hereby declare myself Planetery Governor of the colony upon that planet upon the paramount authority of the Imperial Government. As Planetary Governor, I herewith exercise my powers under Article Nine, Section Twelve, of the Constitution, and pronounce and decree—" he let his eyes sweep over the taut, assembled faces "—that all personnel serving aboard the sublight battleship *Nergal*, Hull Number SBB-One-Seven-Seven-Two-Nine-One-One-Three, are, for extraordinary services to the Imperium and the human race, pardoned for all crimes and, if they so desire, are restored to service in Battle Fleet with seniority and rank granted by myself as commanding officer of *Dahak*, Hull Number One-Seven-Seven-Two-Nine-One, to date from this day and hour. I now also direct that the findings of the Court and the decree of the Governor be entered immediately in the data base of the said battleship *Nergal* and transferred, as soon as practicable, to the data base of the said ship-of-the-line *Dahak* for transmission to Fleet Central at the earliest possible date.

"This Court," he finished quietly, "is adjourned."

He sat in a ringing silence and turned slowly to look at Horus. It had taken weeks of agonized thought to reach his decision and mind-numbing days studying the relevant regulations to find the authority and precedents he required. In one sense, it might not matter at all, for it was as apparent to the northerners as to anyone in the south that the Imperium might well have fallen. But in another, far more important sense it meant everything . . . and was the very least he could do for the people Horus had so rightly called "extraordinary."

"Thank—" Horus broke off to clear his husky throat. "Thank you, sir," he said softly. "For myself and my fellows."

A sound came from the hangar deck, a sigh that was almost a sob, and then everyone was on his or her feet. The thunder of their cheers bounced back from the battle steel bulkheads, battering Colin with fists of sound, but under the tumult, he heard one voice in his very ear as Jiltanith gripped his arm in fingers of steel.

"I thank thee, Colin MacIntyre," she said softly. "Howsoe'er it chanced, thou'rt a captain, indeed, as wise as thou'rt good. Thou hast gi'en my father and my family back their souls, and from the bottom of my heart, I thank thee."

It took time to restore calm, yet it was time Colin could never begrudge. These were *his* people, now, in every sense of the word, and if mortal man could achieve their purpose, his people would do it.

But a whispering quiet returned at last, and Hector MacMahan stood at Colin's gesture.

MacMahan would never forget the guilt and grief of Operation Stalking-Horse's civilian casualties. There were fresh lines on his face, fresh white in his dark hair, but he was not immune to the catharsis that had swept the hangar deck. It showed in his eyes and expression as he faced the others.

"All right," he said quietly, "to business," and there was instant silence once more.

He touched buttons on the Terran-made keyboard wired into the briefing console, and a detailed holo map glowed to life between the stage and the front row of seats. It hovered a meter off the deck, canted so that its upper edge almost touched the deckhead to give every observer an unobstructed view.

"This," MacMahan said, "is the southern enclave. It's absolutely the best data we've had on it yet, and we owe it to Ninhursag. We only asked her for the access code; obviously she figured out why and ran the considerable risk of compiling the rest of this for us. If we make it, people, we owe her big.

"Now, as you can see, the enclave is a cavern about twelve kilometers across with the armed parasites forming an outer ring against its walls right here." He touched another button, and the small holographic ships glowed crimson. "They aren't permanently crewed and won't matter much as long as they stay that way; if they lift off, *Dahak* should be able to nail them easily.

"*These*, on the other hand"—another group of ships glowed bright, forming a second, denser ring closer to the center of the cavern—"are transports, and they're going to be a problem. Most of their heavy combat equipment is in them, though Ninhursag was unable to determine how it's distributed, and most of their personnel live aboard them, not in the housing units.

"That means the transports are where their people will be concentrated when they realize they're under attack and that the heaviest counter-attacks are going to come from them. The simplest procedure would be to break into the enclave, pop off a nuke, and get the hell out. The next simplest thing would be to go for the transports with everything we've got and blow them apart before any nasty surprises can come out of them. The *hardest* way to do it is to try to take them ship-by-ship."

He paused and studied his audience carefully.

"We're going to do it the hard way," he said quietly, and there was not even a murmur of protest. "For all we know, many of the people in stasis aboard them would've joined us from the beginning if they'd had the chance. Certainly Ninhursag did, and at the risk of a pretty horrible death if she'd been caught. They deserve the chance to pick sides when the fighting's over.

"But more than that, we're going to *need* them. There are close to five thousand trained, experienced Imperial military personnel in stasis aboard those ships, and the Achuultani are coming. We can't count on the Imperium, though we'll certainly try to obtain any help from it that we can. But in a worst-case scenario, we're on our own with little more than two years to get this planet into some kind of shape to defend itself out of its own resources, and we need those people desperately. By the same token, we need the tech base and medical facilities that are also aboard those transports, so mass destruction weapons are out of the question.

"By Ninhursag's estimates, our Imperials are outnumbered almost ten-to-one, and anyone as paranoid as Anu will have automatic weapons in strategic locations. We're taking in a force of just over a thousand people, almost all of them Terra-born, but our own Imperials are going to have to be in the van. Our Terra-born are all trained military people, and they'll have the best mix of Terran and Imperial weaponry we can give them, but they won't be the equal of Imperials. They can't be, and, at the absolute best, the fighting is going to be close, hard, and vicious. Our losses—" he swept the watching eyes without flinching "—will be heavy.

"They're going to be heavy," he repeated, "but we're going to win. We're going to remember every single thing they've ever done to us and to our planet and we're going to kick their asses, but we're also going to take prisoners."

There was a formless protest at his words, but his raised hand quelled it.

"We're going to take prisoners because Ninhursag may not be our only ally inside—we'll explain that in a moment—and because we don't know what sort of booby-traps Anu may have arranged and we'll need guides. So if someone tries to surrender, let them. But remember this: our Senior Fleet Captain has other officers now. We can, and will, convene courts-martial afterward, and the guilty *will be punished.*" He said the last three words with a soft, terrible emphasis, and the sound that answered chilled Colin's blood, but he would not have protested if he could have.

"There's another point, and this is for our own Imperials," MacMahan said quietly. "We Terra-born understand your feelings better than you may believe. We honor you and we love you, and we know you'll be the other side's primary targets. We can't help that, and we won't try to take this moment away from you, but when this is over, we're going to need you more than we ever needed you before. We'll need every single one of you for the fighting, including Colin and all the children, but we also need survivors, so don't throw your lives away! You're our senior officers; if anything happens to Colin, command of *Dahak* will devolve on one of you, and taking out the southerners is only the first step. What really matters is the Achuultani. *Don't get yourselves killed on us now!*"

Colin hoped the old Imperials heard the raw appeal in his voice, but he also remembered his earliest thoughts about Horus, his fear that the northern Imperials were no longer entirely sane themselves. He'd been wrong—but not very. It wasn't insanity, but it was fanaticism. They'd suffered a hell on earth for thousands of years to bring this moment about. He knew, beyond a shadow of a doubt, that even if they heard and understood what Hector was saying, they were going to take chances no cool, calm professional would ever take, and it was going to get all too many of them killed.

"All right," MacMahan said more normally, "here's what we're going to do.

"We're leaving *Nergal* right where she is with a skeleton crew. There will be one Imperial, chosen by lot, to command her in an emergency, backed up by just enough trained Terra-born to get her into space. I hate asking any of you to stay behind, but we have no choice. If it all comes apart on us in the south, we'll take the bastards out with a nuclear demolition charge inside the shield, but that's going to mean none of us will be coming back."

He paused to let that sink in, then went on calmly.

"In that case, the remaining crew members are going to have to take *Nergal* out to rendezvous with *Dahak*. *Dahak* will be expecting you and won't fire as long as you stay clear of Senior Fleet Captain Druaga's kill zone. You will therefore stop at ten thousand kilometers and transmit *Nergal*'s entire memory to *Dahak*, which will include the findings of Senior Fleet Captain MacIntrye's court-martial and his decree of pardon as Planetary Governor. Once that's been received by *Dahak*, you will once more be members of *Dahak*'s crew and the Imperial Fleet. *Nergal*'s memory contains the best projections and advice Colin and the Council have been able to put together, but what you actually do after that will be up to you and *Dahak*.

"But that's an absolute worst case. Think of it as insurance for something we truly don't think will happen.

"The rest of us will take every cutter and ground combat vehicle we can muster and move south under stealth. We will take no fighters; they'd be useless inside the enclave, but more importantly, we'll need every Imperial we have to run our other equipment.

"We'll be going in through the western access point, here." Another portion of the holo map glowed as he spoke. "We have the codes from Ninhursag, and there's no indication they've been changed. We'll advance along these axes—" more lines glowed "—with parties detailed to each transport. Each attack party will be individually briefed on its mission and as much knowledge of the terrain as Ninhursag was able to give us. You'll also have Ninhursag's personal implant codes. Make damned sure you don't kill her by mistake. She's one lady we want around for the victory party.

"If you can get inside on the first rush, well and good. If you can't, the assault parties will try to prevent anyone from leaving any of the transports while the reserve deals with each holdout in turn. Hopefully, if any of them try to lift out to escape, they won't all lift at once. That means *Dahak* may only have to destroy one or two of them before the others realize what's happening. With us inside and an active *Dahak* outside, they'll surrender if they have a grain of sanity left.

"All right. That's the bare—very bare—bones of the plan. My staff will break it down for each group individually, and we'll hold a final briefing for everyone just before we push off. But there's one other thing you all ought to know, and Sergeant Asnani is the one to tell you about it. Sergeant?"

Andrew Asnani stood, wishing for a moment that he was still Abu al-Nasir, the tough, confident terrorist leader accustomed to briefing his men, as he felt their avid eyes and tried to match the colonel's calm tone.

"What Colonel MacMahan means," he said, "is that there were some unexpected developments inside the enclave. Specifically, your agent Ramman tried to betray you."

He almost flinched at his audience's sudden ripple of shock, but he continued in the same calm voice.

"No one's entirely certain what happened, but there were rumors all over the enclave, especially among their Terra-born. The official line is that he was caught out by Ganhar, their chief of operations, admitted he'd been passing you information for decades to earn the right to defect, and tried to shoot his way out, but that Ganhar out-drew and killed him. That's the *official* story, but I don't think it's the truth. Unfortunately, I can't *know* the truth. I can only surmise."

He inhaled deeply. He'd seen the southerners, been

one of their own, in a sense, and he was even more aware than his listeners of the importance of his evaluation.

"It's possible," he said carefully, "that Ramman succeeded in giving his information to Ganhar before he was killed. He hadn't been told any more than Ninhursag, but if she could figure out what was coming, so could he. If that happened, then they may be waiting for us when we come in." His audience noted his use of the pronoun "we," and one or two people smiled tightly at him.

"But I don't believe they will be. If they planned an ambush, they'd've watched the drop site, and if they did, they know no one went near it. Of course, they may realize there could have been a backup, but I watched closely after the news broke. I believe the Imperials themselves believe the official story. And, while it may be that their leadership chose to put out disinformation, I don't think they did.

"I think," he went on, speaking more precisely than ever, "Ganhar told Anu and the others exactly what they told the rest of their people. I *think* he knows we're coming and deliberately helped clear the way for us."

He paused again, seeing disbelief in more than one face, and shrugged.

"I realize how preposterous that sounds, but there are reasons for my opinion. First, Ganhar was in serious trouble before they began their counter-attacks. Jantu, their security head, had his knife out, and from all I could gather, everyone expected him to stick it in. Second, Ganhar only inherited their operational branch after Kirinal was killed; he's new to the top slot, and I think actually being in charge did something to him. I can't put my finger on it exactly, but Abu al-Nasir was important enough to attend several conferences with him, and he let his guard down a bit more with their 'degenerates' than with their own Imperials. That's an unhappy man. A very unhappy man. Something's eating him up from the inside. Even before the news about Ramman broke, I had the impression his heart just wasn't in it anymore.

"You have to understand that their enclave is like feeding time in a snake house. The difference between them and what I've seen here—well, it's like the difference between night and day. If I were in the position of any of their leaders, I'd be looking over my shoulder every second, waiting for the axe to fall. Mix a little guilt with that kind of long-term, gnawing anxiety, and you could just have a man who wants out, any way he can get out.

"I certainly can't guarantee any of that. It's possible we'll walk right into a trap, and if we do, it's my evaluation that is taking us into it. But if they let us through the access point at all, we'll be inside their shield, and Captain MacIntyre has accepted my offer to personally carry one of your one-megaton nuclear demolition charges."

He met their eyes, his own stubborn and determined in the silence.

"I can't guarantee it isn't a trap," he said very, very quietly, "but I can and will guarantee that that enclave *will* be taken out."

General Gerald Hatcher opened his office door in the underground command post and stopped dead. He shot a quick glance back at the outer office, but none of the officers and noncoms bent over their desks had looked up as if they expected to see his surprise.

He inhaled through his nostrils and stepped through the door, closing it carefully behind him before he walked to his own desk. He'd never seen the twenty-five-centimeter-long rectangular case that lay on his blotter, and he examined it closely before he touched it. It was unlikely anyone could have smuggled a bomb or some similar nastiness into his office. On the other hand, it should have been equally difficult to smuggle *anything* into it.

He'd never seen anything quite like it, and he began to question his first impression that it was made of plastic. Its glossy, bronze-colored material had a metallic sheen, reflecting the light from the improbable, three-headed creature that crowned it like a crest, and he sank tensely into his chair as the implications of the starburst between the dragon's forepaws registered. He reached out and touched the case cautiously, smiling in wry self-mockery at his own tentativeness.

Metal, he decided, running a fingertip over it, though he suspected it was an alloy he'd never encountered. And there was a small, raised stud on the side. He drew a deep breath and pressed it, then relaxed and exhaled softly as the case's upper edge sprang up with a quiet click.

He lifted the lid cautiously, laying it back to lie flat on the desk, and studied the interior. There was a small, lift-up panel in what had been the bottom and three buttons to one side of it. He wondered what he was supposed to do next, then grinned as he saw the neatly-typed label gummed over one button. "Press," it said, and its prosaic incongruity tickled his sense of humor. He shrugged and obeyed, then snatched his hand back as a human figure took instant shape above the case.

Somehow, Hatcher wasn't a bit surprised to see Hector MacMahan. The colonel wore Marine battledress and body armor, and a peculiar-looking, stubby weapon with a drum magazine hung from his right shoulder. He was no more than twenty centimeters tall, but his grin was perfectly recognizable.

"Good evening, General," Hector's voice said in time to the moving lips of the image. "I realize this is a bit unusual, but we had to let someone know what was happening, and you're one of the few people I trust implicitly.

"First, let me apologize for my disappearance. You told me to make myself scarce—" another tight grin crossed his leprechaun-sized face while Hatcher stared at him in fascination "—so I did. I'm aware I made myself a bit scarcer than you had in mind, but I'm certain you understand why. I hope to apologize and explain everything in person in the near future, but that may not be possible, which is the reason for this message.

"Now, about what's been happening in the last few weeks. For the moment, just understand that there are two separate factions of . . . well, call them extra-terrestrials, although that's not exactly the best term for them.

At any rate, there are two sides, and they've been fighting one another clandestinely for a very, very long time. Now the fighting's come out into the open and, with any luck, it will come to an end very soon.

"Obviously, I'm a supporter of one side. I apologize for having used you and your resources as we did, but it was necessary. So"—Hector's face turned suddenly grim—"were all the casualties. Please believe that you cannot regret those deaths any more than we do and that we did our best to keep them as low as possible. Unfortunately, our adversaries don't share our own concern for human life.

"This message is to tell you that we're about to kick off an operation that we hope and believe will prove decisive. I realize your own reports—particularly those from New York—may've led you to conclude we're losing. Hopefully, our opponents have reached the same conclusion. If they have, and if our intelligence is correct, they're about to become our *late* opponents.

"Unfortunately, a lot of us are also going to die. I know how you hate terms like 'acceptable casualties,' Ger, but this time we really don't have a choice. If every one of us is killed, it'll still be worth it as long as we take them out, too. But in the process, there may be quite a ruckus in points south, and I'm sorry to say we really aren't positive how thoroughly *their* people may have infiltrated Terran governments or even your own command. I *think* USFC is clean, and you'll find a computer disk in the bottom of this case. I ask you to run it only on your own terminal and not to dump it to the main system, because it contains the names and ranks of eight hundred field grade and general officers in your own and other military forces in whom you may place total confidence.

"The point is that when we attack, your own bad guys may go ape on you. I have no idea what they'll do if they realize their lords and masters have been taken out and, frankly, we don't have the numbers or the organization to deal with all the things they *may* do. You, working with our allies on the disk, do. We ask you to stand by to do whatever you can to control the situation and prevent any more loss of life and destruction than can possibly be avoided.

"Watch your communications. You'll find instructions on the disk for reaching the others via a commo net I'm almost certain is secure. Until you've talked to them, don't use normal channels. Above all, don't talk to *any* civilians until your plans are in place.

"Our attack will kick off approximately eighteen hours from the time you get this. I know it's not much time, but it's the best I can do. When you talk to the others on the disk, *don't* mention the attack. To succeed, we need total surprise, and they already know what's coming down. They'll be waiting to discuss 'general contingency plans' with you.

"I'm sorry to dump this on you, Ger, but you're a good man. If I don't make it back, it's been an honor to serve under you. Give my love to Sharon and the kids, and take care of yourself. Good luck, Ger."

The tiny Hector MacMahan vanished, and General Gerald Hatcher sat staring at the flat, open case. He never knew exactly how long he sat there, but at last he reached out to press the button again and replay the message. Then he stopped himself. In the wake of that message, every moment was precious.

He lifted the panel and took out the computer disk, then swiveled his chair and switched on his terminal.

Chapter Twenty-three

Nergal's hangar deck was crowded once more. The Imperials stood out from their allies in the soot-black gleam of combat armor, limbs swollen and massive with jump gear and servo-mech "muscles." They were festooned with weapons, and their faces were grim in their opened helmets.

The far more numerous Terra-born wore either the close-fitted blackness of Imperial commando smocks or the battledress of a score of nations. There were only so many smocks, and the people who wore them wore no body armor, for they were better protection than any Terran armor. The other Terra-born wore the best body protection Earth could provide—pathetic against Imperial weapons, but the best they could do. And there were still many Terra-born inside the enclave; it was highly probable they would face Terran weapons, as well.

Their own weapons were as mixed as their uniforms. Cut-down grav guns hung from as many shoulders as possible, while the very strongest carried lightweight energy guns, like the one Tamman had used in Tehran and La Paz, and a few teams carried ten-millimeter grav guns mounted on anti-grav generators as crew-served weapons. Most, however, carried Terran weapons. There were quite a few battle rifles (and the proliferation and improvement of body protection meant those rifles had a lot more punch than the infantry weapons of even a few decades back), but grenade launchers, squad and heavy machineguns (the latter also fitted with anti-grav generators), and rocket launchers were the preferred weapons. Goggles hung around every neck, the fruit of *Nergal's* fabrication shops. They provided vision almost as good as an Imperial's and, equally important, would "read" any Imperial implants within fifty meters.

Horus was absent, for, to his unspeakable disappointment, the lot for who must remain to command *Nergal* had fallen to him. He'd wanted desperately to argue, but he hadn't. The assault vehicles would carry maxium loads, but even so, too many people who wanted to be there could not. His own crew would consist entirely of the oldest and least combat-ready adult Terra-born, with Isis as his executive officer. Children and those with no combat or shipboard training had been dispersed to carefully-hidden secondary locations, protected by the combat-trained adults who couldn't cram into the assault craft. His people were going to war, and he could no more shirk his responsibilities than could any of the others.

Even now, he and his bridge crew were watching their sensor arrays and completing last-minute equipment checks while Colin and Hector MacMahan stood on the launch bay stage.

"All right," Colin said quietly, "we've been over the plan backward and forward. You all know what you're supposed to do, and you also know that no plan survives contact with the enemy. Remember the objectives and keep yourselves alive if you possibly can. As Horus would say, this time we're going banco, but if anybody in this galaxy can pull it off, you can. Good luck, good hunting, and God protect you all."

He started to turn away, but MacMahan's suddenly raised voice stopped him.

"Attention on deck!" the colonel rapped, and every one of those grim-faced warriors snapped to attention in the first formal military courtesy since Colin had boarded *Nergal*. Every right hand whipped up in salute, and his chest suddenly seemed too small and tight. He tried to think of some proper response, but he could not even trust his voice to speak, and so he simply brought his hand up in response, then snapped it down.

There were no cheers as they followed him to the waiting assault craft, but he felt like a giant as he climbed into the shuttle he would pilot.

Night cloaked the western hemisphere of the planet, and a full, silvery moon rode high and serene. But deep within that moon, passive instrumentation watched the world below. *Dahak* knew, as Anu did not, precisely where to watch, and now he noted the brief, tiny, virtually indetectable flares of energy as *Nergal*'s auxiliaries floated out into the night.

It was happening, he realized calmly. For better or worse, his captain had launched his attack, and energy pulsed through the web of his circuitry, waking weapons that had been silent for fifty-one millennia.

The attack force headed south, and a vast storm front covered much of the southern Pacific, smashing at the assault craft with mighty fists. Colin was grateful for it. He led his warriors into its teeth, scant meters above the rearing, angry wave crests, and the miles dropped away behind them.

They moved scarcely above mach two, for they dared not come in at full bore. There were still southern fighters abroad in the night; they knew that, and they hid in the maw of the storm under their stealth fields, secure in the knowledge that *Dahak* would be watching over them from above. All five of *Nergal*'s other assault shuttles followed Colin, but there were far too few of them to transport all of his troops. Cutters and both pinnaces carried additional personnel, and all six of *Nergal*'s heavy tanks floated on their own gravitonics, able to keep pace at this slow speed. The tanks were a mixed blessing, for each used up two of his scant supply of Imperials, but their firepower was awesome, and very little short of a direct nuclear hit could stop them. Which was the point Horus and he had carefully not discussed with their crews; those six tanks protected twelve of *Nergal's* eighteen Imperial children.

The tingle of active scanner systems reached out to them from the south, still faint but growing in intensity, as he checked his position for the thousandth time. Another twenty minutes for the tanks, he estimated, but they'd be picked up by those scanners within ten. He drew a deep breath, and his voice was crisp over the com link.

"Shuttle pilots—go!" he said, and the heavily armed and armored assault boats suddenly screamed ahead at nine times the speed of sound.

Alarms clangored aboard the sublight battleship *Osir*, and the man who had been Fleet Captain (Engineering) Anu shot upright in bed.

He blinked furiously, banishing the rags of sleep, and his face twisted in a snarl. Those gutless, sniveling *bastards* were daring to attack *him*! His neural feed dropped data into his brain with smooth efficiency, and he saw six assault shuttles shrieking towards his enclave. It was incredible! What did they think they were *doing*?! He'd blow them away like insects!

A command snapped out to the automated perimeter weapon emplacements, another ordered his distant fighters to abandon stealth and rally to the defense of the enclave, and a third woke every alarm within the shield.

"Here they come!" Colin muttered, wincing as missiles and energy beams suddenly shredded the darkness. This was the riskiest moment of the approach but it was also something assault shuttles were designed for, and those automated defenders were outside the main shield.

Decoys and jammers went to work, fighting the defensive computers, and Tamman's weapon systems sprang to life beside him. Colin felt him bending forward as if to urge his electronic minions to greater efforts, but he had little attention to spare. He was too busy wrenching the shuttle through every evasive maneuver he could devise, and the night was full of death.

He bit off a groan as one of the shuttles took a direct hit and blew apart in a ball of fire. Hanalat and Carhana, he thought sickly, and sixty Terra-born with them. A missile exploded dangerously close to a second shuttle, and his heart was in his throat as Jiltanith clawed away from the fireball. Energy guns snarled, and his own craft shuddered as something smashed a glancing blow against her armor.

But then Tamman had his own solution, and a salvo of mass missiles screamed away, too fast, too close, for defensive systems to stop. They were ballistic weapons, impervious to decoys, and they struck in a blast that wracked a continent and flooded the American Highland plateau with dreadful light. Other shuttles were firing, their missiles crossing and criss-crossing with the ones charging up to destroy them, and energy guns raved back at the ground. Explosions and smoke, pulverized stone and vaporized ice and killing beams of energy—that was all the world there was as *Nergal's* people thundered into the attack. . . .

Anu crowed in triumph as the first assault shuttle exploded, then cursed savagely as the others struck back. He struggled into his uniform as the enclave trembled to the fury of the assault. Breaker! Breaker take them *all!* His defenses were designed to stop the all-out attack of an eighty-thousand ton battleship, not an assault landing, and fire stations were being blown into oblivion—not one-by-one, but in twos and threes and dozens! They'd gotten in by surprise, too close for his heavy anti-ship weapons, and his lightly-protected outer defenses crumbled and burned as he cursed.

It had been too long since he'd seen the Imperium wage war; he'd forgotten what it was like.

Ninhursag stumbled out of her shower, dragging wet hair frantically from her eyes, and shot down the apartment block transit shaft like a wet, naked otter. The sub-basement was built to withstand anything short of a direct hit with a nuke or a warp charge, and she had no business in what was about to happen out there. Not when she was as likely to be killed by a friend—or an accident—as by an enemy!

She was closing the reinforced blast door before it caught up with her. They were here! *They'd done it!*

"Shuttle Two, on my wing!" Colin snapped, and Jiltanith plummeted out of the flame-sick clouds. The two of them charged straight into the weakening defenses while their companions continued to savage Anu's weaponry. There! The access point beacon!

Colin MacIntrye drew a deep breath. At this speed, there would be no time to alter course if the shield stayed up, not even with a gravitonic drive. His implant triggered the code Ninhursag had stolen.

"NO!!"

Anu bellowed the protest in a burst of white-hot fury as he felt the shield open. How? *HOW?!* There was no way they could have the code! Ramman had *died*, and no other Imperial had left the enclave!

But they had it. The gates of his fortress yawned wide as two night-black shuttles screamed down the western tunnel, and its rock walls glowed with the compression heat of their passage.

"In!" Colin screamed to his passengers, and Tamman's exultation was a fire cloud beside him. The shuttles bucked and heaved, bare meters from destruction against the tunnel walls or one another, but neither Colin nor Jiltanith spared a thought for that. They hurtled onward, and their heavy, nose-mounted batteries of energy guns bellowed, destroying the very air in their path. Colin rode the thunder of his guns, blazing and invincible, and the

inner portal of Imperial battle steel blew open like a gate of straw.

They crashed through into the enclave, drives howling in torment as they threw full power into deceleration. Even Imperial technology had its limits, and they were still moving at over a hundred kilometers per hour when they smashed through the trees in the central park and plowed into the apartment blocks. The hapless Terra-born traitors in their path had mere seconds to realize death had come as the buildings exploded outward and the shuttles slammed to a halt amid the wreckage, no more than thirty meters apart. Their passengers were battered and bruised, but assault shuttles were built for just such mistreatment. The hatches opened, and the waiting troops charged out.

One or two fell, but only a spattering of fire met them. It was no trap, Colin thought exultantly. No trap!

He activated his jump gear, vaulting over a heap of smoking rubble, his own energy gun snarling. Only a handful of armed security men confronted him, and he bared his teeth as he blew the first unarmored enemy apart.

A tremendous boom of displaced air burst out of the tunnel as the next pair of shuttles shot into the enclave, and then the true madness began.

Anu dashed onto *Osir's* command deck, cursing his henchmen for the unrealiability that had spawned his distrust and made him order the other warships deactivated. Not even *Osir's* crew was permitted to live on board, but she was his command post, and he skidded to a halt beside the captain's console, activating his automatic defensive systems. They were intended to deal with an uprising among his own, not a full-scale invasion, but maybe they could buy his minions time to get into action.

Concealed weapons roused to life throughout the enclave. There was no time to give them precise directions even had Anu wanted to; they opened fire on anything that moved.

o   o   o

Ganhar tumbled from his bed as the alarms shrieked, and his eyes lit. Doubt, fear, and anguished uncertainty vanished in a blaze of triumph, and he laughed wildly. *There, maniac! Let's see you deal with these people!*

He dragged out his own combat armor. He was going to die, he thought calmly, and unless there truly was an afterlife, he would never know why he'd permitted this to happen, but it no longer mattered. He'd done it, and it wasn't in him to leave any task half-done.

The last surviving shuttle crashed into the wreckage and disgorged its troops, and *Nergal's* people began to die. Energy beams raked the park, attracted by movement, and the Terra-born could detect neither the targeting systems nor the weapons that killed them. But their Imperials' armor scanners could find both, and they moved to engage them.

Colin wanted to weep as Rohantha vaulted onto a wreckage-bared structural beam, exposing herself recklessly, energy gun ripping two heavy weapons from the cavern wall before they could rake her team of Terraborn. She almost made it back into cover herself, and Nikan, her cabin mate and lover, blew the gun that killed her to rubble.

Colin spun on his own toes, dodging as an energy bolt whipped past him and tore a twenty-centimeter hole through an Israeli paratrooper. His own weapon silenced the Israeli's automated executioner, and he dashed on, racing for the battleships while a corner of his mind tried to remember the dead man's name.

Three of Anu's stealthed fighters abandoned concealment, screaming through the heavens under maximum power as they stooped upon the clumsy gaggle of cutters and pinnaces and tanks still streaming towards the enclave. Their tracking systems found targets, but the lead pair vanished in cataclysmic balls of flame before they could fire. The third flight crew had a moment to gape at one another in horror as their instruments told them what had happened. Hyper missiles—*shipboard* missiles!—which could only have been launched from vacuum!

They died before they could warn their commander that *Dahak* was not dead.

Anu grimaced in hate and triumph. Even the computers could give him only a confused impression of what was happening, but he felt armory lockers being wrenched open aboard the transports while his weapons spewed death outside them.

Yet his triumphant snarl faded as the intensity of the fighting grew and grew. The attackers weren't human! They were demons out of Breaker's darkest hell, and they soaked up his fire and kept right on coming!

A surge of *Nergal*'s raiders swept up the boarding ramp of the transport *Bislaht*, and a trio of French Marines set up a fifty-caliber machine-gun in the lock. Their teammates rushed past them behind Nikan, racing for the armory before *Bislaht*'s mutineers could find their weapons.

They almost won their race. Barely half a dozen defenders were in armor when they crashed out of the transit shaft. Nikan roared in fury as he cut two of them down and charged the others, his energy gun on full automatic, filling the air with death. A third armored mutineer went down, then a fourth, but the fifth got his weapon up in time. Nikan exploded in a fountain of blood and a crackling corona of ruptured energy packs, and the SAS commando behind him hosed his killer with a grav gun.

Smoke and the stink of blood filled the armory, and the Terra-born commandos, now with no Imperial to lead them, crouched for cover just inside the hatch and killed anything that moved.

Ganhar stepped out of the transit shaft inside Security Central aboard the transport *Cardoh*. Security men shoved past or bounced off his armor as they funneled towards the transit shaft, heading for the armory below, and he waded through them like a Titan. Jantu's outer office was deserted, and he felt a momentary surge of disappointment. But then the inner hatch licked open, and Jantu stood in the opening, an energy pistol clutched in his hand.

Ganhar smiled through his armored visor, savoring the wildness of Jantu's eyes. It was worth it, he thought coldly. It was all worth it, if only for this moment.

He lifted his grav gun slightly, and Jantu's crazed eyes narrowed with sudden comprehension as his implants recognized Ganhar's. The Operations head saw it all in that fleeting instant, saw the recognition and understanding, the sudden, intuitive grasp of what had *really* happened when Ramman came to him.

"You lose," he said softly, and his gun hissed.

Colin went flat on his face as an armored form tackled him from behind, and he rolled over, snatching out his sidearm before he recognized Jiltanith. The reason she'd hit him became instantly clear as an energy bolt whipped above him, and he raised himself on one elbow, sighting back along its path. The unarmored security man was lining up for a second shot when Colin's grav gun ripped him to shreds.

Dahak felt almost cheerful, despite a gnawing anxiety over Colin. His scanners showed that the northerners had breached the enclave. One way or the other, that shield would soon fall.

In the meantime, he busied himself locating all of Anu's deployed fighters as they abandoned stealth mode to streak back south. He tracked each of them precisely, allocated his hyper missiles with care, and fired a single salvo.

Twenty-nine more Imperial fighters died in a span of approximately two-point-seven-five Terran seconds.

The huge cavern was hideous with smoke and flame as more southerners found weapons and armor, emerging as isolated knots of warring figures that sought to link with one another amid the nightmare that had burst upon them. They were badly outnumbered, but they were all Imperials. Even without combat armor, they were more than a match for any Terra-born opponent. Or would have been, had they understood what was happening.

Most of Anu's automatics were silent now, for both sides were equally at risk from them, and both had been taking them out from the start. But they'd blunted the first rush while more of his people got themselves armed. It was helping, but they'd yielded a dangerous amount of ground. So far he'd lost touch completely only with *Bislaht*, but fighting raged aboard three other transports, and six more were surrounded, their hatches under intense fire.

Breaker! Who would have thought degenerates could *fight* like this? There were only a handful of old, worn out Imperials among them, but they were like madmen!

He winced as his scanners watched a quintet of Terra-born suddenly pop up out of a tangle of wreckage. They formed a gantlet, with three of his own Imperials between them. Two of the degenerates went down, but the others swept his armored henchmen with an unbelievable mix of Imperial and Terran weapons. Grav gun darts exploded inside armored bodies, a flamethrower hosed them with liquid fire, and a Terran anti-tank rocket blew the last survivor six meters backward. The surviving degenerates ducked back down under cover and went scuttling off in search of fresh prey.

This couldn't be happening—he saw it with his own eyes, and he still couldn't believe it!

But then came the report he'd hoped for. *Transhar's* people had finally gotten some of their vehicles powered up, and he grinned again as the first light tank floated towards the hatch on its gravitonics.

Andrew Asnani slid to a halt, sucking in air as he scrubbed sweat from his face. He'd become separated from the rest of his team, and the deafening bellow and crash of battle pounded him like a fist, but for all its horror, it was the sweetest sound he'd ever heard. It proved he hadn't led the colonel and his people into a trap, and he'd been able to shuck off his demolition charge.

He drew another breath and took a firmer grip on his assault rifle as he eased around the rubble of a broken wall. He was in the section that had housed Anu's terrorists, and he still wasn't certain how he'd gotten here. Habit, perhaps. Or possibly something else. . . .

He dropped suddenly as shapes loomed in the dust-heavy smoke. Terra-born, not Imperials, for his goggles saw no signature implants. But neither were they *his* people, he thought grimly, hunkering deeper into the shadow of his broken wall. There were at least twenty of them, all armed, though he had no idea how they'd gotten their hands on weapons. It didn't matter. The odds sucked, and with a little luck, he'd just let them slip . . .

But he had no luck. They were coming straight towards him, and the copper taste of fear filled his mouth. Unfair! To have come so far, risked so much, and blunder into contact with—

His mind froze, panic suddenly a thing of the past, and he stopped trying to ease further back out of sight. *Abgram!* The man leading that group was *Abgram*, and that changed everything, for it had been Abgram whose operation had planted a truck bomb in New Jersey five years before.

For eleven months, Asnani had known who had killed his family, yet he could do nothing without blowing his own cover and Colonel MacMahan's op. But the thunder and screams were in his ears, and his own life was no longer essential to success.

He ejected his partially used magazine, replacing it with a fresh one, checking his safety, gathering his legs under him. The terrorists were coming closer, dodging in and out of shadows even as he had. He couldn't leave his cover without being seen, but they'd see him anyway in another twenty seconds. Ten meters. He'd let them come another ten meters. . . .

Sergeant Andrew Asnani, United States Army, exploded from concealment with his weapon on full auto.

Six men died almost instantly, and the man called Abgram went down, screaming, even as his fellows poured fire into the apparition that had erupted in their midst. He stared up in agony, watching bullets hammer body armor and flesh, seeing blood burst from the man who had shot him.

It was the last thing Abgram ever saw, for only one purpose remained to Andrew Asnani, and his last, short burst blew Abgram's head apart.

"Shit!"

Colin killed his jump gear and slithered to a halt in a tangle of smashed greenery as the light tank let fly. A solid rod of energy ripped through two of Anu's madly fleeting Terran allies and what had once been a fountain before it struck an armored figure. Rihani, he thought, one of *Nergal*'s engineers, but there was too little left to ever know. He watched the tank settle onto its treads for added stability as grenades and rockets exploded about it. Its thick armor and invisible shield shrugged off the destruction as the turret swiveled, seeking fresh prey. The long energy cannon snouted in his direction, and he grabbed Jiltanith's ankle and hauled her down beside him, not that—

A lightning bolt whickered out of the shattered portal, and the southern tank exploded with a roar. Its killer rumbled into sight, squat and massive on its own treads, grinding out onto the cavern floor, and Colin pounded the dirt beside him in jubilation.

Nergal's heavy tank moved forward confidently, cannon seeking, anti-personnel batteries flashing, heavy grav guns whining from its upper hull.

Anu roared in fury as *Transhar*'s tank was killed, but his fury redoubled as the enemy tank took up a firing position that covered *Transhar*'s vehicle ramp. Another tank tried to come down it, and *Nergal*'s heavy blew it to wreckage with a single, contemptuous shot.

A warp grenade bounced and rolled, bringing up against the edge of its shield, but nothing happened.

Both sides had their suppressers out, smothering the effect of a grenade's tiny hyper generator. Normally that favored the defense, but now he watched a second enemy tank charge out of the portal—and a third!—and nothing *but* a nuke or a warp warhead was going to stop those things. That or a proper warship giving ground support. But he had only one active battleship, and the rest of her crew had not yet arrived.

It was a race, he thought grimly. A race between *Osir's* personnel and whatever horror *Nergal's* people would produce next.

Ganhar leapt lightly down from *Cardoh's* number six personnel lock, letting his jump gear absorb the twelve-meter drop. *Osir* was over that way, he thought, still queerly calm, almost detached, and that was where Anu would be.

"There!" Colin shouted, pointing across two hundred meters of fire-swept ground at the battleship *Osir*. "Feel it, 'Tanni? Her systems are live! Anu must be aboard her!"

"Aye," Jiltanith agreed, then broke off to nail a fleeing southerner with a snapshot from her energy gun. In her armor her strength was the equal of any full Imperial's, and her reflexes had to be seen to be believed.

"Aye," she said again, "yet 'twill be no lightsome thing to cross yon kill zone, Colin!"

"No, but if we can get in there . . ."

"We've none t'guard our backs and we 'compass it," she warned.

"I know." Colin scanned the smoking bedlam, but they'd outdistanced their own people, and few of the southerners seemed to be in the vicinity. It was the automatics sweeping the area that made the approach so deadly.

"Look over there, to the left," he said suddenly. Some of the robotic weapons had been knocked out, leaving a gap in the defenses. "Think we can get through there before they fry us?"

"I know not," Jiltanith replied, "yet may we assay it."

"I knew you'd like the idea," he panted, and then they were off.

Hector MacMahan ducked, then swore horribly as an enemy grav gun spun Darnu's shattered armor in a madly whirling circle. The Imperial crashed to the ground, and Hector hosed a stream of darts at the spot he thought the fire had come from.

An armored southerner lurched up and fell back into death, but it was hardly a fair trade, MacMahan thought savagely, leading the surviving members of his team forward. Darnu had been worth any hundred southerners, and he was far from the first Imperial *Nergal* had lost this bloody night.

But they were pushing the bastards back. The tanks were making the difference—that and the teams who'd gotten aboard the other transports and kept their armored vehicles from ever being manned. They had a chance, a good chance, if they could only keep moving. . . .

The last of *Nergal*'s cutters swept out of the tunnel and exploded in mid-air. MacMahan swore again, and his men went forward in a crouching run.

Ganhar darted a look over his shoulder. He didn't recognize the implants on either of those two armored figures. Breaker! There was a third unknown looming up behind them! It was always possible that if they'd known he'd let them through the door they would have greeted him as an ally, but they couldn't know that, could they? Besides, he was closer to *Osir* than they were.

He reached a ramp and hurled himself up it, seeking the cover of the battle steel hull while beams and grav gun darts lashed at his heels. He landed on a shoulder and rolled in a clatter of armor, coming up onto his feet and running for the transit shaft. Anu would be on the command deck.

Jiltanith and Colin went up the main ramp under a hurricane of fire from the automatics, but none of the surviving weapons could depress far enough to hit them. The hatch was open, and Colin crashed through it first, dodging to the right. Jiltanith followed, spinning to the left, but the lock was empty and the inner hatch stood open as well. They edged forward as cautiously as they dared in their need for haste.

It was quieter in here, and the clank of an armored foot was loud behind them. They wheeled, but it was one of their own—Geb, his armor as smoke and soot-smutted as their own. Something had hit him in the chest, hard enough to crack even bio-enhanced ribs, but the dished-in armor had held, though Colin didn't like the way the old Imperial was favoring his left side.

"Glad to see you, Geb," he said, suppressing a half-hysterical giggle at how inane the greeting sounded. "Feel like a little walk?"

"As long as it's upstairs," Geb panted back.

"Good. Watch our backs, then, will you?" Geb nodded and Colin slapped Jiltanith's armored shoulder. "Let's go find Anu, 'Tanni," he said, and led the way towards the central transit shaft.

Ganhar stepped out of the transit shaft twelve decks below the command deck, for the shaft above was inactive. So, a security measure he hadn't known about, was it? There were still the crawl ways, and he pressed the bulkhead switch to open the nearest of them.

"Hello, Ganhar." He froze at the soft voice and did a quick three-hundred-sixty-degree scan. She was unarmored, but her energy gun was trained unwaveringly on his spine.

"Hello, Inanna." He spoke quietly, knowing he could never turn fast enough to get her with the grav gun. "I thought we were on the same side."

"I told you before, Ganhar—I'm a bright girl. I had my own bugs in Jantu's outer office."

Ganhar swallowed. So she'd seen it all, and she knew why he was here.

"My quarrel's with Anu," he said. "If I can take him out, maybe they'll let us surrender."

"Wrong idea, Ganhar," Inanna said calmly. "I told you that before."

"But *why*, Inanna?! He's a fucking maniac!"

"Because I love him, Ganhar," she said, and fired.

Colin and Jiltanith rode the transit shaft as high as they could, but someone had deactivated it above deck ninety. They stepped out of it, looking for another way up, and Colin gasped in sudden alarm as the blast of an energy gun echoed down the passageway behind him. He was trying to turn towards it when a second beam from the same weapon slashed across the open bore of the shaft. It missed him by a centimeter as he heard Jiltanith's weapon snarl and looked up to see an unarmored figure tumble to the deck.

"Jesus!" he muttered. "That one was too fucking close!"

"Aye," Jiltanith replied, then paused. "Methinks our way lieth thither wi' all speed, Colin. Unless mine eyes deceive me, there lie two bodies 'pon yonder deck. I'll warrant well the first o' them did seek out Anu as do we."

"Methinks you're probably right," he grunted, stepping back across the transit shaft. Jiltanith's shot had caught the unarmored woman in mid-torso, and the gruesome sight made him look away quickly. He had no time to examine her, anyway, yet an odd sense of familiarity tugged at a corner of his brain. He glanced at her again, but he'd never seen her before and he turned his attention to the half-opened crawl way, stepping over the mangled, armored figure lying before it.

"Wonder who the hell *he* was?" he muttered, opening the hatch fully.

Geb came out of the transit shaft and paused for breath as Jiltanith eeled into the crawl way after Colin. His ribs must be pretty bad, he decided. His implants were suppressing the pain, but it was hard to breathe, and they were using enough painkillers to make him dizzy. Best not to squeeze into quarters that narrow. Besides, they'd need someone here to watch their retreat.

He squatted on his heels, trying not to think about how many friends were dying beyond this quiet hull, and glanced at the dead, armored figure beside him, wondering, like Colin and Jiltanith, who he'd been and why his fellow mutineer had killed him. Then he glanced at the dead woman and froze.

No, he thought. Please, Maker, let me be wrong!

But he wasn't wrong. He knew that face well, had known it millennia ago when it belonged to a woman named Tanisis. A beautiful young woman, married to one of his closest friends. He'd thought her dead in the mutiny and mourned her, as had her husband ... who had named a Terran-born daughter "Isis" in her memory.

And now, so many years later, Geb cursed the Maker Himself for not making that the truth. She'd lived, he thought sickly, slept away the dreamless millennia in stasis, alive, still young and beautiful ... only to be obscenely murdered, butchered so that one of Anu's ghouls could don her flesh.

He rose slowly, blinded by tears, and adjusted his energy gun to wide-angle focus, breathing a prayer of thanks that Jiltanith either had not remembered her mother's face or else had not looked closely at the body. Nor would she have the chance to, for there was one last service Geb could perform for his friend Tanisis. He pressed the firing stud and a fan of gravitonic disruption wiped the mangled body out of existence.

Hector MacMahan looked about cautiously. All six of *Nergal's* tanks were in action now, and only one southern heavy had gotten free of its transport hold to challenge them. Its half-molten wreckage littered two hundred square meters of cavern floor, spewing acrid, choking smoke to join the fog shrouding the hellish scene.

An awful lot of their Imperials were dead, he thought bitterly. Their own hatred, coupled with their need to protect their weaker Terra-born, had cost them. He doubted as many as half were still alive, even counting the tank crews, but their sacrifice had given *Nergal's* raiders control of the entire western half of the enclave and four of the seven transports on the eastern side. They were closing in on pockets of resistance, Terra-born moving cautiously under covering fire from the tanks.

Unless something went dreadfully wrong in the next thirty minutes, they were going to win this thing.

Colin let his armor's "muscles" take the strain of the climb, questing ahead with his *Dahak*-modified implants as he neared the humming intensity of the command deck. They were only one deck below it when he felt the automatic weapons. They were covered by a stealth field, but it needed adjustment, and even in its prime it hadn't been a match for his implants.

"Hold it," he grunted to Jiltanith.

"What hast thou spied?"

"Booby traps and energy guns," he replied absently, examining the intricate field of interlocking fire. "Damn, it's a bitch, too. Well . . ."

He plucked his grav gun from its webbing. The energy gun might have been better, but the quarters were far too cramped for it.

"What dost thou?"

"I'm going to open us a little path," he said, and squeezed the trigger.

A hurricane of needles swept the crawl way, drilling half their lengths even into battle steel before they exploded. Scanner arrays, trip signals, and targeting systems shredded under his fire, and the weapons went mad. The shaft above him became a crazy-quilt of exploding energy beams and solid projectiles.

Anu's head jerked up as bedlam erupted in one of the crawl ways. His automatic defenses had been triggered, but there was something wrong. They weren't firing under proper control—they were tearing themselves apart!

*   *   *

The carnage lasted a good thirty seconds, and Colin probed the smoking wreckage carefully.

"That's got it. On the other hand, we just rang the doorbell. Think we should keep going?"

"'Twould seem we ha' scant choice."

"I was afraid you'd say that. C'mon."

Anu turned away from his console, and his face was almost relaxed.

It would take a while yet, but the sheer audacity of the attack had been decisive. Those heavy tanks had hurt, but it was surprise that had done in the enclave. The dreams of fifty thousand years were crumbling in his fingers, and it was all the fault of those crawling traitors from *Nergal*. Their fault, and the fault of his own gutless subordinates.

But if he'd lost, he could still see to it they lost, too. He walked calmly across the command deck to the fire control officer's couch, insinuating his mind neatly into the console. He really should have provided a proper bomb, but this would do.

He initiated the arming sequence, then paused. No, wait. Let whoever was in the crawl way get here first. He wanted to watch at least one of the bastards *know* what was going to happen to his precious, putrid world.

Colin helped Jiltanith out of the crawl way, then paused, his face white. Jesus! The son-of-a-bitch was arming every warhead in the magazines!

"Come on!" he shouted, and hurled himself toward the command deck. His gauntleted hand slapped the emergency over-ride, and he charged through as the hatch licked open. His energy gun was ready, swinging to cover the captain's console, but even as he burst onto the command deck, he knew he'd guessed wrong. The heavy hand of a grab field smashed at him, seizing him in fingers of iron. He stopped instantly, not even rocking with the impetus of his charge, unable even to fall in the armor that had become a prison.

"Nice of you to drop by," a voice said, and he turned

his head inside his helmet. A tall man sat at the gunnery console with an energy pistol in one hand. He didn't look like the images of Anu from the records, but he wore the midnight blue of Battle Fleet with an admiral's insignia.

"It's over, Anu," Colin said. "You might as well give it up."

"No," Anu said calmly, "I don't think I'm the surrendering kind."

"I know what kind you are," Colin said contemptuously, keeping his eyes on Anu while his implants watched Jiltanith creeping closer and closer. She was belly-down on the deck, trying to work her way under the plane of the grab field, but her enhanced senses were less keen than his. Could she skirt it safely, or not?

"Do you, now?" Anu mocked. "I doubt that. None of you ever had the wit to understand me, or you would have joined me instead of trying to pull me down to your own miserable level."

"Sure," Colin sneered. "You've done a wonderful job, haven't you? Fifty thousand years, and you're still stuck on one piddling little planet."

Anu's face tightened and he started to trigger the warheads, then stopped and uncoiled from the couch like a serpent.

"No," he murmured. "I think I'll watch you scream a bit first. I'm glad you're in armor. It'll take a while to burn through with this little popgun, and you'll *feel* it so nicely. Let's start with an arm, shall we? If I start with a leg, you'll just fall over, and that won't be any fun."

He came nearer, and sweat beaded Colin's forehead. If the bastard came another three meters closer, Jiltanith would have a shot through the hatch—but he'd be able to see her, and she was flat on her belly. He wracked his brain as Anu took another step. And another. There had to be a way! There *had* to! They'd come so far. . . .

Wait! Anu had been so damned confident, he might not have changed—

Anu took another step, and Jiltanith raised her grav gun. Her armor scuffed the deck so gently normal ears would not have heard it, but Anu was an Imperial. He whirled snake-quick, his eyes widening in shock, and the energy pistol swung down and fired like lightning.

It was all one blinding nightmare. Anu's pistol snarled. Its energy bolt hit Jiltanith squarely in the spine and held there. Smoke burst from her armor, but she pressed the trigger and an explosive dart hit blew his right leg into tatters an instant before a sparkling corona of ruptured power packs glared above her armored body.

Colin heard her scream over his com link. Her grav gun fell from her hand and her armored body convulsed, and his world vanished in a boil of fury.

Anu hit the deck, screaming until his implants took control. They damped the pain, sealed the ruptured tissues, drove back the fog of shock, but it took precious seconds, and Colin's implants—his bridge officer implants—reached out and demanded access to *Osir's* computers.

There was a flicker of electronic shock, and then, like *Nergal*, *Osir* recognized him, for Anu hadn't changed the command codes; it hadn't even occurred to him to try. He stared at Colin in horror, momentarily stunned as even the loss of his leg had not stunned him, unable to believe what he was seeing. There *were* no bridge officers! *He'd killed them all!*

Colin's mind flooded into *Osir's* computers, killing the grab field. But hate and madness spurred Anu's own efforts, and his command licked out to the fire control console. He enabled the sequenced detonation code.

Colin raced after it, trying to kill it, but he was in the wrong part of *Osir's* brain. He couldn't get to it, so he did the only other thing he could. He slammed down a total freeze of the entire command network, and every single system in the ship locked.

Anu screamed in frustration, and Colin staggered as the pistol snarled again. Energy slammed into his chest, but his armor held long enough for him to hurl himself aside. Anu swung the pistol, trying to hold it on his fleeing target, but he hadn't counted on the adjustments *Dahak* had made to Colin's implants. He misjudged his enemy's reaction speed, and Colin slammed into a bulk-

head in a clangor of armor and battle steel. He richo-
cheted off like a bank shot, bouncing himself back
towards Anu, and Anu screamed again as an armored
foot reduced his pistol hand to paste. He tried to roll
away, but Colin was on him like a demon. He reached
down, jerking him up in a giant's embrace, and his hands
twisted.

Anu shrieked as his arms shattered, and for just an
instant their eyes met—Anu's mad with terror and pain,
his own equally mad with hate and a pain not of his
flesh—and Colin knew Anu's life was his.

But he didn't take it. He tossed his victim aside, cold
in his fury, and the mutineer bounced off a bulkhead
with another wail of agony. He slid to the deck, helpless
in his broken body, and Colin ignored him as he flung
himself to his knees beside Jiltanith. He couldn't read
her bio-read-outs through her badly damaged armor, and
he lifted her in his arms, calling her name and peering
into her helmet visor in desperation.

Her eyes opened slowly, and he gasped in relief.

" 'Tanni! How . . . how badly are you hurt?"

"Certes, 'twas like unto an elephant's kick," she murmured dazedly, "yet 'twould seem I am unhurt."

"Thank God!" he whispered, and she smiled.

"Aye, methinks He did have more than summat t'do
wi' it," she replied, her voice a bit stronger. " 'Twas that,
or mine armor, or mayhap a bit o' both. Yet having saved
me, it can do no more, good Colin. I must come forth
if I would move. That blast hath fused my servo circuits
all."

"You're out of your mind if you think I'm letting you
out of there yet!"

"So, thou art a tyrant after all," she said, and he
hugged her close.

"Rank hath its privileges, 'Tanni, and I'm getting you
out of here in one piece, damn it!"

"As thou wilt," she murmured with a small smile. "Yet
what of Anu?"

"Don't worry," Colin said coldly.

He eased her dead armor into a sitting position where

she could see the crippled mutineer, then returned his attention to the computers. He activated a stand-alone emergency diagnostic system and felt his cautious way down the frozen fire control circuits to the detonation order, then sought the next circuit in the sequence. He disabled it and withdrew, then reactivated the core computers and swung to face Anu, and his face was cold.

"How?" the mutineer moaned. Even his implants couldn't fully deaden the agony of his broken limbs, and his face was white. "How could you *do* that?"

"Dahak taught me," Colin said grimly, and Anu shook his head frantically.

"*No!* No, *Dahak's* dead! I *killed* it!" The agony of failure, utter and complete, filled Anu's face, overshadowing his physical pain.

"Did you, now?" Colin asked softly, and his smile was cruel. "Then you won't mind this a bit."

He bent over the broken body and snatched it up, careless of Anu's wail of anguish.

"What wouldst thou, Colin?" Jiltanith asked urgently.

"I'm giving him what he wanted," Colin said coldly, and crossed the command deck. A hatch hissed open at his command to reveal the cabin of a lifeboat, and he dumped Anu into the lead couch. The mutineer stared at him with desperate, hating eyes, and Colin smiled that same cold, cruel smile as his neural feed programmed the lifeboat with a captain's imperative, locking out all attempts to change it.

"You wanted Dahak, you son-of-a-bitch? Well, Dahak wants you, too. I think he'll enjoy the meeting more than you will."

"No!" Anu shrieked as the hatch began to close. "*Noooooooooo! Ple—*"

The hatch cut him off, and *Osir* twitched as the lifeboat launched.

The gleaming minnow arced upward through the enclave's shield, fleeing the planet its mother ship had come to so long before. It altered course, swinging uneeringly to line its nose on the white, distant disk of the moon, and its passenger's terrified mind hammered futilely at the commands locked into its computers. The lifeboat paid no heed, driving onward toward the mighty starship it had left millennia ago. Tracking systems aboard that starship locked upon it, noting its origin and course, and a fold-space signal pulsed out before it, identifying its single passenger to *Dahak*.

The computer watched it come, and Alpha Priority commands within his core programming tingled to life. *Dahak* could have fired the instant he identified the target, but he held his fire, waiting, letting the lifeboat bear its cargo closer and closer, and the human emotion of anticipation filled his circuitry.

The lifeboat reached the kill zone about the warship, and a single, five-thousand-kilometer streamer of energy erupted from beneath the crater men had named Tycho. It lashed out, fit to destroy a ship like *Osir* herself, and the silver minnow vanished.

There were tiny sounds aboard the leviathan called *Dahak*. The targeting systems shut themselves down with a quiet click. The massive energy mount whined softly as it powered down, its glowing snout cooling quickly in the vacuum of its weapon bay. Then there was only silence. Silence and yet another human emotion ... completion.

Chapter Twenty-four

Two months to the day after the fall of the enclave, Senior Fleet Captain Colin MacIntyre, Imperial Battle Fleet, commanding officer of the ship-of-the-line *Dahak* and Governor of Planet Earth and the Solarian System, stepped out of the hoverjeep and breathed deep of the crisp, clear morning of a Colorado autumn. The usual frenzy of Shepherd Space Center was stilled, and he felt his NASA driver staring at the bronze-sheened tower of alloy thrusting arrogantly heavenward before them. The sublight battleship *Osir* had been sitting here for a week, waiting for him, but a week hadn't been long enough for NASA to get used to her.

He adjusted his cap and moved to join the small group at the foot of *Osir's* ramp. He was grateful that those same people had let him have a few moments of privacy to stand alone with the permanent honor guard before The Cenotaph. That was the only name it had, probably the only name it ever would have, and it was enough. The polished obsidian shaft reared fifty meters into the air in front of White Tower, glittering and featureless,

309

and its plain battle steel plinth bore the name and birth-planet of every person who had died fighting the southerners.

It was a long list. He'd stepped close, scanning the endless names until he found the two he sought. "SANDRA YVONNE TILLOTSON, LT. COL., USAF, EARTH" and "SEAN ANDREW MACINTYRE, US FORESTRY SERVICE, EARTH." His brother and his friend were in good company, he thought sadly. The best.

Now he tried to put the sorrow aside as he reached the waiting group. Horus stood with General Gerald Hatcher, Sir Frederick Amesbury, and Marshal Vassily Chernikov—the three men who, most of all, had held the planet together in the wake of the preposterous reports coming out of Antarctica. Once the truth of those fantastic tales registered, virtually every major government had fallen overnight, and Colin still wasn't quite certain how these men had managed to hang onto a semblance of order, even with the support of Nergal's allies within the military.

"Horus," Colin nodded to his friend. "It looks like I'm leaving you in good hands."

"I think so, too," Horus replied with a small, slightly wistful smile.

Only eleven of Nergal's senior Imperials had lived through the fighting, and they had chosen to remain behind with the planet on which they'd spent so much of their long lives. Colin was glad. They'd far more than earned their right to leave, but it would have seemed wrong, somehow. In a very real sense, they were the surviving godparents of the human race, Terran branch. If anyone could be trusted to look after Earth's interests, they could.

And Earth's interests would need looking after. A second line of automated stations had gone off the air, which meant the Achuultani's scouts were no more than twenty-five months away. He had that long to reach the Imperium, find out why no defense was being mounted, summon assistance, and get back to Sol. It was a tall order, and he frankly doubted he could do it. Nor was the fact reassuring that no one had yet answered the non-stop messages *Dahak* had been transmitting ever since they recovered the hypercom spares from the enclave.

It looked like the only way they could find help—if there was any to find—was to go out and get it in person, and only *Dahak* could do that. Which meant Earth would be on her own until *Dahak* could return.

The situation wasn't quite as hopeless as it might have been. Assuming *Dahak*'s records of previous incursions were any guide, the Achuultani scouts would be anywhere from a year to eighteen months ahead of the main incursion, and Earth would not be fangless when they arrived. Except for *Osir* herself, all of *Dahak*'s sublight warships had been debarked, along with the vast majority of the old starship's fighters and enough combat and ground vehicles to conquer the planet five times over. They would remain behind to form the nucleus of Sol's defense.

Two of *Dahak*'s four Fleet repair units, each effectively a hundred-fifty-thousand-ton spaceborne industrial complex in its own right, had also been debarked. Their first task had been the construction of the gravity generator *Dahak* would leave in his place to avoid disturbing such things as the Lagrange point habitats, not to mention little items like Earth's tides. Since completing that assignment, they had split their capacity between replicating themselves and producing missiles, mines, fighters, and every other conceivable weapon of war. The technological and industrial base Anu had hoarded for fifty millennia was coming into operation, as well, with every Terrestrial assistance a badly frightened planet could provide.

No, Earth would not be helpless when the Achuultani arrived. But a strong hand would be needed to lead Colin's birth-world through the enormous changes that awaited it, and that hand would belong to Horus.

Colin had declared himself Governor of Earth, but he'd never meant to claim the title seriously. He'd seen it only as a means to make his pardon of *Nergal*'s Imperials "official," yet it had become clear his temporary expedient was in fact a necessity. It would be a long time before Terrans really trusted *any* politician again, and Hatcher, Amesbury, and Chernikov agreed unanimously with Horus: Earth needed a single, unquestioned source of authority, or her people would be too busy fighting one another to worry about the Achuultani.

So Colin had declared peace and, backed by *Dahak's* resources, made it stick with very little difficulty. When he then proclaimed himself Planetary Governor in the name of the Imperium (once more with *Dahak's* newly-revealed potential hovering quietly in the background) and promised local autonomy, most surviving governments had been only too happy to hand their problems over to him. The Asian Alliance might still make problems, but Horus and his new military aides seemed confident that they could handle that situation.

Once they had, all existing militaries were to be merged (and Colin was profoundly grateful he would be elsewhere while his henchmen implemented *that* decision), and he'd named Horus Lieutenant Governor and appointed all ten of his surviving fellows Imperial Councilors for Life to help him mind the store while "the Governor" was away.

All of which, he reflected with an inner smile, would certainly keep Horus's "retirement" from being boring.

The thorniest problem, in many ways, had been the surviving southerners. Of the four thousand nine hundred and three mutineers from stasis, almost all had declared their willingness to apply for Terran citizenship and accept commissions in the local reserves and militia. Colin had re-enlisted a hundred of them for service aboard *Dahak* (on a probationary basis) to help provide a core of experienced personnel, but the rest would remain on Earth. Since they had been sitting under an Imperial lie detector at the time they declared their loyalty anew, he felt reasonably confident about leaving them behind. Horus would keep an eagle eye on them, and they would furnish him with a nucleus of trained, fully-enhanced Imperials to get things rolling while the late Inanna's medical facilities began providing biotechnics to Earth's Terra-born defenders.

But that left over three hundred Imperials who had joined Anu willingly or failed the lie detector's test, all of them guilty, at the very least, of mutiny and multiple murder. Imperial law set only one penalty for their crimes, and Colin had refused to pardon them. The executions had taken almost a week to complete.

It had been his most agonizing decision, but he'd made it. There had been no option ... and deep inside he knew the example—and its implicit warning—would stick in the minds he left behind him, Terra-born and Imperial alike.

So now he was leaving. *Dahak's* crew was tremendously understrength, but at least the ship had one again. The survivors of Hector MacMahan's assault force, all fourteen of *Nergal's* surviving children, and his tentatively rehabilitated mutineers formed its core, but it had been fleshed out just a bit. A sizable chunk of the USFC and SAS, and the entire US Second Marine Division, Russian Nineteenth Guards Parachute Division, German First Armored Division, and Japanese Sendai Division would provide the bulk of his personnel, along with several thousand hand-picked air force and navy personnel from all over the First World. All told, it came to barely a hundred thousand people, but with so many parasites left behind it would suffice. They'd rattle around like peas in the vastness of their ship, but taking any more might strain even *Dahak's* ability to provide biotechnics *and* training before they reached the borders of the Imperium.

"Well, we'll be going then," Colin said, shaking himself out of his thoughts. He reached out to shake hands with the three military men, and smiled at Marshal Chernikov. "I expect my new Chief Engineer will be thinking of you, sir," he said.

"Your Chief Engineer with two good arms, Comrade Governor," Chernikov replied warmly. "Even his mother agrees that his temporary absence is a small price to pay for that."

"I'm glad," Colin said. He turned to Gerald Hatcher. "Sorry about Hector, but I'll need a good ops officer."

"You've got one, Governor," Hatcher said. "But keep an eye on him. He disappears at the damnedest times."

Colin laughed and took Amesbury's hand.

"I'm sorry so much of the SAS is disappearing with me, Sir Frederick. I hope you won't need them."

"They're good lads," Sir Frederick agreed, "but we'll make do. Besides, if you run into a spot of bother, my chaps should pull you out again—even under Hector's command."

Colin smiled and held out his hand to Horus. The old Imperial looked at it for a moment, then reached out and embraced him, hugging him so hard his reinforced ribs creaked. The old man's eyes were bright, and Colin knew his own were not entirely dry.

"Take care of yourself, Horus," he said finally, his voice husky.

"I will. And you and 'Tanni take care of each other." Horus gave him one last squeeze, then straightened, his hands on Colin's shoulders. "We'll take care of the planet for you, too, Governor. You might say we've had some experience at that."

"I know." Colin patted the hand on his right shoulder, then stepped back. A recorded bosun's pipe shrilled—he was going to have to speak to *Dahak* about this perverse taste for Terran naval rituals he seemed to have developed—and his subordinates snapped to attention. He returned their salutes sharply, then turned and walked up the ramp. He did not look back as the hatch closed behind him, and *Osir* floated silently upward as he stepped into the transit shaft.

His executive officer looked up as he arrived on the command deck.

"Captain," she said formally, and started to rise from the captain's couch, but he waved her back and took the first officer's station. The gleaming disk of *Dahak*'s hull, no longer hidden by its millennia-old camouflage, floated before him as the visual display turned indigo blue and the first stars appeared.

"Sorry you missed the good-byes?" he asked quietly.

"Nay, my Colin," she said, equally softly. "I ha' said my farewells long since. 'Tis there my future doth lie."

"All of ours," he agreed. They sped onward, moving at a leisurely speed by Imperial standards, and *Dahak* swelled rapidly. The three-headed dragon of his ensign faced them, vast and proud once more, loyal beyond the imagining of humans. Most humans, at any rate, Colin reminded himself. Not all.

The starship grew and grew, stupendous and overwhelming, and a hatch yawned open on Launch Bay Ninety-One. *Osir* had come full circle at last.

The battleship threaded her way down the cavernous bore, and *Dahak*'s voice filled her bridge with the old, old ritual announcement of Colin's own navy.

"Captain, arriving," it said.